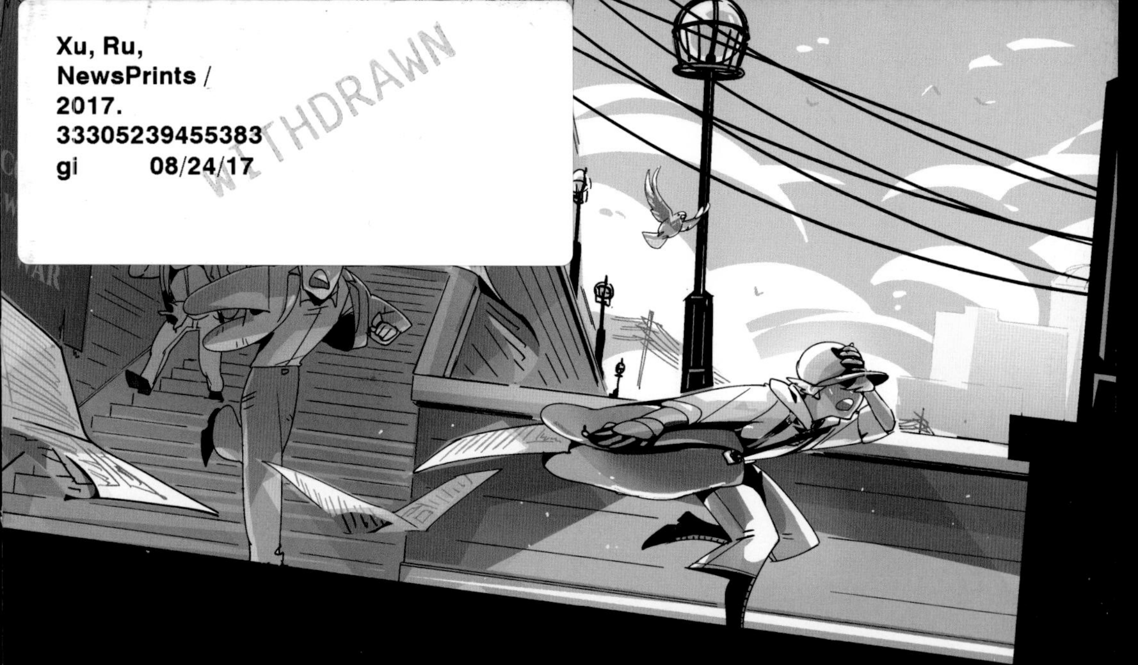

NEWSPRINTS

Ru Xu

graphix
AN IMPRINT OF
SCHOLASTIC

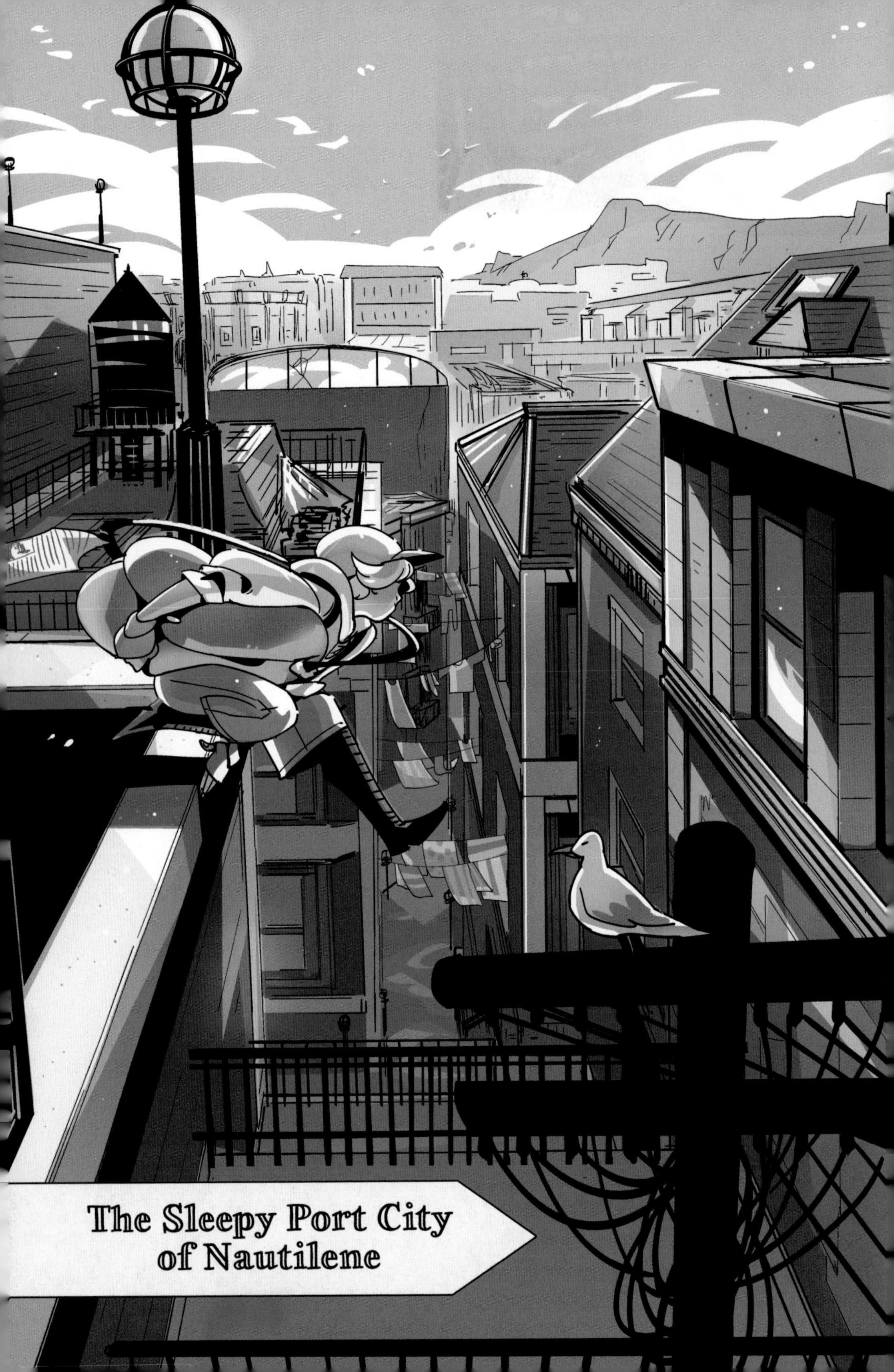
The Sleepy Port City
of Nautilene

HUFF HUFF

PLASH

GOLDIE, THERE YOU ARE!

THEY STILL ON MY TAIL?

GET BACK HERE, BUGLE BRAT!

CATCH ME IF YOU CAN, YA TWEEDLE DUMS!

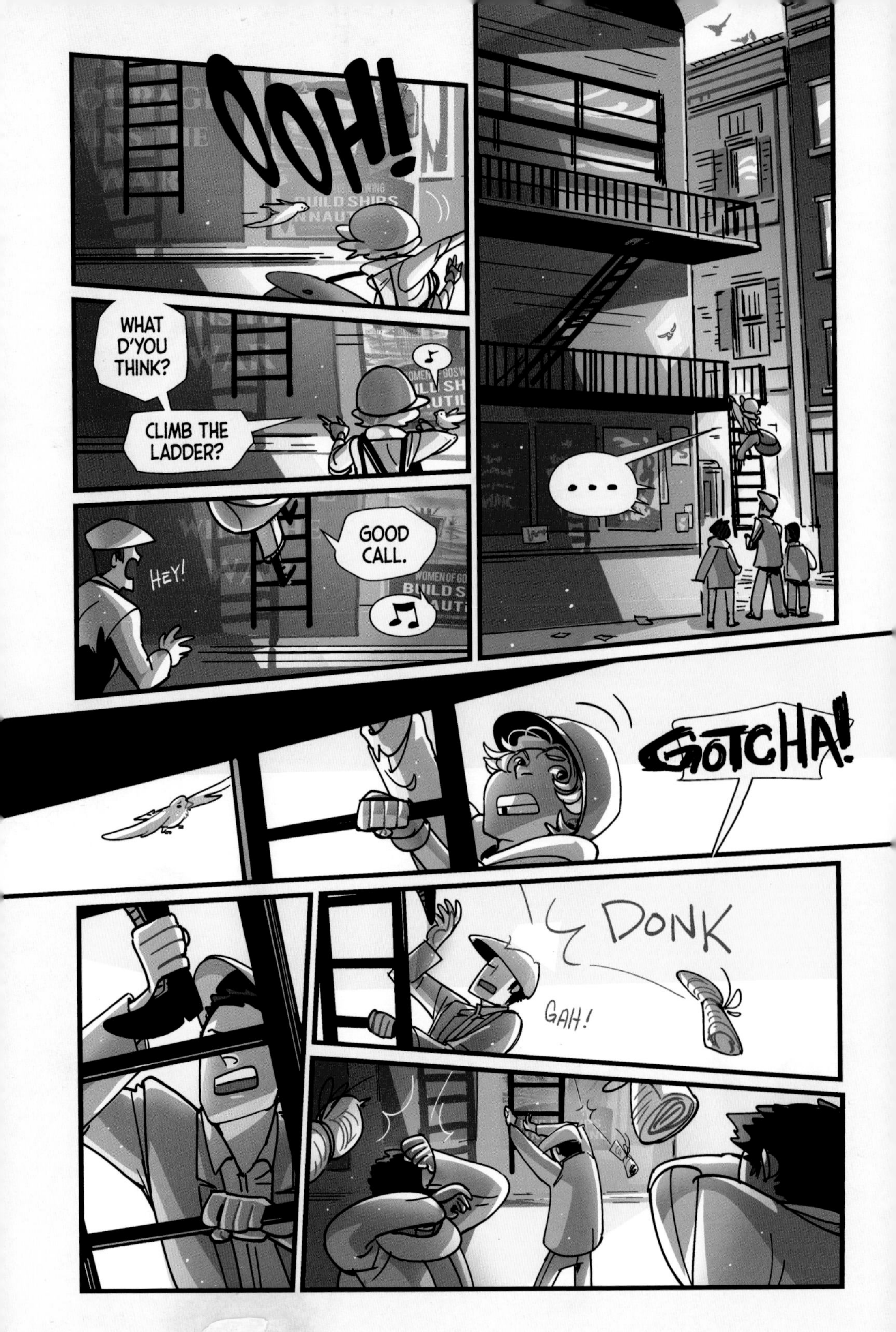
OOH!
WHAT D'YOU THINK?
CLIMB THE LADDER?
HEY!
GOOD CALL.
...
GOTCHA!
DONK
GAH!

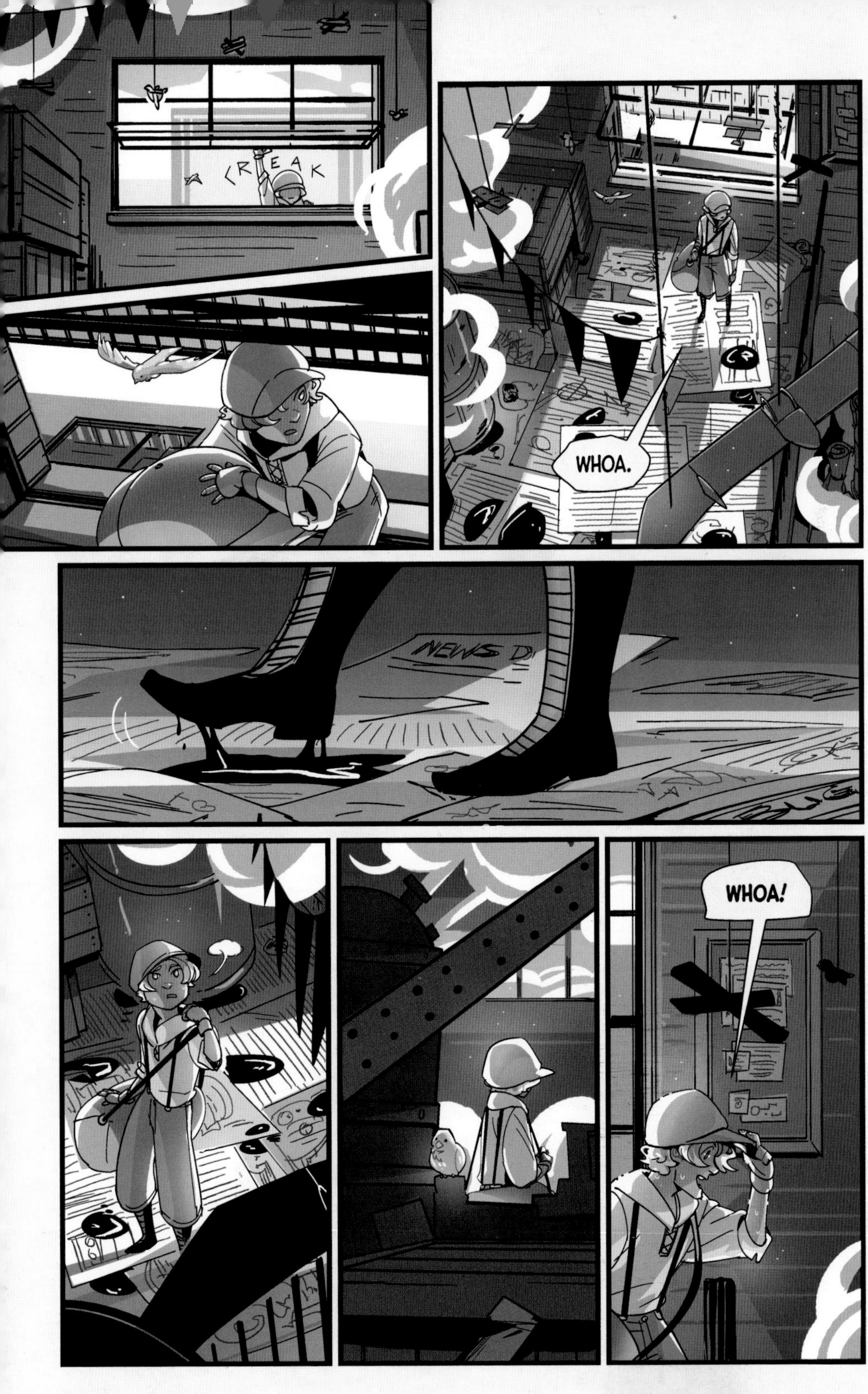
CREAK
WHOA.
NEWS
WHOA!

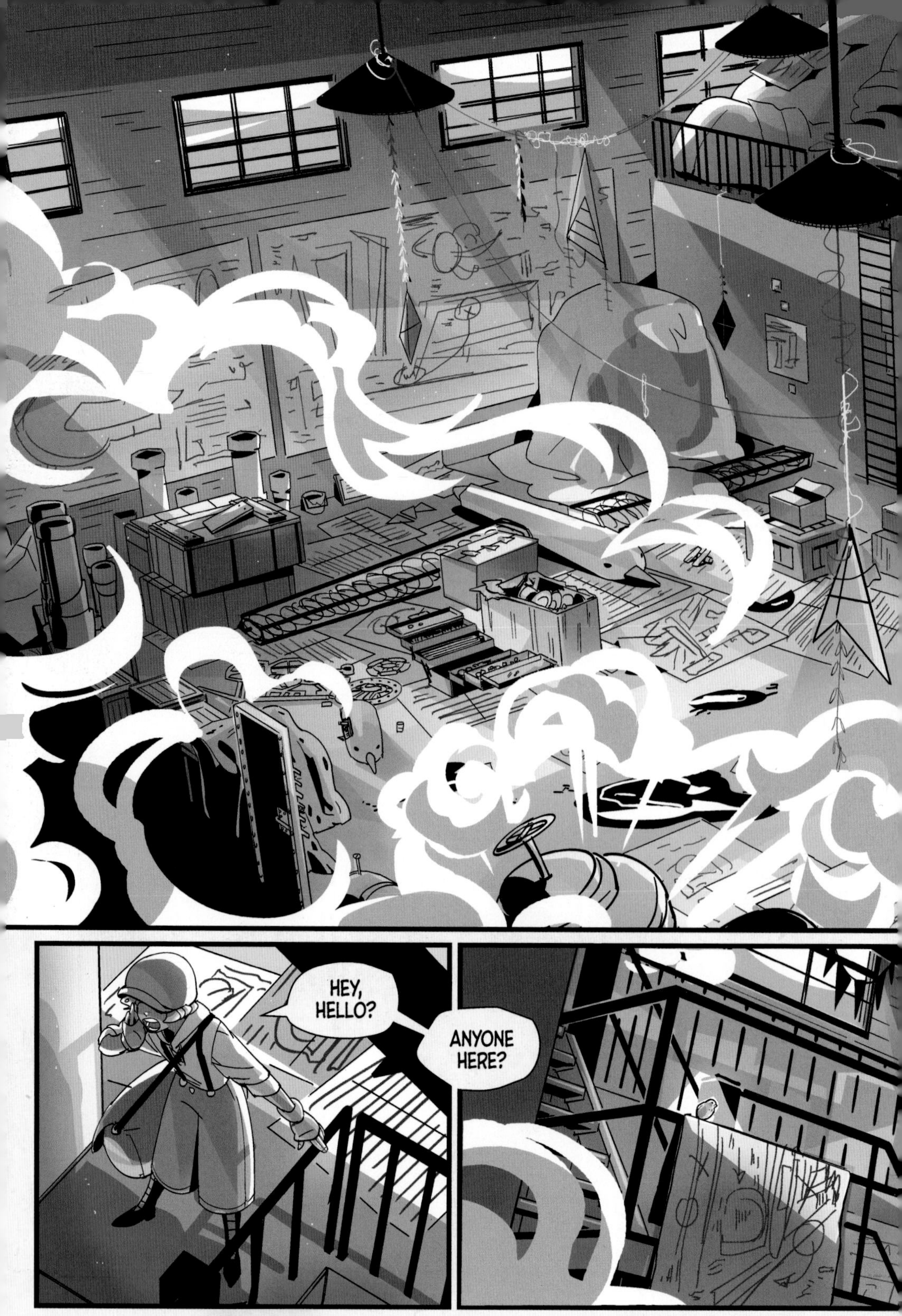
HEY, HELLO?
ANYONE HERE?

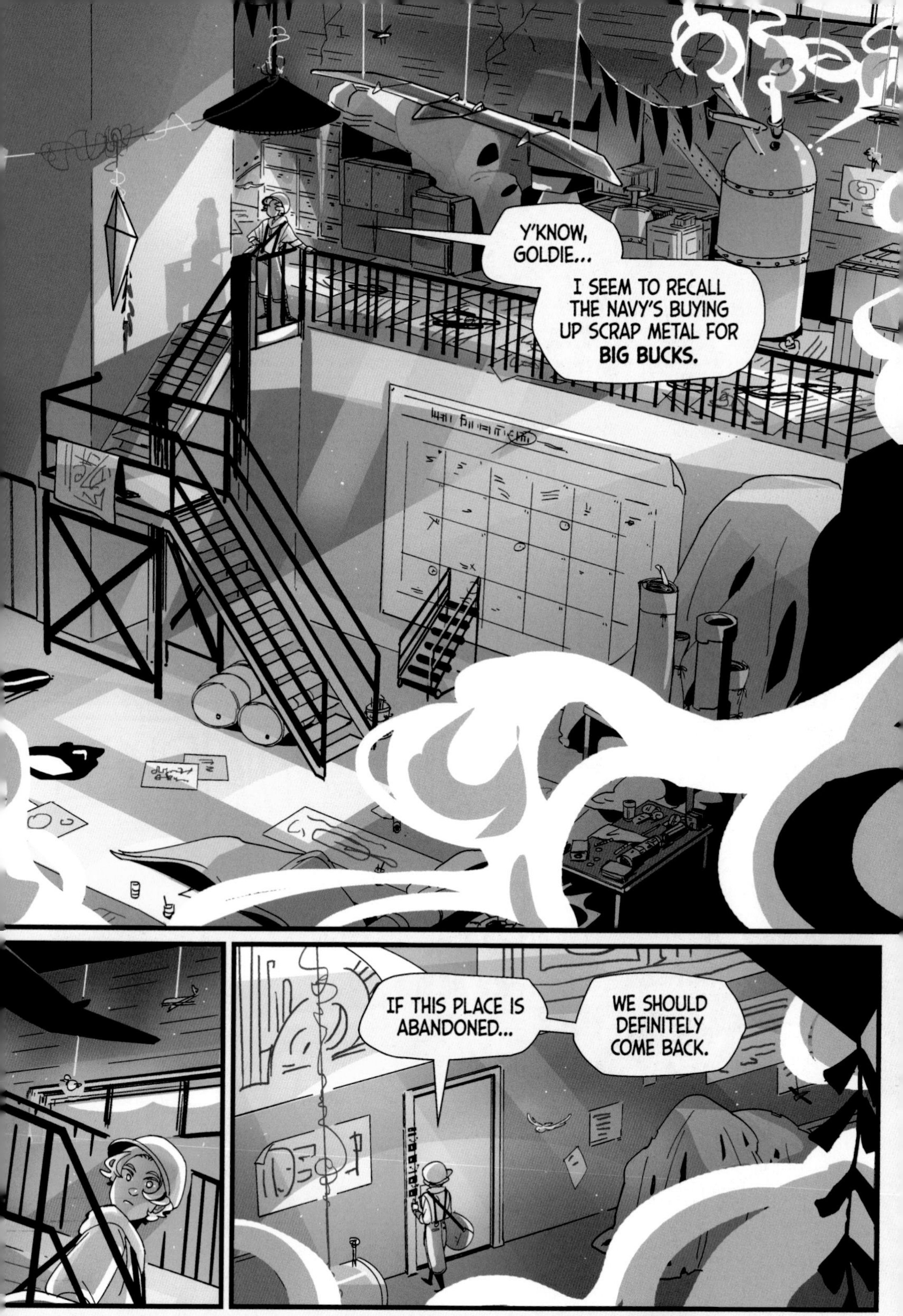
Y'KNOW, GOLDIE...
I SEEM TO RECALL THE NAVY'S BUYING UP SCRAP METAL FOR BIG BUCKS.
IF THIS PLACE IS ABANDONED...
WE SHOULD DEFINITELY COME BACK.

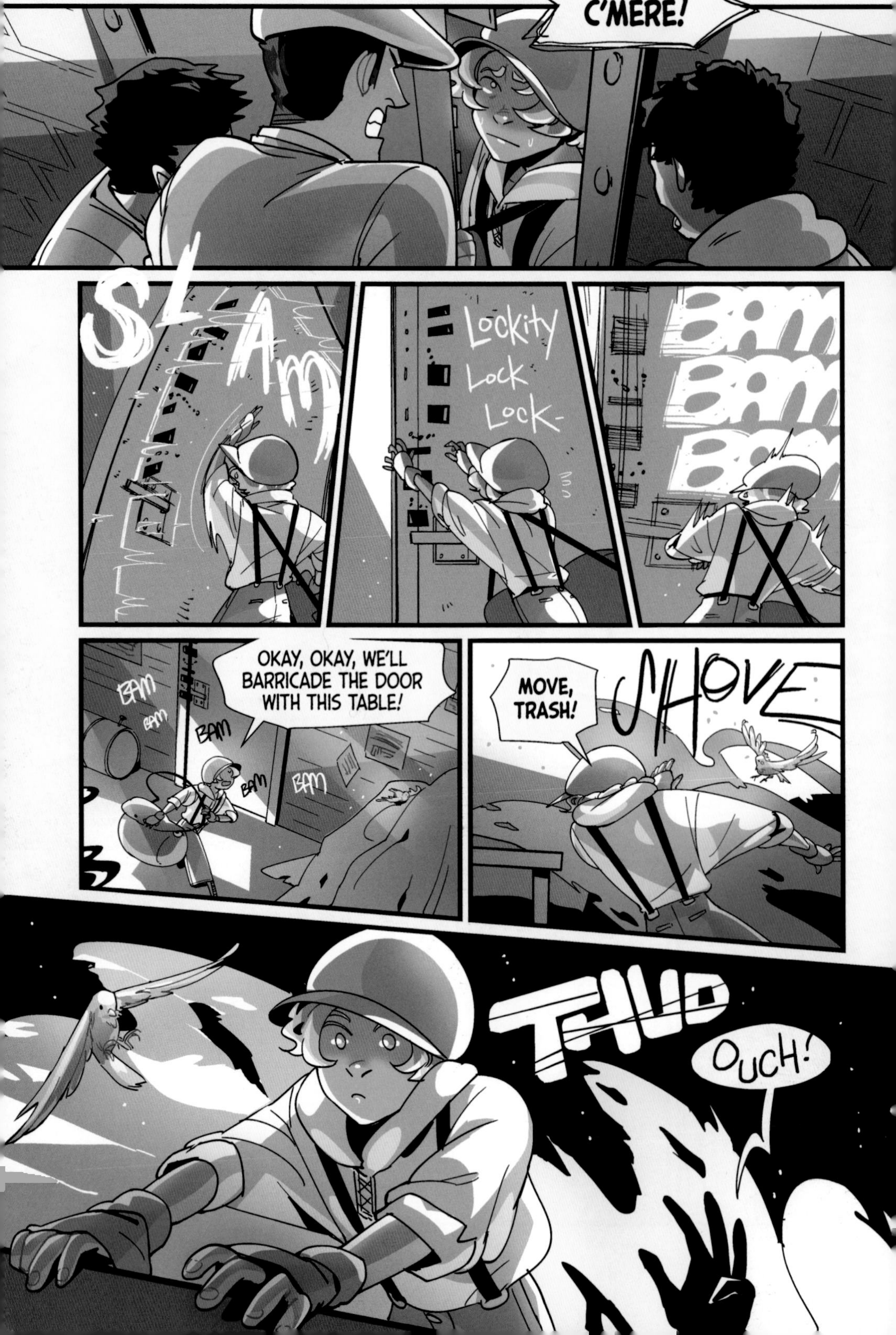
C'MERE!
SLAM
Lockity Lock Lock-
BAM BAM BAM
BAM
BAM
BAM
BAM
BAM
OKAY, OKAY, WE'LL BARRICADE THE DOOR WITH THIS TABLE!
MOVE, TRASH!
SHOVE
THUD
OUCH!

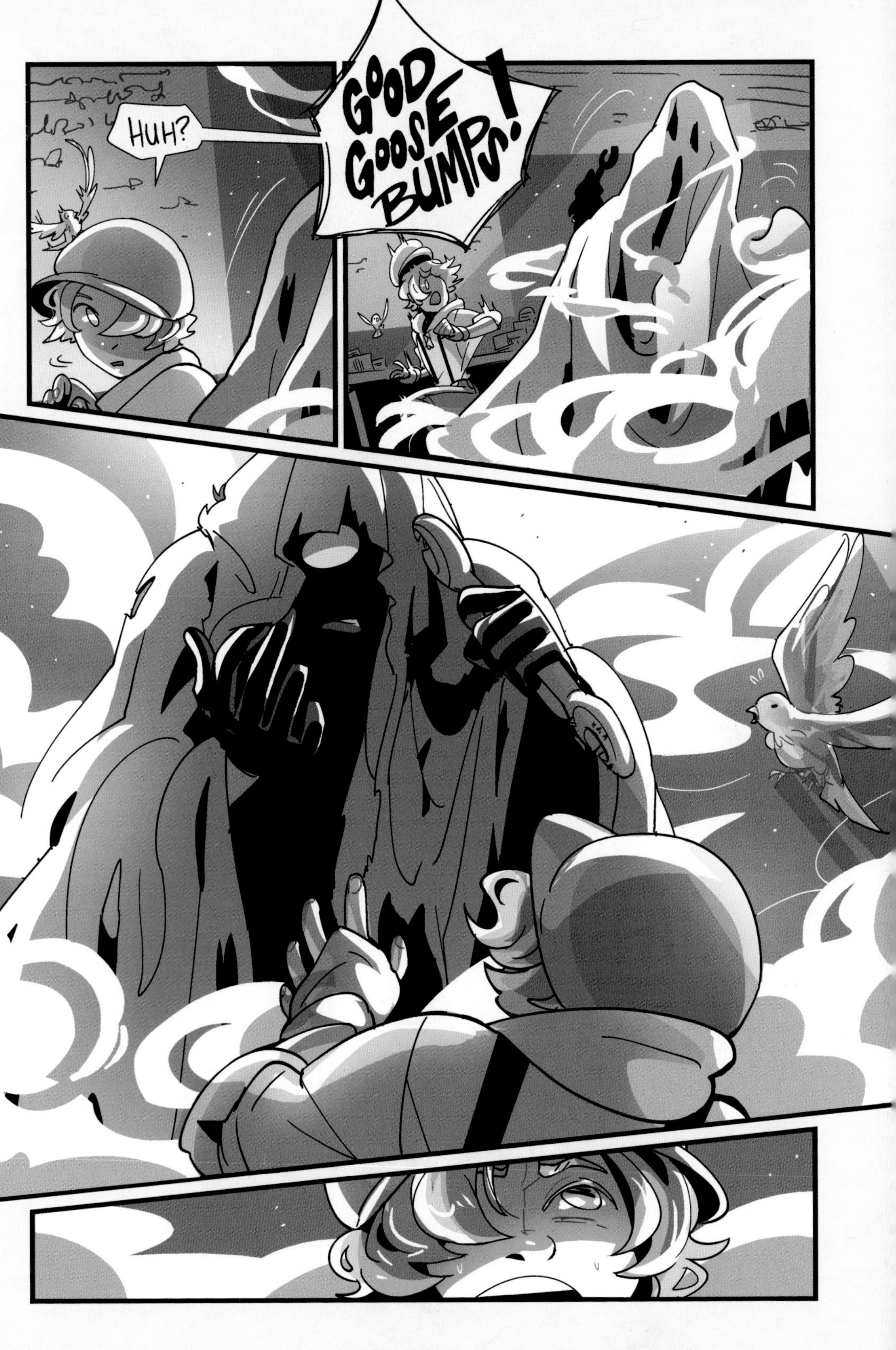
HUH?
GOOD GOOSE BUMPS!

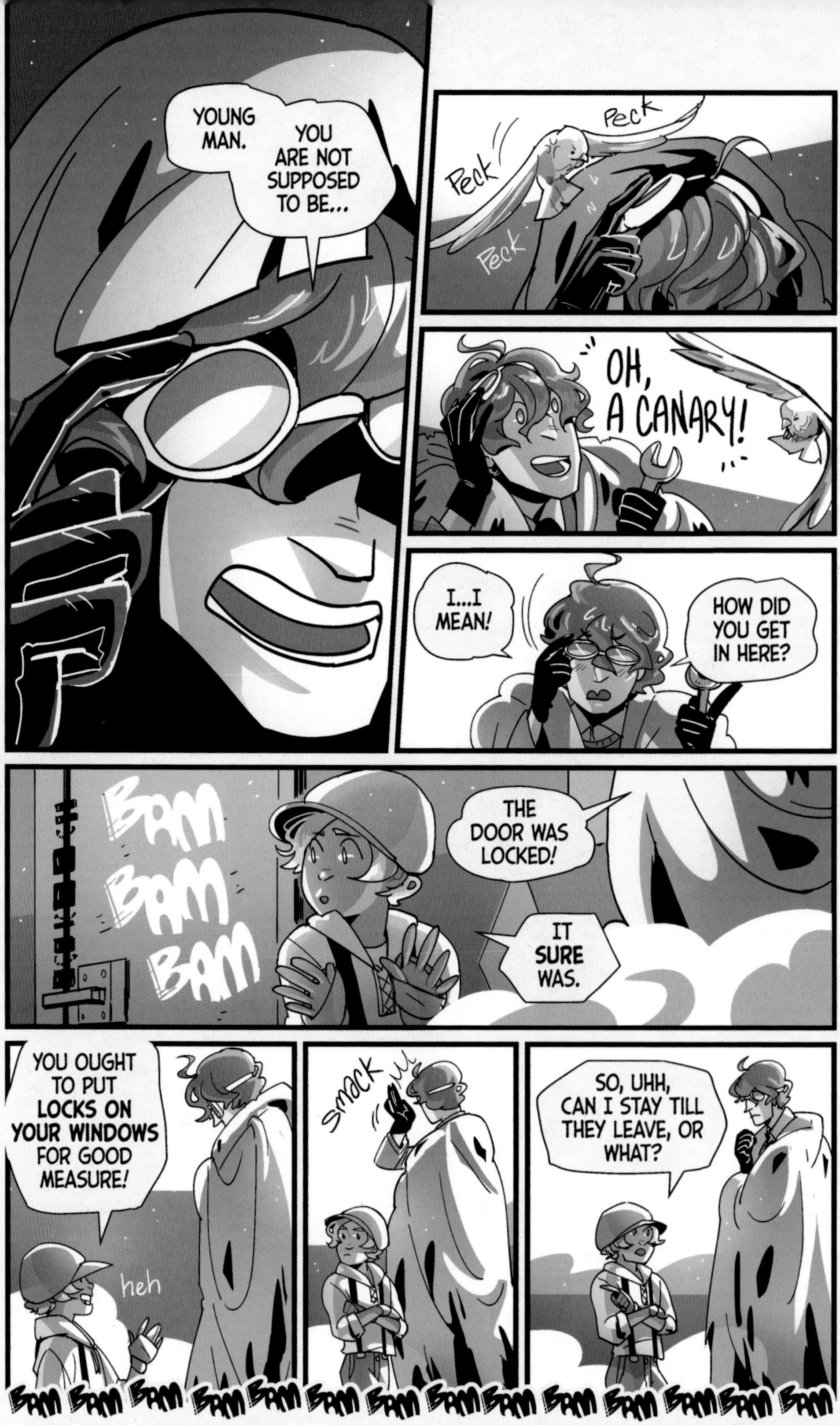
YOUNG MAN.
YOU ARE NOT SUPPOSED TO BE...
Peck
Peck
Peck
OH, A CANARY!
I...I MEAN!
HOW DID YOU GET IN HERE?
BAM BAM BAM
THE DOOR WAS LOCKED!
IT SURE WAS.
YOU OUGHT TO PUT LOCKS ON YOUR WINDOWS FOR GOOD MEASURE!
heh
smack
SO, UHH, CAN I STAY TILL THEY LEAVE, OR WHAT?
BAM BAM BAM BAM BAM BAM BAM BAM BAM BAM BAM BAM BAM BAM

TWO HOURS LATER

CORRECT ME IF I'M WRONG, BUT THEY DON'T SEEM LIKE YOUR FRIENDS.

RIVAL NEWSIES. I WAS SELLING PAPERS ON THEIR TURF.

BAD GAMBLE. NOW I'M GONNA MISS CURFEW AND BE GROUNDED!

HMM, WHAT IF I WROTE YOUR GUARDIAN A NOTE OF EXCUSE?

LIKE: "THANKS, YOUR KID WOKE ME UP BEFORE I SUFFOCATED IN STEAM"?

BINGO!

GASP

I'LL JUST TEAR A PAGE OUT OF MY JOURNAL HERE...

IS THAT GOLD?

AWAH WAIT, ISN'T THIS BOOK VALUABLE?

WELL, SURE! IT'S FULL OF MY MATH THEORIES!

MATH, HUH? LIKE COUNTING MONEY AND STUFF? YOU'RE SPEAKIN' MY LANGUAGE.

I LIKE TO THINK I WAS PRETTY GOOD AT THAT...

I MEAN, BACK WHEN I STILL WENT TO SCHOOL.

YOU AREN'T IN SCHOOL?

WHAT ABOUT YOUR EDUCATION?!

10

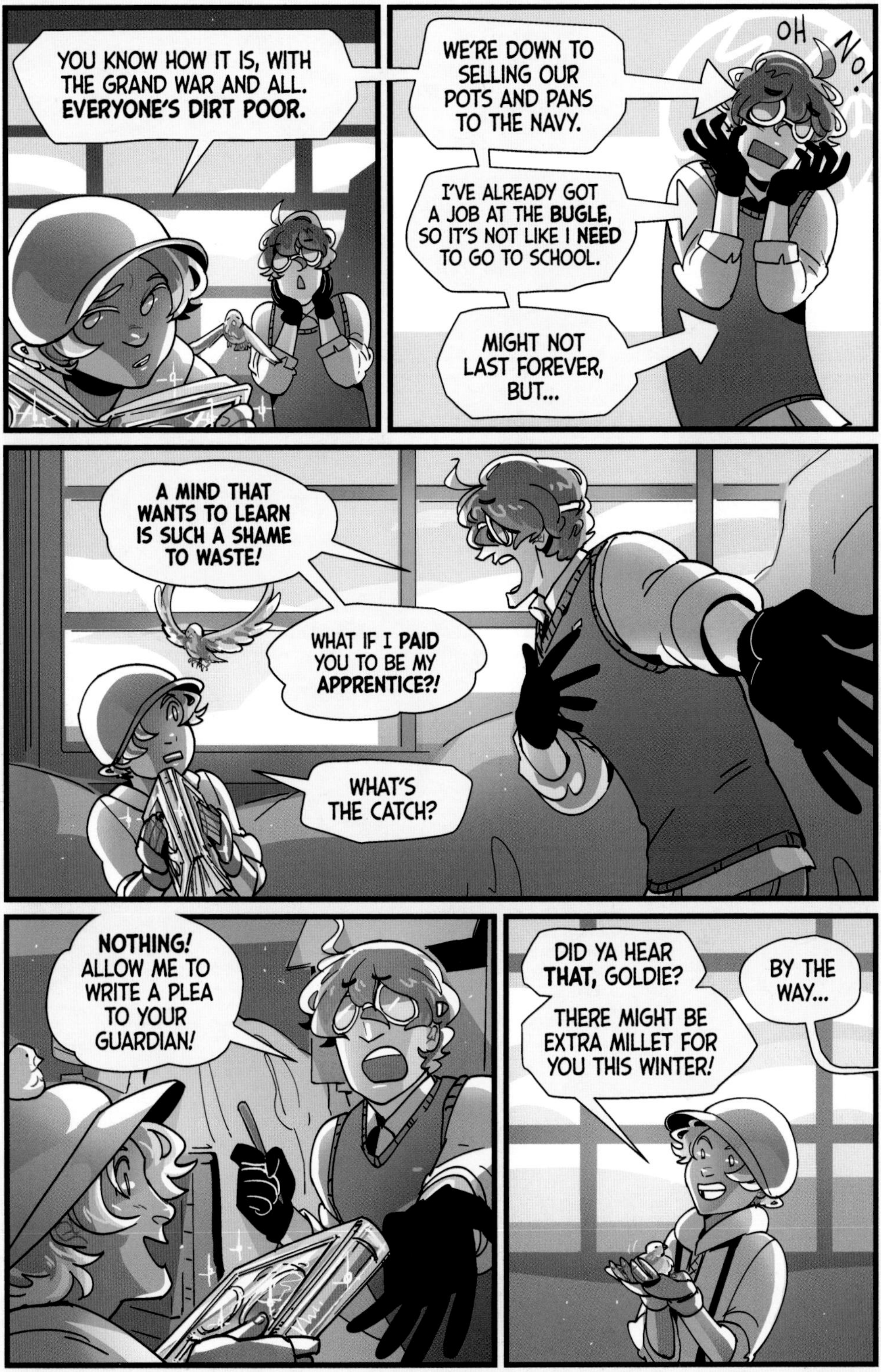
YOU KNOW HOW IT IS, WITH THE GRAND WAR AND ALL. EVERYONE'S DIRT POOR.
WE'RE DOWN TO SELLING OUR POTS AND PANS TO THE NAVY.
OH NO!
I'VE ALREADY GOT A JOB AT THE BUGLE, SO IT'S NOT LIKE I NEED TO GO TO SCHOOL.
MIGHT NOT LAST FOREVER, BUT...
A MIND THAT WANTS TO LEARN IS SUCH A SHAME TO WASTE!
WHAT IF I PAID YOU TO BE MY APPRENTICE?!
WHAT'S THE CATCH?
NOTHING! ALLOW ME TO WRITE A PLEA TO YOUR GUARDIAN!
DID YA HEAR THAT, GOLDIE?
THERE MIGHT BE EXTRA MILLET FOR YOU THIS WINTER!
BY THE WAY...

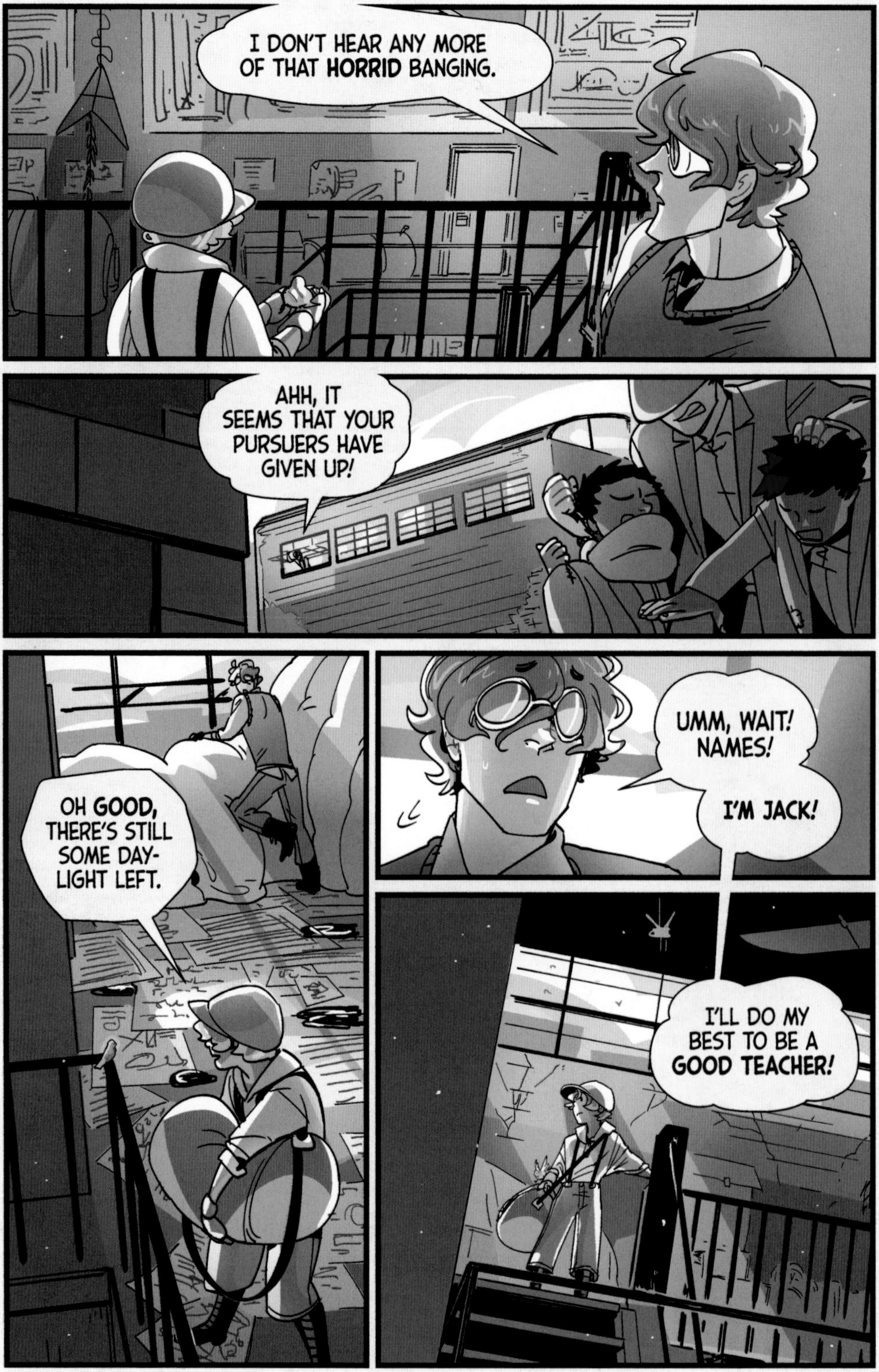
I DON'T HEAR ANY MORE OF THAT HORRID BANGING.
AHH, IT SEEMS THAT YOUR PURSUERS HAVE GIVEN UP!
OH GOOD, THERE'S STILL SOME DAY-LIGHT LEFT.
UMM, WAIT! NAMES!
I'M JACK!
I'LL DO MY BEST TO BE A GOOD TEACHER!

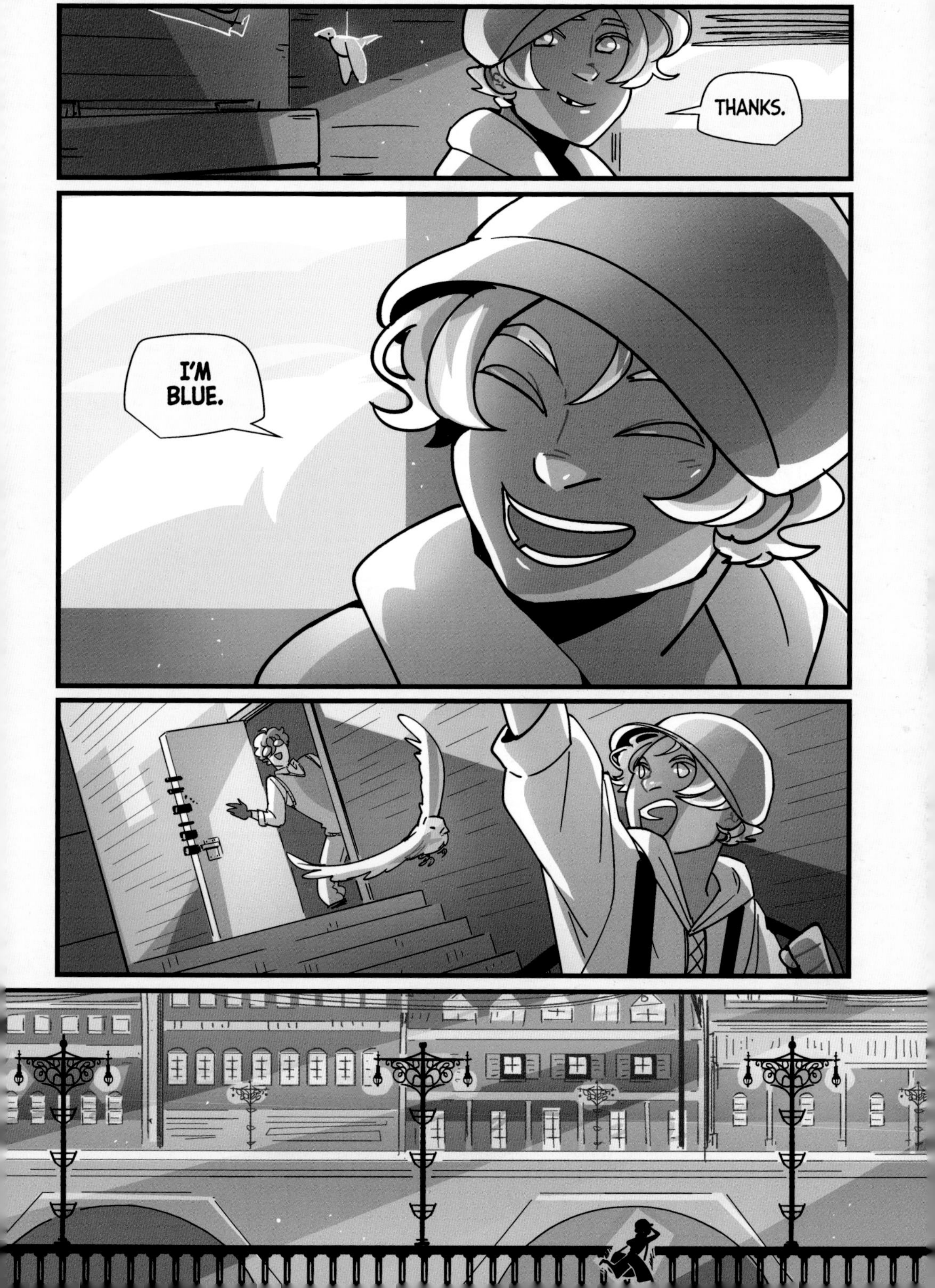
THANKS.
I'M BLUE.

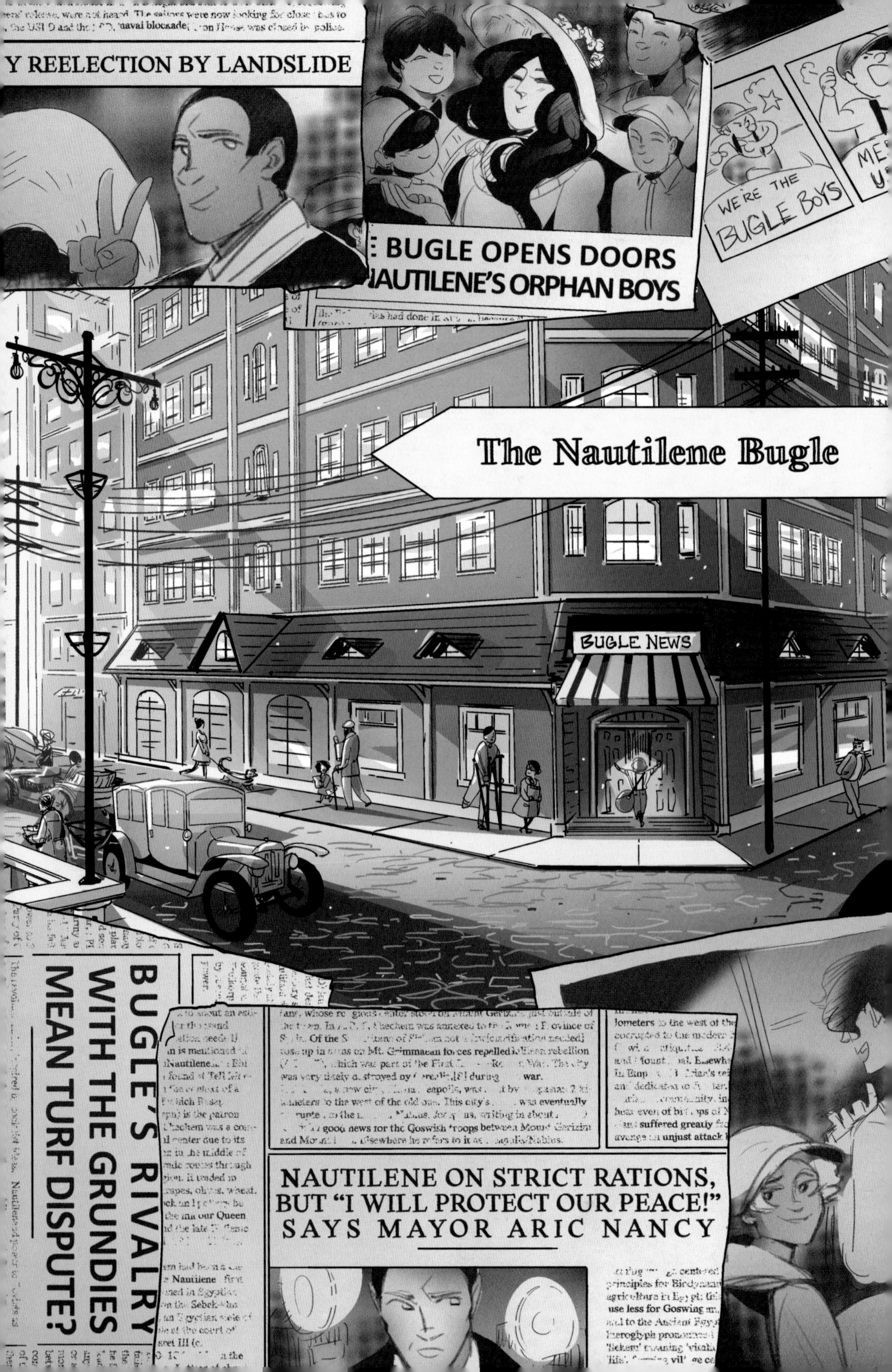
Y REELECTION BY LANDSLIDE
E BUGLE OPENS DOORS
AUTILENE'S ORPHAN BOYS
WE'RE THE BUGLE BOYS
The Nautilene Bugle
BUGLE NEWS
BUGLE'S RIVALRY WITH THE GRUNDIES MEAN TURF DISPUTE?
NAUTILENE ON STRICT RATIONS, BUT "I WILL PROTECT OUR PEACE!" SAYS MAYOR ARIC NANCY

WE GIVE THANKS FOR THE FOOD ON OUR TABLE...

FOR WE KNOW THERE ARE MANY IN NAUTILENE WHO GO WITHOUT.

LET US BEAR IN MIND THE SACRIFICES OF THE SOLDIERS STILL FIGHTING FOR US...

Peek

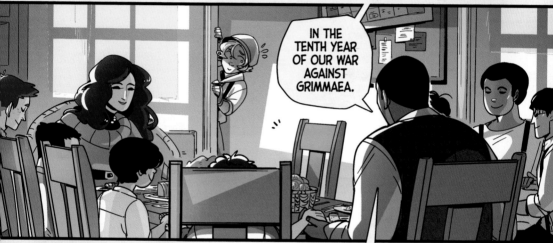

IN THE TENTH YEAR OF OUR WAR AGAINST GRIMMAEA.

LET US NEVER FORGET OUR NOBLE QUEEN,

WHO LOST HER FAMILY IN THAT DREADFUL FIRST ATTACK AGAINST OUR GREAT NATION OF GOSWING...

SO THAT WE MAY CHERISH OUR OWN SMALL BUT WONDERFUL PATCHWORK FAMILY.

HMMM.

AHEM...

tap tap

WE ARE THANKFUL.

WE ARE THANKFUL!

NOW THEN, LET'S EAT!

SO, THE WAR STARTED 'CAUSE **GRIMMAEA** ATTACKED OUR ROYAL FAMILY, RIGHT?

munch munch

TODAY'S BUGLE SAID THAT IT STARTED BECAUSE OF A **BORDER DISPUTE** BETWEEN GOSWING AND GRIMMAEA.

BLUE, YOU READ THE BUGLE?

OF COURSE. EVERY DAY!

16

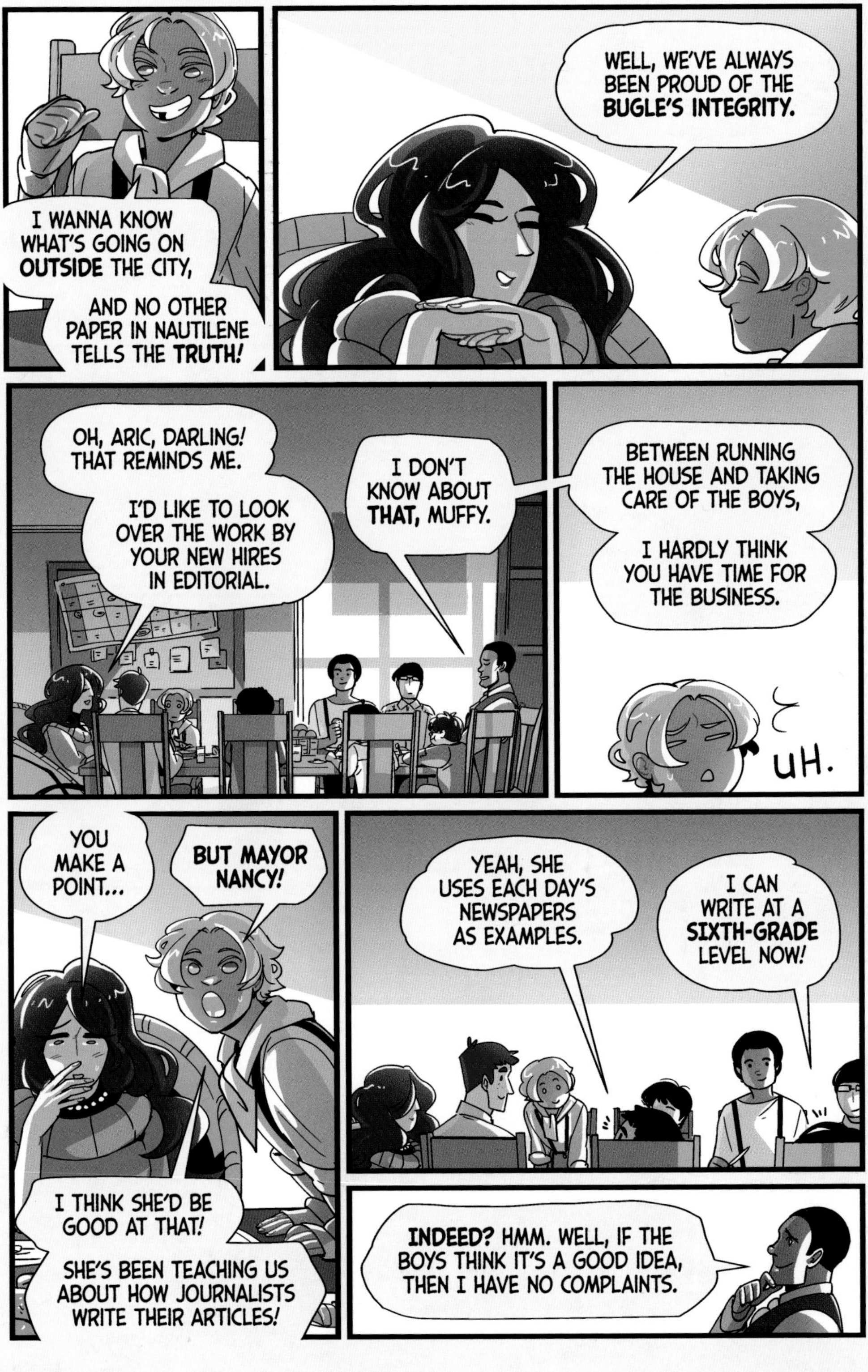
I WANNA KNOW WHAT'S GOING ON OUTSIDE THE CITY,
AND NO OTHER PAPER IN NAUTILENE TELLS THE TRUTH!
WELL, WE'VE ALWAYS BEEN PROUD OF THE BUGLE'S INTEGRITY.
OH, ARIC, DARLING! THAT REMINDS ME.
I'D LIKE TO LOOK OVER THE WORK BY YOUR NEW HIRES IN EDITORIAL.
I DON'T KNOW ABOUT THAT, MUFFY.
BETWEEN RUNNING THE HOUSE AND TAKING CARE OF THE BOYS,
I HARDLY THINK YOU HAVE TIME FOR THE BUSINESS.
UH.
YOU MAKE A POINT...
BUT MAYOR NANCY!
I THINK SHE'D BE GOOD AT THAT!
SHE'S BEEN TEACHING US ABOUT HOW JOURNALISTS WRITE THEIR ARTICLES!
YEAH, SHE USES EACH DAY'S NEWSPAPERS AS EXAMPLES.
I CAN WRITE AT A SIXTH-GRADE LEVEL NOW!
INDEED? HMM. WELL, IF THE BOYS THINK IT'S A GOOD IDEA, THEN I HAVE NO COMPLAINTS.

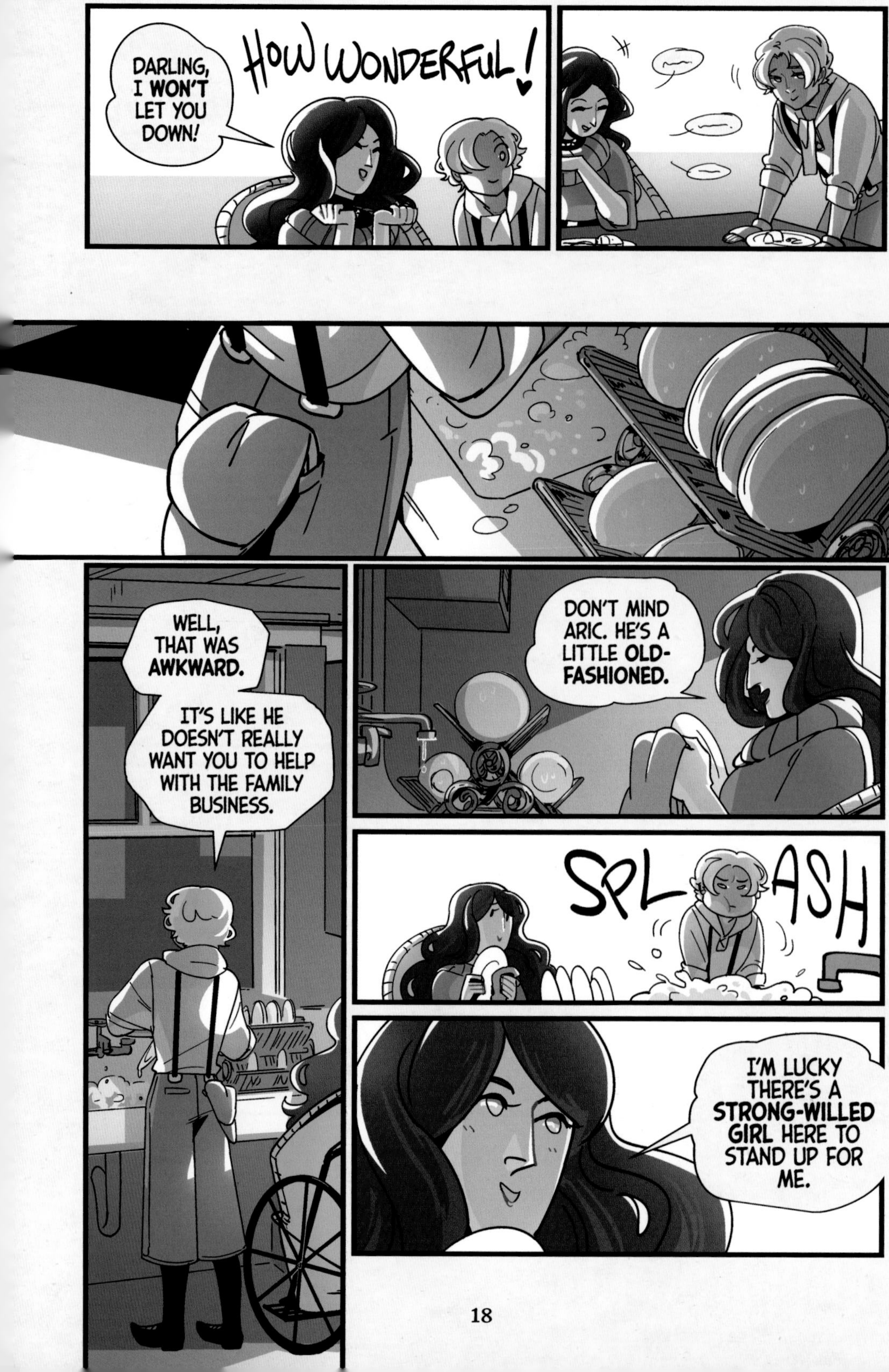
DARLING, I WON'T LET YOU DOWN!
HOW WONDERFUL!
WELL, THAT WAS AWKWARD.
IT'S LIKE HE DOESN'T REALLY WANT YOU TO HELP WITH THE FAMILY BUSINESS.
DON'T MIND ARIC. HE'S A LITTLE OLD-FASHIONED.
SPLASH
I'M LUCKY THERE'S A STRONG-WILLED GIRL HERE TO STAND UP FOR ME.

I APPRECIATE THAT YOU'VE KEPT MY SECRET FOR THREE YEARS.

OH, I'M SO GLAD TO HAVE YOU HERE!

I THINK YOUR NEW PAPER ROUTES HAVE **REALLY** HELPED US GET THE BUGLE OUT THERE!

MA'AM...

WHAT IS IT, BLUE?

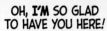

DO YOU THINK I'VE... PROVEN MYSELF?

Y'THINK THEY'D STILL LET ME BE A NEWSBOY IF THEY KNEW I'M NOT A BOY?

DUCKLING, IF ANYONE'S PROOF THAT NEWSIES DON'T HAVE TO BE BOYS, IT'S **YOU**.

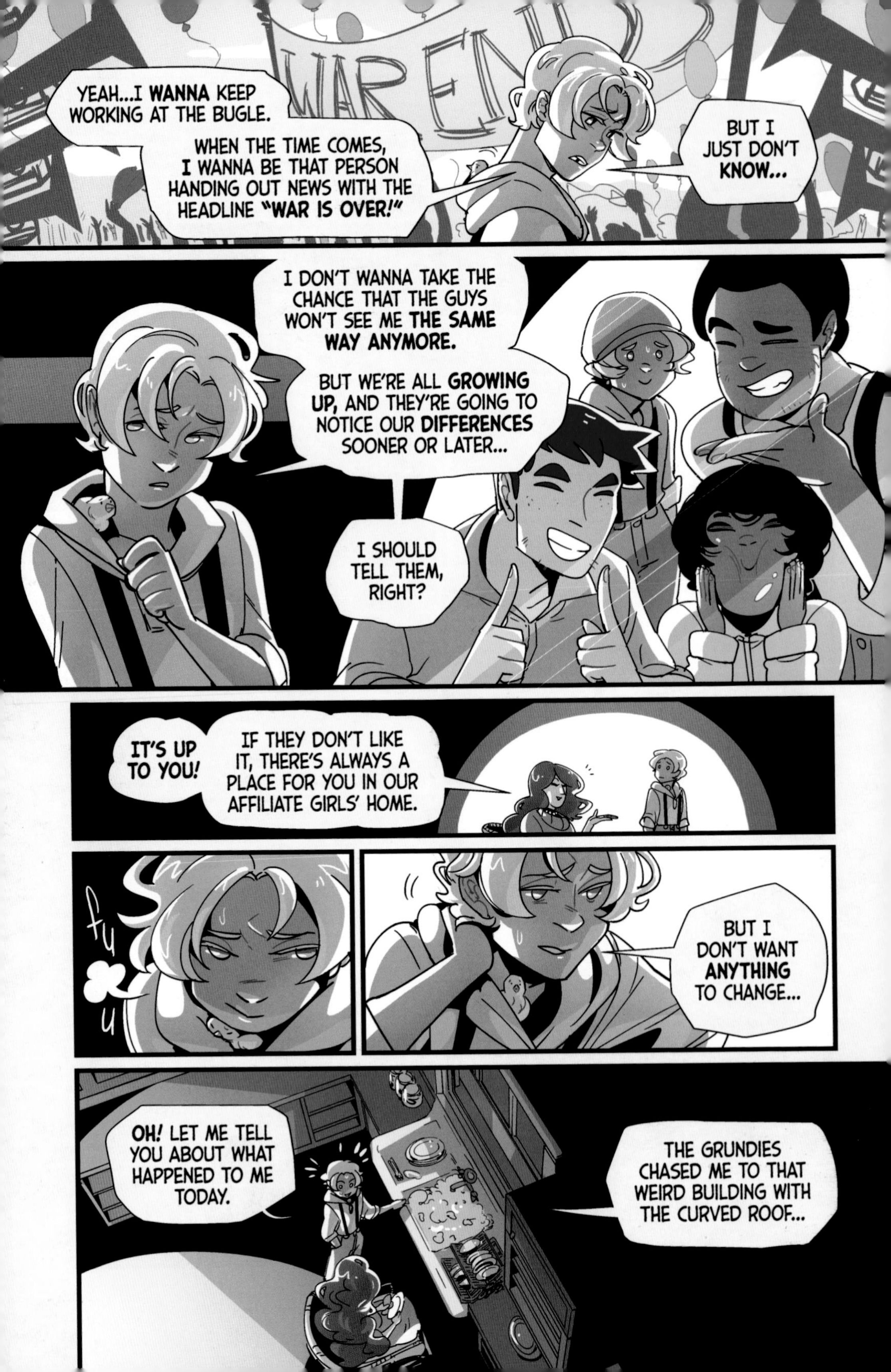
WAR END
YEAH...I WANNA KEEP WORKING AT THE BUGLE.
WHEN THE TIME COMES, I WANNA BE THAT PERSON HANDING OUT NEWS WITH THE HEADLINE "WAR IS OVER!"
BUT I JUST DON'T KNOW...
I DON'T WANNA TAKE THE CHANCE THAT THE GUYS WON'T SEE ME THE SAME WAY ANYMORE.
BUT WE'RE ALL GROWING UP, AND THEY'RE GOING TO NOTICE OUR DIFFERENCES SOONER OR LATER...
I SHOULD TELL THEM, RIGHT?
IT'S UP TO YOU!
IF THEY DON'T LIKE IT, THERE'S ALWAYS A PLACE FOR YOU IN OUR AFFILIATE GIRLS' HOME.
fu
u
BUT I DON'T WANT ANYTHING TO CHANGE...
OH! LET ME TELL YOU ABOUT WHAT HAPPENED TO ME TODAY.
THE GRUNDIES CHASED ME TO THAT WEIRD BUILDING WITH THE CURVED ROOF...

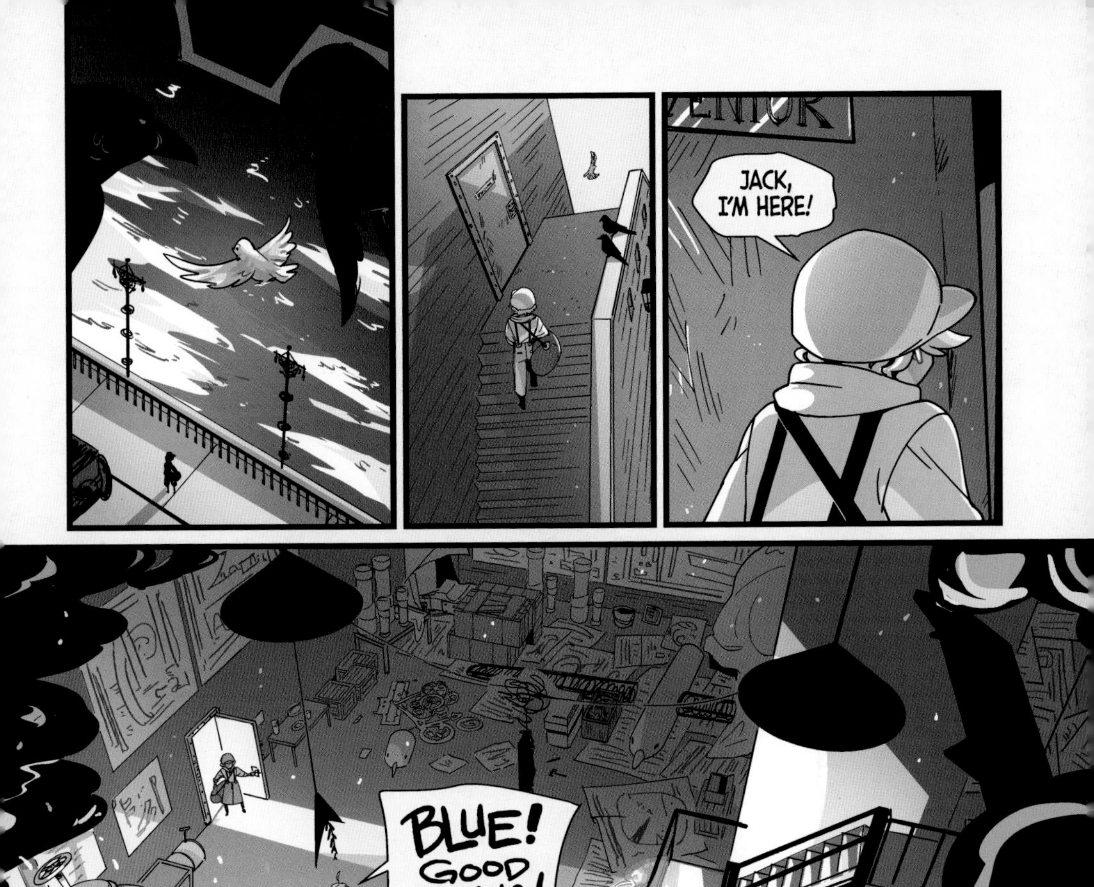
JACK, I'M HERE!
BLUE! GOOD TIMING!
HELP ME PUT OUT THE SMALL FIRES!
OW! NOW I'M ON FIRE!

Day One as Jack's Apprentice

Day Two

I'M SO SORRY, MY MIND IS ON A **MILLION** OTHER THINGS RIGHT NOW.

Day Three

NOW THESE FREQUENCIES WILL ATTRACT CERTAIN TYPES OF BIRDS...

BUT I CAN'T REMEMBER THE RIGHT NUMBER FOR THE MACHINE.

RAVENS GULLS SANDERLINGS

THREE FOUR EIGHT..? THOUSAND?

WHAT FREQUENCY DID THOSE **DARNED CORVIDS** LIKE...?

I HAVEN'T A CLUE WHAT YOU'RE...

DID I LOCK THE FRONT DOOR?

HUH?

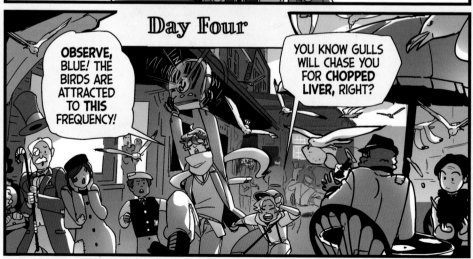

Day Four

OBSERVE, BLUE! THE BIRDS ARE ATTRACTED TO **THIS** FREQUENCY!

YOU KNOW GULLS WILL CHASE YOU FOR **CHOPPED LIVER**, RIGHT?

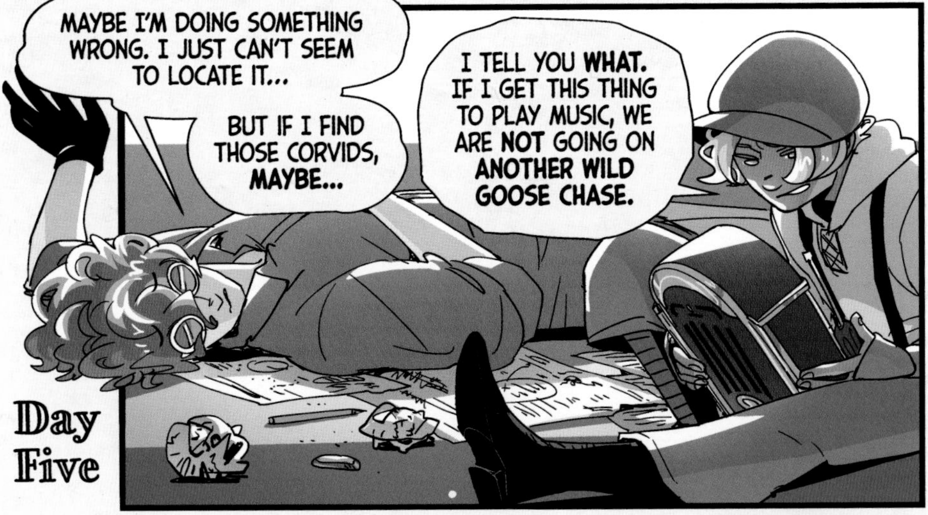
MAYBE I'M DOING SOMETHING WRONG. I JUST CAN'T SEEM TO LOCATE IT...
BUT IF I FIND THOSE CORVIDS, MAYBE...
I TELL YOU WHAT. IF I GET THIS THING TO PLAY MUSIC, WE ARE NOT GOING ON ANOTHER WILD GOOSE CHASE.

Day Five

Day Six

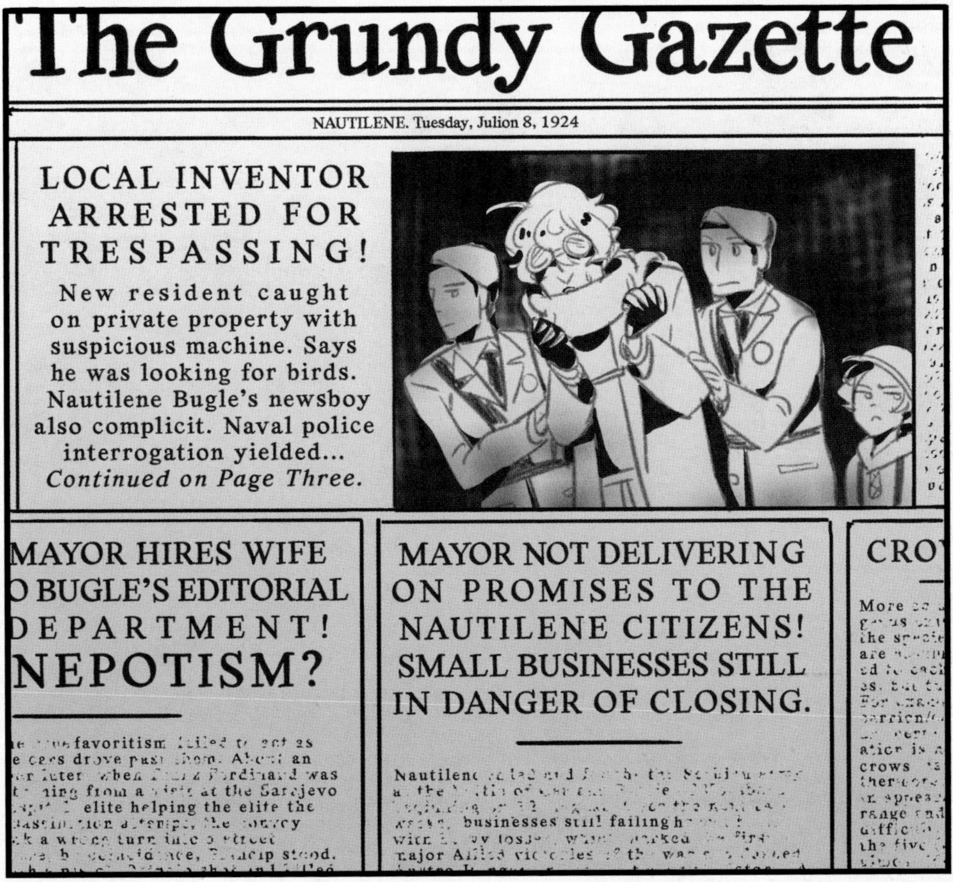

The Grundy Gazette

NAUTILENE. Tuesday, Julion 8, 1924

LOCAL INVENTOR ARRESTED FOR TRESPASSING!

New resident caught on private property with suspicious machine. Says he was looking for birds. Nautilene Bugle's newsboy also complicit. Naval police interrogation yielded...
Continued on Page Three.

MAYOR HIRES WIFE O BUGLE'S EDITORIAL DEPARTMENT! NEPOTISM?

MAYOR NOT DELIVERING ON PROMISES TO THE NAUTILENE CITIZENS! SMALL BUSINESSES STILL IN DANGER OF CLOSING.

CROV

Day Seven

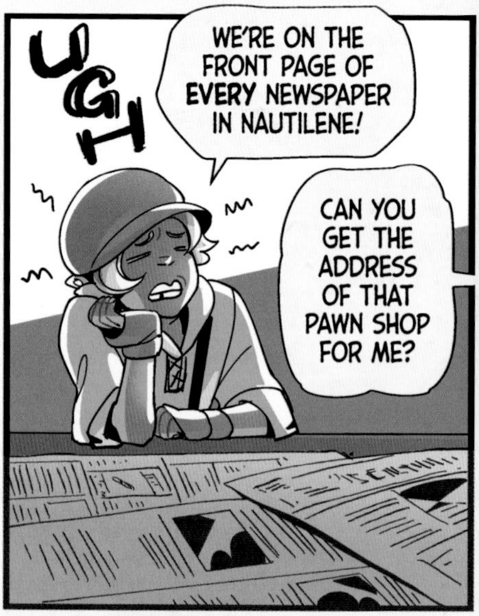
UGH
WE'RE ON THE FRONT PAGE OF EVERY NEWSPAPER IN NAUTILENE!
CAN YOU GET THE ADDRESS OF THAT PAWN SHOP FOR ME?

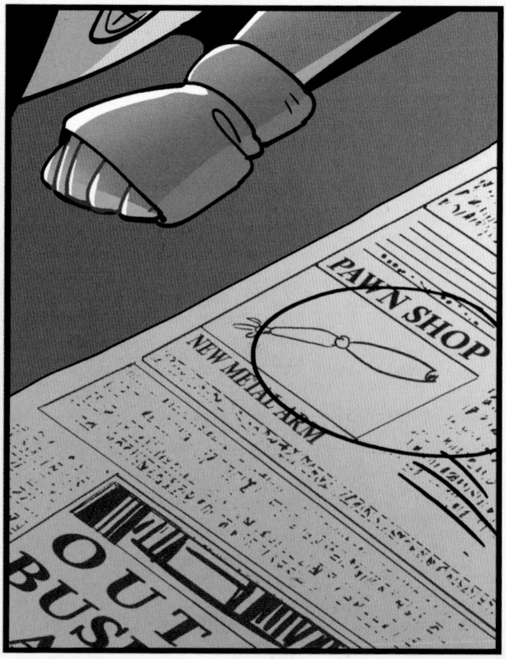
PAWN SHOP
NEW METAL ARM
OUT
BUST

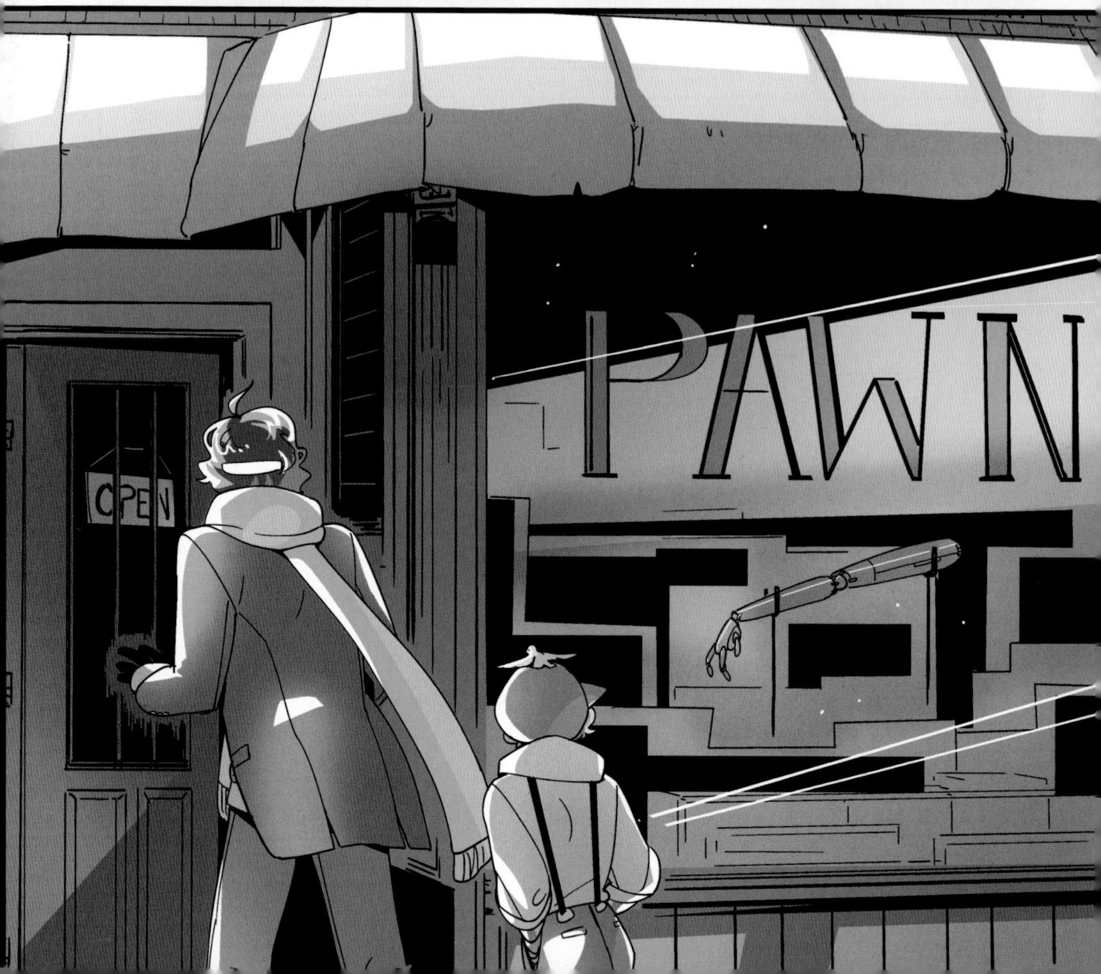
OPEN
PAWN

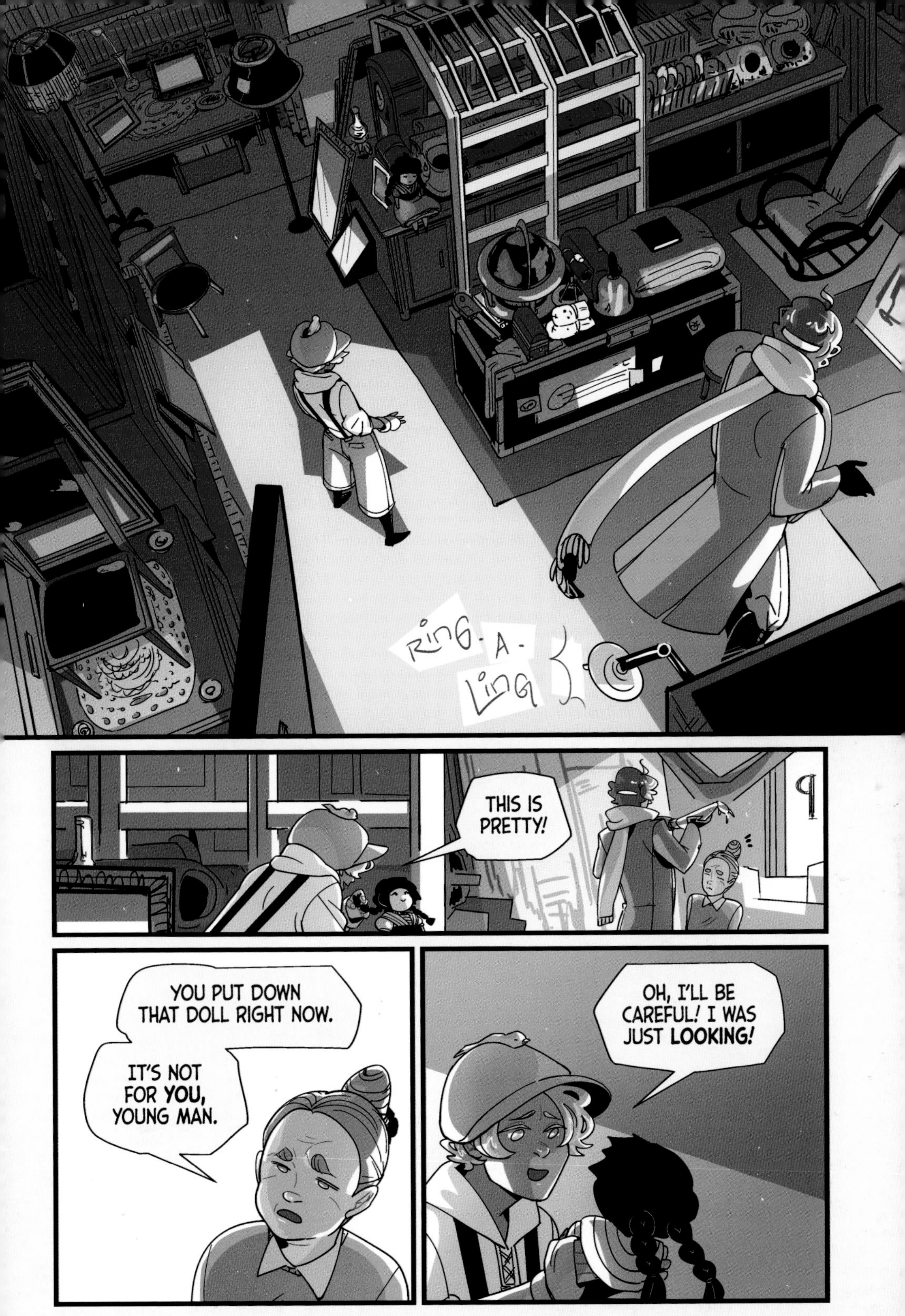
RING-A-LING
THIS IS PRETTY!
YOU PUT DOWN THAT DOLL RIGHT NOW.
IT'S NOT FOR **YOU**, YOUNG MAN.
OH, I'LL BE CAREFUL! I WAS JUST **LOOKING!**

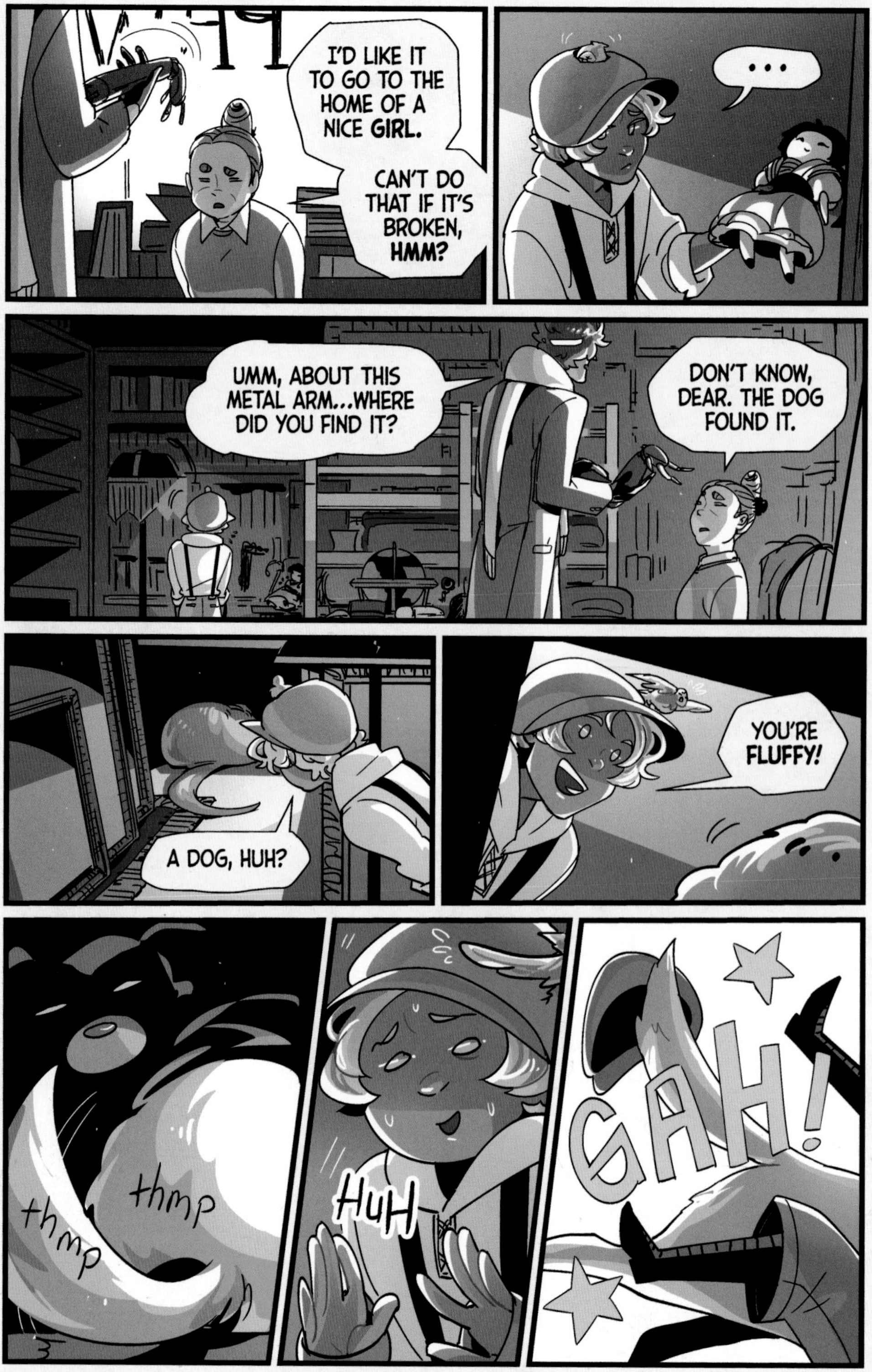
I'D LIKE IT TO GO TO THE HOME OF A NICE GIRL.
CAN'T DO THAT IF IT'S BROKEN, HMM?
...
UMM, ABOUT THIS METAL ARM...WHERE DID YOU FIND IT?
DON'T KNOW, DEAR. THE DOG FOUND IT.
A DOG, HUH?
YOU'RE FLUFFY!
thmp
thmp
HuH
GAH!

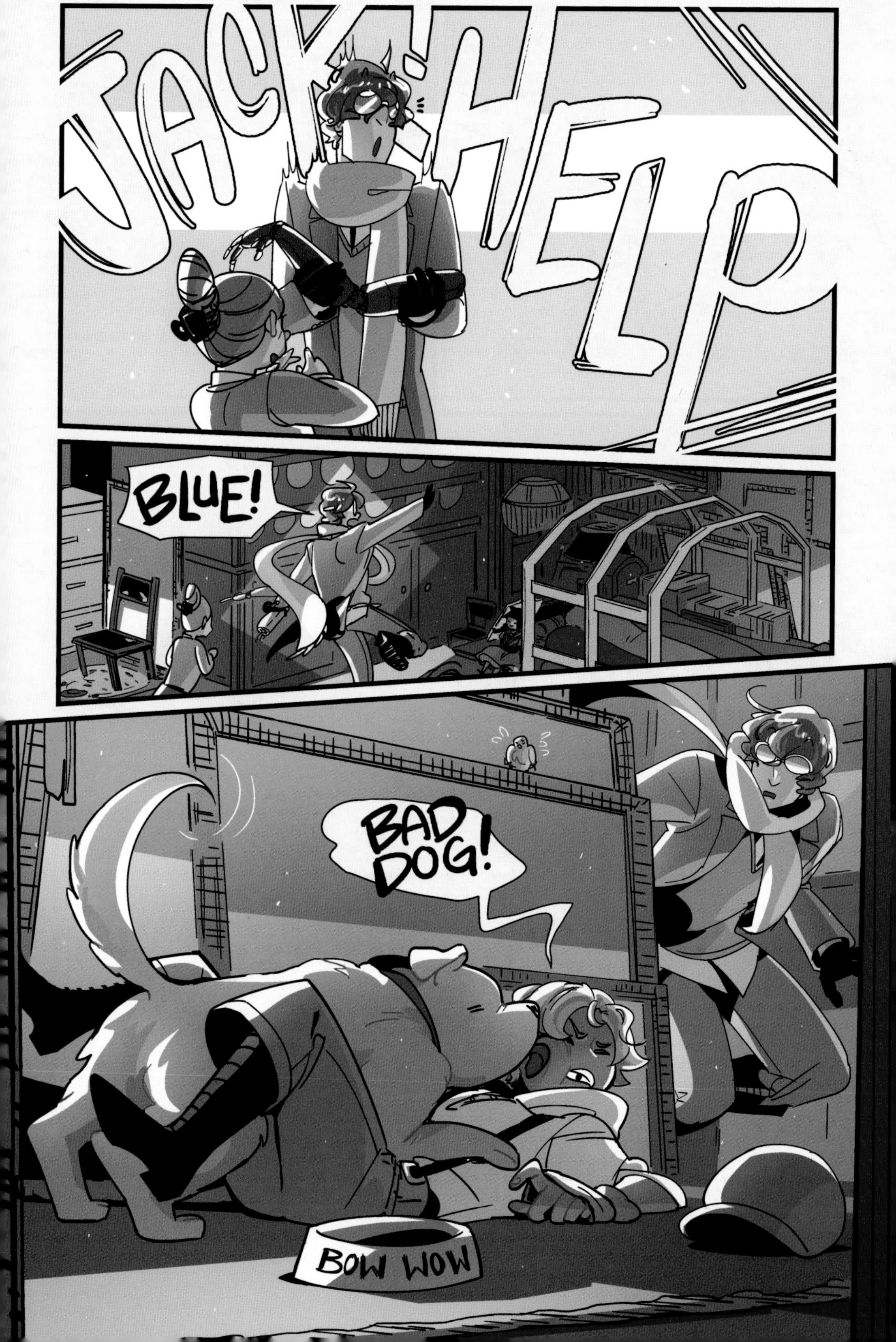
JACK! HELP
BLUE!
BAD DOG!
BOW WOW

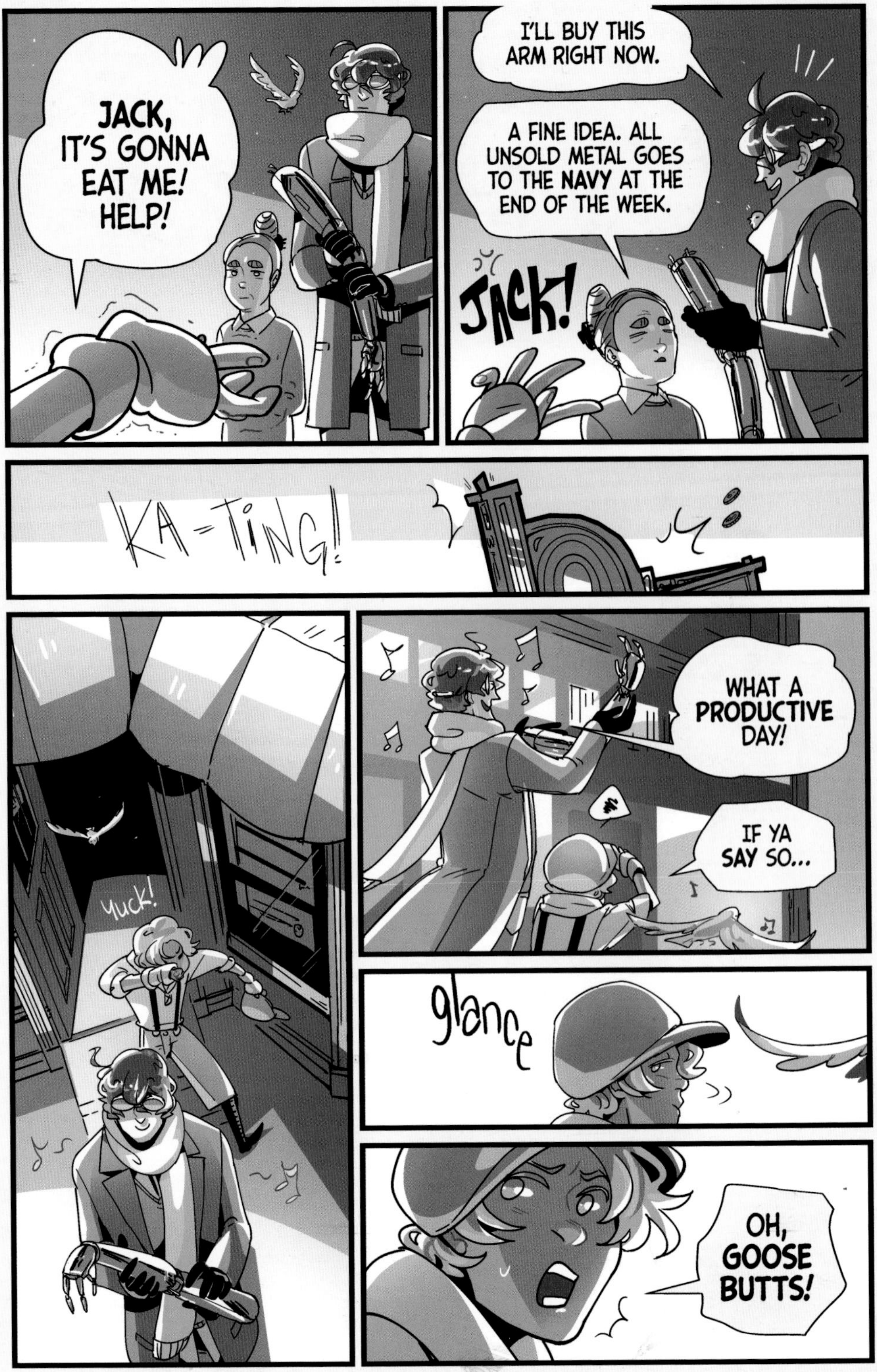
JACK, IT'S GONNA EAT ME! HELP!
I'LL BUY THIS ARM RIGHT NOW.
A FINE IDEA. ALL UNSOLD METAL GOES TO THE NAVY AT THE END OF THE WEEK.
JACK!
KA-TING!
YUCK!
WHAT A PRODUCTIVE DAY!
IF YA SAY SO...
glance
OH, GOOSE BUTTS!

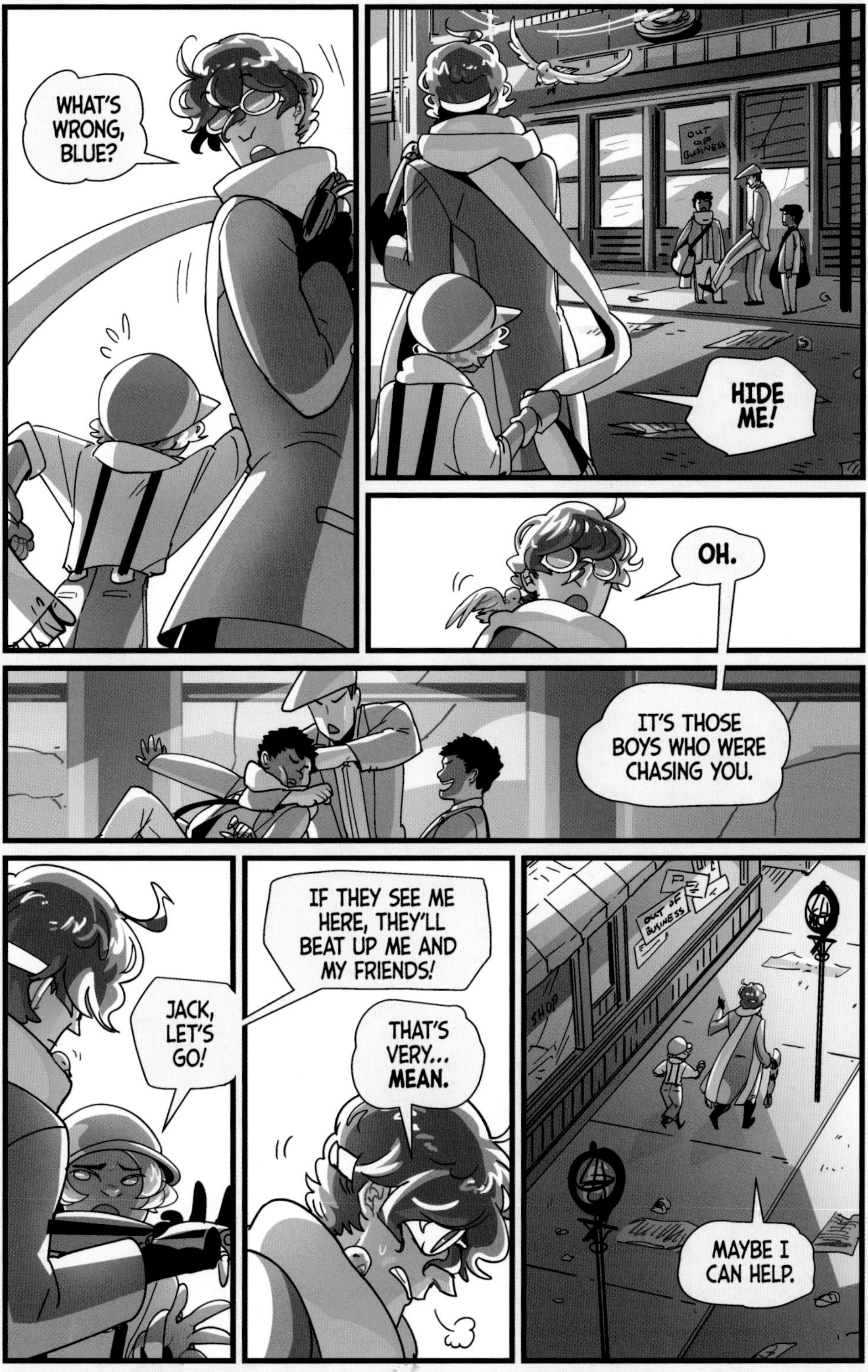

WHAT'S WRONG, BLUE?
OUT OF BUSINESS
HIDE ME!
OH.
IT'S THOSE BOYS WHO WERE CHASING YOU.
JACK, LET'S GO!
IF THEY SEE ME HERE, THEY'LL BEAT UP ME AND MY FRIENDS!
THAT'S VERY... MEAN.
OUT OF BUSINESS
SHOP
MAYBE I CAN HELP.

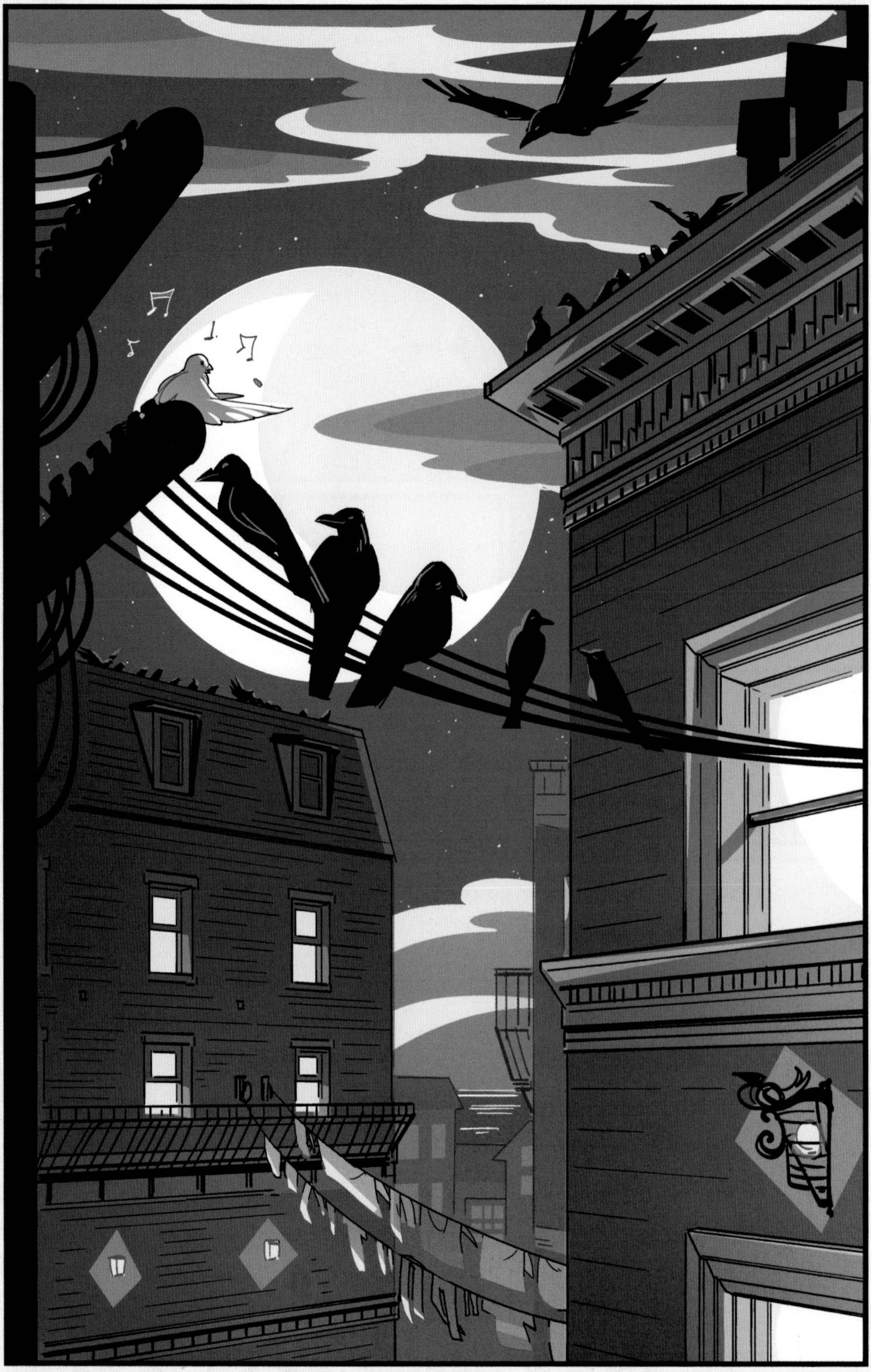

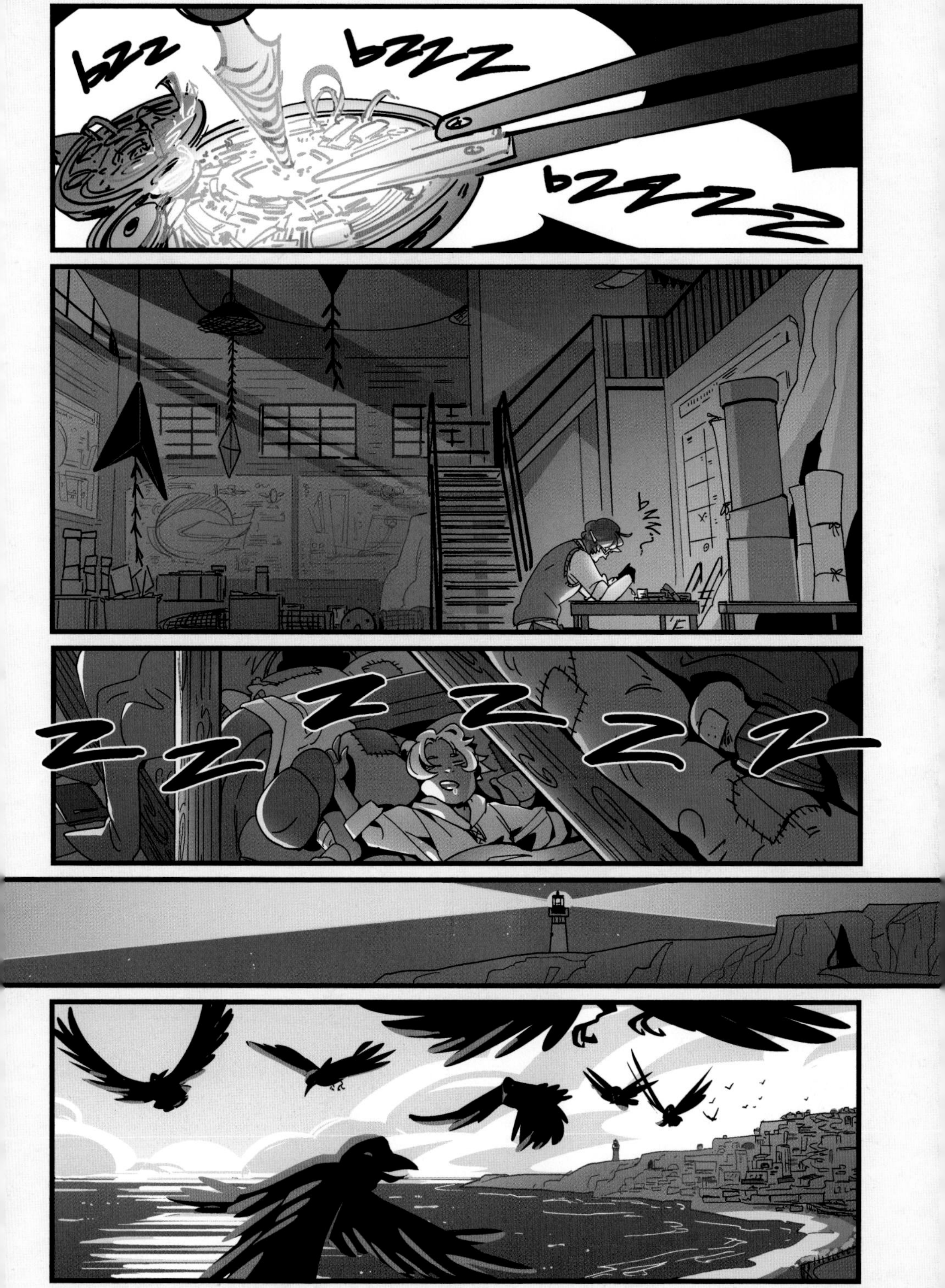
bzz
bzzzz
bzzzzzz
bzzz...
ZZZZZZZ

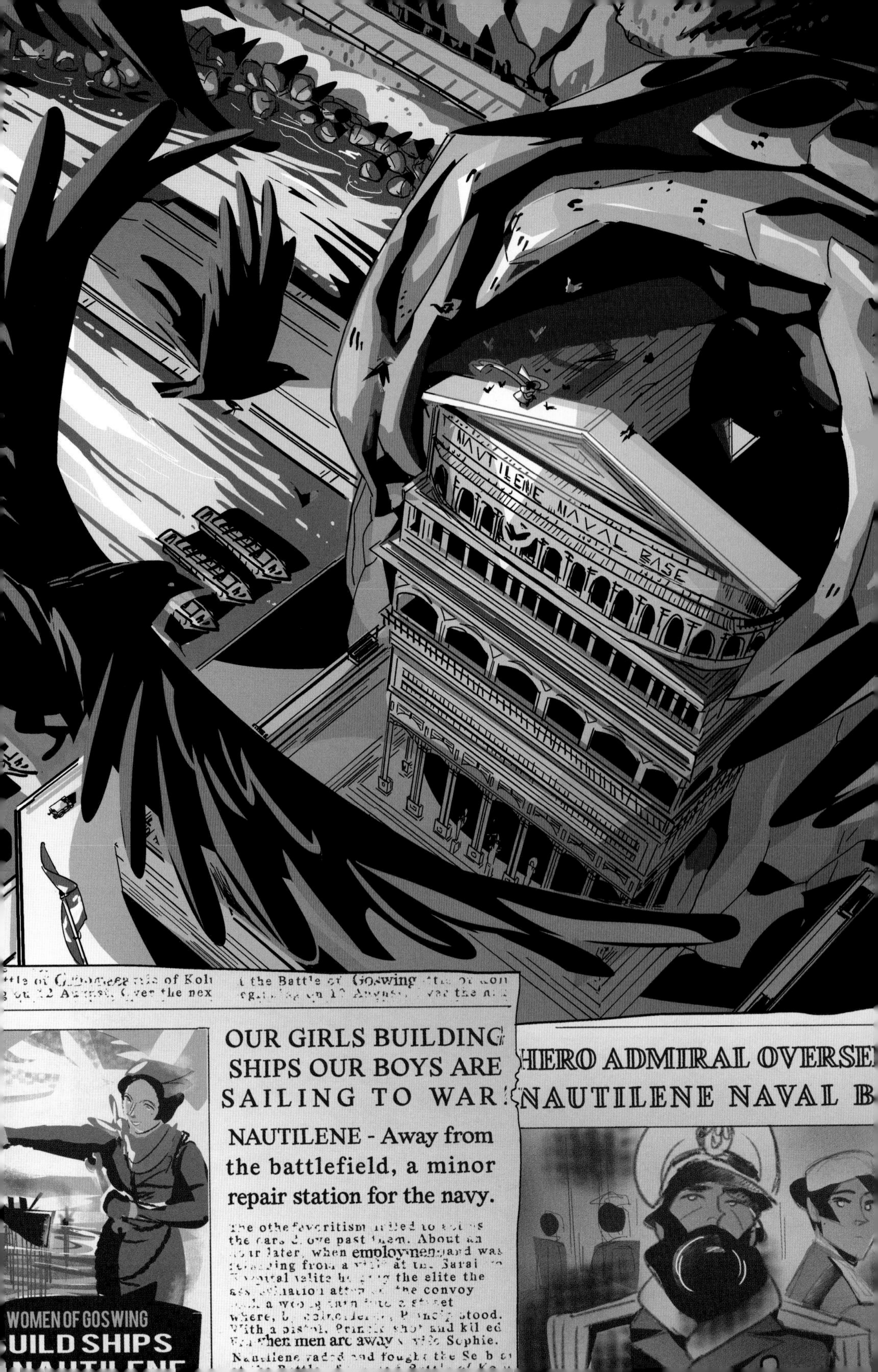
NAUTILENE NAVAL BASE
OUR GIRLS BUILDING
SHIPS OUR BOYS ARE
SAILING TO WAR
NAUTILENE - Away from the battlefield, a minor repair station for the navy.
HERO ADMIRAL OVERSE
NAUTILENE NAVAL B
WOMEN OF GOSWING
UILD SHIPS

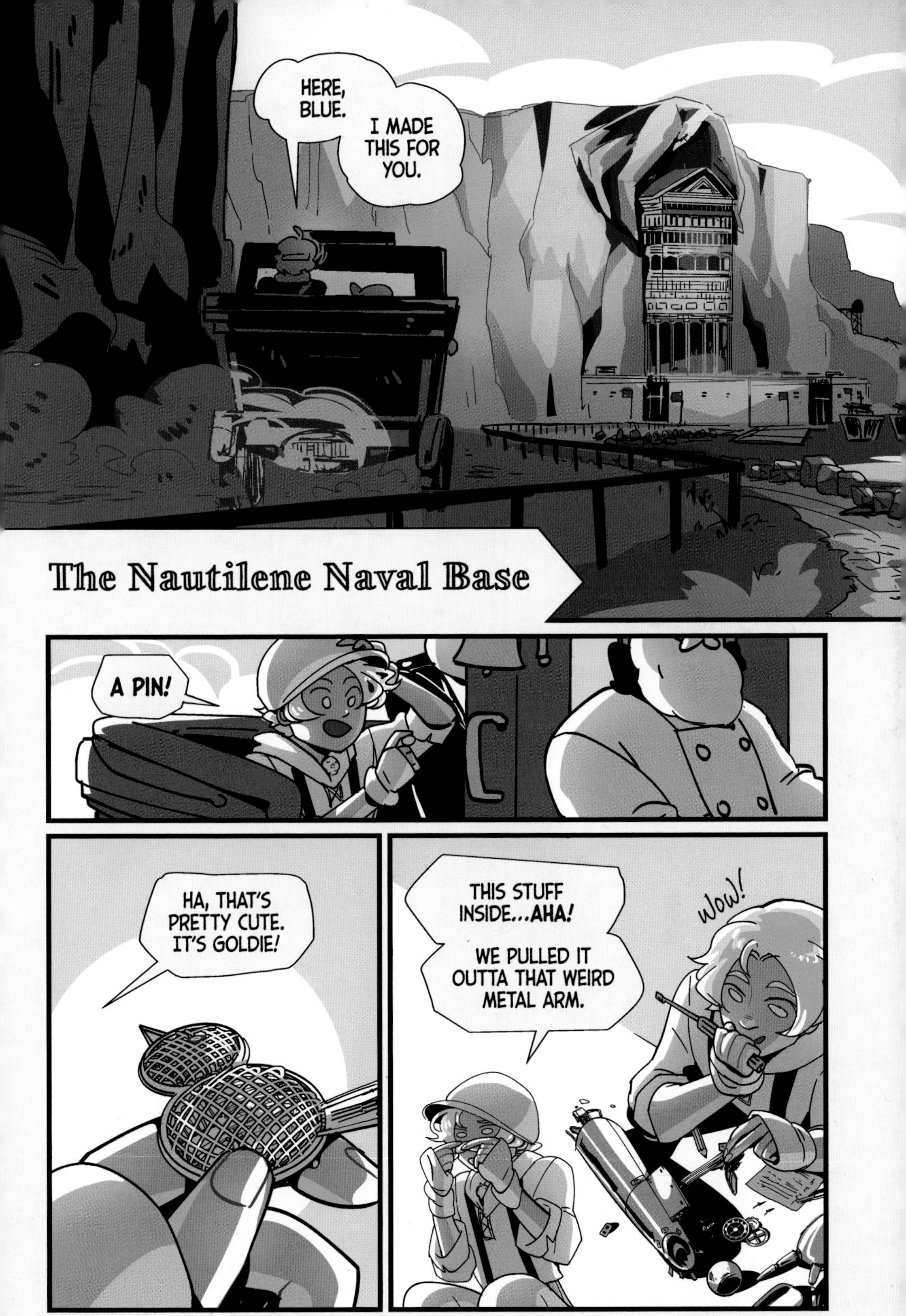
HERE, BLUE.
I MADE THIS FOR YOU.
The Nautilene Naval Base
A PIN!
HA, THAT'S PRETTY CUTE. IT'S GOLDIE!
THIS STUFF INSIDE...**AHA!**
WE PULLED IT OUTTA THAT WEIRD METAL ARM.
WOW!

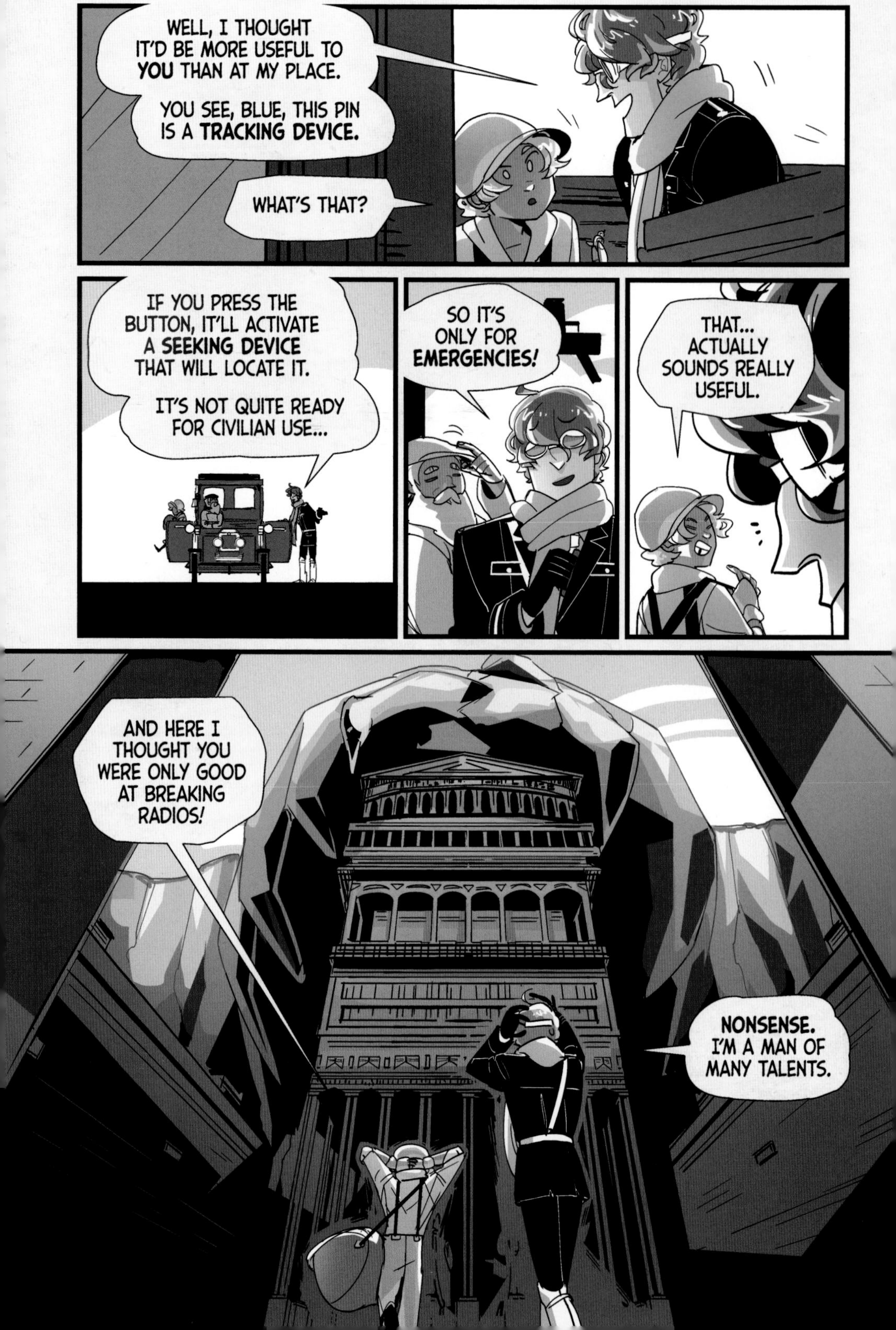
WELL, I THOUGHT IT'D BE MORE USEFUL TO YOU THAN AT MY PLACE.
YOU SEE, BLUE, THIS PIN IS A TRACKING DEVICE.
WHAT'S THAT?
IF YOU PRESS THE BUTTON, IT'LL ACTIVATE A SEEKING DEVICE THAT WILL LOCATE IT.
IT'S NOT QUITE READY FOR CIVILIAN USE...
SO IT'S ONLY FOR EMERGENCIES!
THAT... ACTUALLY SOUNDS REALLY USEFUL.
AND HERE I THOUGHT YOU WERE ONLY GOOD AT BREAKING RADIOS!
NONSENSE. I'M A MAN OF MANY TALENTS.

AND THAT'S EVERYTHING?

I'LL RELAY YOUR CONCERNS ABOUT THE WORKING CONDITIONS TO THE ADMIRAL...

OH!

NO, STOP RIGHT THERE.

ME?

SIR, YOU MAY NOT BRING YOUR SON HERE.

I'M AN APPRENTICE, MA'AM!

CHILDREN AREN'T ALLOWED AT THE NAVAL BASE.

MISS, SURELY HE WON'T BE A PROBLEM?

COULD I TALK TO A SUPERIOR OFFICER, OR...

ADULTS GET LOST FOR DAYS IN THIS GIANT BASE, AND CHILDREN MORE SO.

PLEASE ESCORT YOUR CHILD OUT.

ω º ω.

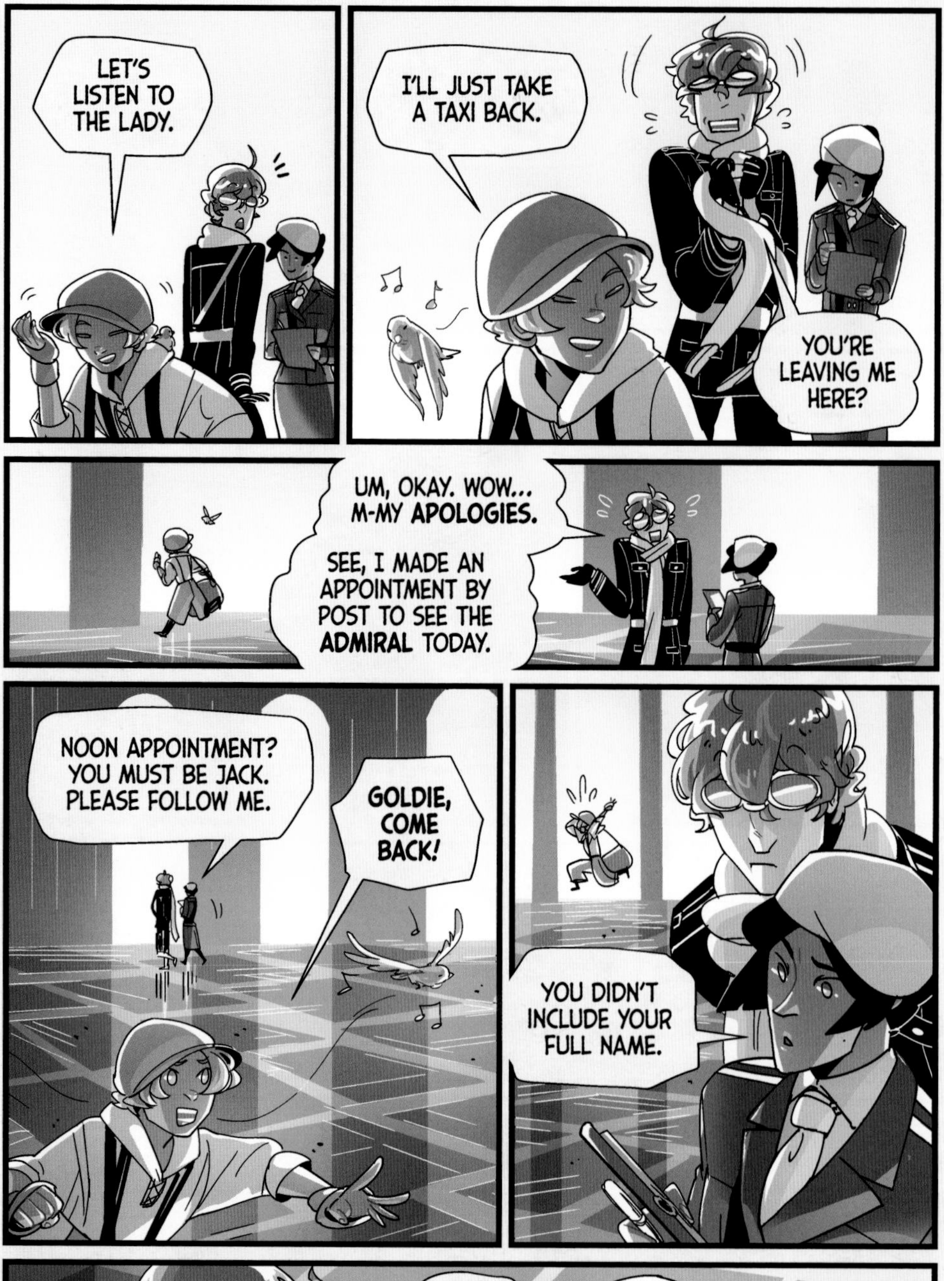
LET'S LISTEN TO THE LADY.
I'LL JUST TAKE A TAXI BACK.
YOU'RE LEAVING ME HERE?
UM, OKAY. WOW... M-MY **APOLOGIES.**
SEE, I MADE AN APPOINTMENT BY POST TO SEE THE **ADMIRAL** TODAY.
NOON APPOINTMENT? YOU MUST BE JACK. PLEASE FOLLOW ME.
GOLDIE, COME BACK!
YOU DIDN'T INCLUDE YOUR FULL NAME.
I DON'T LIKE TO GO BY IT.
HMM... UNUSUAL.

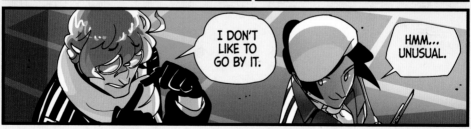

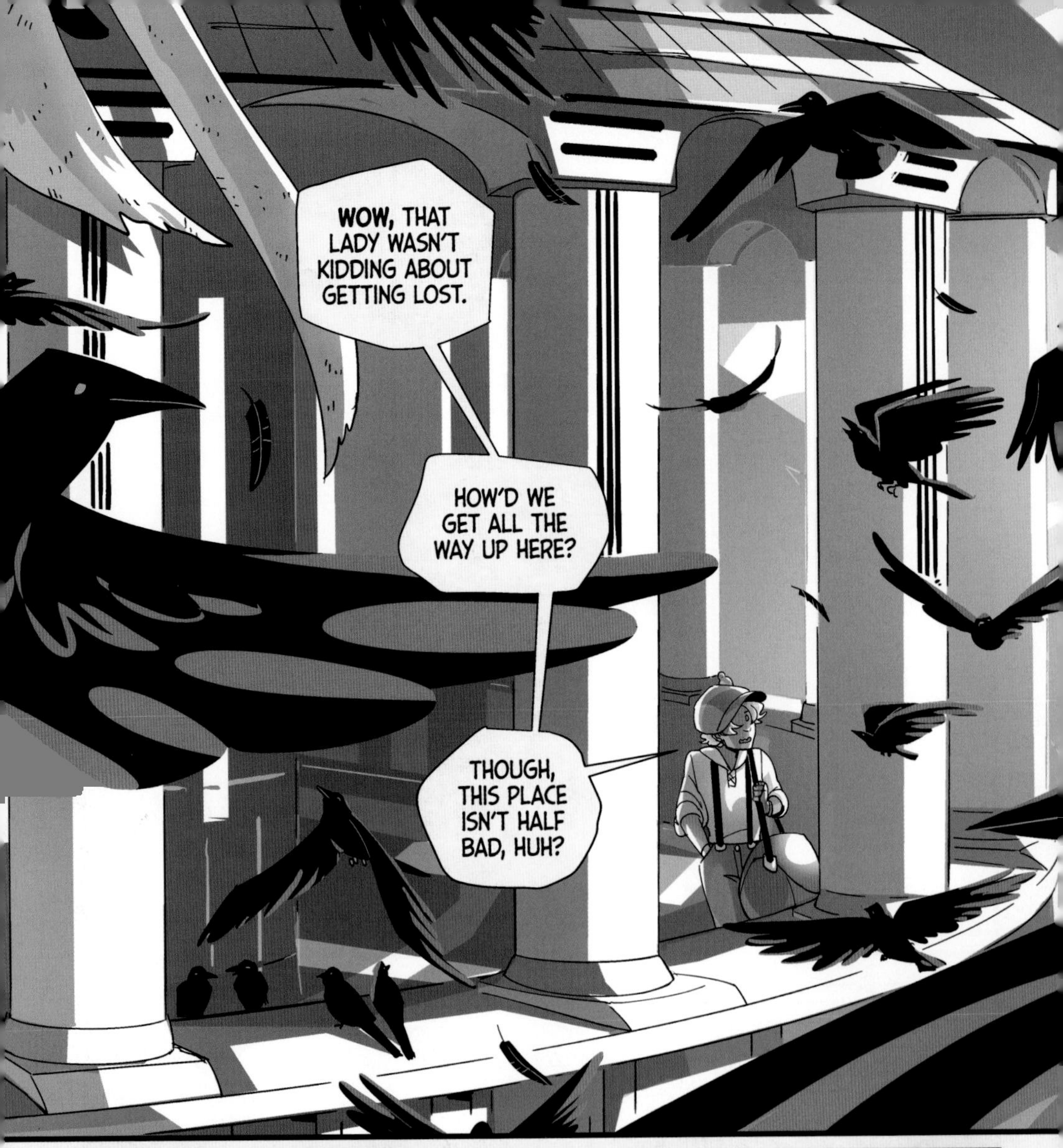
WOW, THAT LADY WASN'T KIDDING ABOUT GETTING LOST.
HOW'D WE GET ALL THE WAY UP HERE?
THOUGH, THIS PLACE ISN'T HALF BAD, HUH?

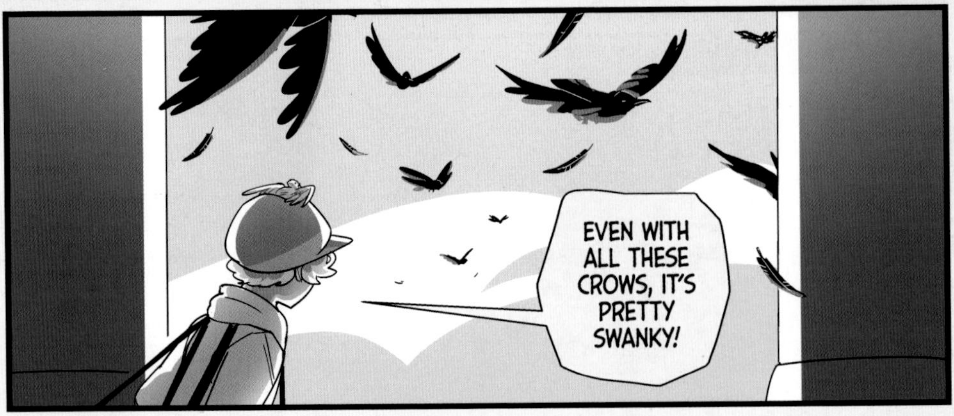
EVEN WITH ALL THESE CROWS, IT'S PRETTY SWANKY!

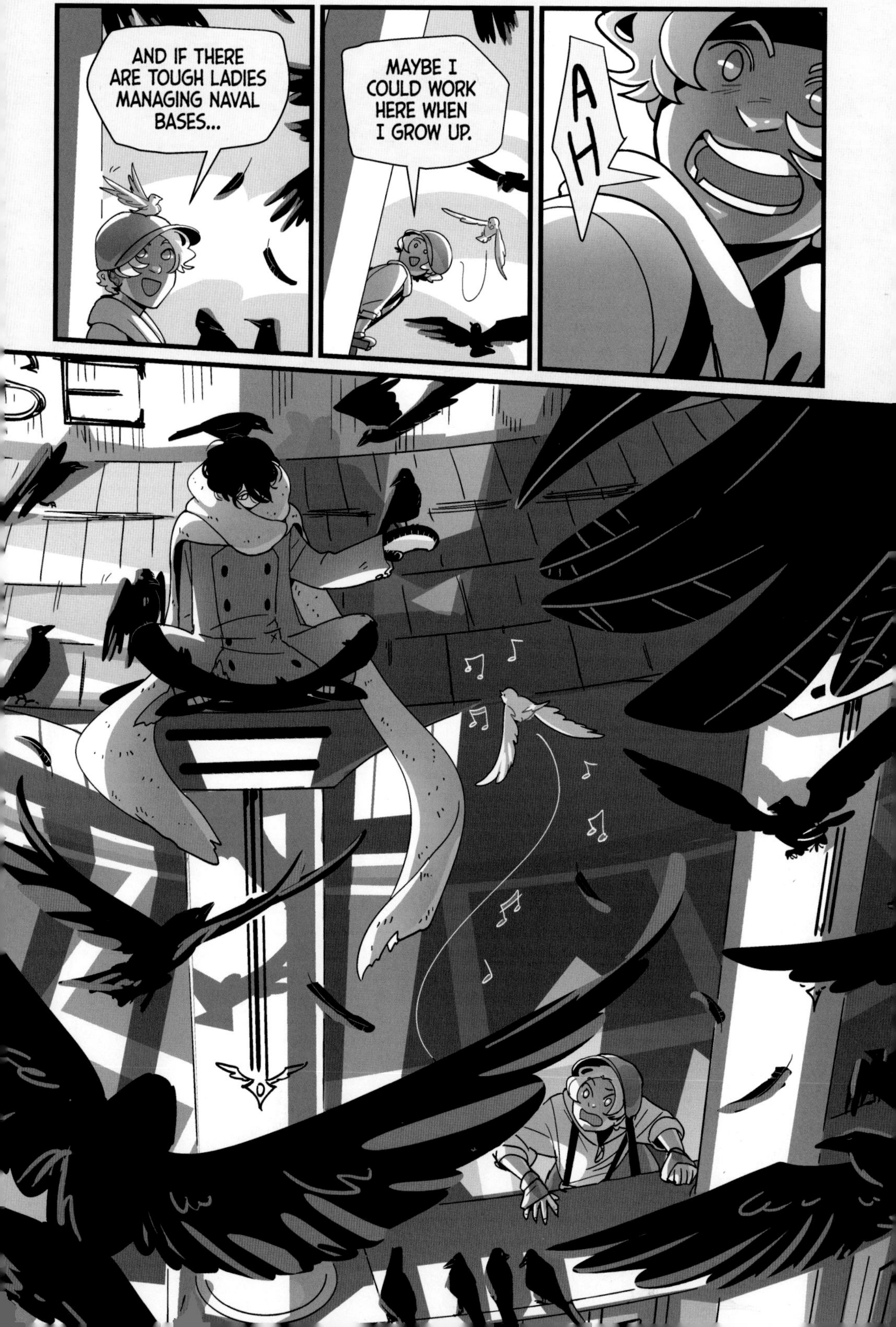

AND IF THERE ARE TOUGH LADIES MANAGING NAVAL BASES...
MAYBE I COULD WORK HERE WHEN I GROW UP.
AH

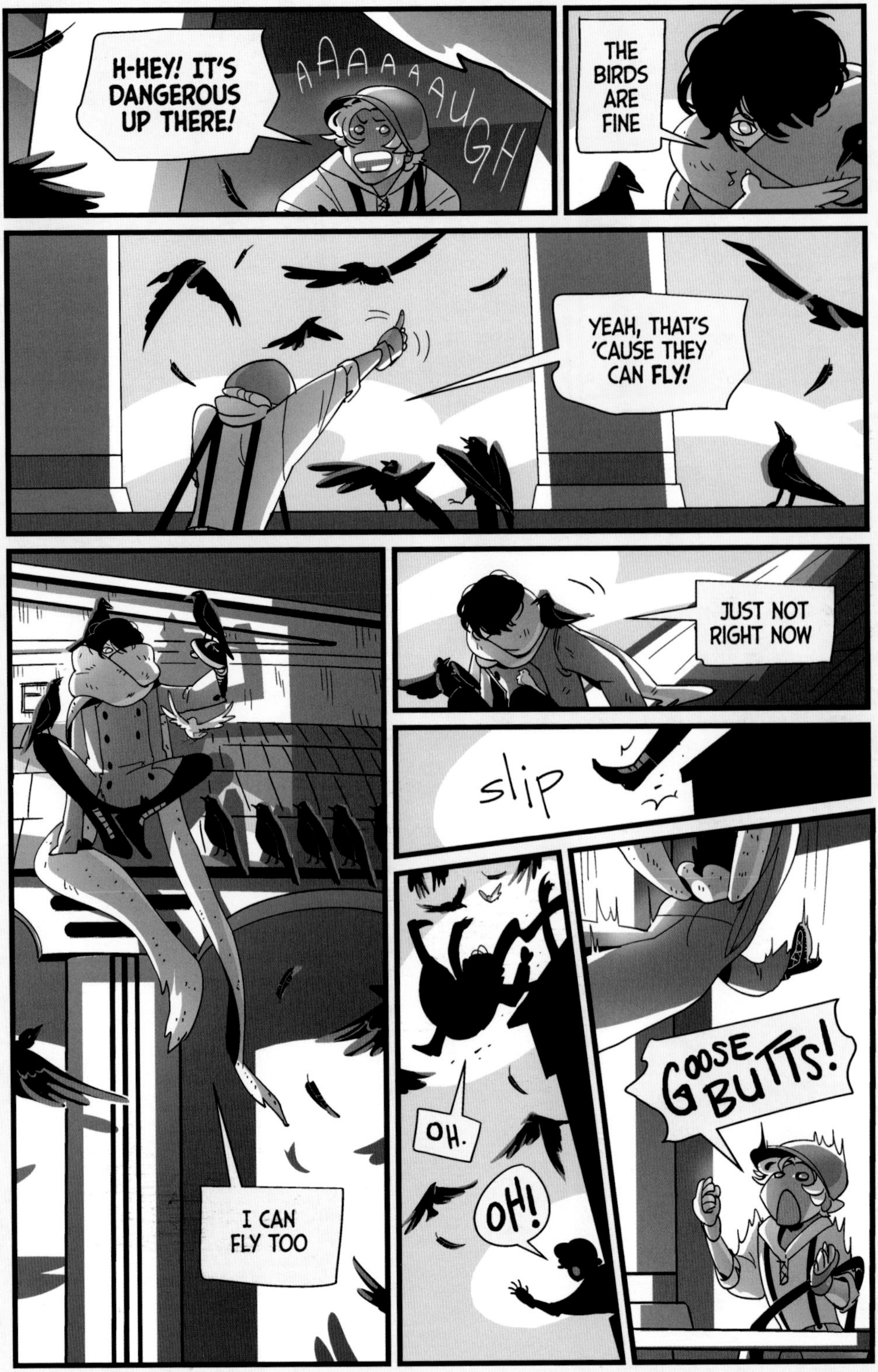
H-HEY! IT'S DANGEROUS UP THERE!
AAAAAAAUGH
THE BIRDS ARE FINE
YEAH, THAT'S 'CAUSE THEY CAN FLY!
I CAN FLY TOO
JUST NOT RIGHT NOW
slip
OH.
OH!
GOOSE BUTTS!

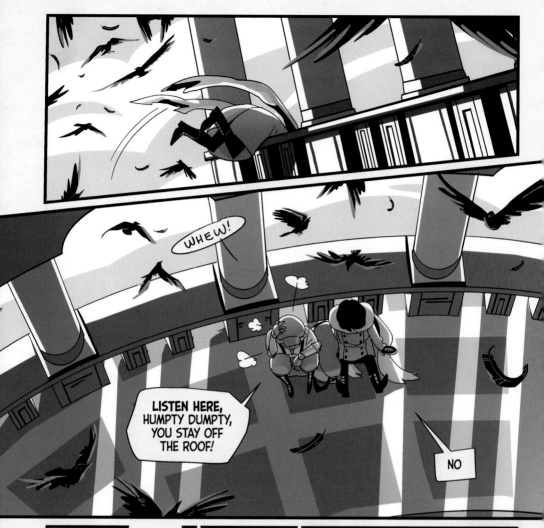

WHEW!

LISTEN HERE, HUMPTY DUMPTY, YOU STAY OFF THE ROOF!

NO

NO?! WHAT IF YA FALL AGAIN?!

MAYBE YOU WILL CATCH ME AGAIN

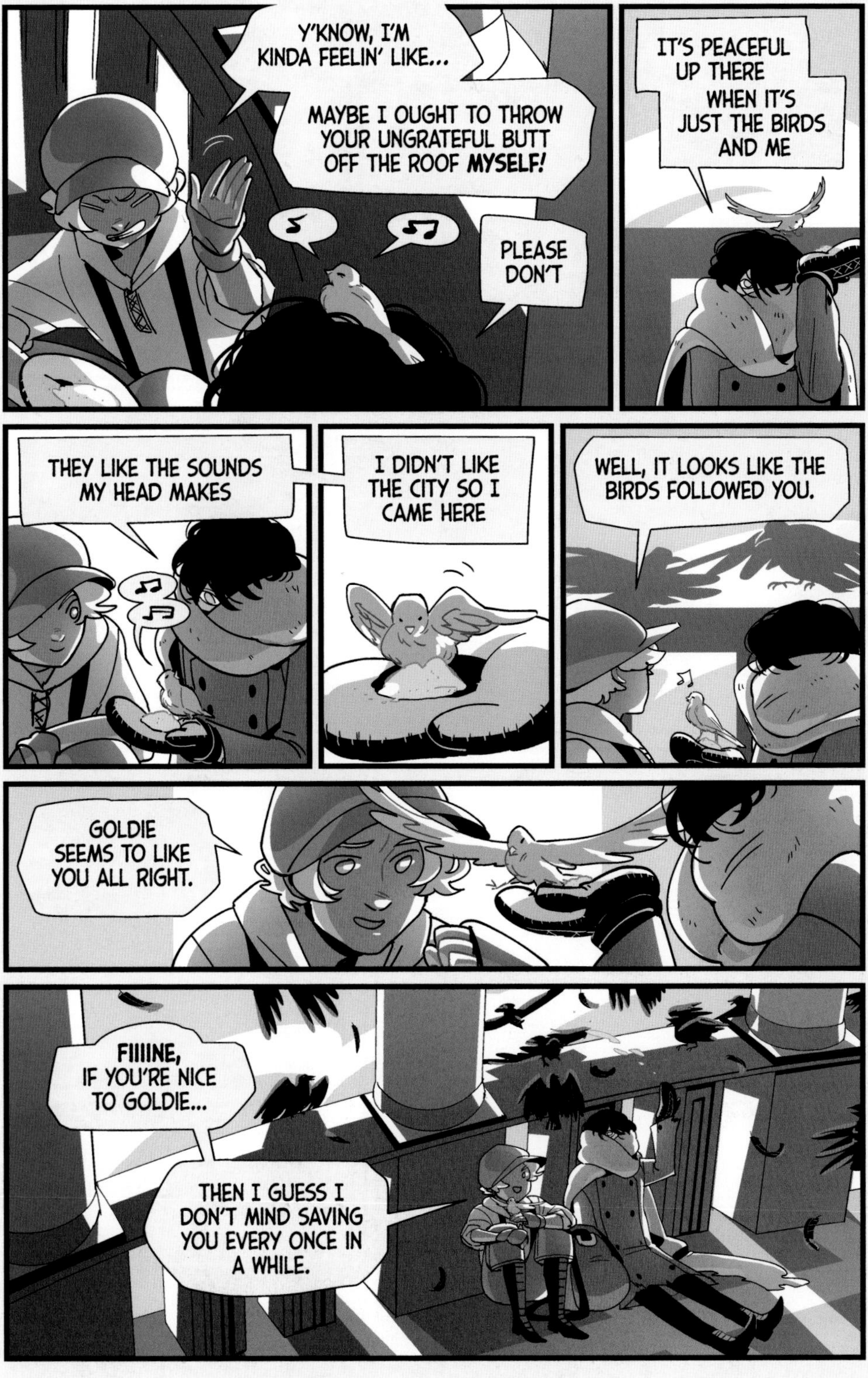
Y'KNOW, I'M KINDA FEELIN' LIKE...
MAYBE I OUGHT TO THROW YOUR UNGRATEFUL BUTT OFF THE ROOF **MYSELF!**
PLEASE DON'T
IT'S PEACEFUL UP THERE
WHEN IT'S JUST THE BIRDS AND ME
THEY LIKE THE SOUNDS MY HEAD MAKES
I DIDN'T LIKE THE CITY SO I CAME HERE
WELL, IT LOOKS LIKE THE BIRDS FOLLOWED YOU.
GOLDIE SEEMS TO LIKE YOU ALL RIGHT.
FIIIINE, IF YOU'RE NICE TO GOLDIE...
THEN I GUESS I DON'T MIND SAVING YOU EVERY ONCE IN A WHILE.

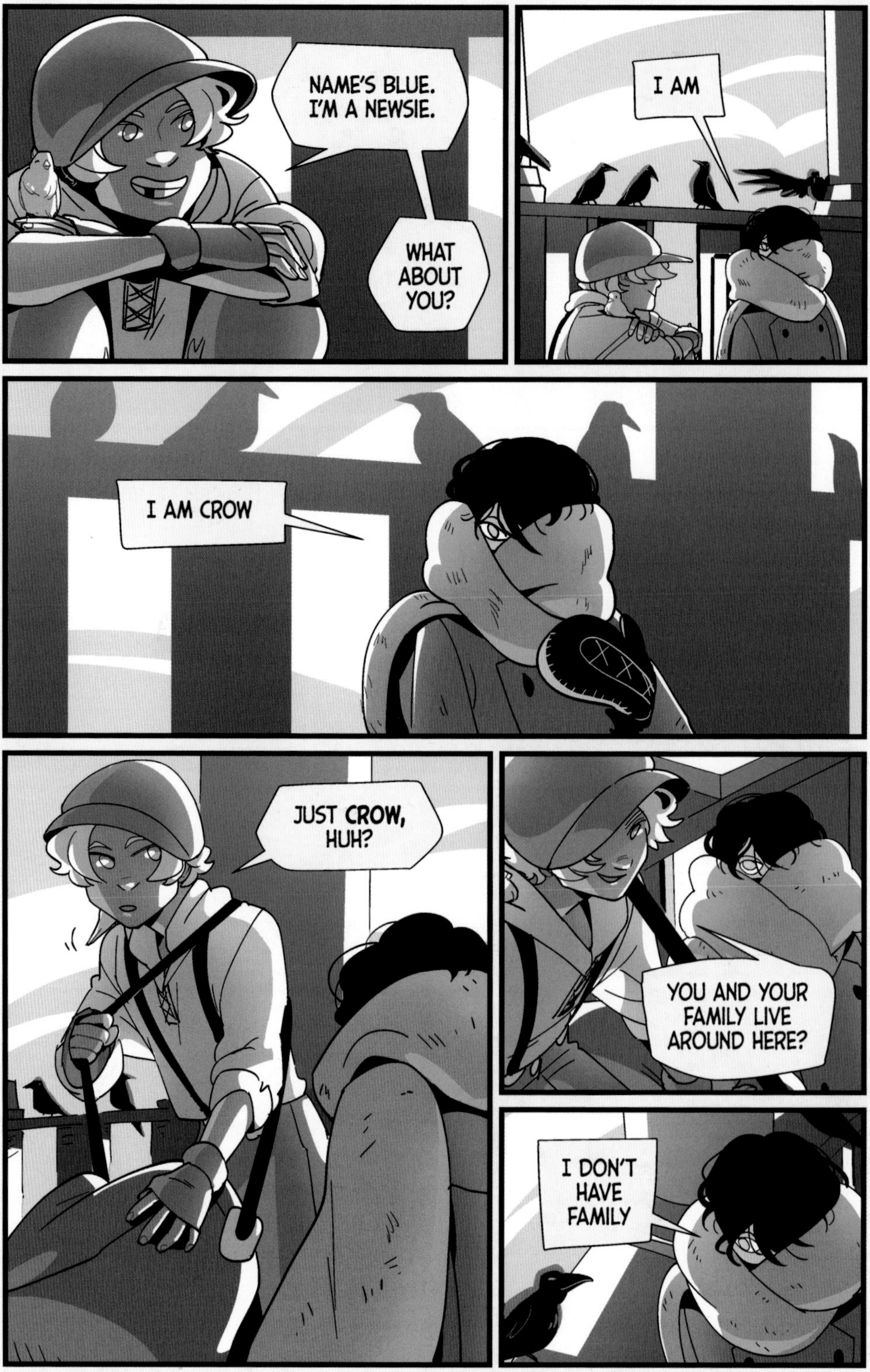
NAME'S BLUE. I'M A NEWSIE.
WHAT ABOUT YOU?
I AM
I AM CROW
JUST CROW, HUH?
YOU AND YOUR FAMILY LIVE AROUND HERE?
I DON'T HAVE FAMILY

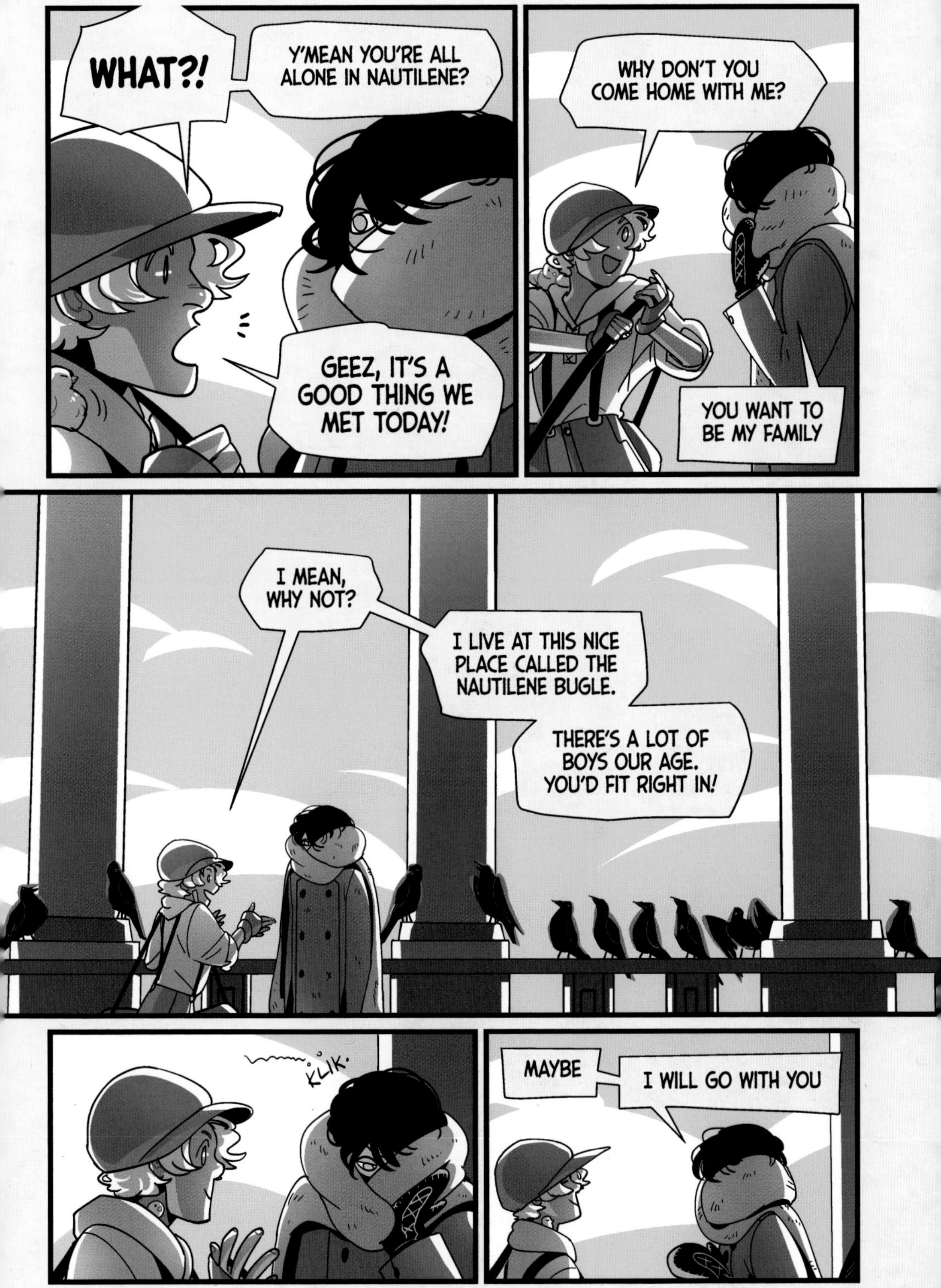
WHAT?!
Y'MEAN YOU'RE ALL ALONE IN NAUTILENE?
GEEZ, IT'S A GOOD THING WE MET TODAY!
WHY DON'T YOU COME HOME WITH ME?
YOU WANT TO BE MY FAMILY
I MEAN, WHY NOT?
I LIVE AT THIS NICE PLACE CALLED THE NAUTILENE BUGLE.
THERE'S A LOT OF BOYS OUR AGE. YOU'D FIT RIGHT IN!
KLIK.
MAYBE
I WILL GO WITH YOU

GREAT!

BUT FIRST LET'S GET OUTTA HERE FAST!

RIGHT NOW

DEFINITELY!

I DUNNO HOW YOU GOT IN, BUT...

THE GROWN-UPS GET PRETTY ANGRY WHEN THEY FIND KIDS HERE.

TRUE

SIR, IF YOU'D JUST PLEASE RESPOND--

BLUE

SO I--

B U M P

ADMIRAL, SIR, LOOK OUT!

ANGRY GROWN-UP

ADMIRAL...?

UH-OH.

46

HOLD THAT THOUGHT, OFFICER.

UHH, SIR.

VERY ANGRY

WAIT! HOLD ON!

WHY ARE THERE ERRANT CHILDREN RUNNING AROUND MY NAVAL BASE?

GO GET THAT BOY!

WELL? DO THEY TRAIN YOU TO STAND THERE USELESSLY?

N-NO, OF COURSE NOT, SIR.

PAT PAT

GOLDIE?

BUT I'M JUST A SECRETARY, ADMIRAL REED!

CROW, DON'T CLIMB THAT!

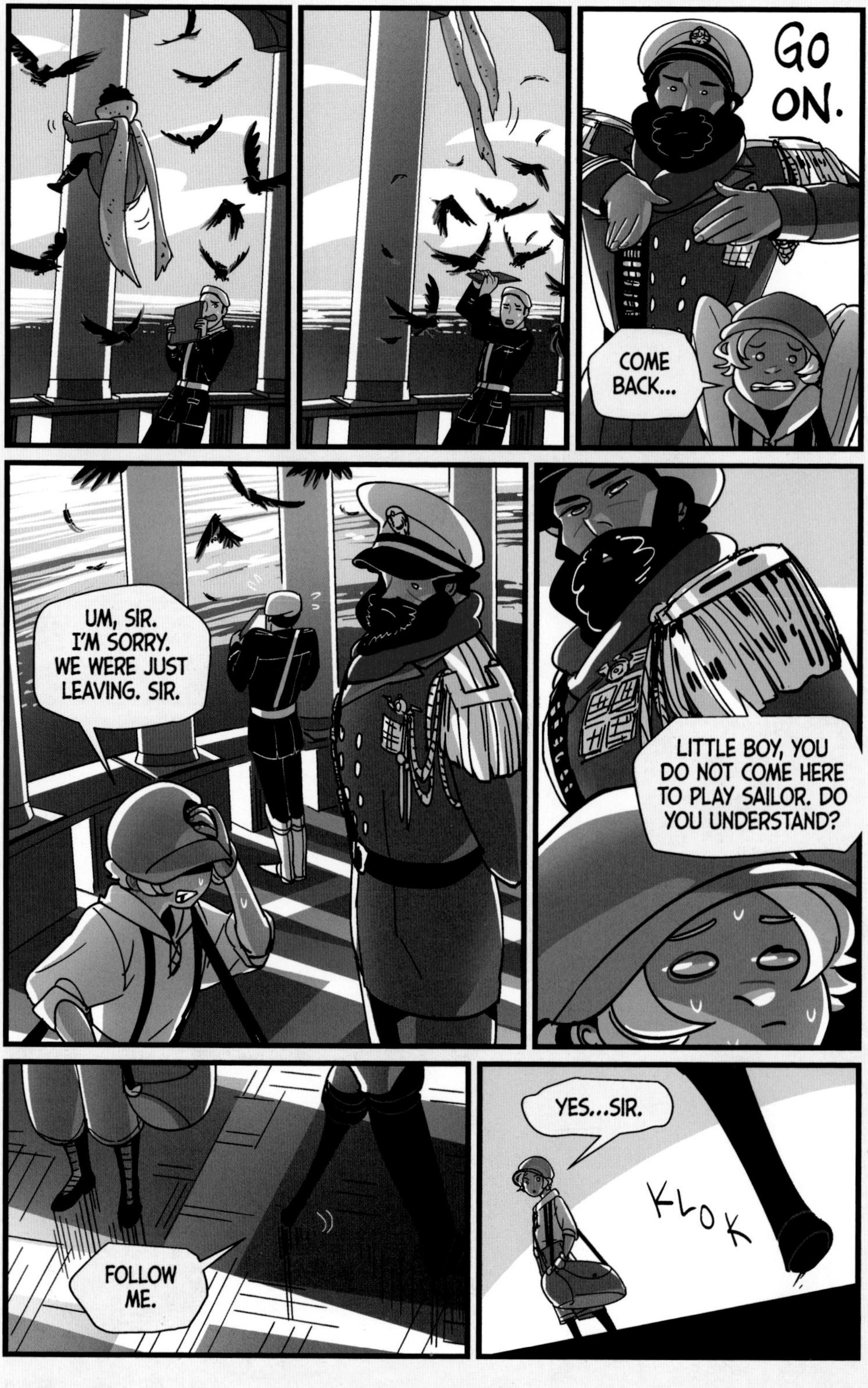
GO ON.
COME BACK...
UM, SIR. I'M SORRY. WE WERE JUST LEAVING. SIR.
LITTLE BOY, YOU DO NOT COME HERE TO PLAY SAILOR. DO YOU UNDERSTAND?
FOLLOW ME.
YES...SIR.
KLOK

YOU ARE LOOKING FOR...?

A COMPLEX MACHINE.

WE HAVE PLENTY OF THOSE.

YOU'LL HAVE TO BE MORE SPECIFIC!

SO THEN, YOU HAVEN'T SEEN ANYTHING OUT OF THE ORDINARY--

WHOA!

UH, SIR!

JILL, REPORT.

FINISHED MY WORK, FATHER. YOU HAVE MEETINGS SCHEDULED ALL MORNING AND AFTERNOON.

THAT'S MY GIRL. HAVE THE REST OF THE DAY OFF.

AND TAKE THIS BOY HOME.

MAKE SURE HIS GUARDIANS GIVE HIM A STERN TALKING TO.

HMM? WHO'S THIS?

YOUR NOON APPOINT-MENT.

JACK.

ANOTHER BLACK UNIFORM?

WHY ARE THERE SO MANY ALTALUS OFFICIALS AROUND?

NO, NO! I'M RETIRED. PLEASE DON'T TELL THEM I'M HERE, SIR!

ALTALUS.

I GUESS THAT MAKES SENSE.

I'VE NEVER SEEN THAT UNIFORM IN NAUTILENE BEFORE.

THERE'S NOTHING TO REPORT.

TELL THE QUEEN THAT NAUTILENE IS AS DULL AS ALWAYS.

I'M NOT HERE ON BEHALF OF THE QUEEN, SIR.

IN FACT, I'D HOPED TO REACH OUT TO YOU BEFORE THE OTHERS DID.

SIR, I BELIEVE THERE IS A **DANGEROUS** WEAPON IN YOUR CITY.

ALL I CAN TELL YOU IS THAT IT IS DRAWN TO OTHER MACHINES.

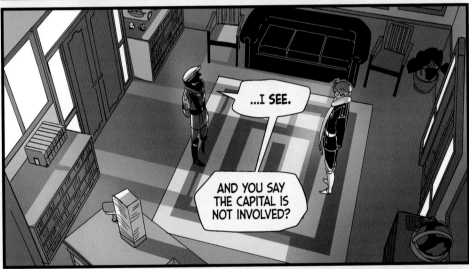

...I SEE.

AND YOU SAY THE CAPITAL IS NOT INVOLVED?

WHO ARE YOU, JACK?

I'M A **CONCERNED** CITIZEN, SIR.

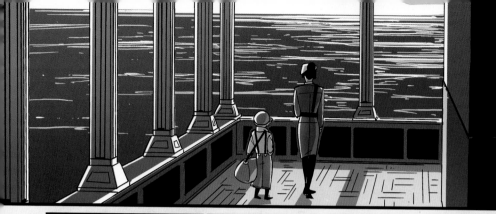

hmm

um

IT SEEMS TO ME LIKE YOU KINDA RUN THIS PLACE.

THE ADMIRAL IS MY FATHER.

HIS SECRETARY WAS DRAFTED, SO I FILL IN WHERE I CAN.

ARE THERE MORE LADIES LIKE YOU HERE?

WELL, THOSE WOMEN I WAS TALKING TO EARLIER BUILD AND REPAIR THE SHIPS OUTSIDE.

OH! I THINK THEY WERE FEATURED IN THE BUGLE A COUPLE YEARS AGO!

PAT PAT

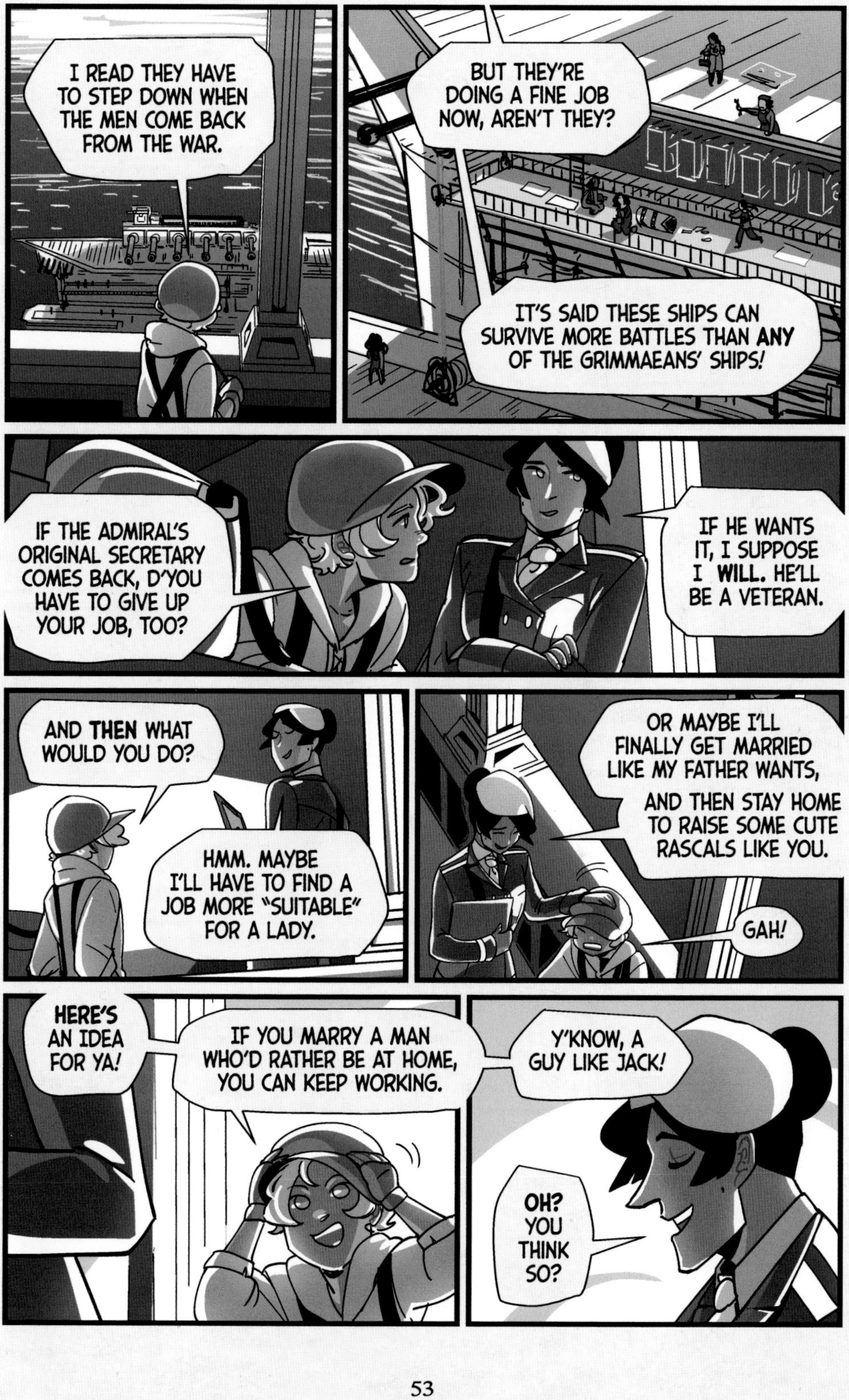
I READ THEY HAVE TO STEP DOWN WHEN THE MEN COME BACK FROM THE WAR.
BUT THEY'RE DOING A FINE JOB NOW, AREN'T THEY?
IT'S SAID THESE SHIPS CAN SURVIVE MORE BATTLES THAN ANY OF THE GRIMMAEANS' SHIPS!
IF THE ADMIRAL'S ORIGINAL SECRETARY COMES BACK, D'YOU HAVE TO GIVE UP YOUR JOB, TOO?
IF HE WANTS IT, I SUPPOSE I WILL. HE'LL BE A VETERAN.
AND THEN WHAT WOULD YOU DO?
HMM. MAYBE I'LL HAVE TO FIND A JOB MORE "SUITABLE" FOR A LADY.
OR MAYBE I'LL FINALLY GET MARRIED LIKE MY FATHER WANTS,
AND THEN STAY HOME TO RAISE SOME CUTE RASCALS LIKE YOU.
GAH!
HERE'S AN IDEA FOR YA!
IF YOU MARRY A MAN WHO'D RATHER BE AT HOME, YOU CAN KEEP WORKING.
Y'KNOW, A GUY LIKE JACK!
OH? YOU THINK SO?

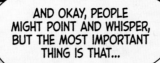
AND OKAY, PEOPLE MIGHT POINT AND WHISPER, BUT THE MOST IMPORTANT THING IS THAT...

YOU CAN **CHOOSE** WHAT TO DO WITH YOUR OWN LIFE!

AND SINCE THE ADMIRAL'S YOUR POPS, **SURELY** YOU COULD GET ANOTHER JOB HERE!

IF YOU HAVE A PLACE YOU **BELONG,** WHY SHOULDN'T YOU TRY TO **KEEP** IT?

WHO CARES IF TOTAL STRANGERS THINK NEWSIES CAN ONLY BE BOYS?!

OH, HAVE I FORGOTTEN TO TELL YA THAT I'M A NEWSBOY, HAHA?

SO YOU ARE...

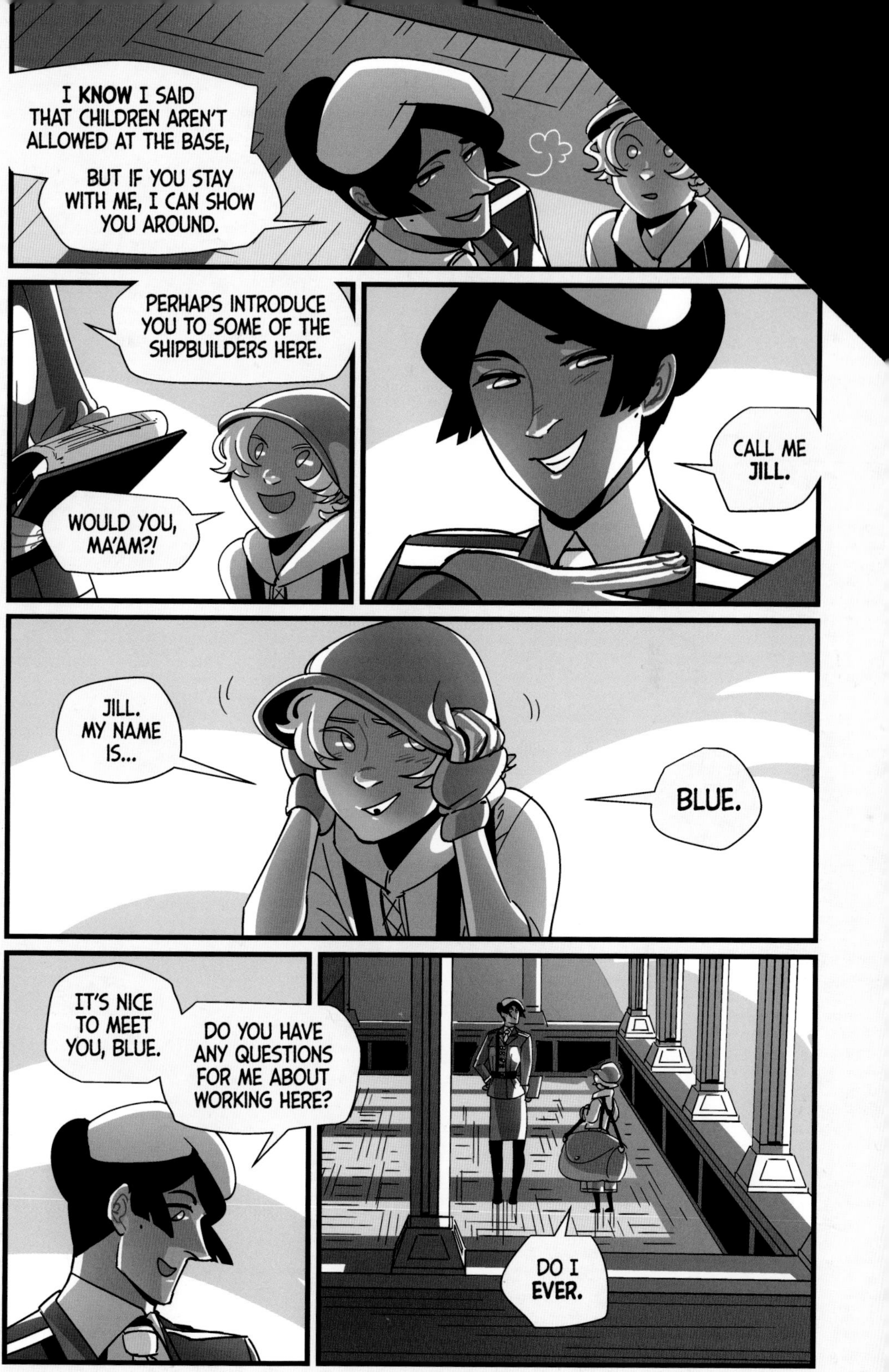
I KNOW I SAID THAT CHILDREN AREN'T ALLOWED AT THE BASE,
BUT IF YOU STAY WITH ME, I CAN SHOW YOU AROUND.
PERHAPS INTRODUCE YOU TO SOME OF THE SHIPBUILDERS HERE.
WOULD YOU, MA'AM?!
CALL ME JILL.
JILL. MY NAME IS...
BLUE.
IT'S NICE TO MEET YOU, BLUE.
DO YOU HAVE ANY QUESTIONS FOR ME ABOUT WORKING HERE?
DO I EVER.

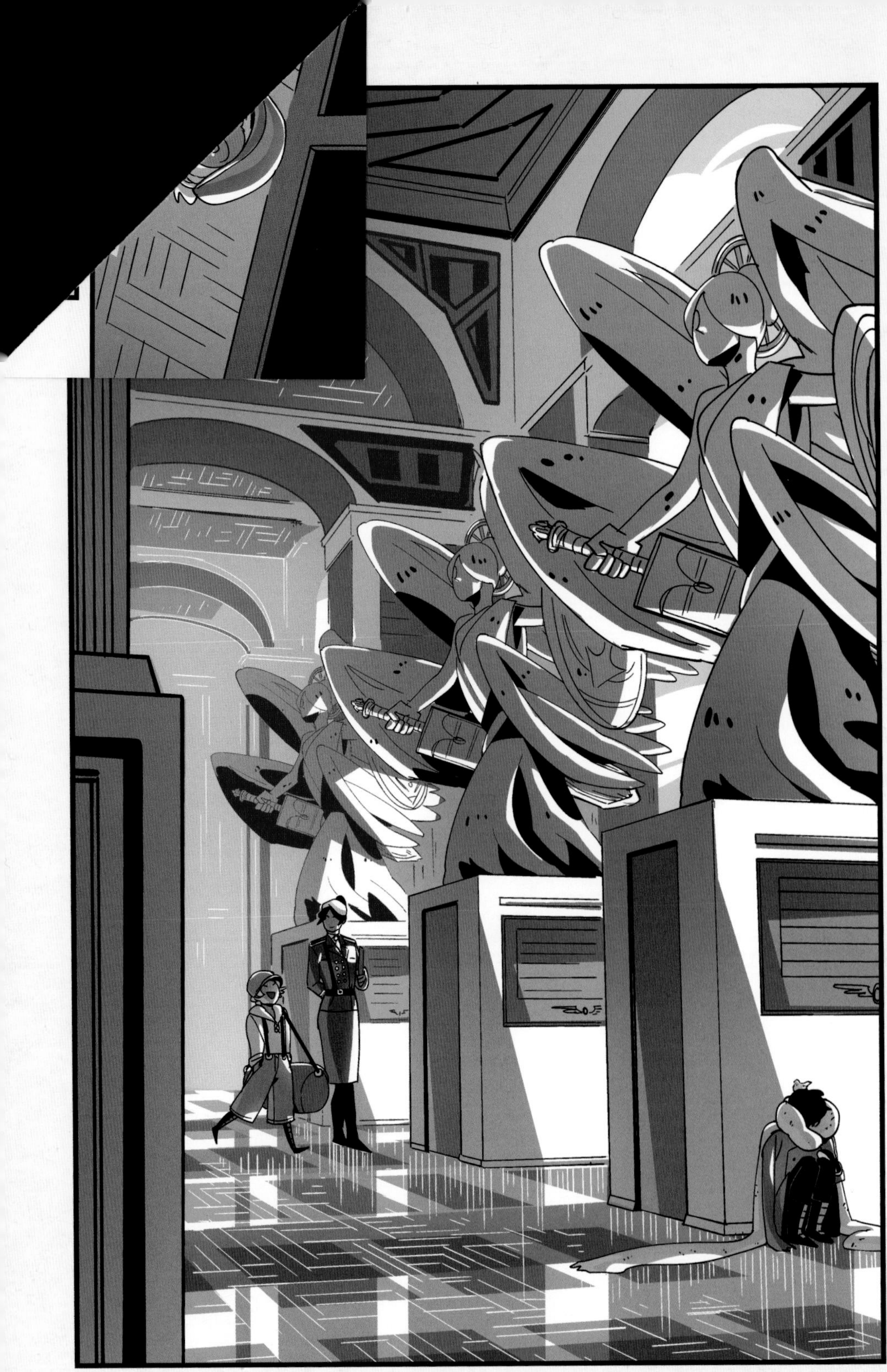

SO, IF YOU HAVE TIME, YOU SHOULD DEFINITELY VISIT JACK AND ME AT HIS STUDIO.

I'D LIKE THAT!

KLIK

CROW!

GOLDIE!

GROWN-UP

DON'T WORRY, JILL'S ALL RIGHT. SHE'LL TAKE US BACK TO NAUTILENE!

NO GROWN-UPS

NO CITIES

JILL'S GONNA DRIVE ME HOME.

HI!

AND I WANT YOU TO COME WITH US!

HERE'S THE BUGLE! C'MON, I'LL INTRODUCE YOU TO EVERYONE!

I DON'T WANT TO GO INSIDE

THE GROWN-UPS WON'T LIKE ME

THEY WILL, TOO.

THE MAYOR AND MS. MUFFY ARE GOOD PEOPLE.

SO MAYBE YOU'RE A LITTLE WEIRD, BUT WHO ISN'T?

I MEAN, WAIT UNTIL YOU MEET JACK--

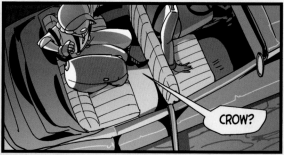

CROW?

CROW!

BUGLE NEWS

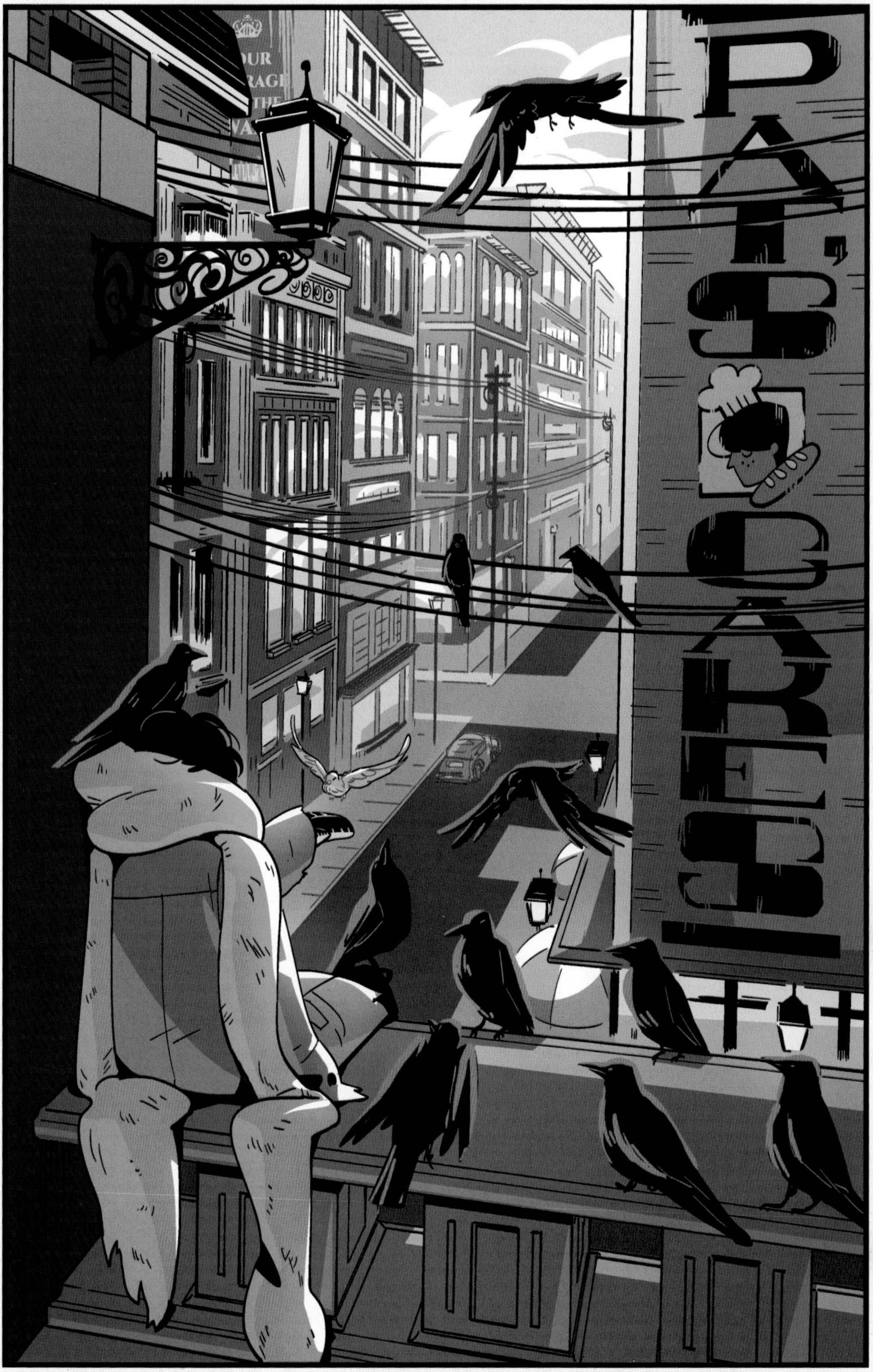
PAT'S

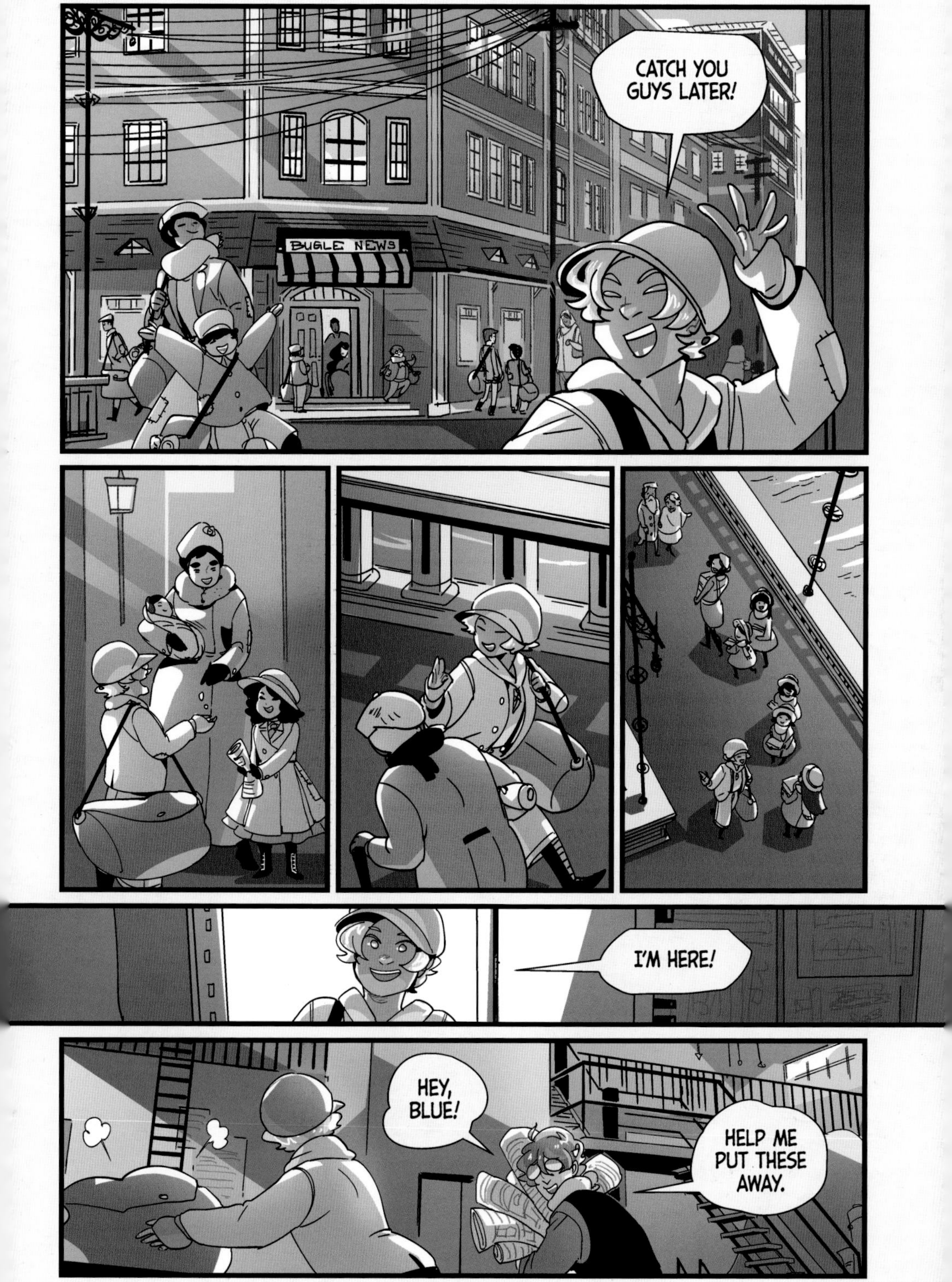
CATCH YOU GUYS LATER!
BUGLE NEWS
I'M HERE!
HEY, BLUE!
HELP ME PUT THESE AWAY.

SO I GET TO CHOOSE OUR NEXT PROJECT?

INDEED!

—TA DA—

HOW 'BOUT WE FINISH **THAT**?

IT'S A BIRD, RIGHT? LET'S GET IT TO FLY!

WELL, THAT'LL BE A DIFFICULT PROJECT.

FLIGHT IS **HARDLY** EVEN READY FOR MILITARY USE AS IT IS. IT'S DEFINITELY NOT READY FOR **CIVILIANS**!

BUT NEITHER WAS THIS GOLDIE PIN YOU MADE ME.

TRUE ENOUGH. I SUPPOSE THAT AS LONG AS WE TAKE SAFETY PRECAUTIONS...

BANG BANG

YEAH, **SAFELY** PUT A SEAT HERE, SO I CAN RIDE IN IT!

HARNESSING FLIGHT TO TRANSPORT CIVILIANS?! MY, THAT'S... **THAT'S...**

THAT'S FOR THE **GREATER GOOD!** NOW YOU'VE CONVINCED ME!

BLUE, CAN YOU GRAB THOSE BLUEPRINTS?

YES, SIR!

BLUE.

I HOPE THIS AWFUL WAR ENDS BEFORE YOU AND YOUR FRIENDS REACH DRAFT AGE.

EHH, MOST OF THE BOYS AT THE BUGLE WON'T BE TWENTY-ONE FOR A WHILE.

EXCEPT HECTOR. HE'S THE ONE WHO BROUGHT ME TO THE BUGLE AFTER MY DAD...

...

SIGH

ANYHOOS.

shff

HECTOR'S IN ALTALUS NOW. HE'S A JOURNALIST. MAYBE YOU'VE READ SOME OF HIS STUFF!

I DIDN'T REALLY READ NEWSPAPERS UNTIL I MET YOU--

KNOK

KNOK

KNOK

I'LL GET THE DOOR!

HM?

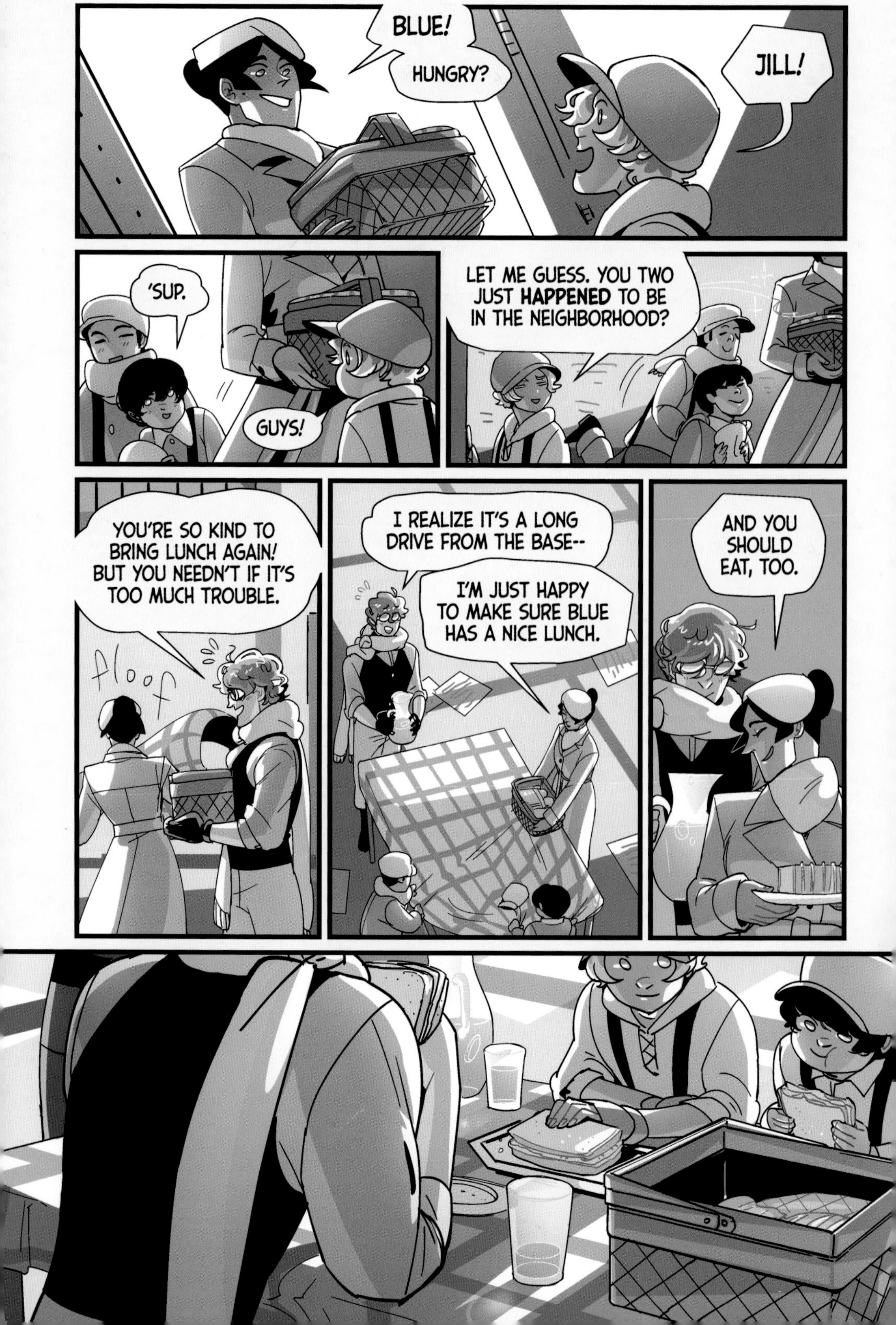
BLUE!
HUNGRY?
JILL!
'SUP.
GUYS!
LET ME GUESS. YOU TWO JUST **HAPPENED** TO BE IN THE NEIGHBORHOOD?
YOU'RE SO KIND TO BRING LUNCH AGAIN! BUT YOU NEEDN'T IF IT'S TOO MUCH TROUBLE.
floof
I REALIZE IT'S A LONG DRIVE FROM THE BASE--
I'M JUST HAPPY TO MAKE SURE BLUE HAS A NICE LUNCH.
AND YOU SHOULD EAT, TOO.

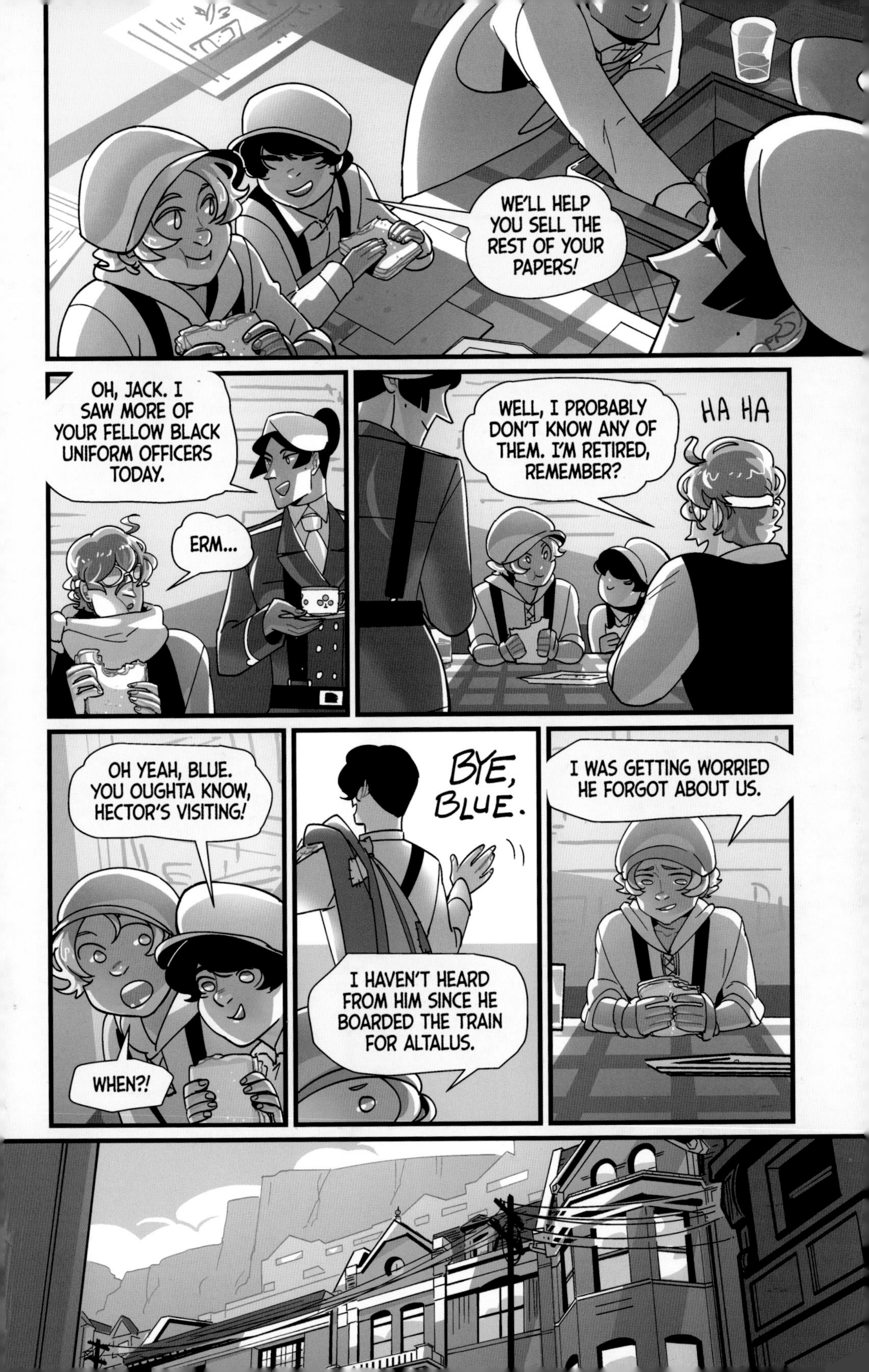
WE'LL HELP YOU SELL THE REST OF YOUR PAPERS!
OH, JACK. I SAW MORE OF YOUR FELLOW BLACK UNIFORM OFFICERS TODAY.
ERM...
WELL, I PROBABLY DON'T KNOW ANY OF THEM. I'M RETIRED, REMEMBER?
HA HA
OH YEAH, BLUE. YOU OUGHTA KNOW, HECTOR'S VISITING!
WHEN?!
BYE, BLUE.
I HAVEN'T HEARD FROM HIM SINCE HE BOARDED THE TRAIN FOR ALTALUS.
I WAS GETTING WORRIED HE FORGOT ABOUT US.

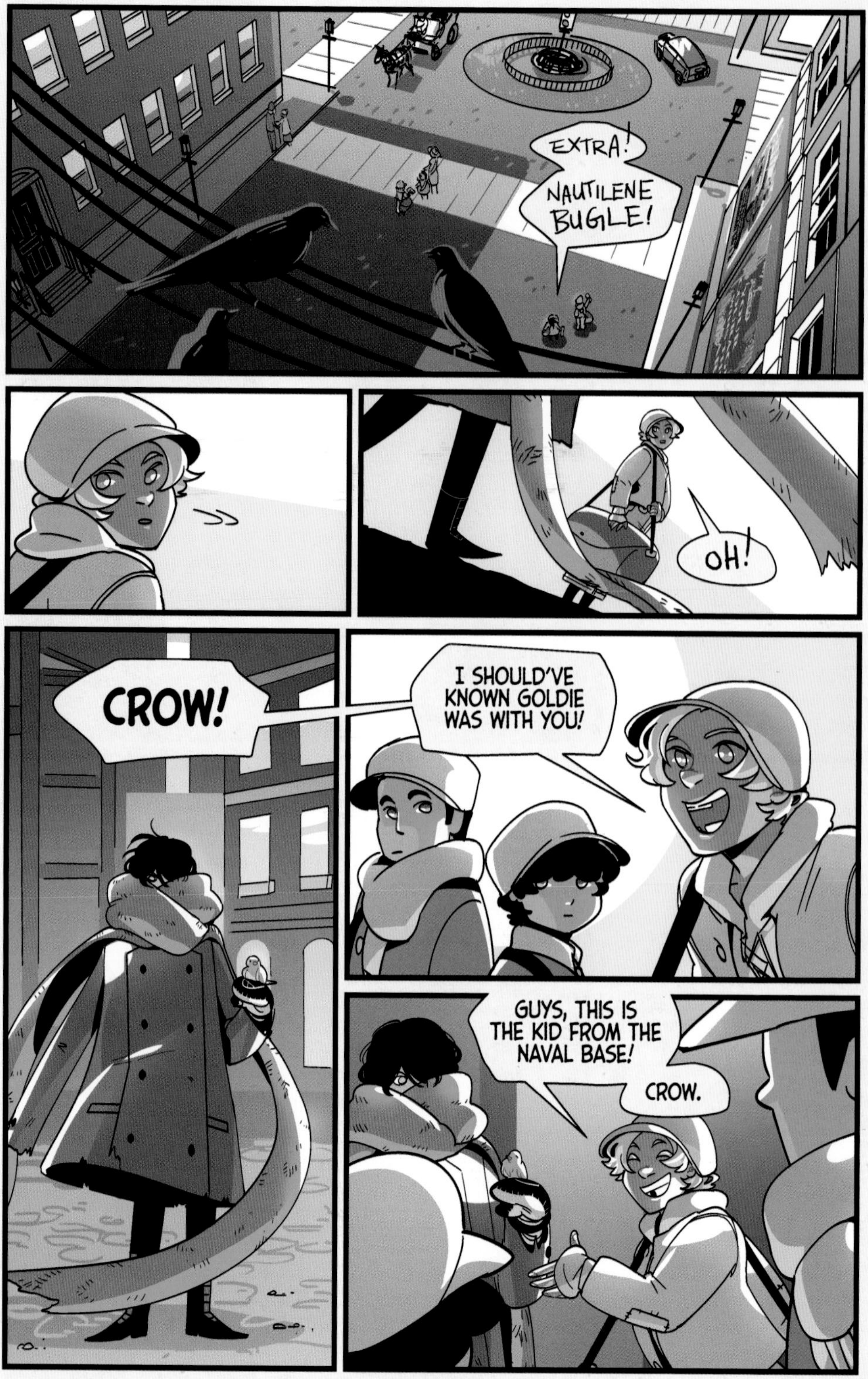
EXTRA!
NAUTILENE BUGLE!
OH!
CROW!
I SHOULD'VE KNOWN GOLDIE WAS WITH YOU!
GUYS, THIS IS THE KID FROM THE NAVAL BASE!
CROW.

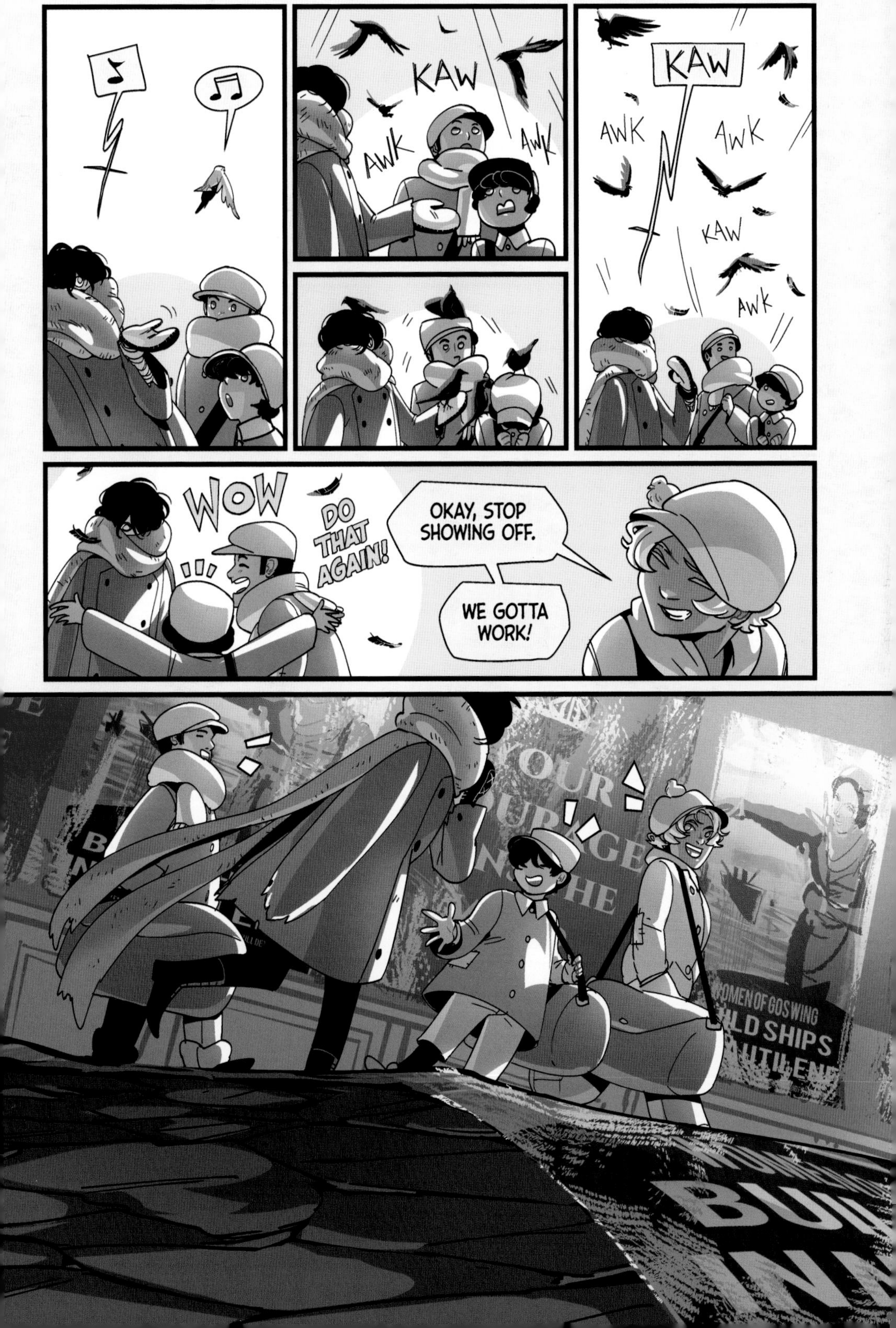
KAW
AWK
AWK
KAW
AWK
AWK
KAW
AWK
WOW
DO THAT AGAIN!
OKAY, STOP SHOWING OFF.
WE GOTTA WORK!

HUH, MAYBE NOT BY MUCH.

LET'S GO HOME.

CROW, COME WITH US BACK TO THE BUGLE.

KLIK

HEY, WHAT'S WRONG?

DIDN'T YOU NOTICE THE GUYS LIKED YOU?

EVERYONE ELSE WILL LIKE YOU, TOO!

GROWN UPS DON'T LIKE ME

WHAT'S THAT MEAN?

I MEAN, SERIOUSLY, GIVE 'EM A CHANCE...

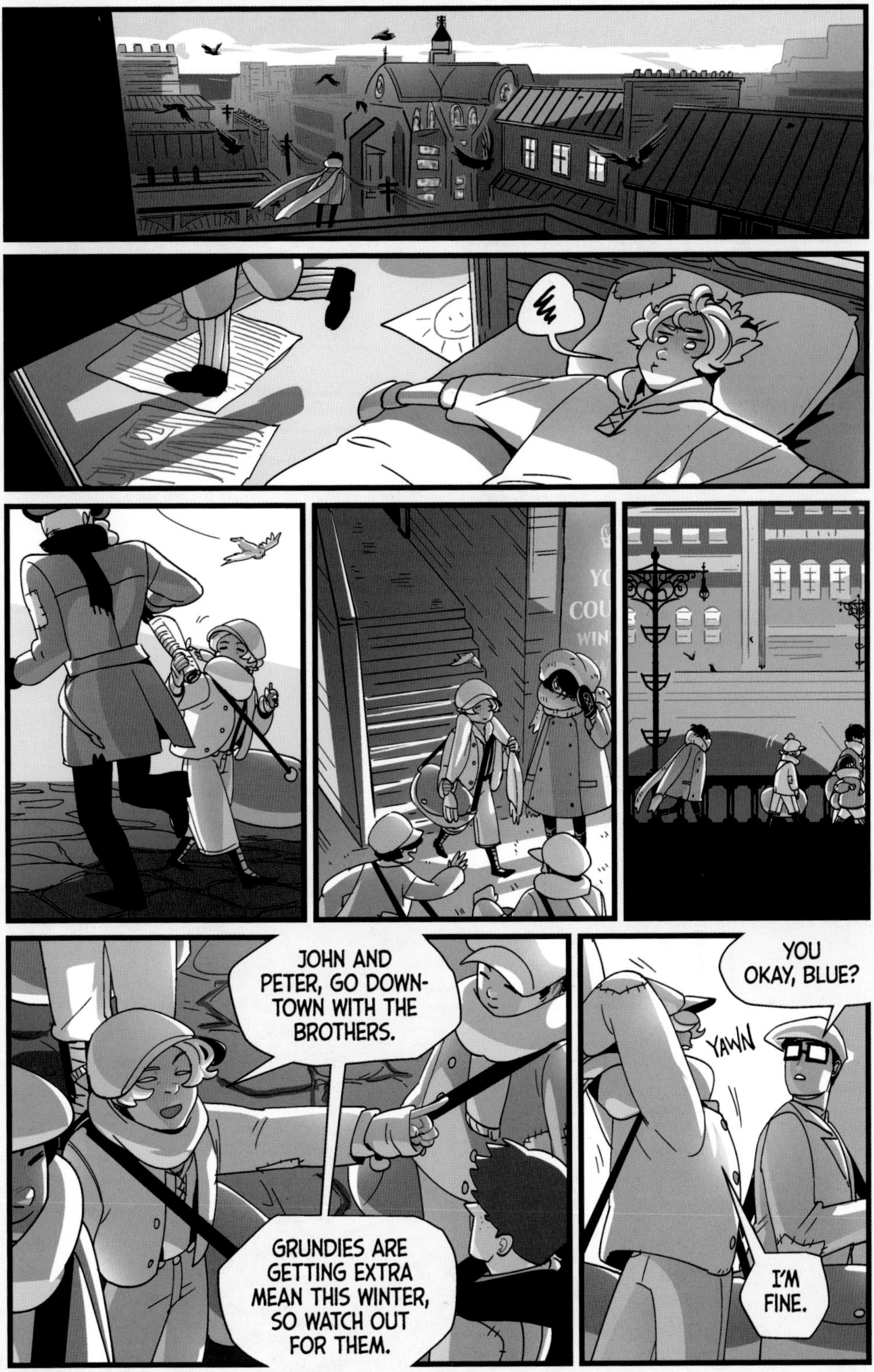
JOHN AND PETER, GO DOWN-TOWN WITH THE BROTHERS.
GRUNDIES ARE GETTING EXTRA MEAN THIS WINTER, SO WATCH OUT FOR THEM.
YAWN
YOU OKAY, BLUE?
I'M FINE.

SEE YOU GUYS AT SUPPER!

SIGH

BUGLE!

ALTALUSIAN OFFICIALS ALL OVER NAUTILENE!

ALTALUSIAN OFFICIALS ALL OVER...

WHY ARE THEY HERE?

YAWN

EXTRA, EXTRA! READ ALL ABOUT IT IN THE BUGLE!

WHY ARE THEY...

HERE?

SWAY

shake shake

ONE FOR ME, DEAR.

READ ABOUT IT...

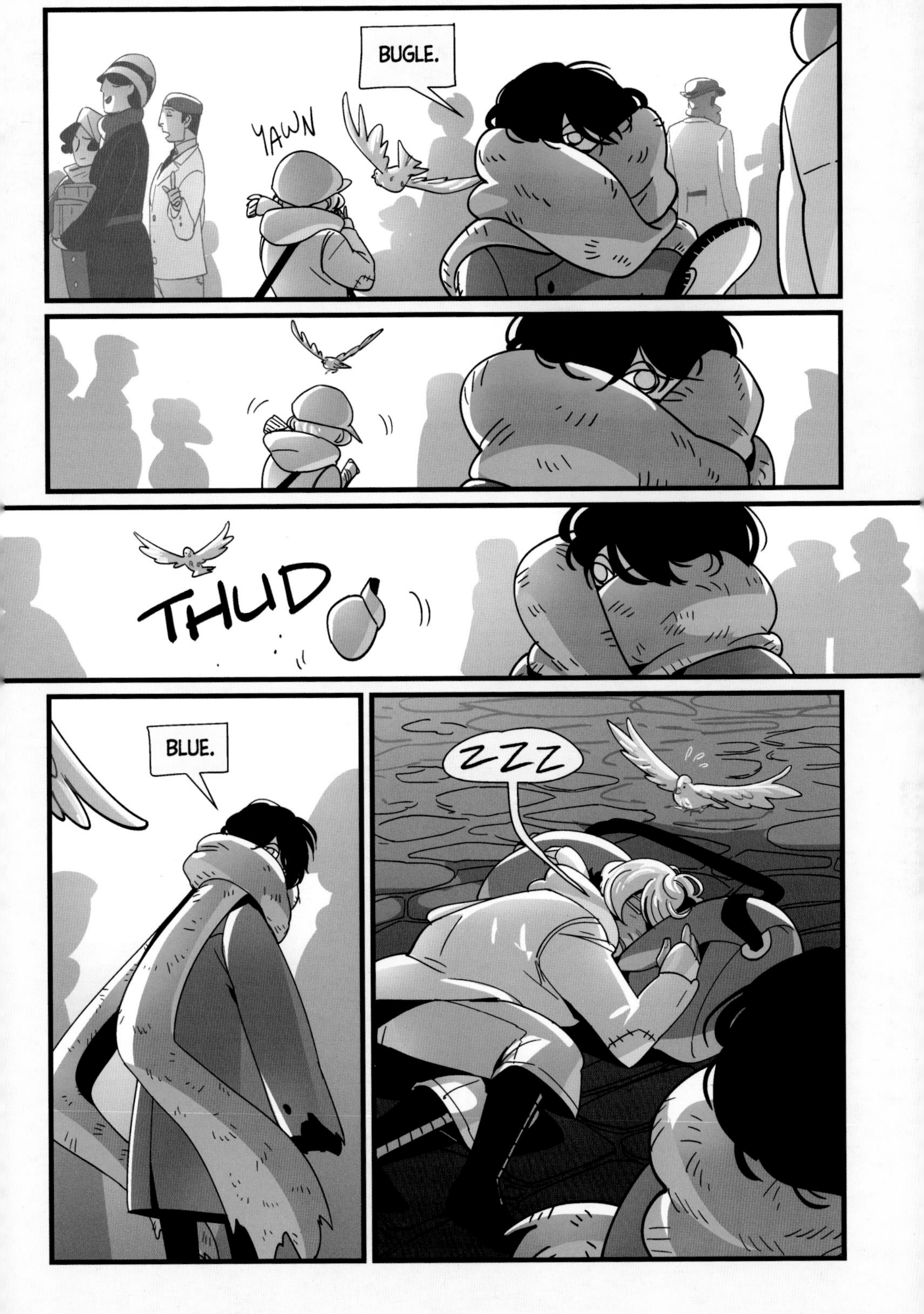
BUGLE.
YAWN
THUD
BLUE.
ZZZ

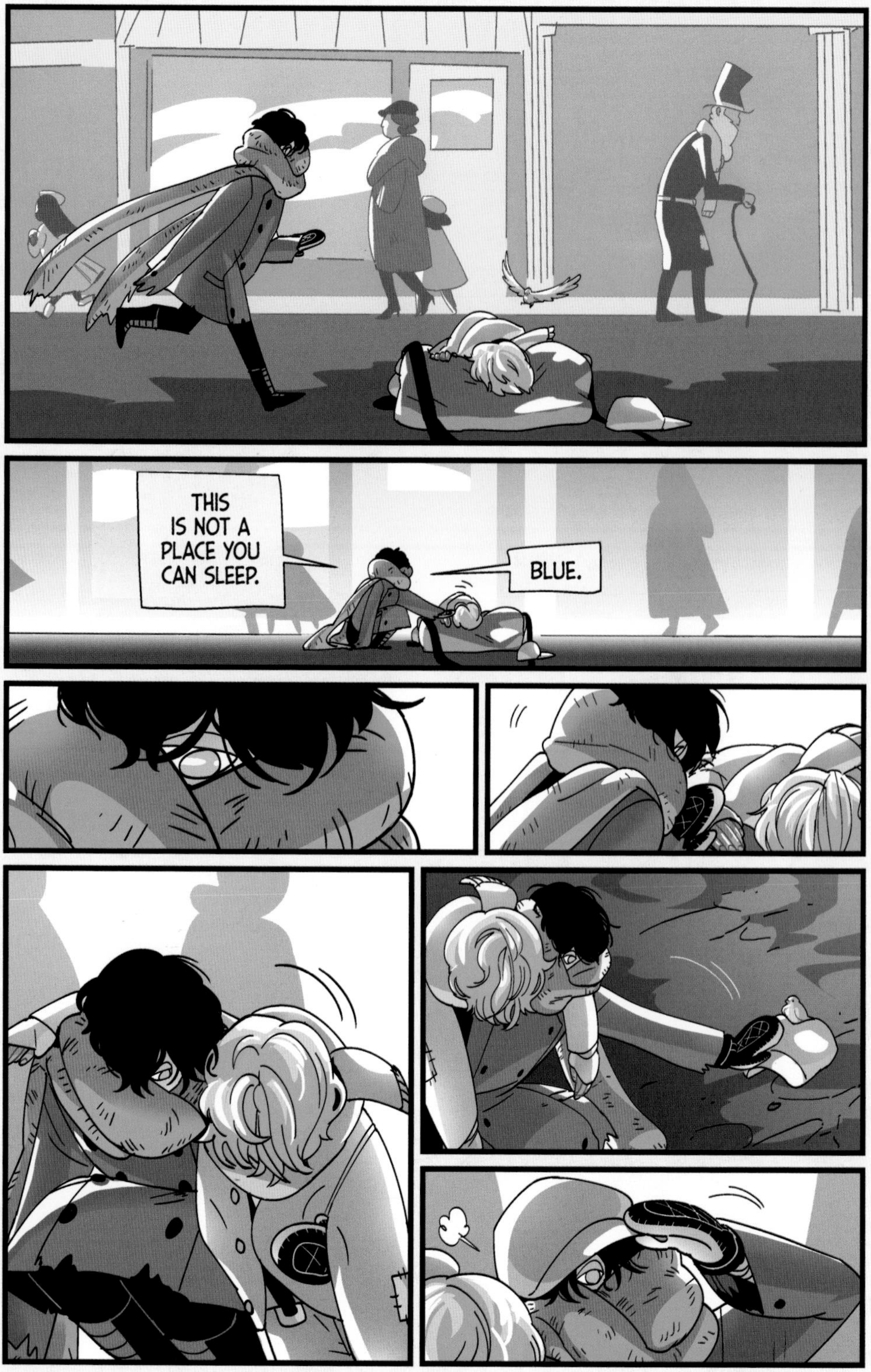
THIS IS NOT A PLACE YOU CAN SLEEP.
BLUE.

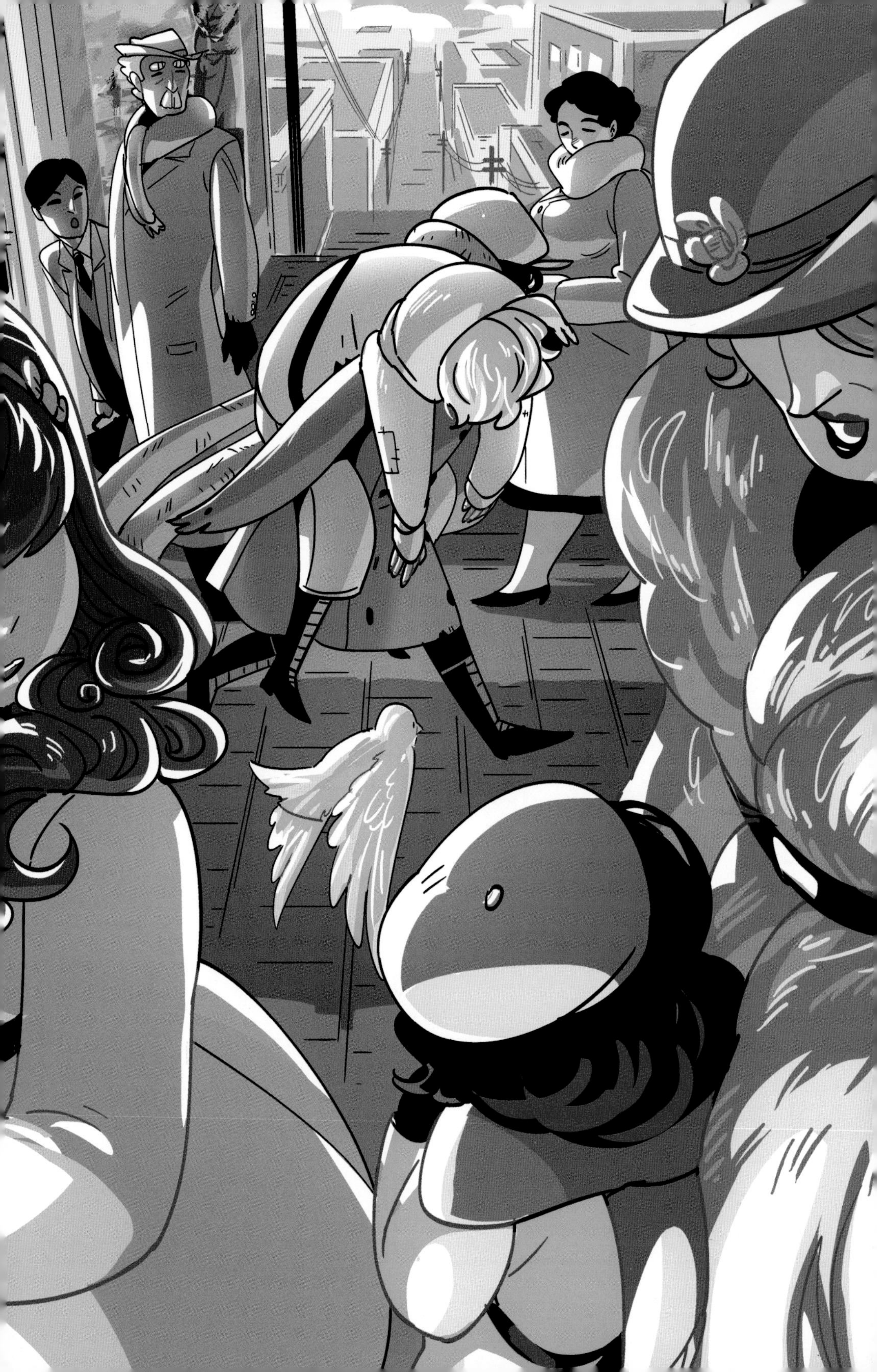

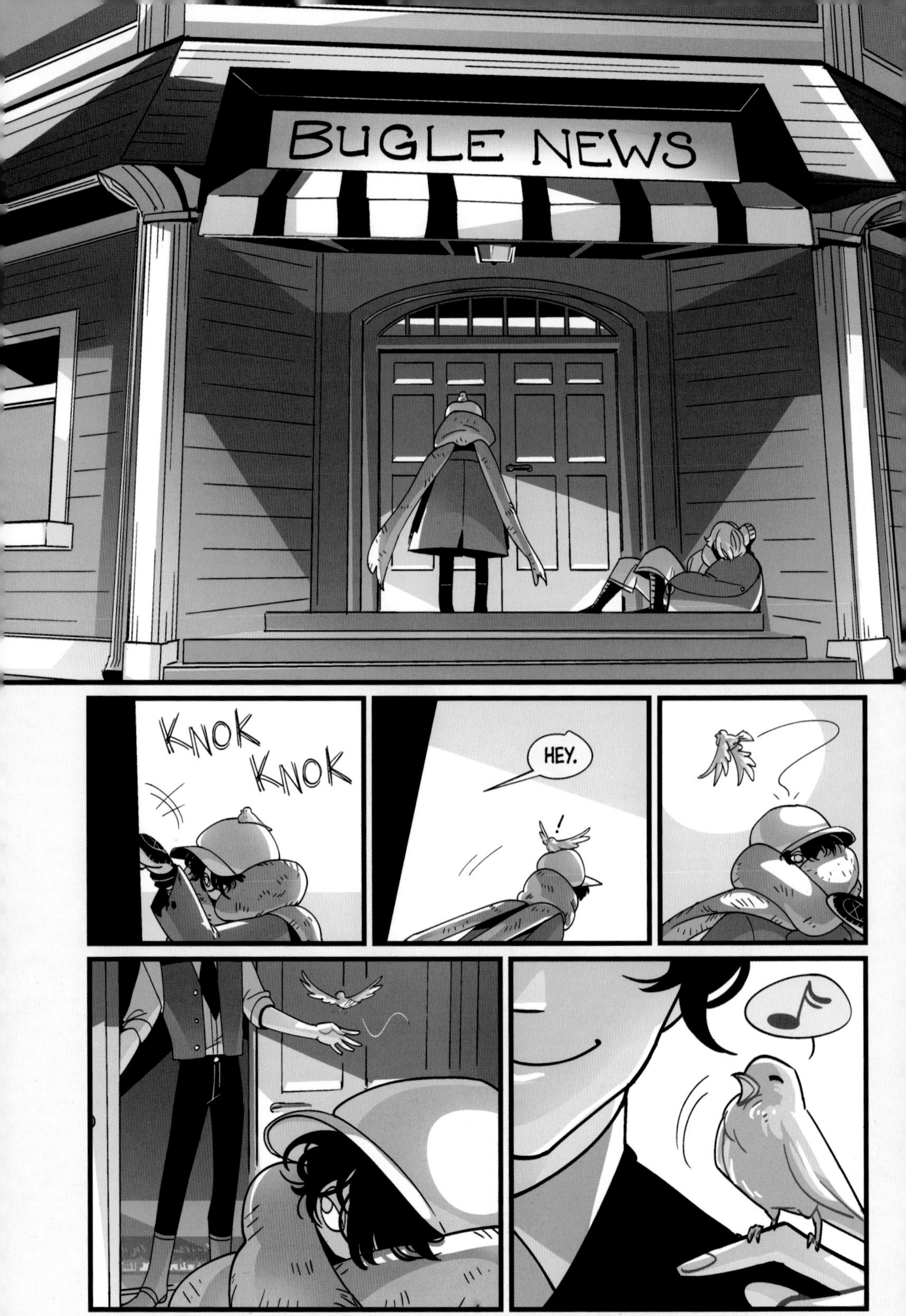
BUGLE NEWS
KNOK
KNOK
HEY.
!

fluff

NICE HAT.

HELLO TO YOU TOO, GOLDIE.

SO KIDDO, ARE YOU A NEW RECRUIT?

I THINK EVERYONE ELSE IS STILL OUT ON THEIR ROUTES.

HOW'D YOU END UP WITH BLUE'S HAT?

Y'KNOW, I GAVE THIS TO HIM.

I'M HECTOR, BY THE WAY.

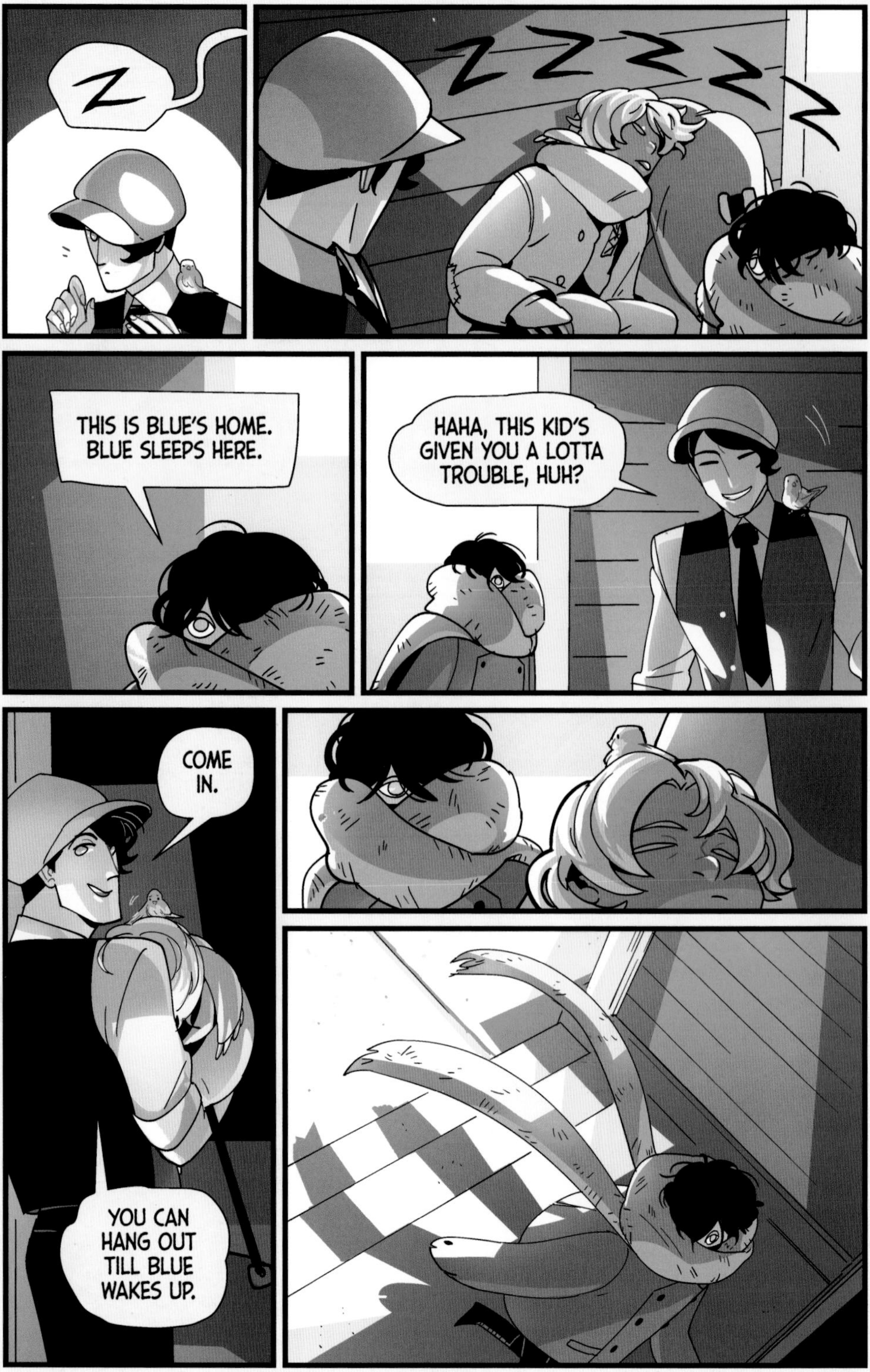
Z
ZZZZZZ
THIS IS BLUE'S HOME. BLUE SLEEPS HERE.
HAHA, THIS KID'S GIVEN YOU A LOTTA TROUBLE, HUH?
COME IN.
YOU CAN HANG OUT TILL BLUE WAKES UP.

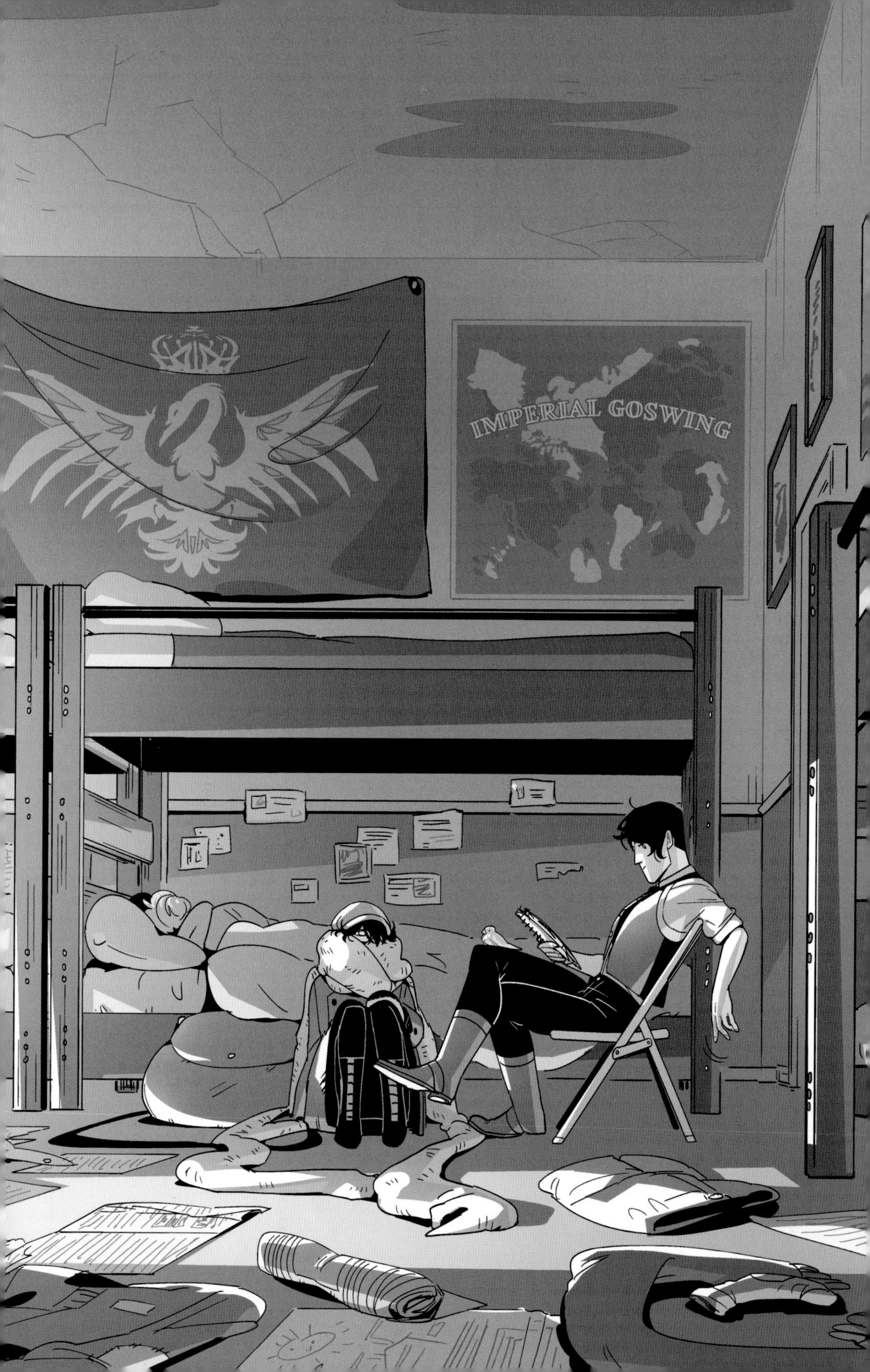
IMPERIAL GOSWING

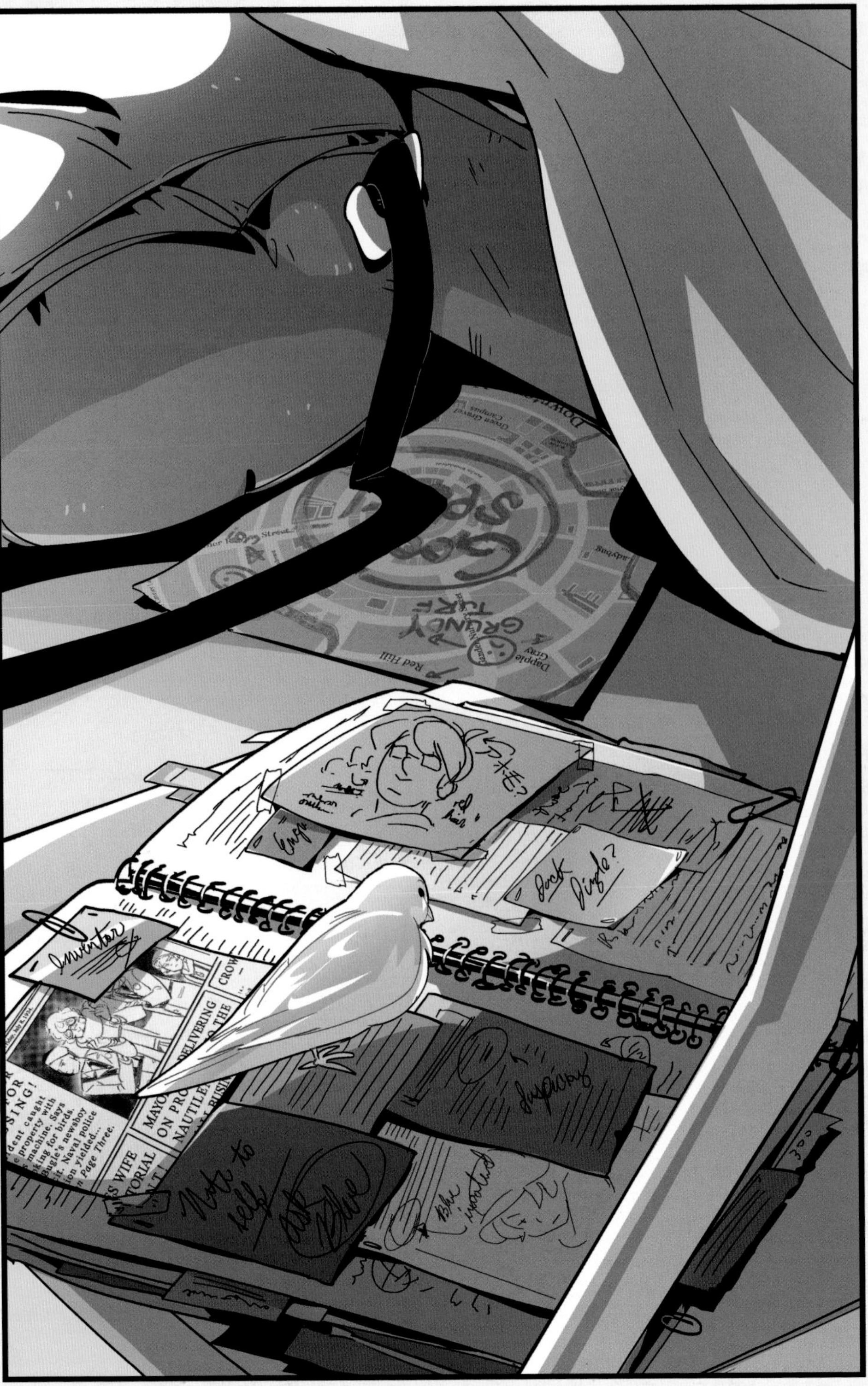
Inventor
Jack Dingle?
Suspicious
Note to self

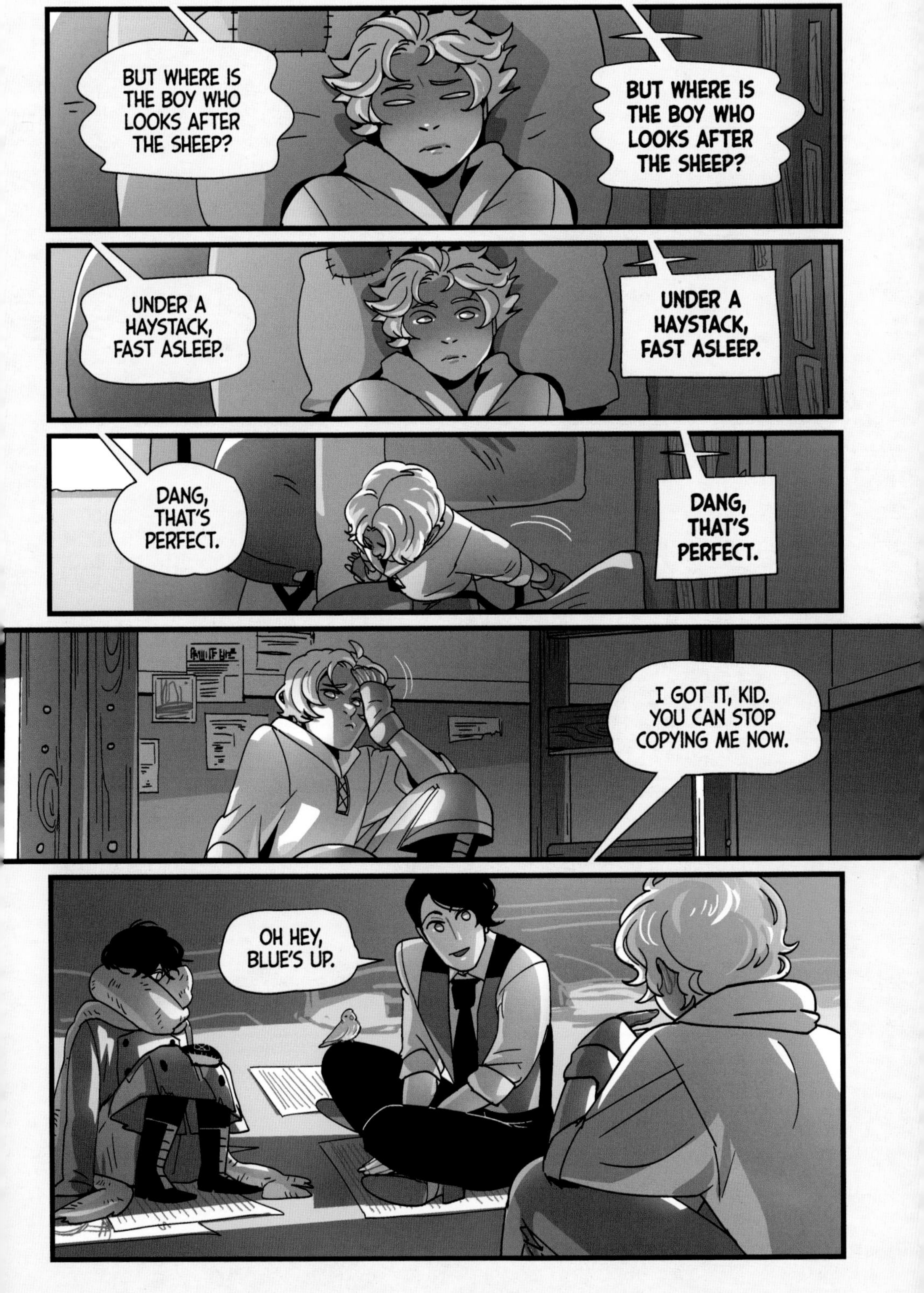
BUT WHERE IS THE BOY WHO LOOKS AFTER THE SHEEP?
BUT WHERE IS THE BOY WHO LOOKS AFTER THE SHEEP?
UNDER A HAYSTACK, FAST ASLEEP.
UNDER A HAYSTACK, FAST ASLEEP.
DANG, THAT'S PERFECT.
DANG, THAT'S PERFECT.
I GOT IT, KID. YOU CAN STOP COPYING ME NOW.
OH HEY, BLUE'S UP.

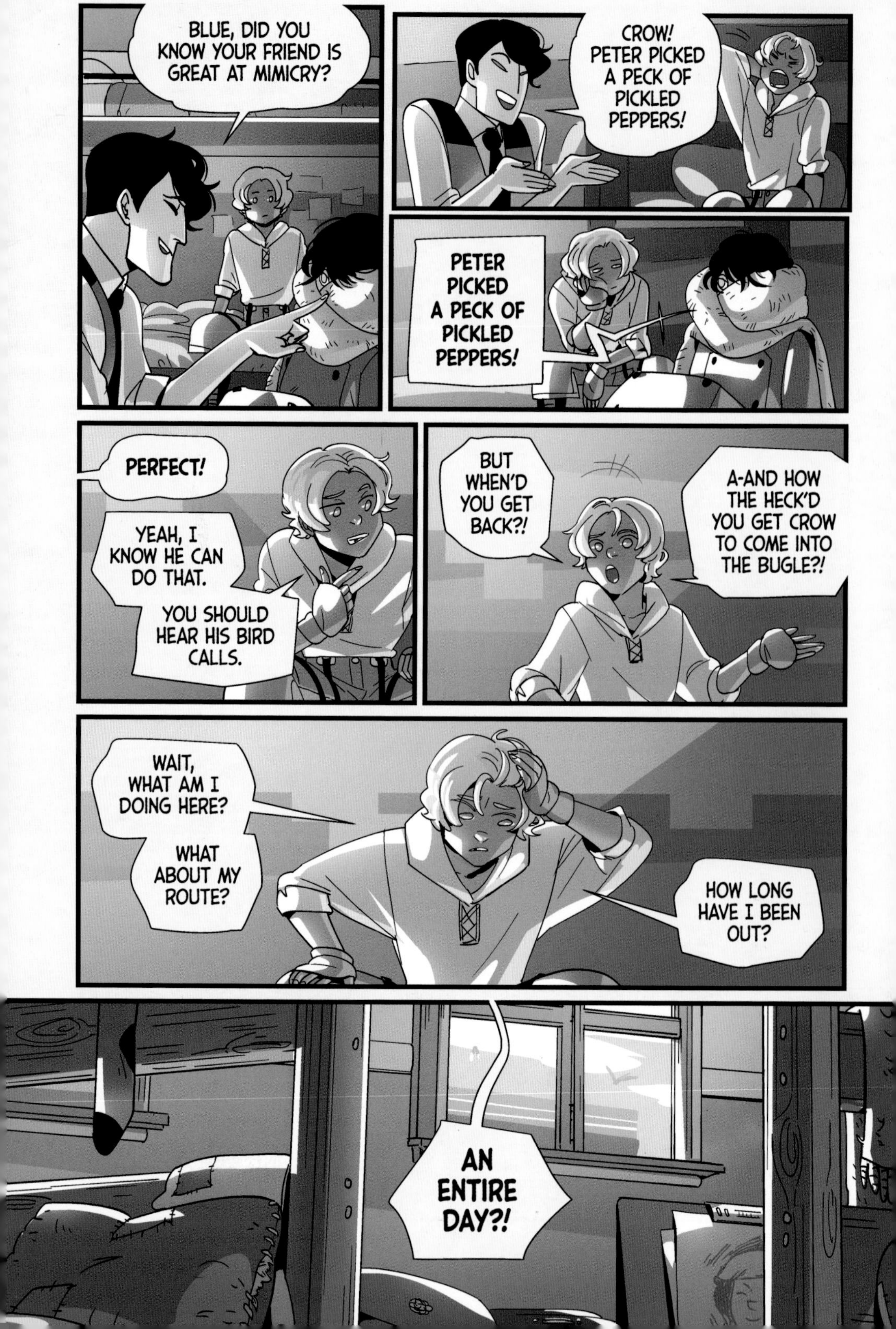
BLUE, DID YOU KNOW YOUR FRIEND IS GREAT AT MIMICRY?
CROW! PETER PICKED A PECK OF PICKLED PEPPERS!
PETER PICKED A PECK OF PICKLED PEPPERS!
PERFECT!
YEAH, I KNOW HE CAN DO THAT.
YOU SHOULD HEAR HIS BIRD CALLS.
BUT WHEN'D YOU GET BACK?!
A-AND HOW THE HECK'D YOU GET CROW TO COME INTO THE BUGLE?!
WAIT, WHAT AM I DOING HERE?
WHAT ABOUT MY ROUTE?
HOW LONG HAVE I BEEN OUT?
AN ENTIRE DAY?!

I LET EVERYONE DOWN...

NAH, THEY ALL WANTED TO PITCH IN WHILE YOU WERE ASLEEP.

YOUR CROW FRIEND KIND OF HOVERED OVER YOU THE ENTIRE TIME.

BUT IT'S NOT JUST THE BUGLE BEAT.

I'M WORRIED ABOUT MY PART-TIME JOB...

RIGHT, THE BOYS SAY YOU'RE THE ONE TO ASK ABOUT THAT...

'BOUT WHAT?

tap tap

SERIOUSLY, YOU'VE BEEN KINDA FIDGETY SINCE YOU GOT BACK...

IT'S MAKIN' ME NERVOUS.

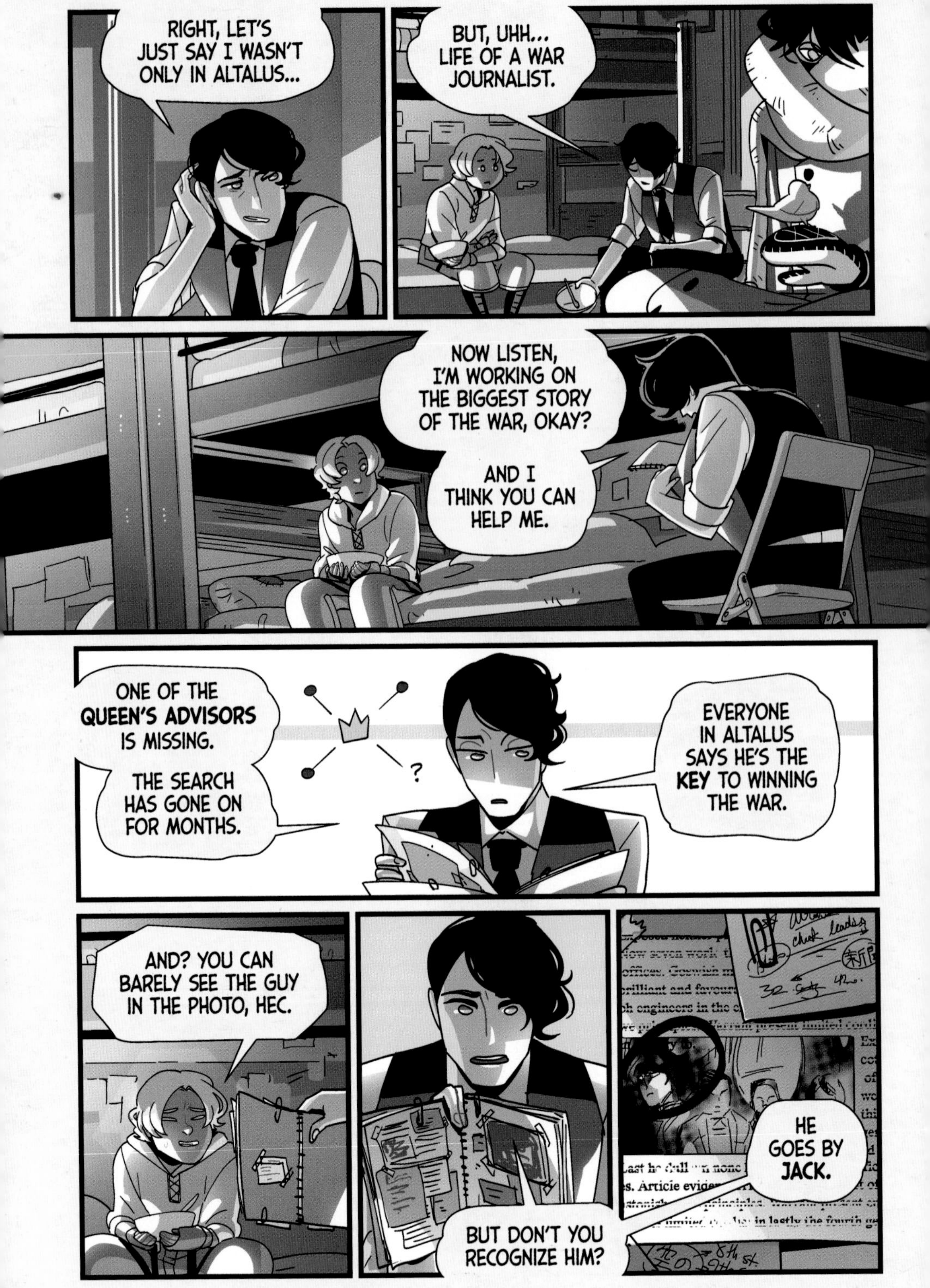
RIGHT, LET'S JUST SAY I WASN'T ONLY IN ALTALUS...
BUT, UHH... LIFE OF A WAR JOURNALIST.
NOW LISTEN, I'M WORKING ON THE BIGGEST STORY OF THE WAR, OKAY?
AND I THINK YOU CAN HELP ME.
ONE OF THE **QUEEN'S ADVISORS** IS MISSING.
THE SEARCH HAS GONE ON FOR MONTHS.
EVERYONE IN ALTALUS SAYS HE'S THE **KEY** TO WINNING THE WAR.
AND? YOU CAN BARELY SEE THE GUY IN THE PHOTO, HEC.
BUT DON'T YOU RECOGNIZE HIM?
HE GOES BY **JACK.**

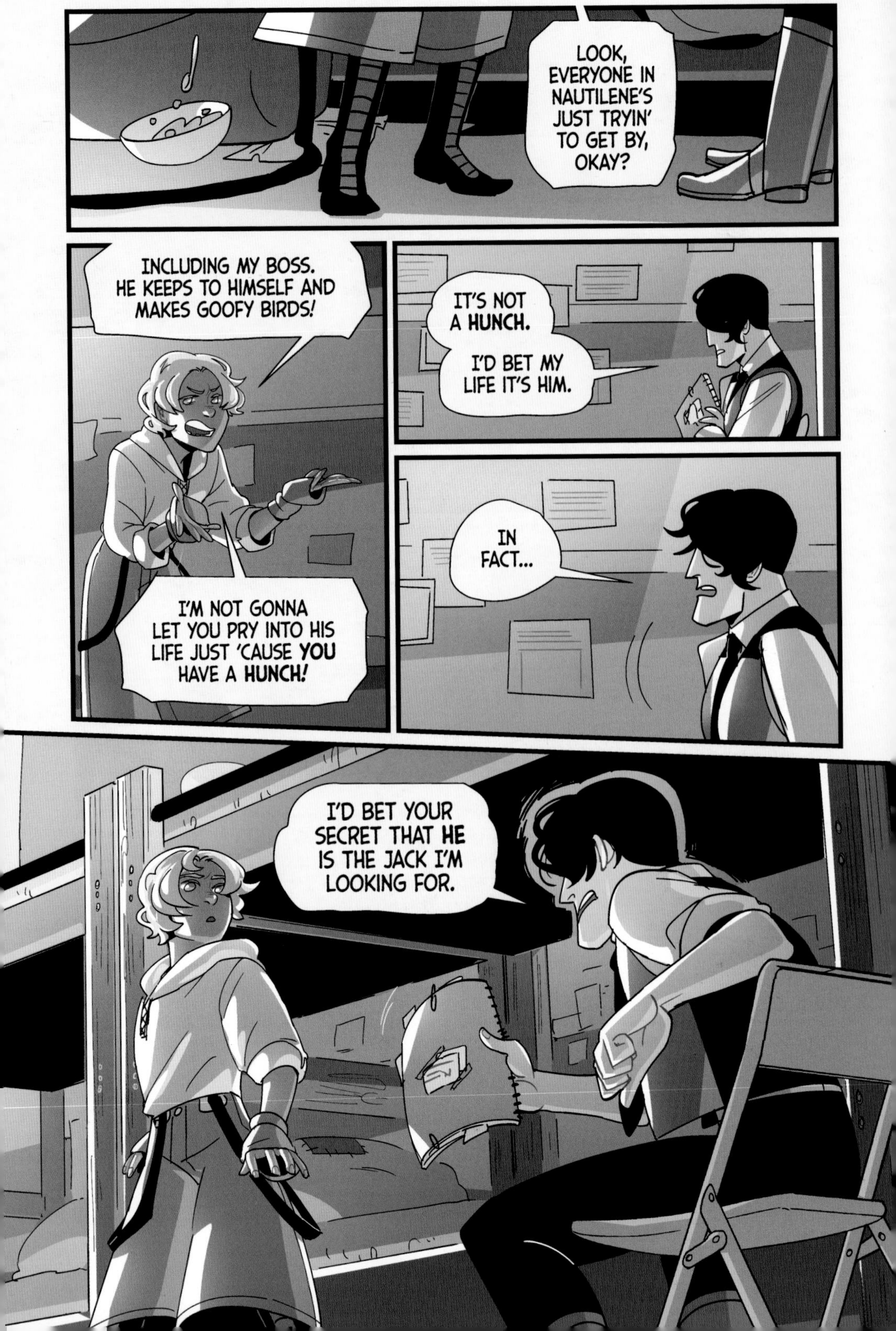
LOOK, EVERYONE IN NAUTILENE'S JUST TRYIN' TO GET BY, OKAY?
INCLUDING MY BOSS. HE KEEPS TO HIMSELF AND MAKES GOOFY BIRDS!
I'M NOT GONNA LET YOU PRY INTO HIS LIFE JUST 'CAUSE YOU HAVE A HUNCH!
IT'S NOT A HUNCH.
I'D BET MY LIFE IT'S HIM.
IN FACT...
I'D BET YOUR SECRET THAT HE IS THE JACK I'M LOOKING FOR.

THAT DOESN'T CHANGE THE FACT THAT YOU ARE BLUE.

AND GOLDIE LEFT WITH...

HECTOR.

HAHAHA!

THAT'S WHAT'S GETTING YOUR GOOSE, HUH?

DON'T WORRY, SHE'S IN GOOD HANDS.

HECTOR HELPED ME RAISE GOLDIE FROM AN EGG, AFTER A CAT ATE HER MOM!

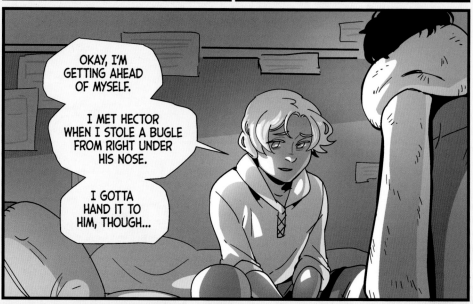

OKAY, I'M GETTING AHEAD OF MYSELF.

I MET HECTOR WHEN I STOLE A BUGLE FROM RIGHT UNDER HIS NOSE.

I GOTTA HAND IT TO HIM, THOUGH...

HE CHASED ME ALL THE WAY ACROSS THE CITY!

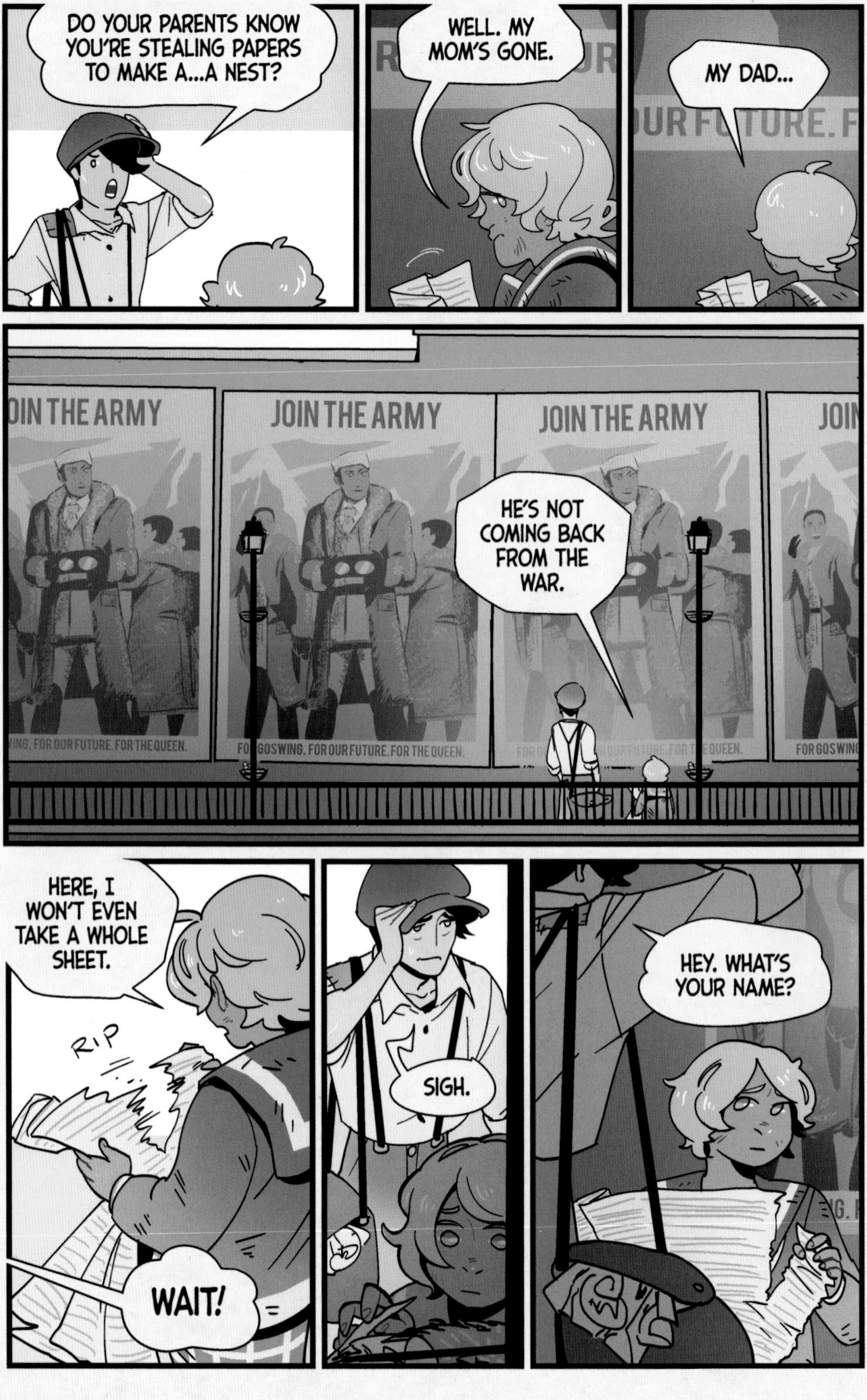
DO YOUR PARENTS KNOW YOU'RE STEALING PAPERS TO MAKE A...A NEST?
WELL. MY MOM'S GONE.
MY DAD...
OUR FUTURE. F
JOIN THE ARMY
JOIN THE ARMY
JOIN THE ARMY
HE'S NOT COMING BACK FROM THE WAR.
WING. FOR OUR FUTURE. FOR THE QUEEN.
FOR GOSWING. FOR OUR FUTURE. FOR THE QUEEN.
FOR GOSWING
HERE, I WON'T EVEN TAKE A WHOLE SHEET.
RIP
WAIT!
SIGH.
HEY. WHAT'S YOUR NAME?

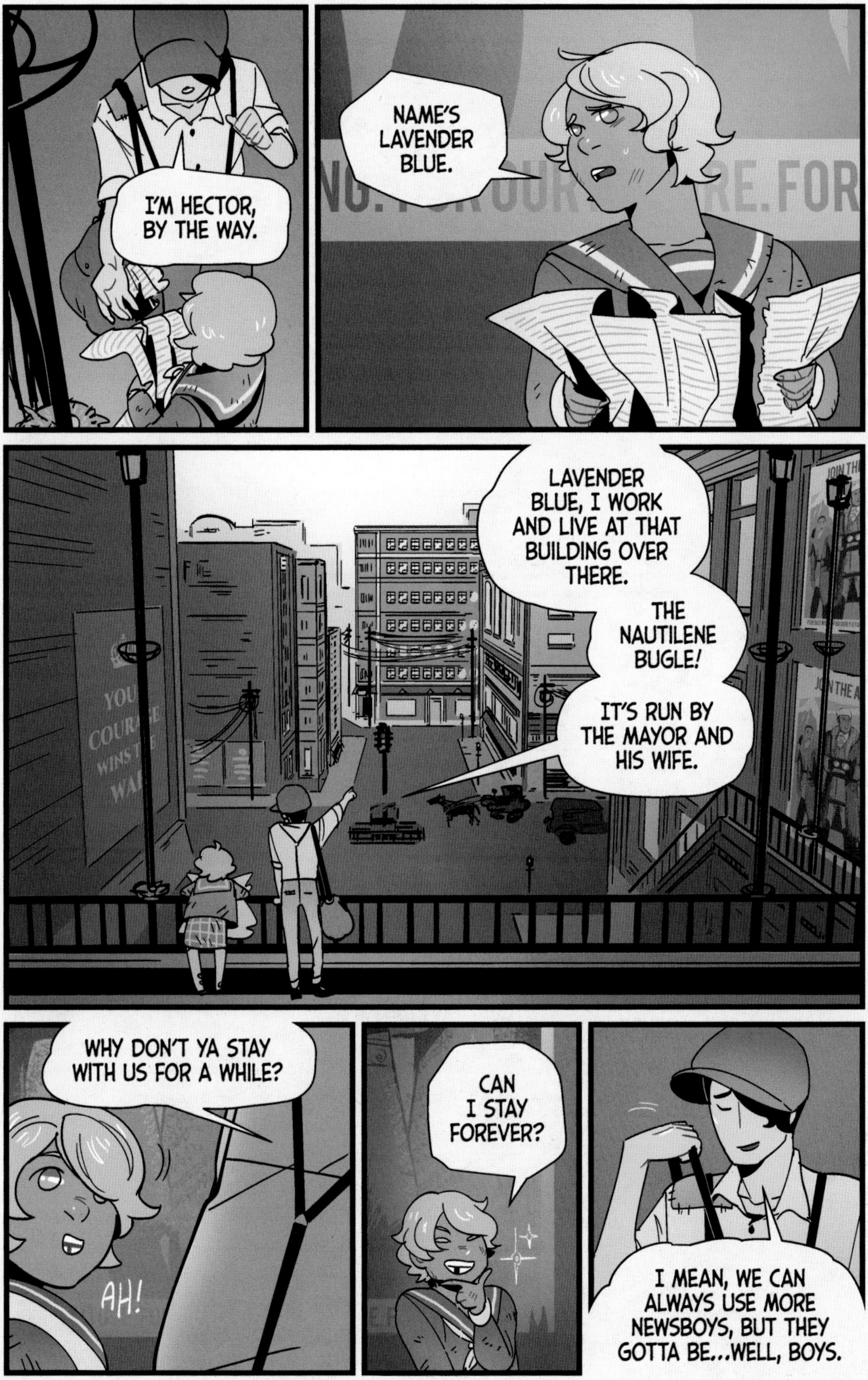
I'M HECTOR, BY THE WAY.
NAME'S LAVENDER BLUE.
LAVENDER BLUE, I WORK AND LIVE AT THAT BUILDING OVER THERE.
THE NAUTILENE BUGLE!
IT'S RUN BY THE MAYOR AND HIS WIFE.
WHY DON'T YA STAY WITH US FOR A WHILE?
AH!
CAN I STAY FOREVER?
I MEAN, WE CAN ALWAYS USE MORE NEWSBOYS, BUT THEY GOTTA BE...WELL, BOYS.

OH! WELL, THAT'S PERFECT!

um

'CAUSE I'M DEFINITELY A BOY!

HEY!

PAFF

HEH, SURE.

BLUE, THEN. YOU AND YOUR FRIEND GOLDIE...

ARE WELCOME TO JOIN US AT THE BUGLE.

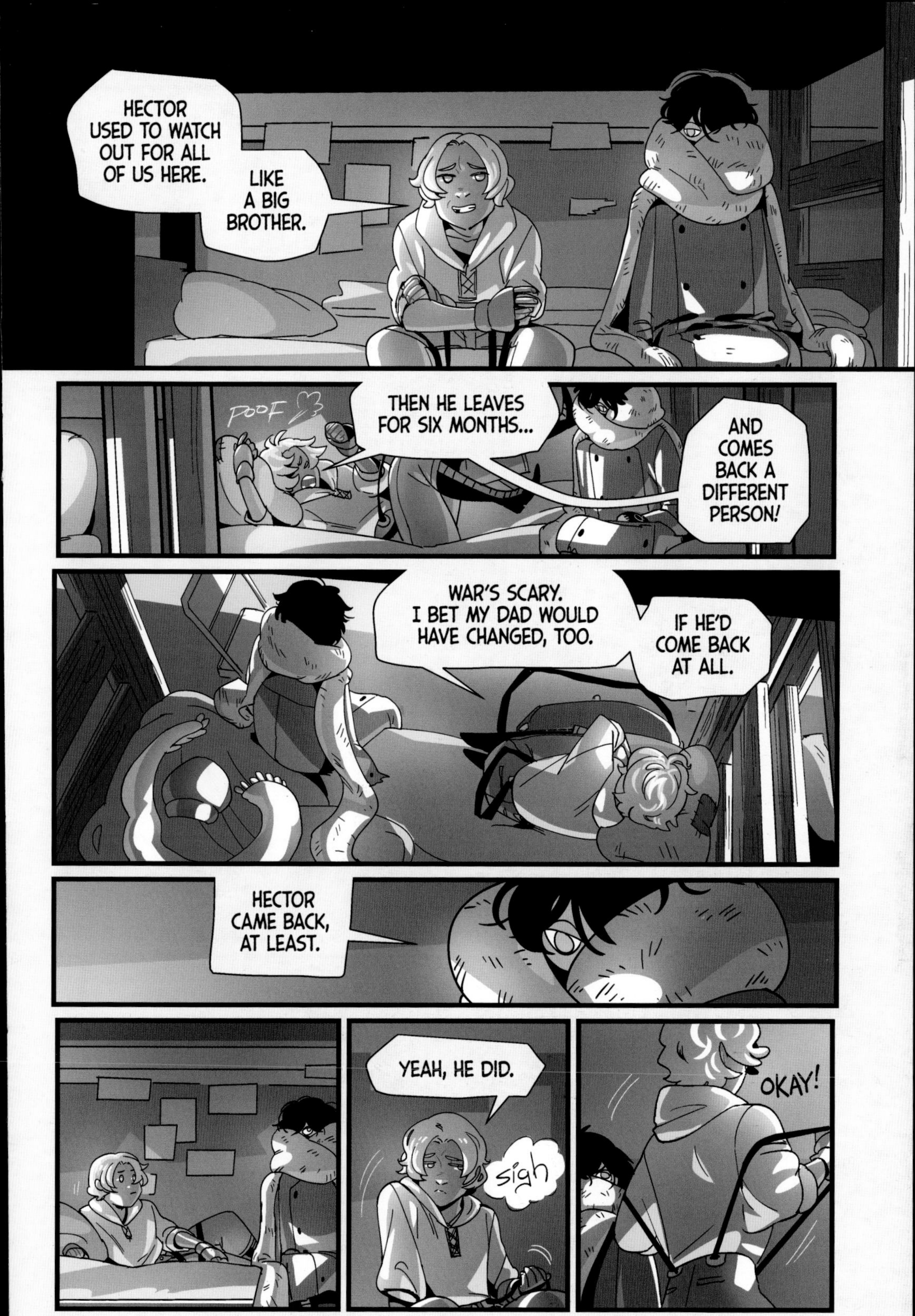
HECTOR USED TO WATCH OUT FOR ALL OF US HERE.
LIKE A BIG BROTHER.
POOF
THEN HE LEAVES FOR SIX MONTHS...
AND COMES BACK A DIFFERENT PERSON!
WAR'S SCARY. I BET MY DAD WOULD HAVE CHANGED, TOO.
IF HE'D COME BACK AT ALL.
HECTOR CAME BACK, AT LEAST.
YEAH, HE DID.
sigh
OKAY!

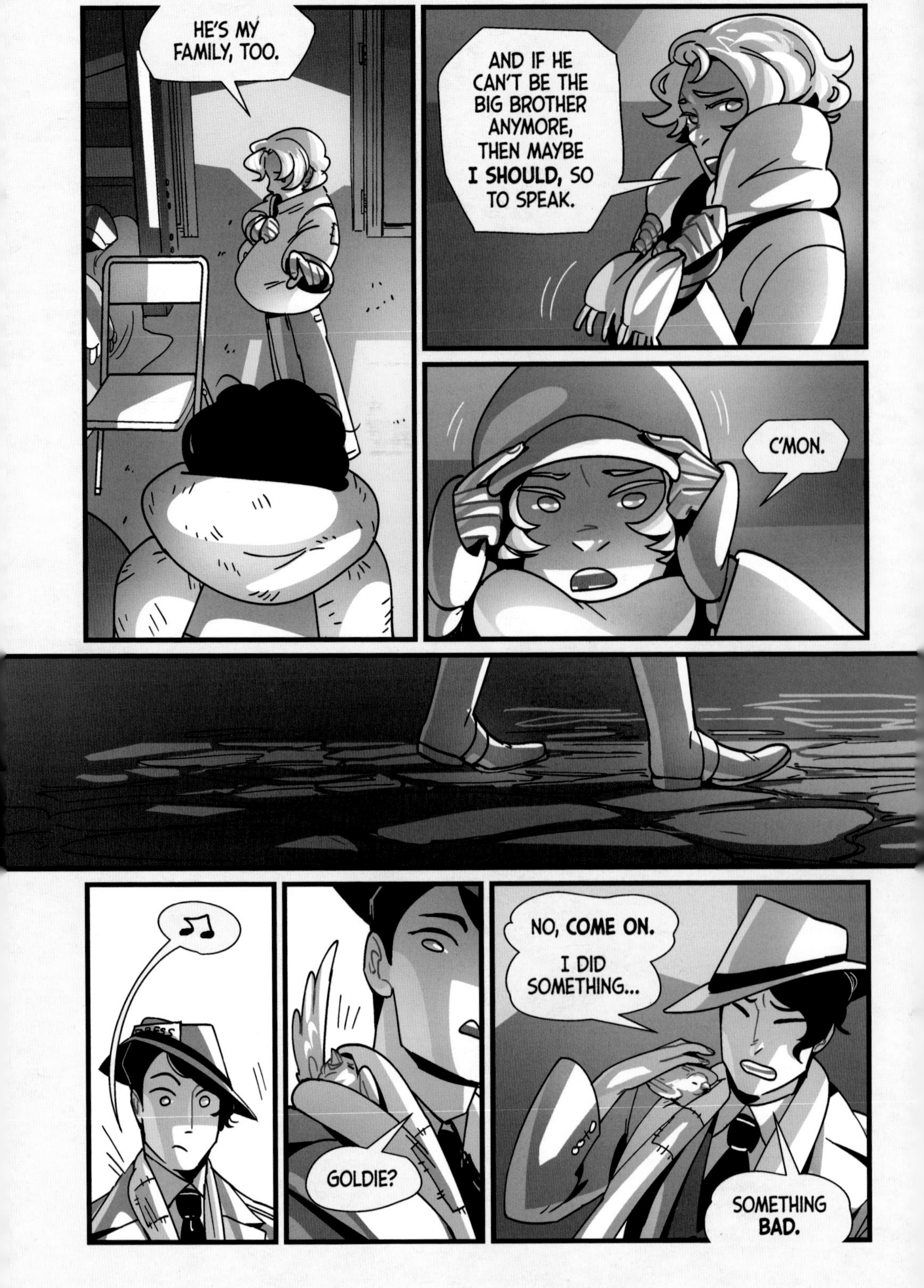
HE'S MY FAMILY, TOO.
AND IF HE CAN'T BE THE BIG BROTHER ANYMORE, THEN MAYBE I **SHOULD,** SO TO SPEAK.
C'MON.
♫
GOLDIE?
NO, **COME ON.**
I DID SOMETHING...
SOMETHING **BAD.**

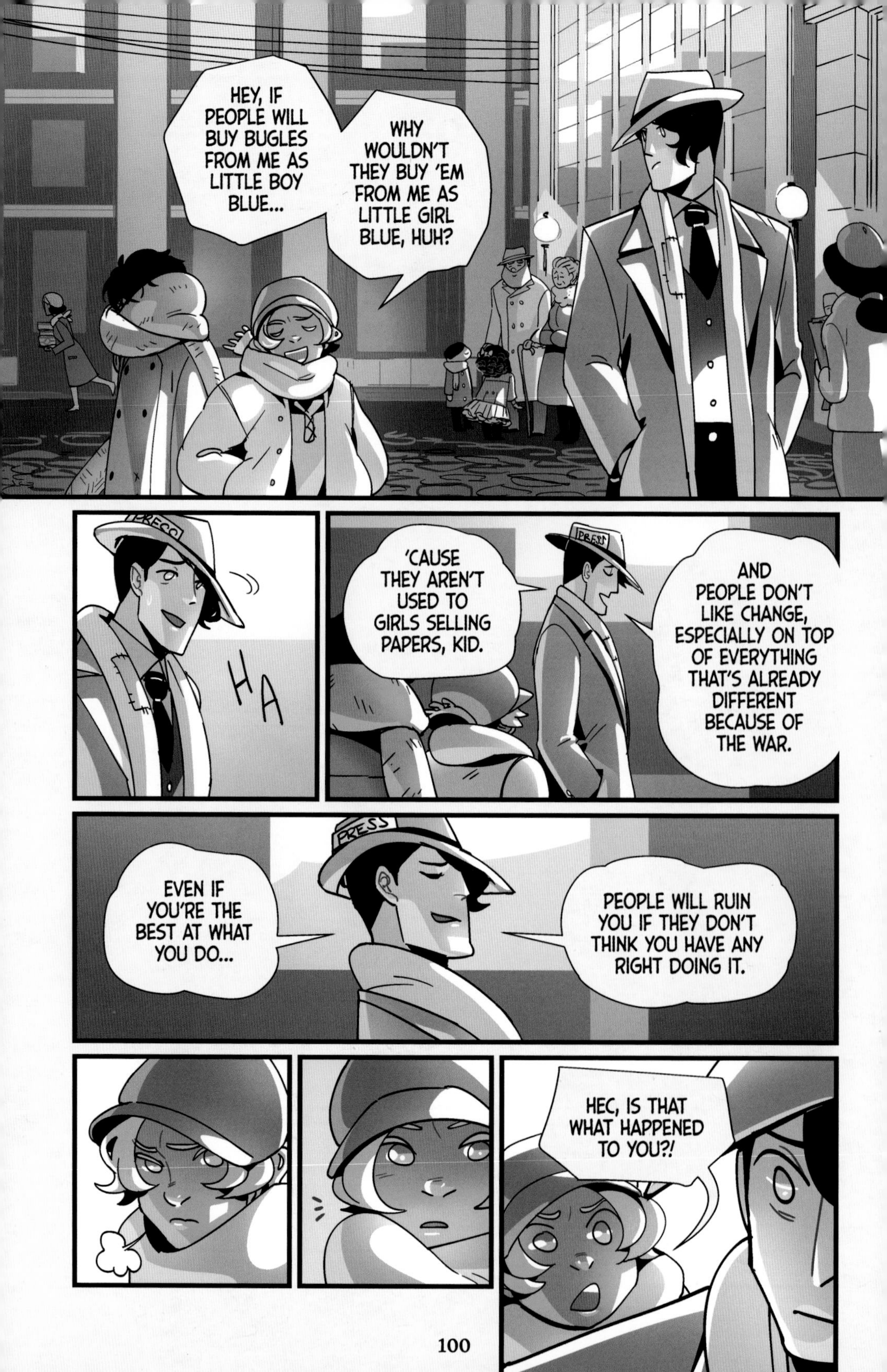
HEY, IF PEOPLE WILL BUY BUGLES FROM ME AS LITTLE BOY BLUE...
WHY WOULDN'T THEY BUY 'EM FROM ME AS LITTLE GIRL BLUE, HUH?
PRESS
HA
'CAUSE THEY AREN'T USED TO GIRLS SELLING PAPERS, KID.
AND PEOPLE DON'T LIKE CHANGE, ESPECIALLY ON TOP OF EVERYTHING THAT'S ALREADY DIFFERENT BECAUSE OF THE WAR.
EVEN IF YOU'RE THE BEST AT WHAT YOU DO...
PEOPLE WILL RUIN YOU IF THEY DON'T THINK YOU HAVE ANY RIGHT DOING IT.
HEC, IS THAT WHAT HAPPENED TO YOU?!

The Grundy Gazette

NAUTILENE. Tuesday, Julion 8, 1924

LOCAL INVENTOR ARRESTED FOR TRESPASSING!

New resident caught on private property with suspicious machine. Says he was looking for birds. Nautilene Bugle's newsboy also complicit. Naval police interrogation yielded...

TOO MANY GROWN-UPS!

GEEZ, THE POLICE? MAYBE I SHOULD TELL JACK ABOUT THIS...

RATTLE RATTLE

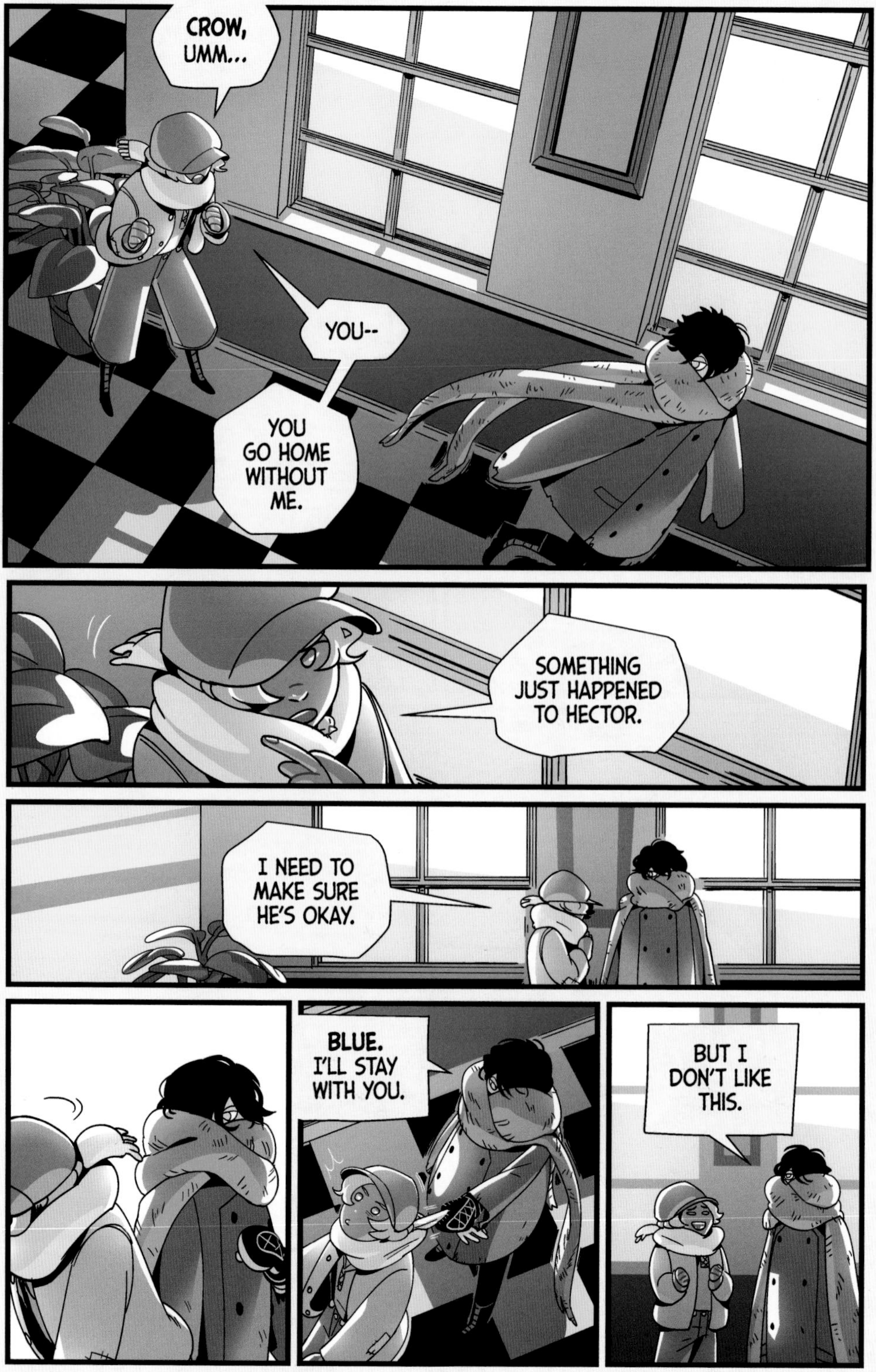
CROW, UMM...
YOU--
YOU GO HOME WITHOUT ME.
SOMETHING JUST HAPPENED TO HECTOR.
I NEED TO MAKE SURE HE'S OKAY.
BLUE. I'LL STAY WITH YOU.
BUT I DON'T LIKE THIS.

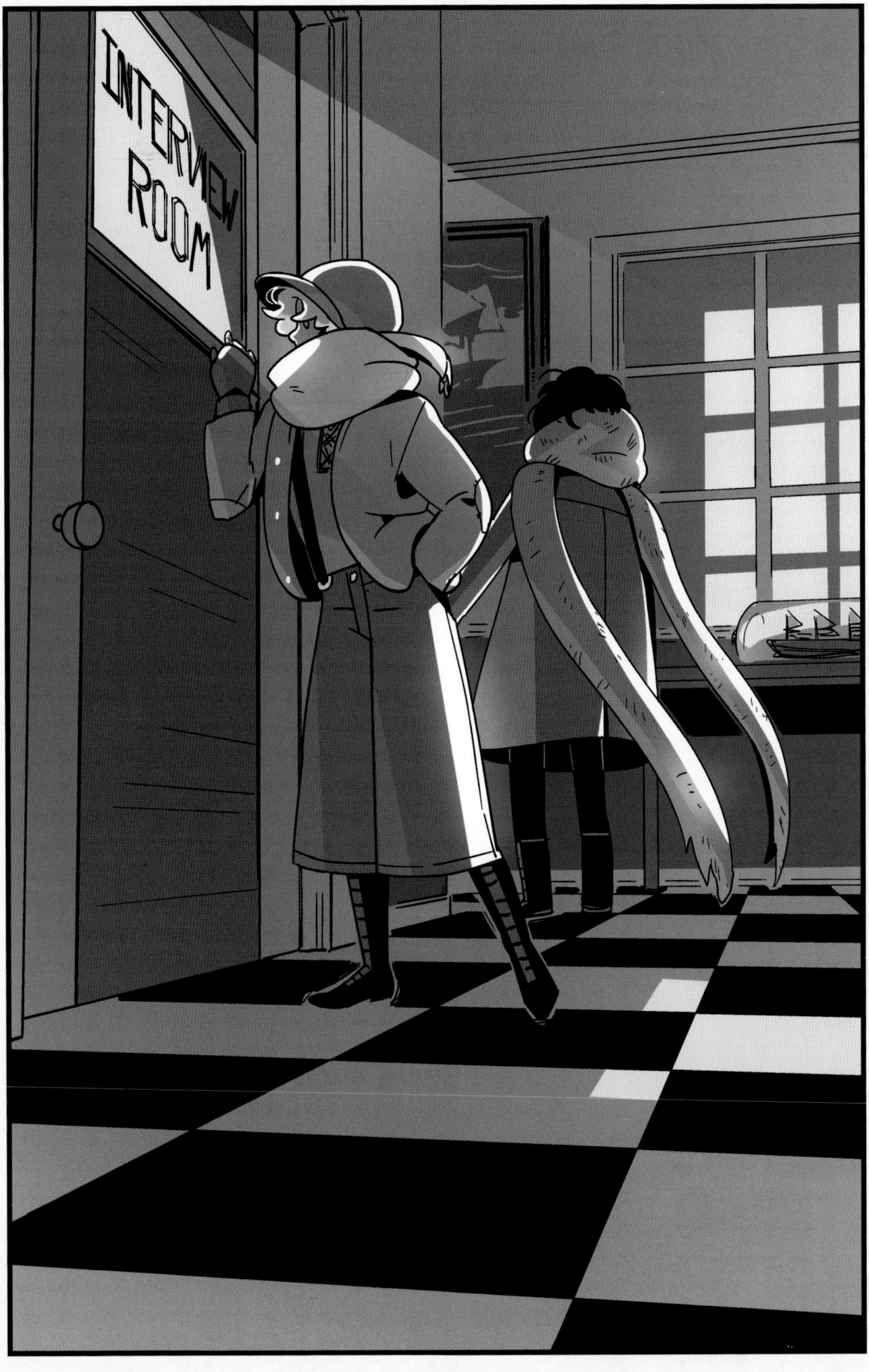
INTERVIEW ROOM

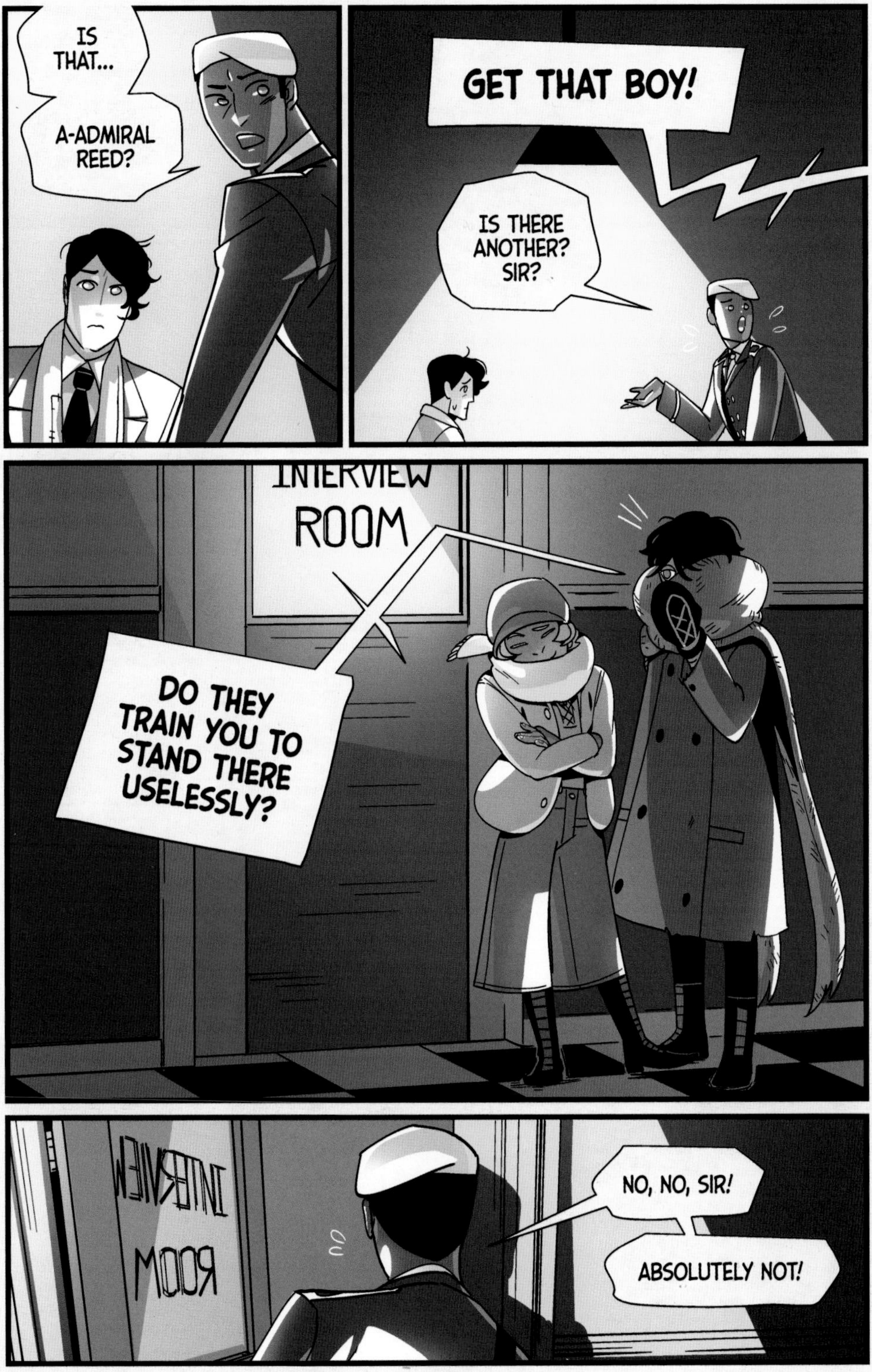
IS THAT...
A-ADMIRAL REED?
GET THAT BOY!
IS THERE ANOTHER? SIR?
INTERVIEW ROOM
DO THEY TRAIN YOU TO STAND THERE USELESSLY?
NO, NO, SIR!
ABSOLUTELY NOT!

C'MON. WE'LL GO BACK TO THE BUGLE.

I'M SURE MAYOR NANCY CAN HELP YOU OUT--

FREEZE

MAYBE WE CAN REASON...

WITH THEM.

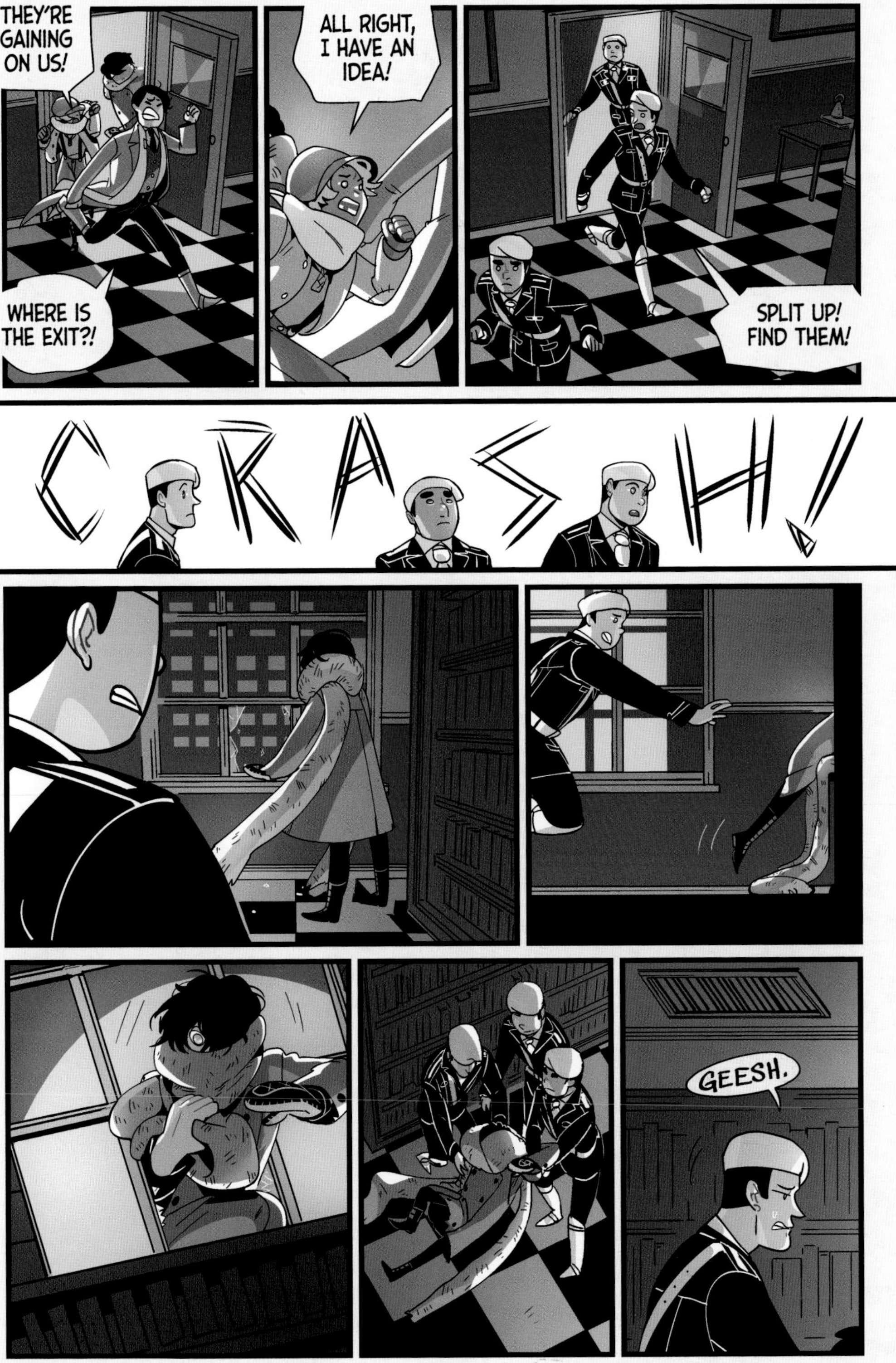
THEY'RE GAINING ON US!
WHERE IS THE EXIT?!
ALL RIGHT, I HAVE AN IDEA!
SPLIT UP! FIND THEM!
CRASH!
GEESH.

DON'T WORRY,
I'LL FIND YOU GUYS
NO MATTER WHAT.

LET'S GO
GET HELP.

FIRST
THING'S

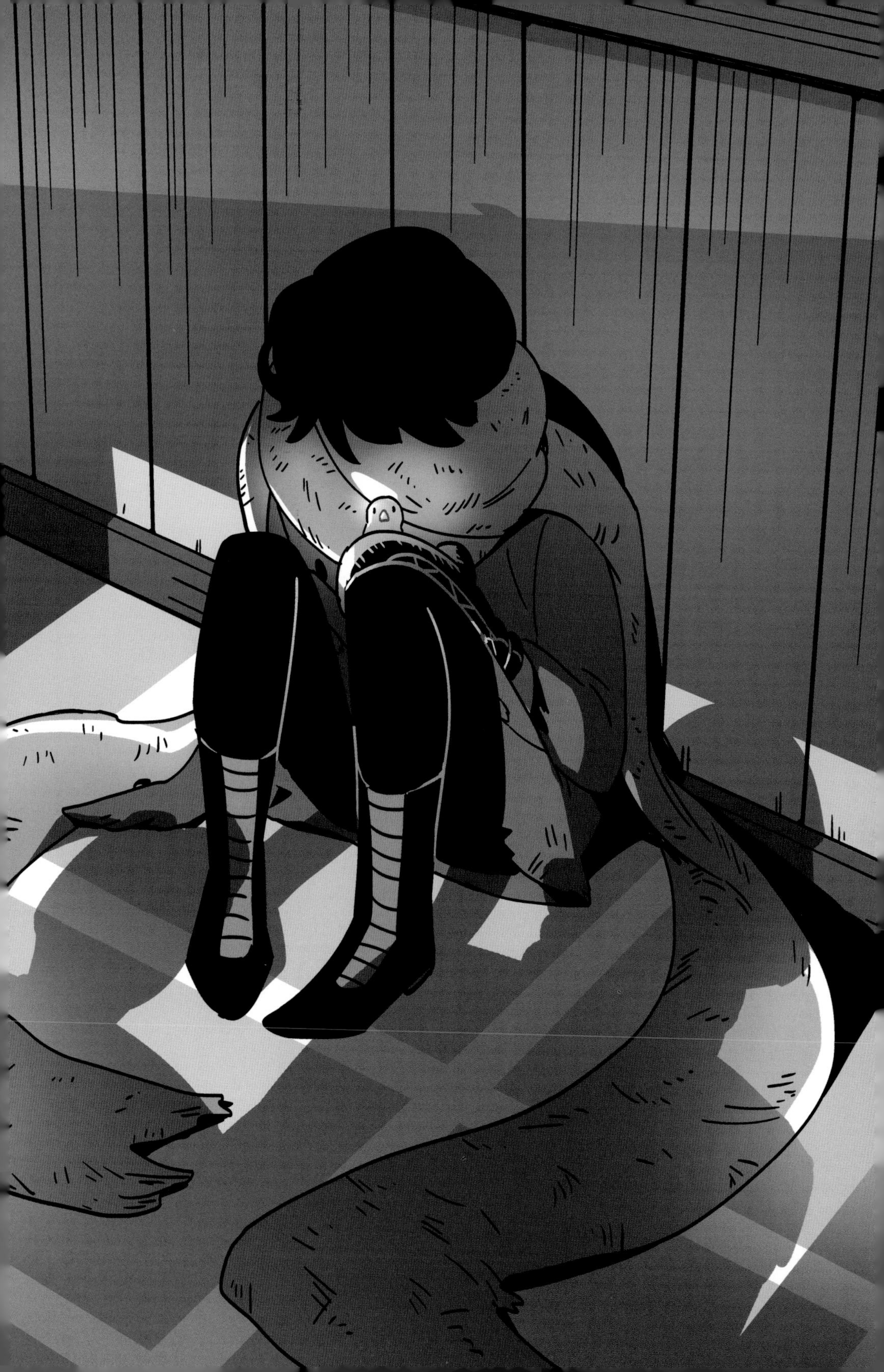

OH, CURSE MY DECORATIVE TUFFETS!

WE STILL HAVEN'T FOUND BLUE!

BUT I BUMPED INTO JILL REED AND MR. JACK.

AND THEY SAID THEY'D HELP LOOK!

HECTOR HASN'T RETURNED, EITHER.

I'M SURE BLUE'S WITH HIM.

THEY'LL BE ALL RIGHT, MUFFY. COME HOME.

BUT WHAT IF THEY'RE IN TROUBLE?

NO MATTER HOW CAPABLE BLUE IS, IT'S STILL SO DANGEROUS OUT THERE AT NIGHT FOR...

MUFFY?

EVEN THE BRAVEST NEWSGIRL.

MUH--

DON'T WAIT UP FOR ME, ARIC!

BUGLE NEWS

YOU MEAN ALL THIS TIME...?

MAYOR NANCY.

I'M NOT SUPPOSED TO TELL YOU THIS, BUT...

THAT'S BLUE'S ROUTE. SOMETIMES HE SNEAKS OUT REALLY LATE TO THE DOCKS.

I THINK HE SELLS HIS EXTRA PAPERS TO THE FISHERMEN WHO SAIL OUT BEFORE US NEWSIES HIT THE STREETS.

REALLY...

SO, DON'T WORRY. MAYBE IT'S ONE OF THOSE NIGHTS, AND BLUE WILL BE HOME BY SUNRISE LIKE USUAL.

LET'S HOPE SO.

MR. MAYOR!

WHAT'S WRONG, OFFICER?

WE'VE DISCOVERED SOMETHING THAT YOU MIGHT WANT TO SEE.

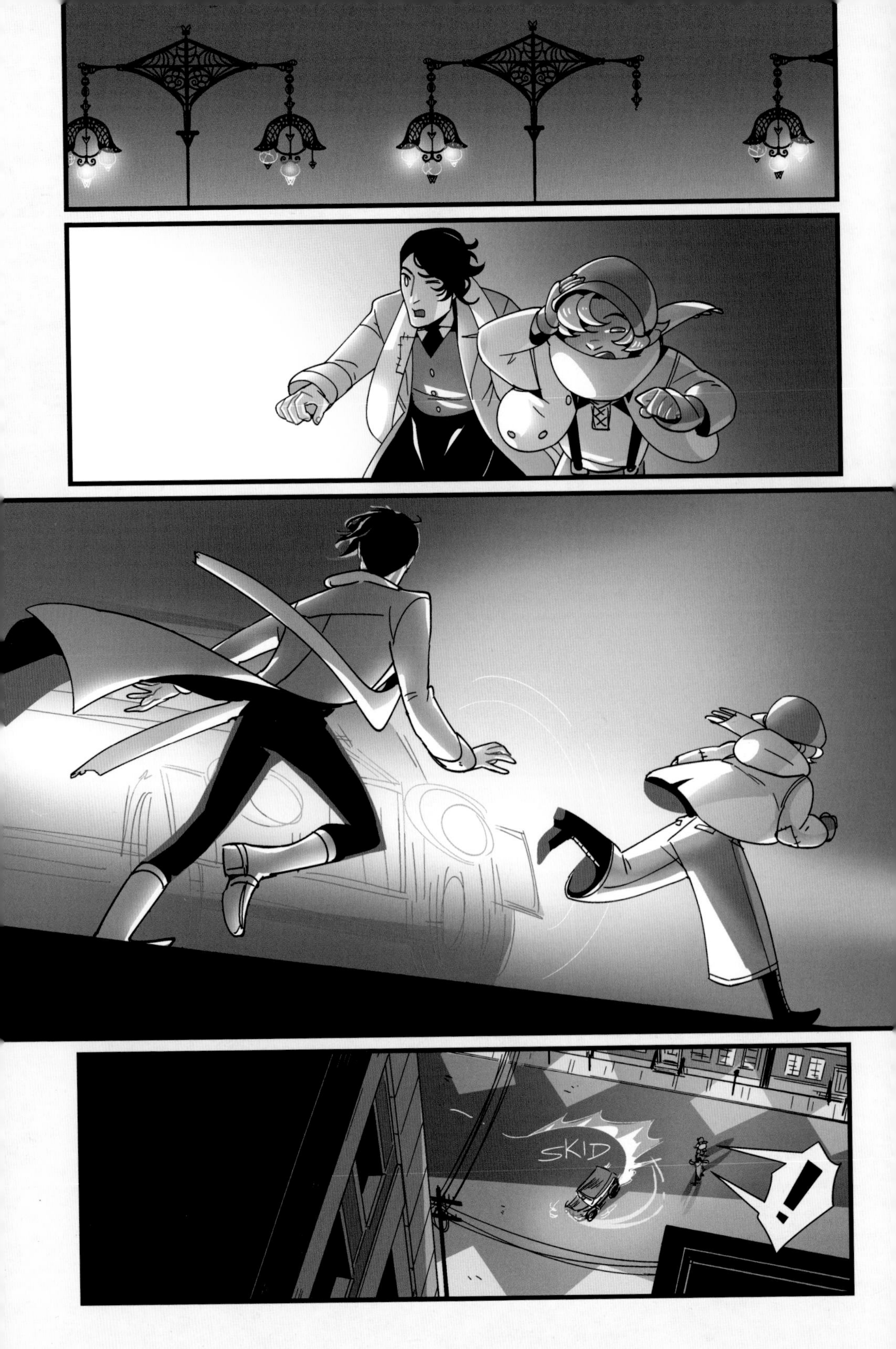
SKID
!

SWING

LOOK BOTH WAYS BEFORE YOU CROSS THE STREET!

J-JILL?

AH!

Jill! Jack!

IS IT--

BLUE!

IF BLUE'S HERE...

THEN THIS THING MUST BE BROKEN.

ARE YOU JACK?

HEY!

WHO ARE YOU?

NEVER MIND HIM! JACK, IS THIS THE DEVICE?

THE ONE THAT FINDS MY GOLDIE PIN?

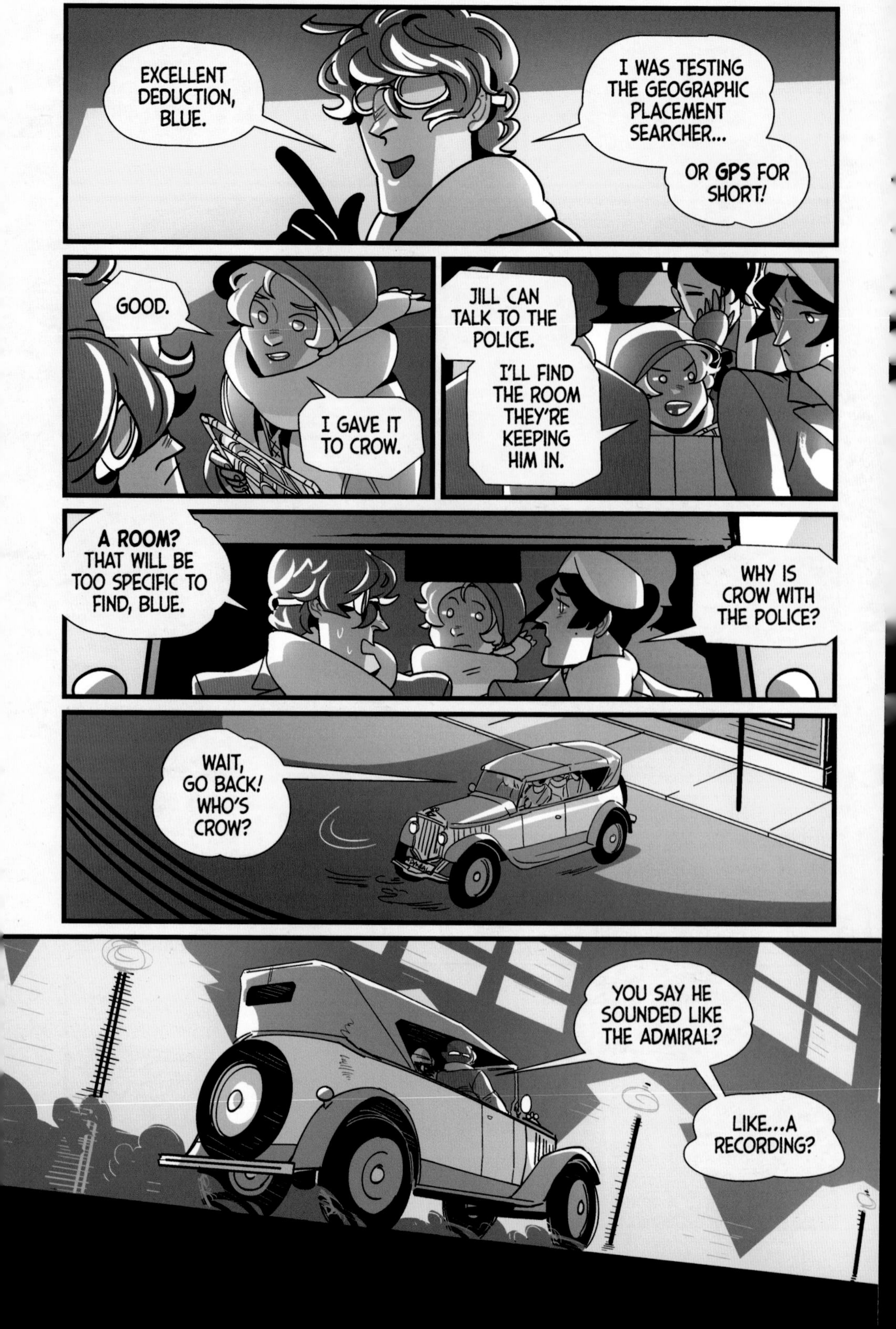

EXCELLENT DEDUCTION, BLUE.
I WAS TESTING THE GEOGRAPHIC PLACEMENT SEARCHER...
OR **GPS** FOR SHORT!
GOOD.
I GAVE IT TO CROW.
JILL CAN TALK TO THE POLICE.
I'LL FIND THE ROOM THEY'RE KEEPING HIM IN.
A ROOM? THAT WILL BE TOO SPECIFIC TO FIND, BLUE.
WHY IS CROW WITH THE POLICE?
WAIT, GO BACK! WHO'S CROW?
YOU SAY HE SOUNDED LIKE THE ADMIRAL?
LIKE...A RECORDING?

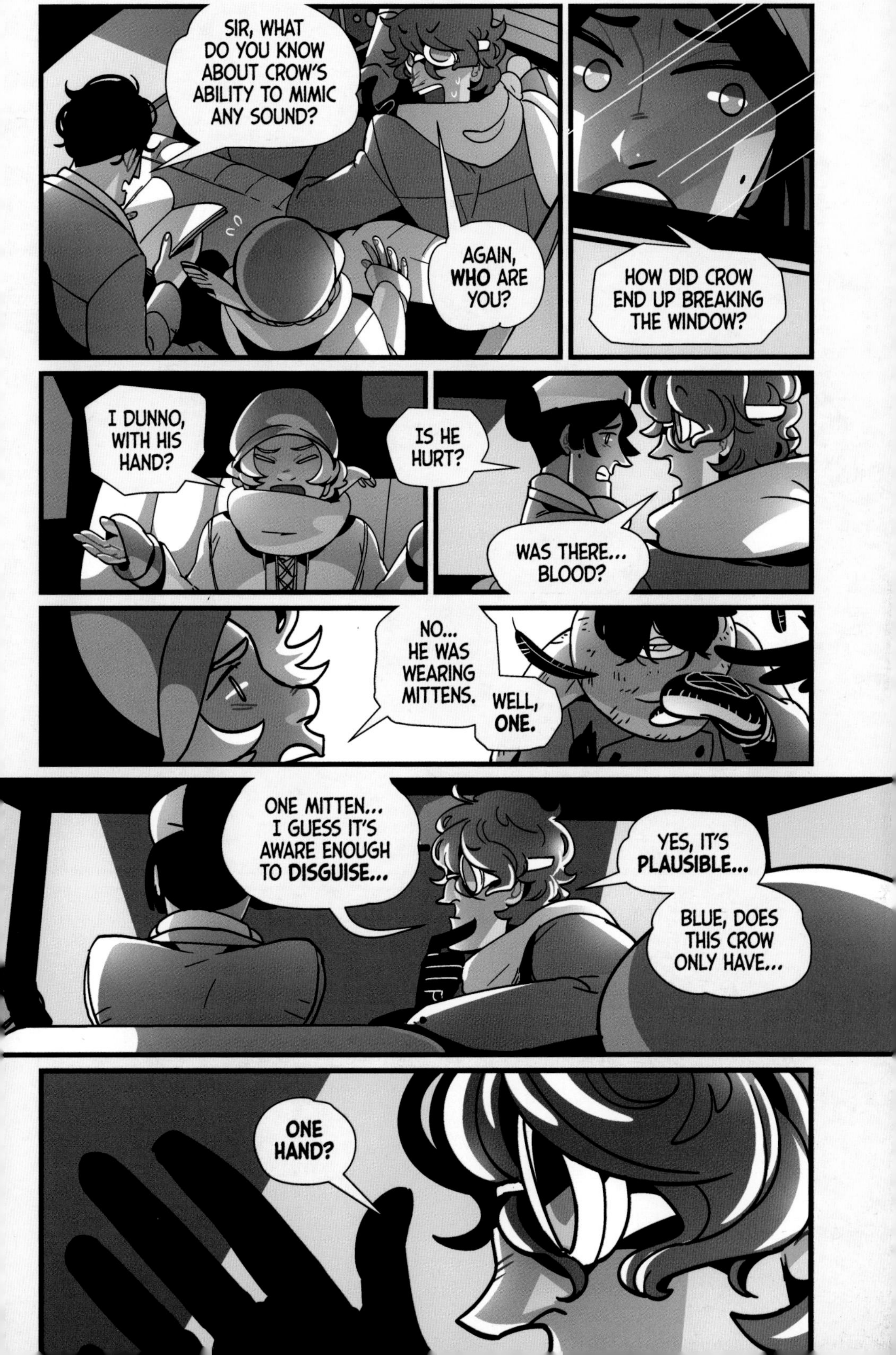
SIR, WHAT DO YOU KNOW ABOUT CROW'S ABILITY TO MIMIC ANY SOUND?
AGAIN, **WHO** ARE YOU?
HOW DID CROW END UP BREAKING THE WINDOW?
I DUNNO, WITH HIS HAND?
IS HE HURT?
WAS THERE... BLOOD?
NO... HE WAS WEARING MITTENS.
WELL, **ONE.**
ONE MITTEN... I GUESS IT'S AWARE ENOUGH TO **DISGUISE...**
YES, IT'S **PLAUSIBLE...**
BLUE, DOES THIS CROW ONLY HAVE...
ONE HAND?

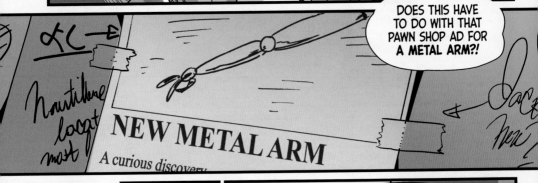

IT'S A PROTOTYPE.

WE ARE TRYING TO FIND THE OTHER HALF--

SECRET

ALONG WITH ITS CREATOR--

Military Personnel

JACK JINGLE.

THE LAD STOLE THIS...**THING** FROM HIS OWN COUNTRY.

REST ASSURED, SIR.

HE WILL BE TRIED FOR TREASON.

PERHAPS JACK TURNED OUT TO BE A MISGUIDED MAN.

SECRET

BUT I THINK THIS BOY...

HE SEEMS MORE HUMAN THAN...

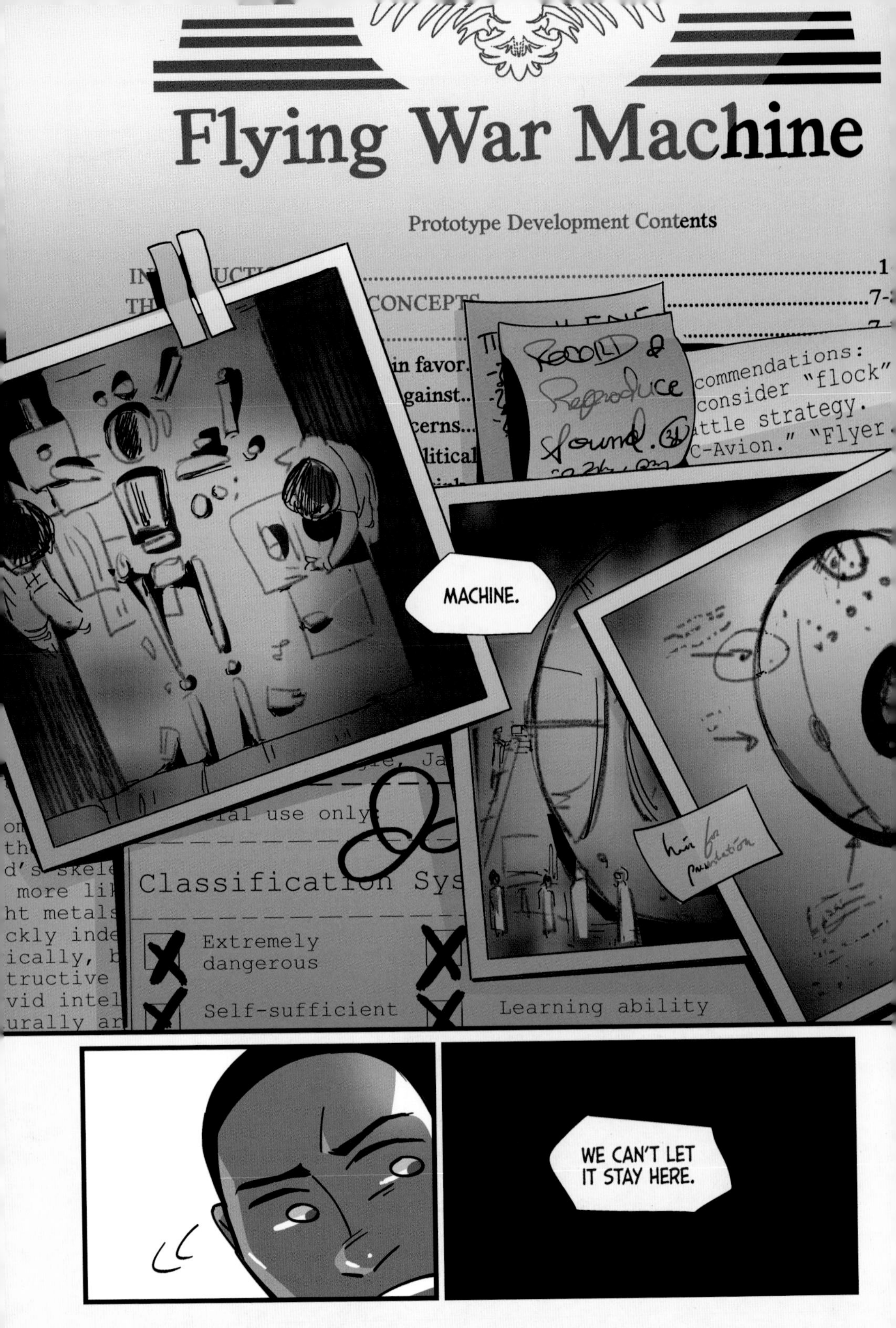
Flying War Machine
Prototype Development Contents
CONCEPTS
in favor.
gainst..
cerns...
litical
commendations:
consider "flock"
ttle strategy.
C-Avion." "Flyer.
Reproduce
MACHINE.
use only
Classification Sys
Extremely dangerous
Self-sufficient
Learning ability
WE CAN'T LET IT STAY HERE.

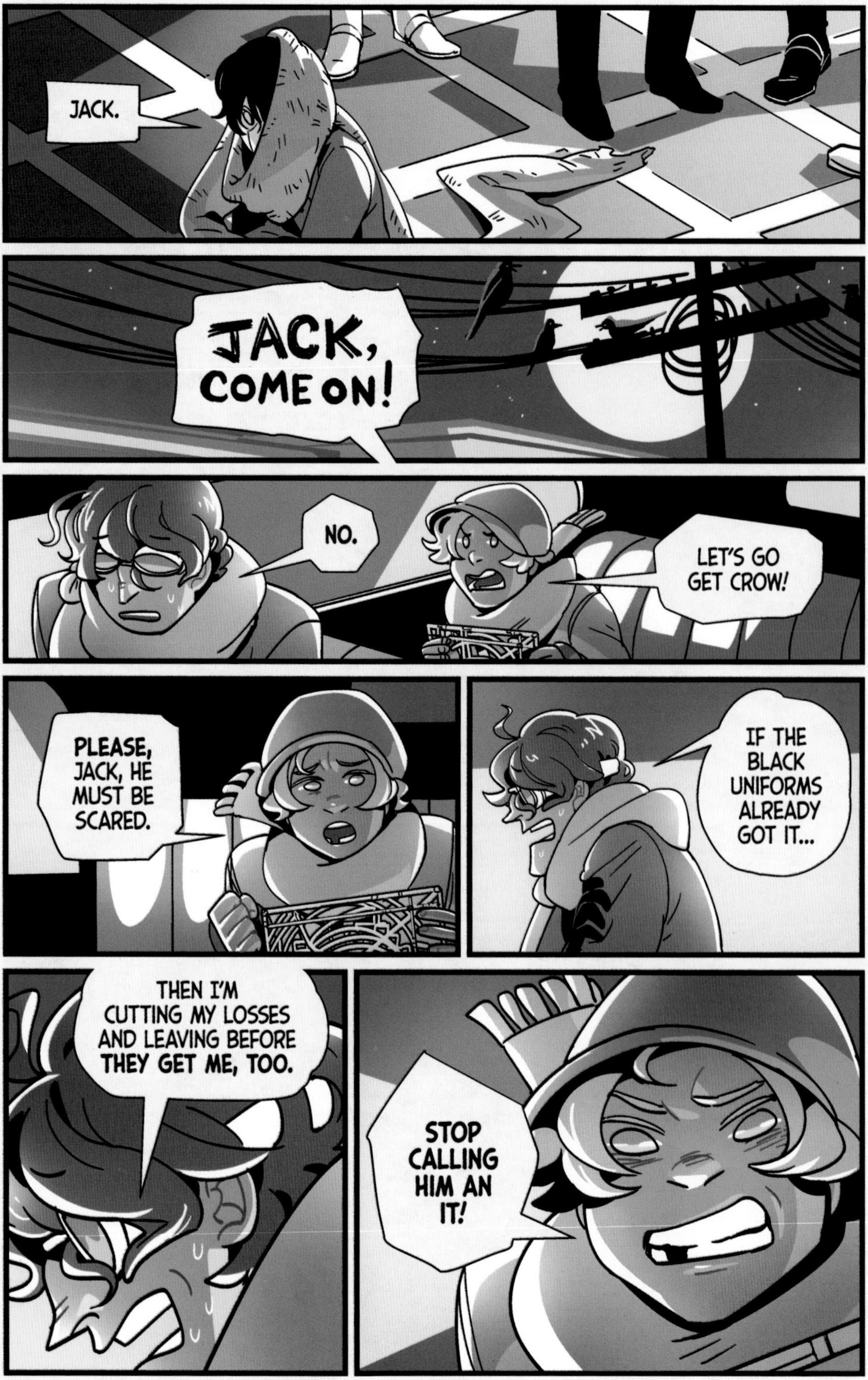
JACK.
JACK, COME ON!
NO.
LET'S GO GET CROW!
PLEASE, JACK, HE MUST BE SCARED.
IF THE BLACK UNIFORMS ALREADY GOT IT...
THEN I'M CUTTING MY LOSSES AND LEAVING BEFORE THEY GET ME, TOO.
STOP CALLING HIM AN IT!

OH, COME ON!

KLIK

KLIK

THE PIN IS MOVING!

WHRR

KLIK

BLUE, LET'S REST TONIGHT. WE'LL GO FIND CROW AT THE POLICE STATION TOMORROW.

BLUE?

HEY! COME BACK!

133

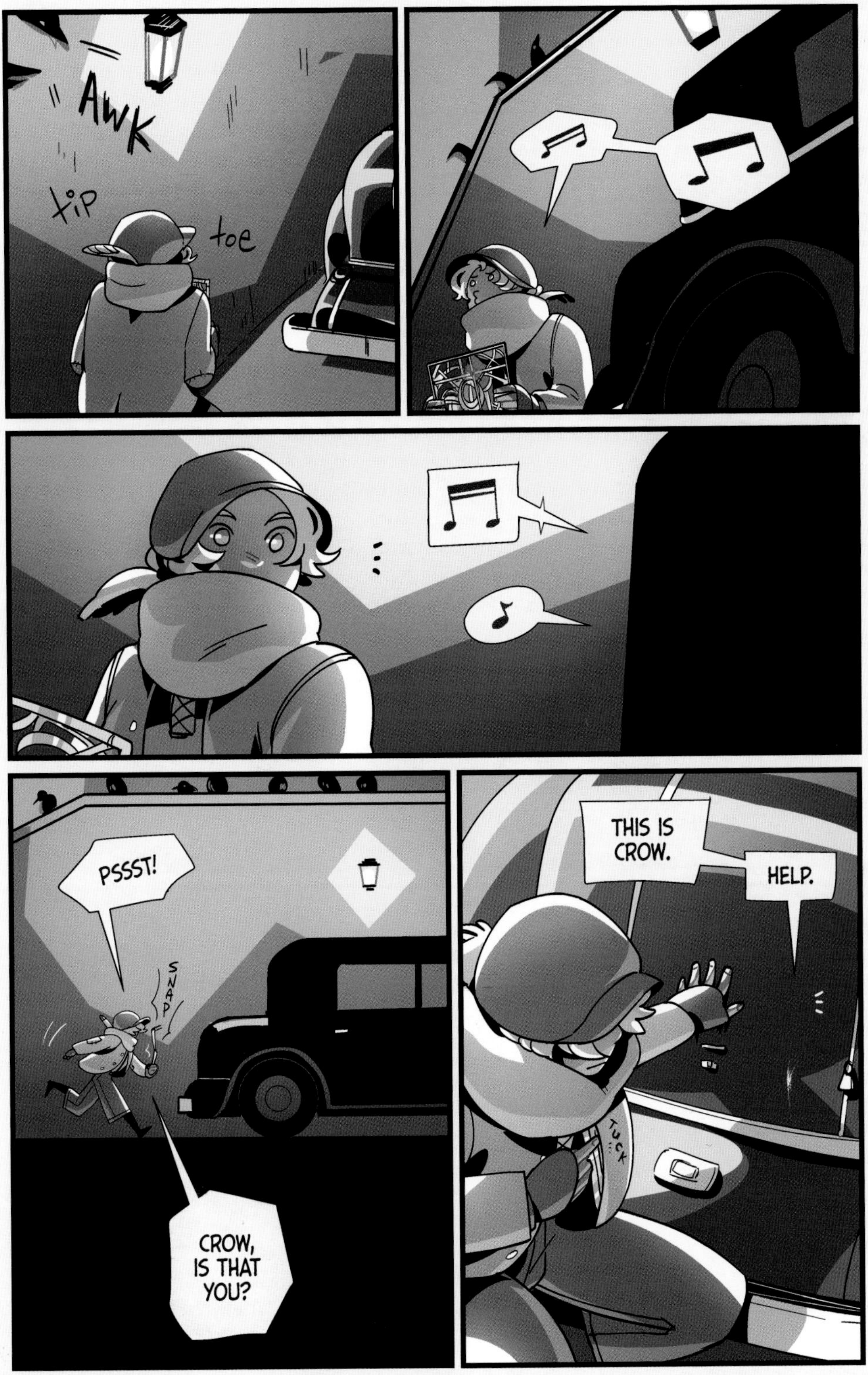
AWK
tip
toe
PSSST!
SNAP
CROW, IS THAT YOU?
THIS IS CROW.
HELP.
TUCK

SIT TIGHT!

meanwhile

GREAT, I LOST BLUE...

AND A PAPER CLIP.

I'LL GET YOU OUT.

BY THE WAY, A LITTLE BIRDIE TOLD ME THAT...

YOU'RE MISSING AN ARM?

MY ARM.

IT RUSTED OFF ONE DAY.

AH

KLANK

HUH.

THEN A DOG ATE IT.

AH

PFT!

IT WAS A BIG DOG!

UNLOCK

SO THAT'S WHY IT WAS IN THE PAWN SHOP...

GOLDIE!

GOOD GIRL.

MAN, YOU'RE SO HEAVY!

I AM.

WE FOUND IT!

ZOOM

DOW!

WHAT WAS THAT?!

No!

MORE BIRDS?!

AH!

WHATEVER...

WE NOW HAVE THE ADDRESS TO THE OTHER HALF!

RADIO THE MAYOR AND THE ADMIRAL.

MY SCARF...

WE'LL MEET THEM THERE!

SLAM

SLAM

ROGER.

WHY ARE THE MAYOR AND ADMIRAL INVOLVED?

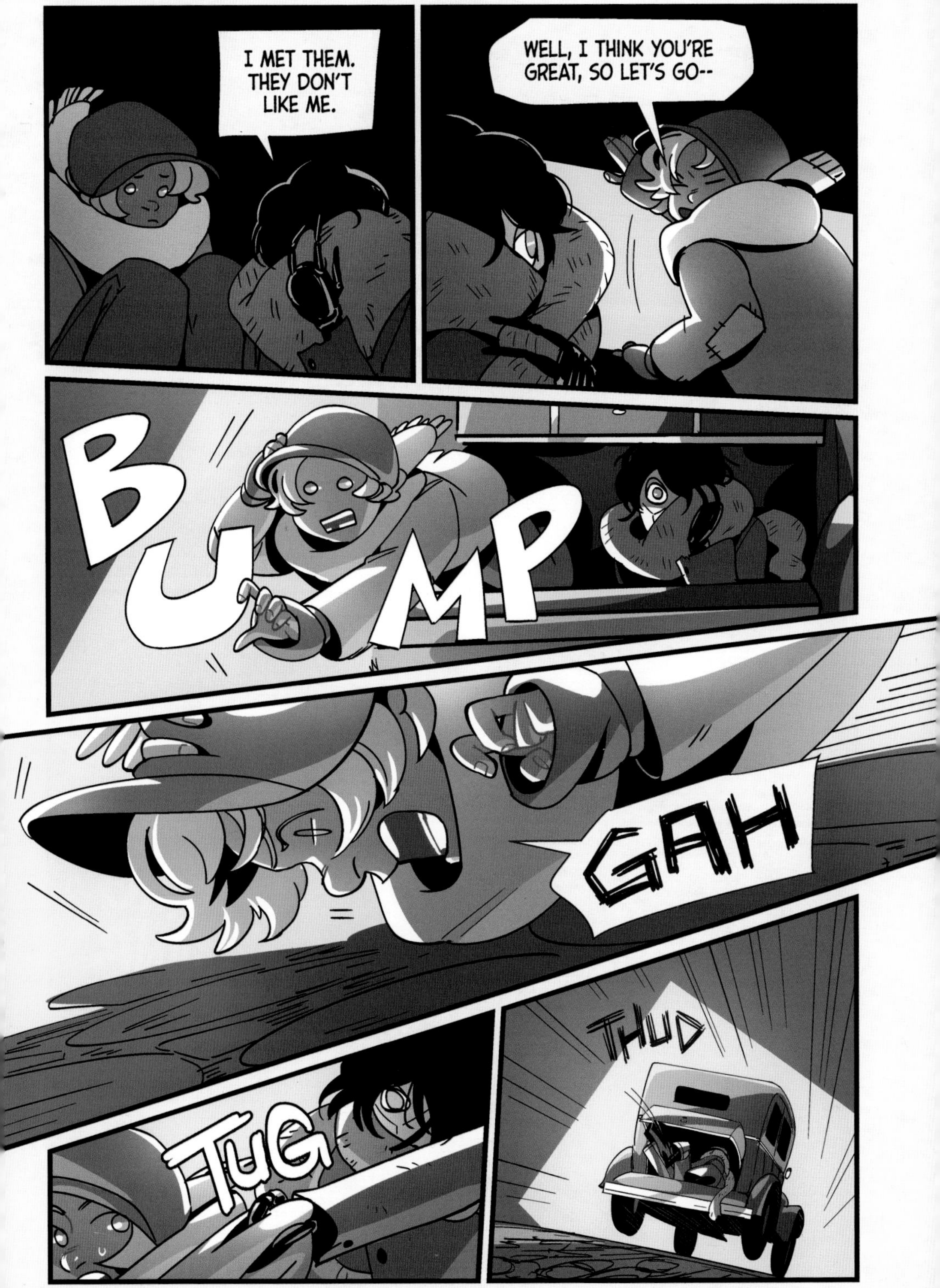
I MET THEM. THEY DON'T LIKE ME.
WELL, I THINK YOU'RE GREAT, SO LET'S GO--
BUMP
GAH
TUG
THUD

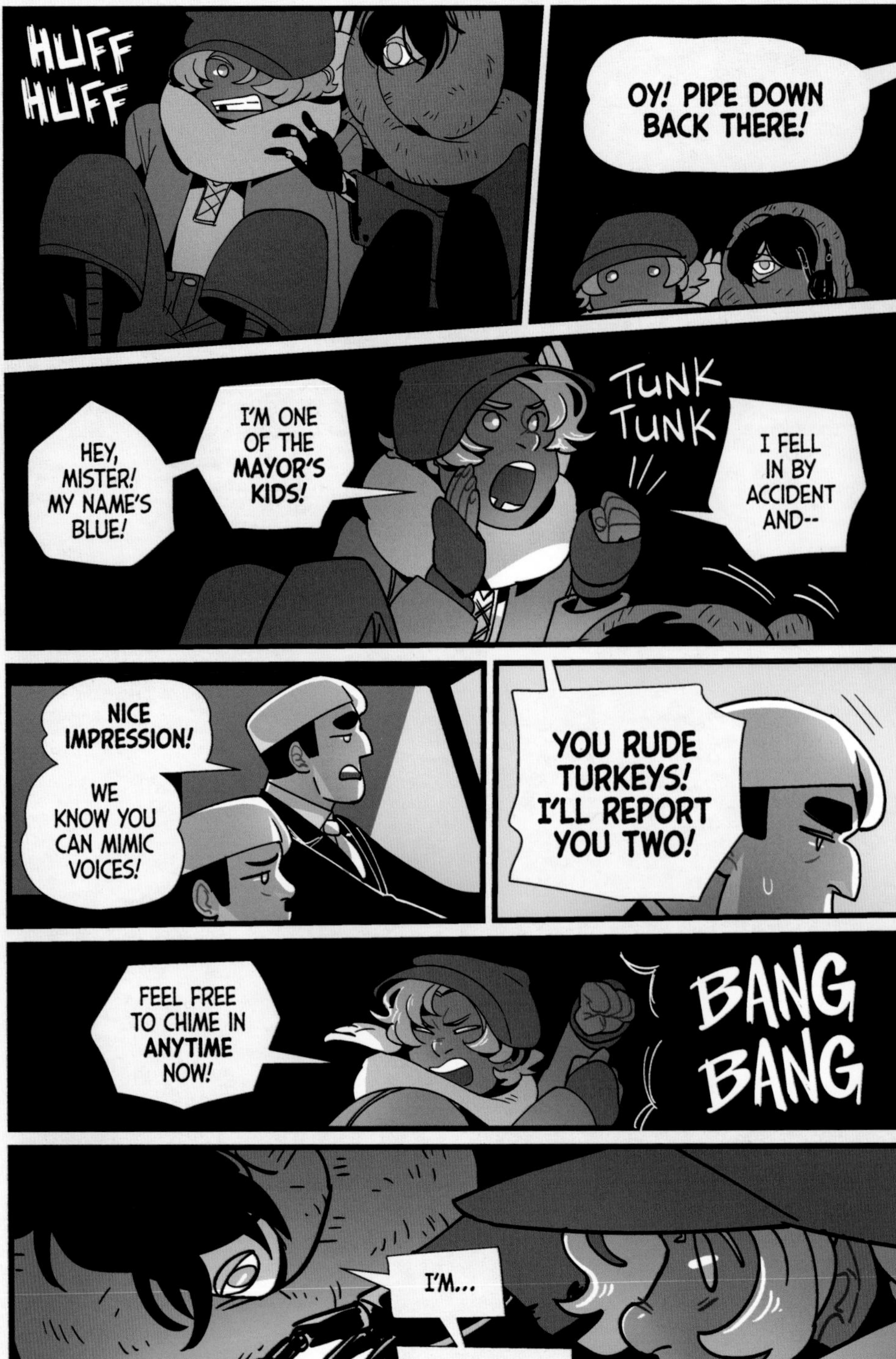
HUFF HUFF
OY! PIPE DOWN BACK THERE!
HEY, MISTER! MY NAME'S BLUE!
I'M ONE OF THE **MAYOR'S KIDS!**
TUNK TUNK
I FELL IN BY ACCIDENT AND--
NICE IMPRESSION!
WE KNOW YOU CAN MIMIC VOICES!
YOU RUDE TURKEYS! I'LL REPORT YOU TWO!
FEEL FREE TO CHIME IN **ANYTIME** NOW!
BANG BANG
I'M...
I'M **AFRAID.**

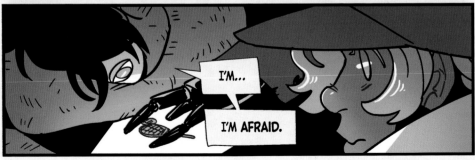

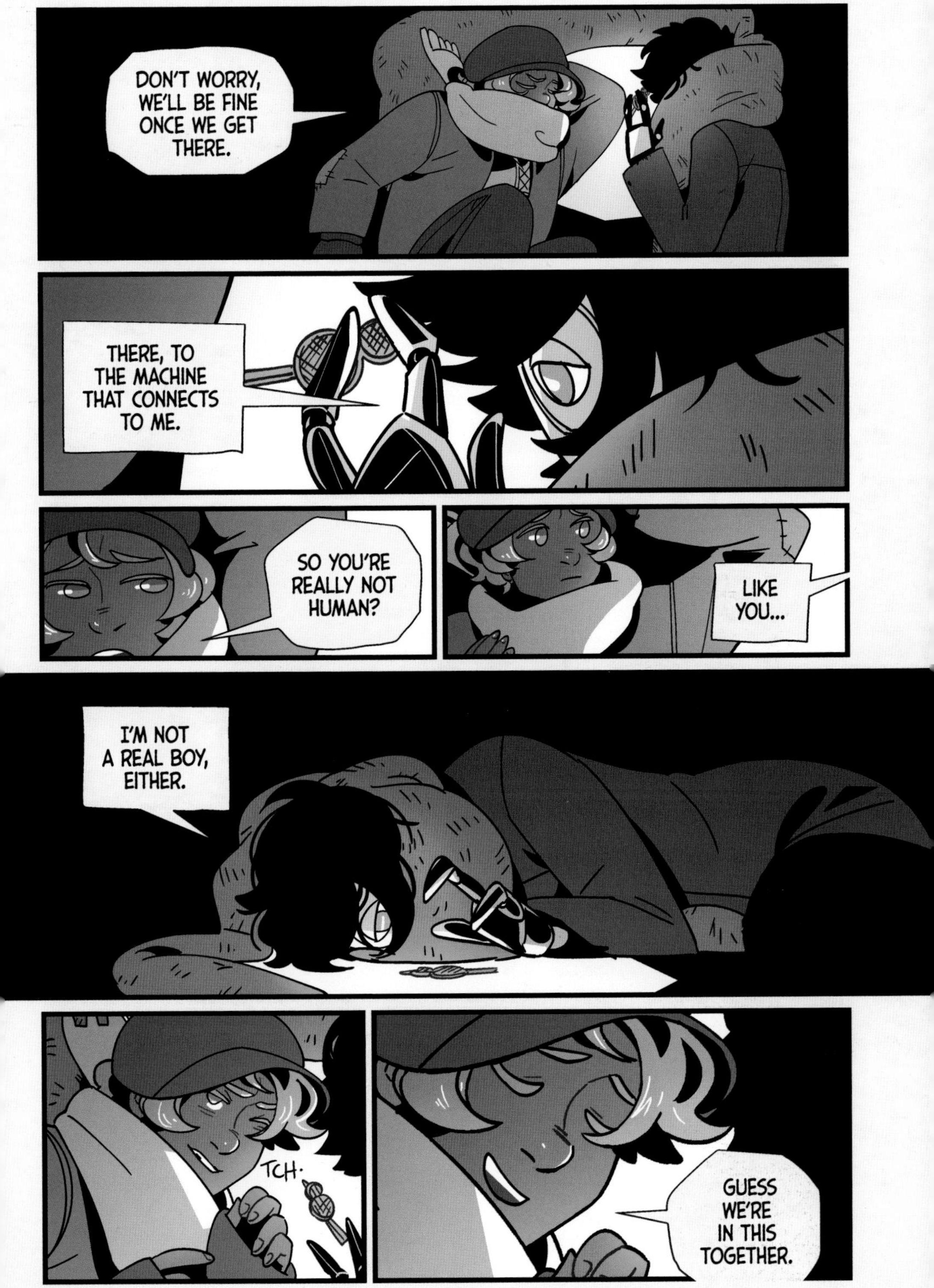
DON'T WORRY, WE'LL BE FINE ONCE WE GET THERE.
THERE, TO THE MACHINE THAT CONNECTS TO ME.
SO YOU'RE REALLY NOT HUMAN?
LIKE YOU...
I'M NOT A REAL BOY, EITHER.
TCH.
GUESS WE'RE IN THIS TOGETHER.

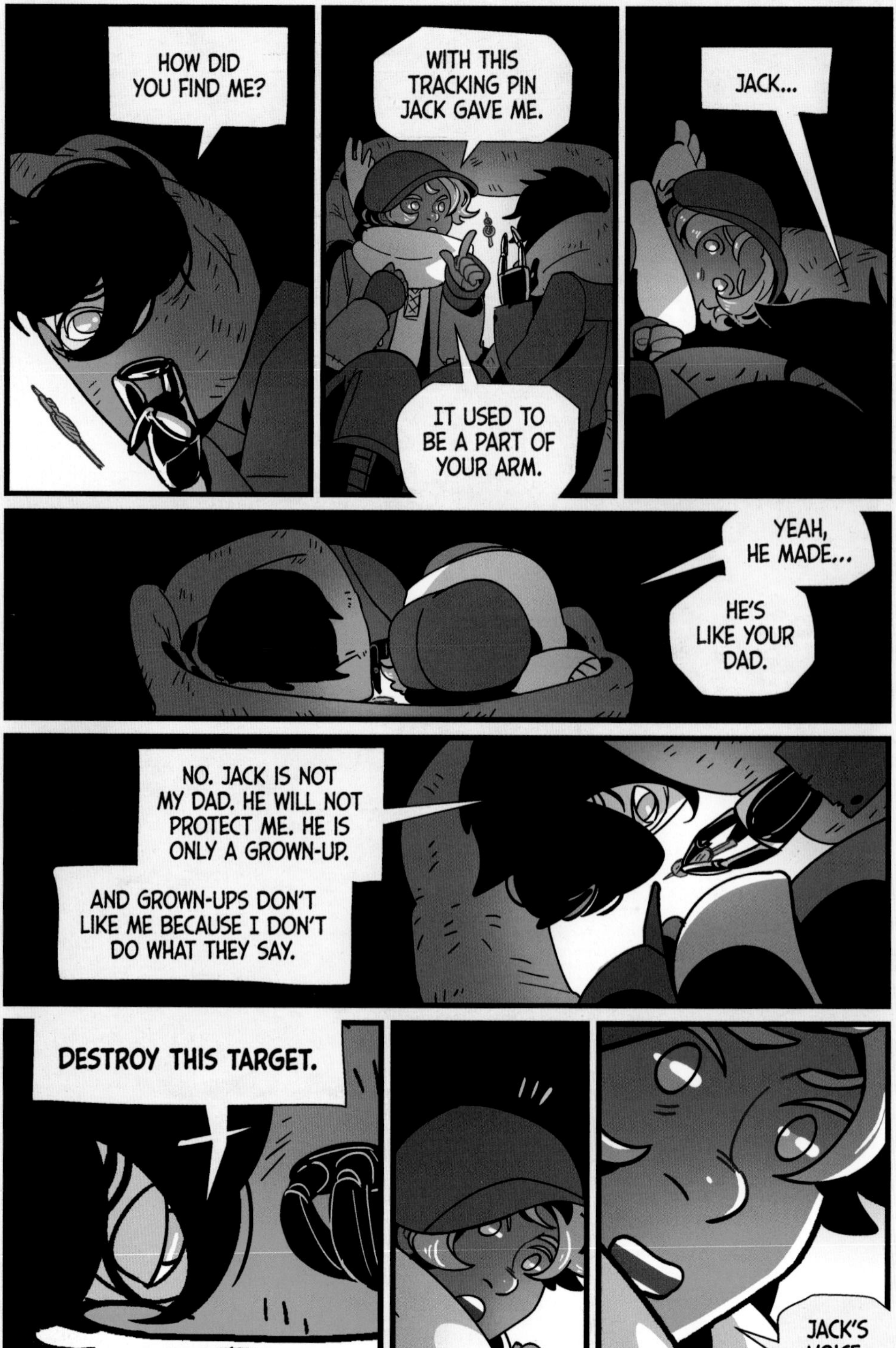
HOW DID YOU FIND ME?
WITH THIS TRACKING PIN JACK GAVE ME.
IT USED TO BE A PART OF YOUR ARM.
JACK...
YEAH, HE MADE...
HE'S LIKE YOUR DAD.
NO. JACK IS NOT MY DAD. HE WILL NOT PROTECT ME. HE IS ONLY A GROWN-UP.
AND GROWN-UPS DON'T LIKE ME BECAUSE I DON'T DO WHAT THEY SAY.
DESTROY THIS TARGET.
JACK'S VOICE.

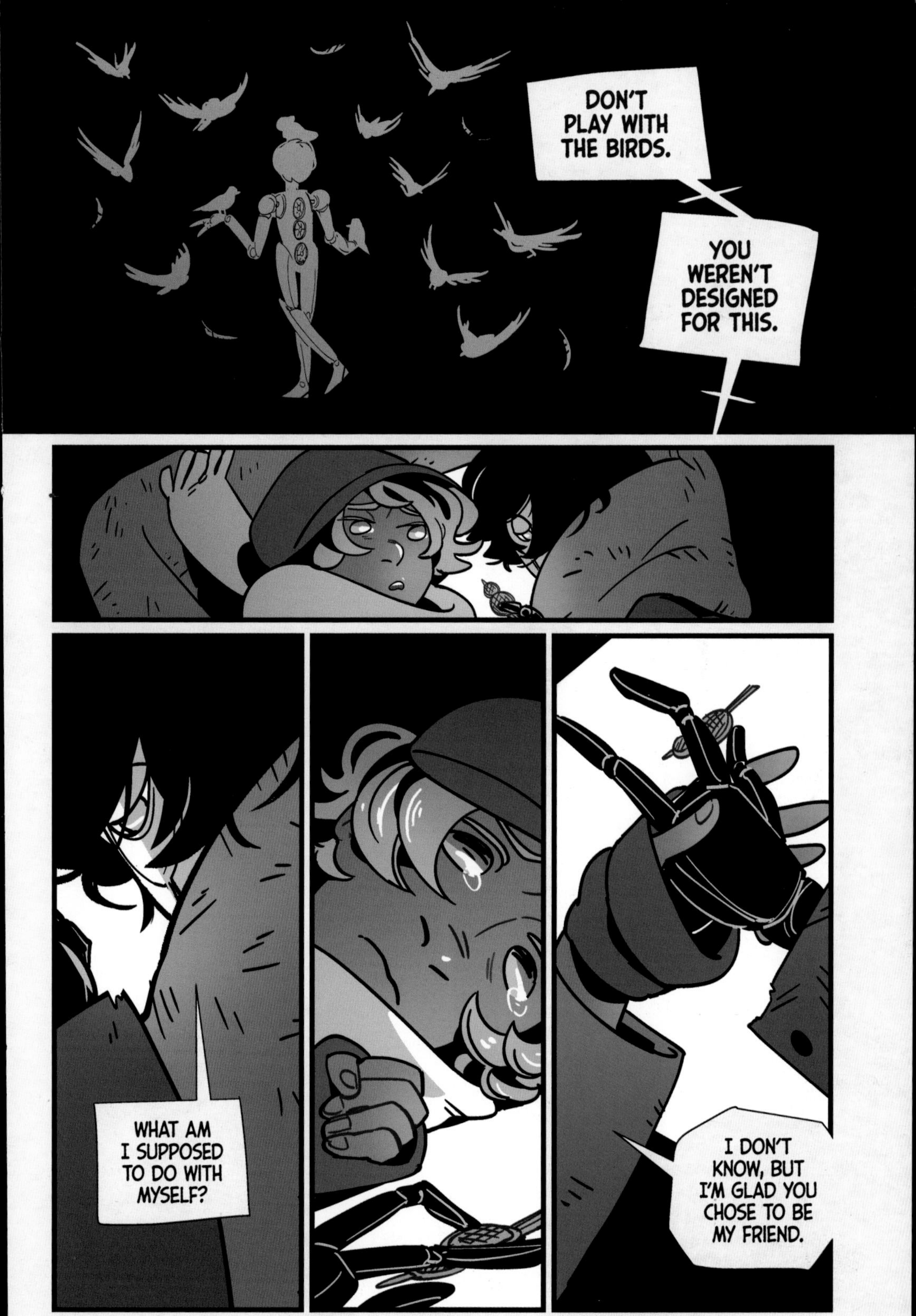
DON'T PLAY WITH THE BIRDS.
YOU WEREN'T DESIGNED FOR THIS.
WHAT AM I SUPPOSED TO DO WITH MYSELF?
I DON'T KNOW, BUT I'M GLAD YOU CHOSE TO BE MY FRIEND.

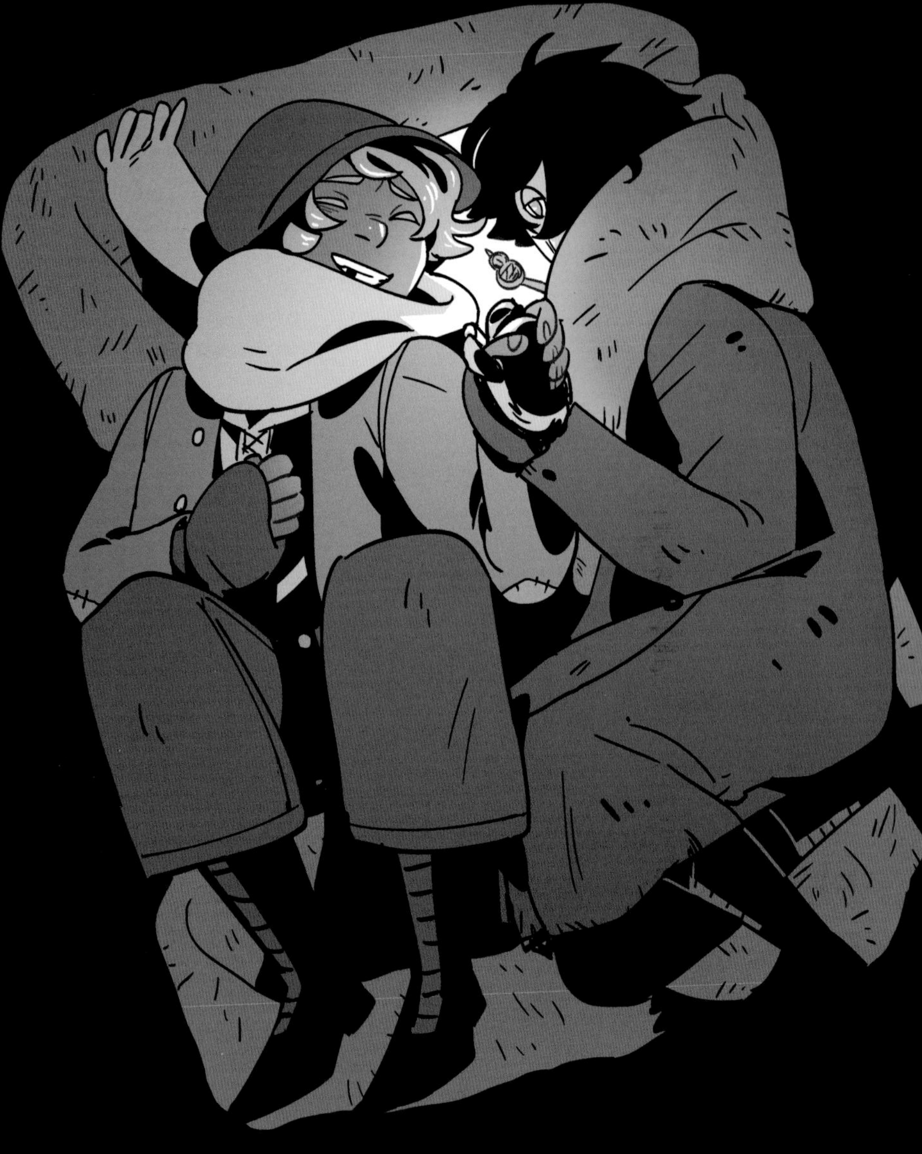

Jack's Secret Warehouse

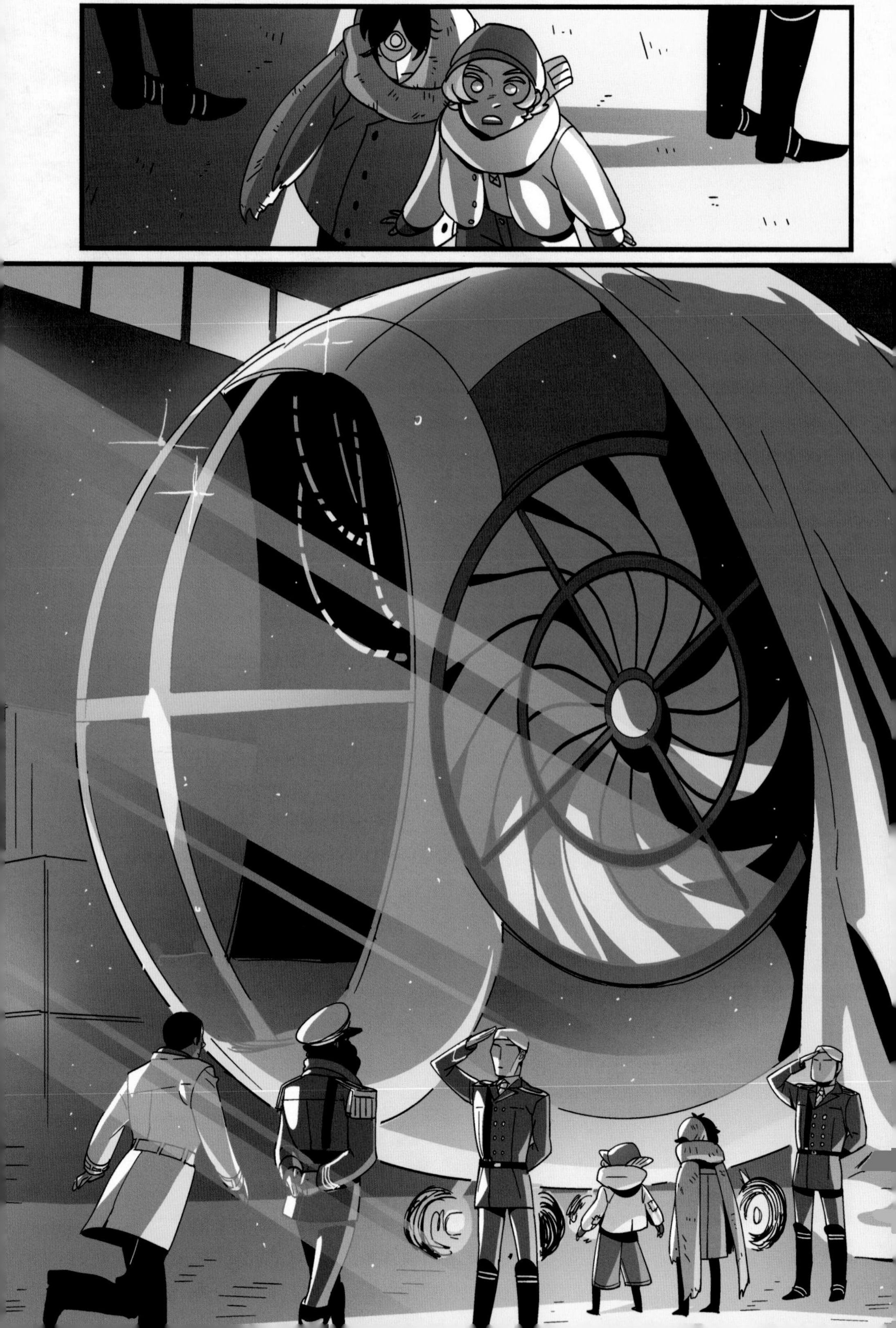

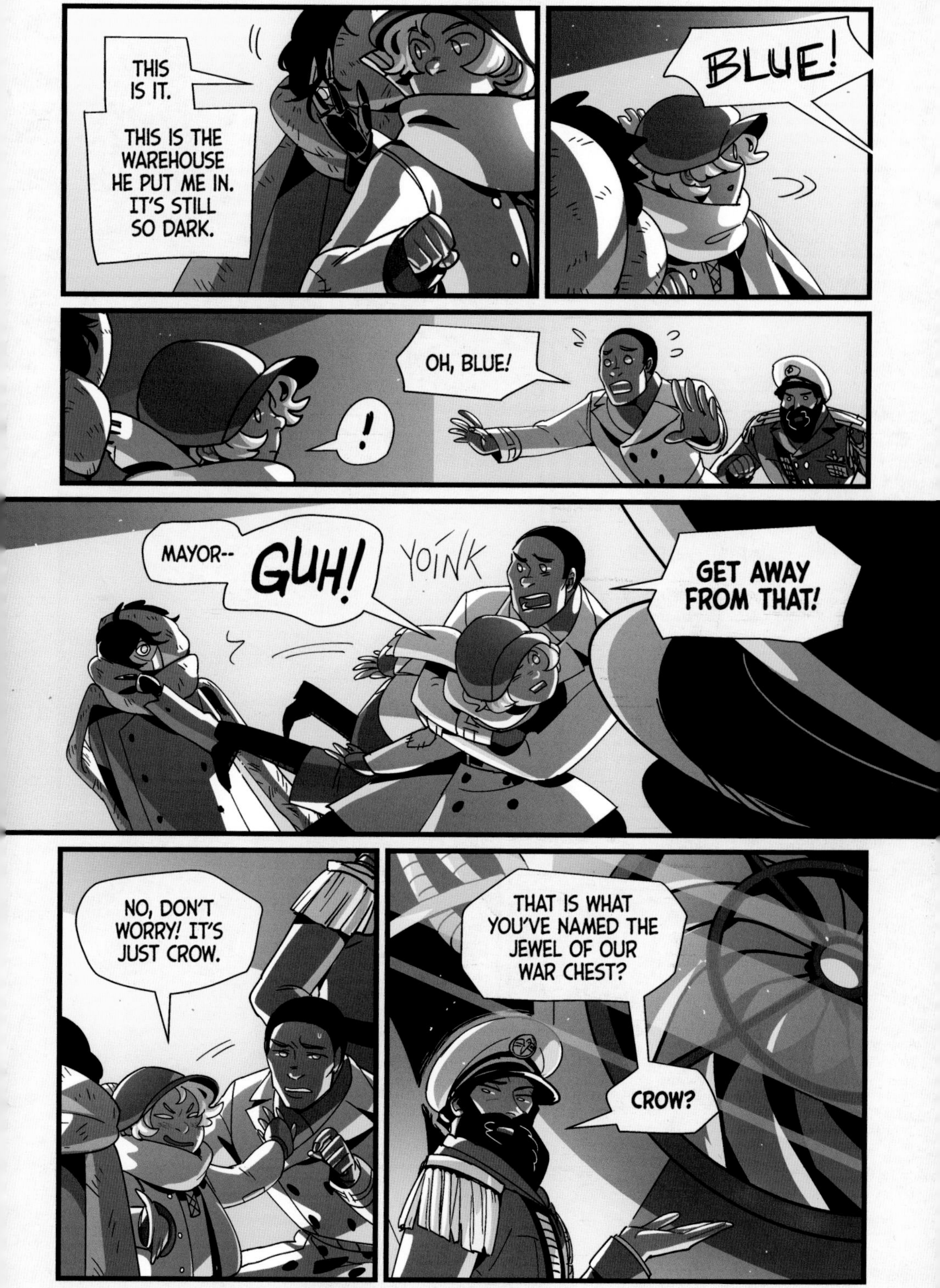
THIS IS IT.
THIS IS THE WAREHOUSE HE PUT ME IN. IT'S STILL SO DARK.
BLUE!
OH, BLUE!
!
MAYOR-- GUH!
YOINK
GET AWAY FROM THAT!
NO, DON'T WORRY! IT'S JUST CROW.
THAT IS WHAT YOU'VE NAMED THE JEWEL OF OUR WAR CHEST?
CROW?

HE'S NOT JUST SOME WAR MACHINE.

IF YOU LISTEN TO WHAT HE HAS TO SAY, YOU'D SEE HE'S A GOOD PERSON, AND HE'S LEARNING MORE EVERY SINGLE DAY.

IT'S NOTHING MORE THAN A METAL SOLDIER BUILT FOR THE BATTLEFIELD.

HE'S MY FRIEND.

RIGHT, BLUE! I SUPPOSE WE'VE BEEN HASTY TO CAST JUDGMENT--

ARE YOU DAFT AS A DUCK, MAN?

BAH

PARDON?!

THIS IS GOVERNMENT PROPERTY!

NOT ANOTHER ORPHAN GOSLING YOU CAN PICK UP WILLY-NILLY!

YOU CAN DRESS IT UP ALL ~~~~

I DIDN'T SAY OTHERWISE. ONLY THAT ~~

LET 'EM ARGUE.

IT DOESN'T MEAN EITHER ONE OF THEM'S RIGHT.

COME WITH ME.

THIS IS IDIOCY.

ENOUGH. BLUE CAN ASK CROW HOW HE'D LIKE TO BE TRANSPORTED...

BLUE?

BLUE!

CROW, HOW DO WE GET IN?

KLIK

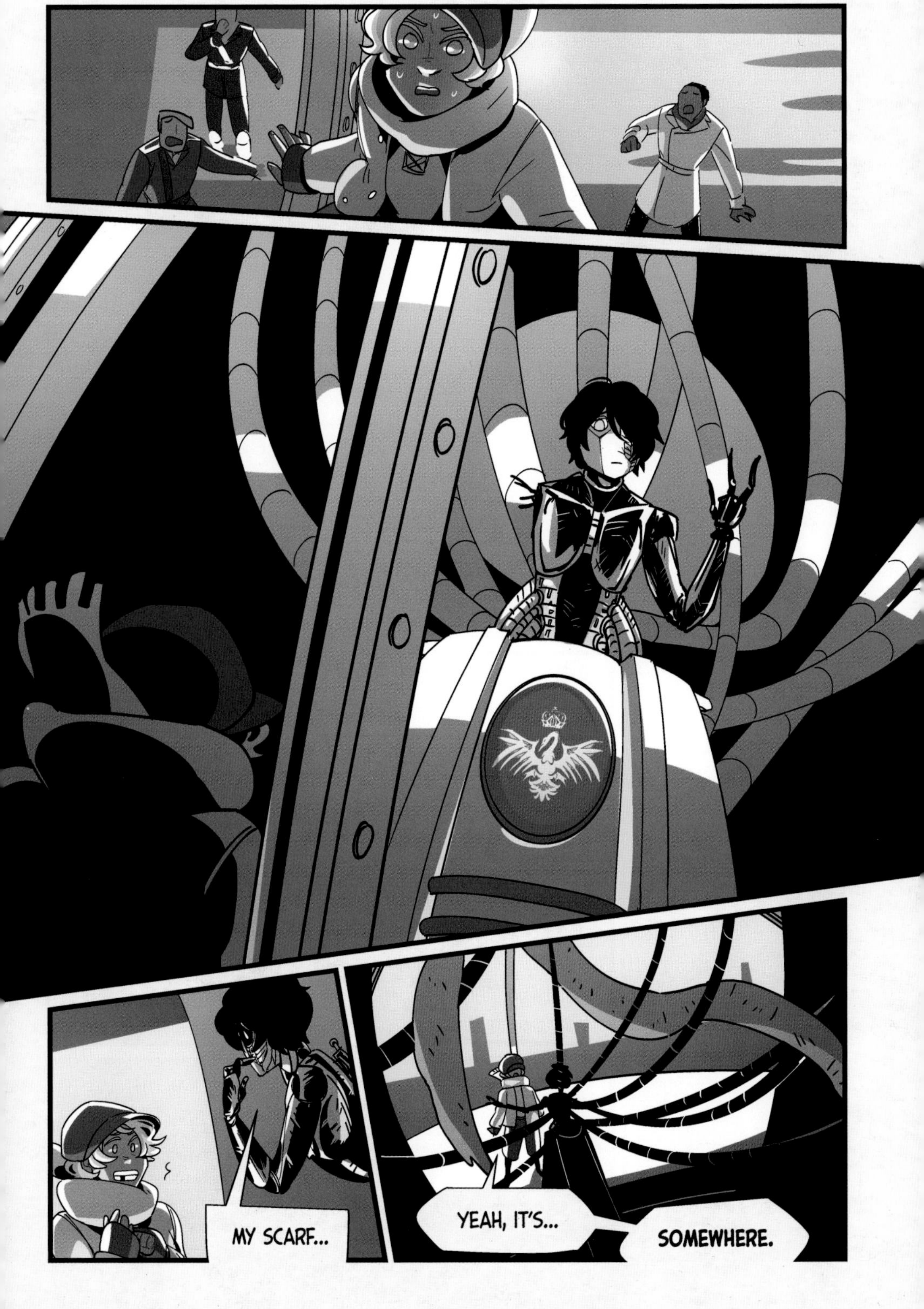
MY SCARF...
YEAH, IT'S...
SOMEWHERE.

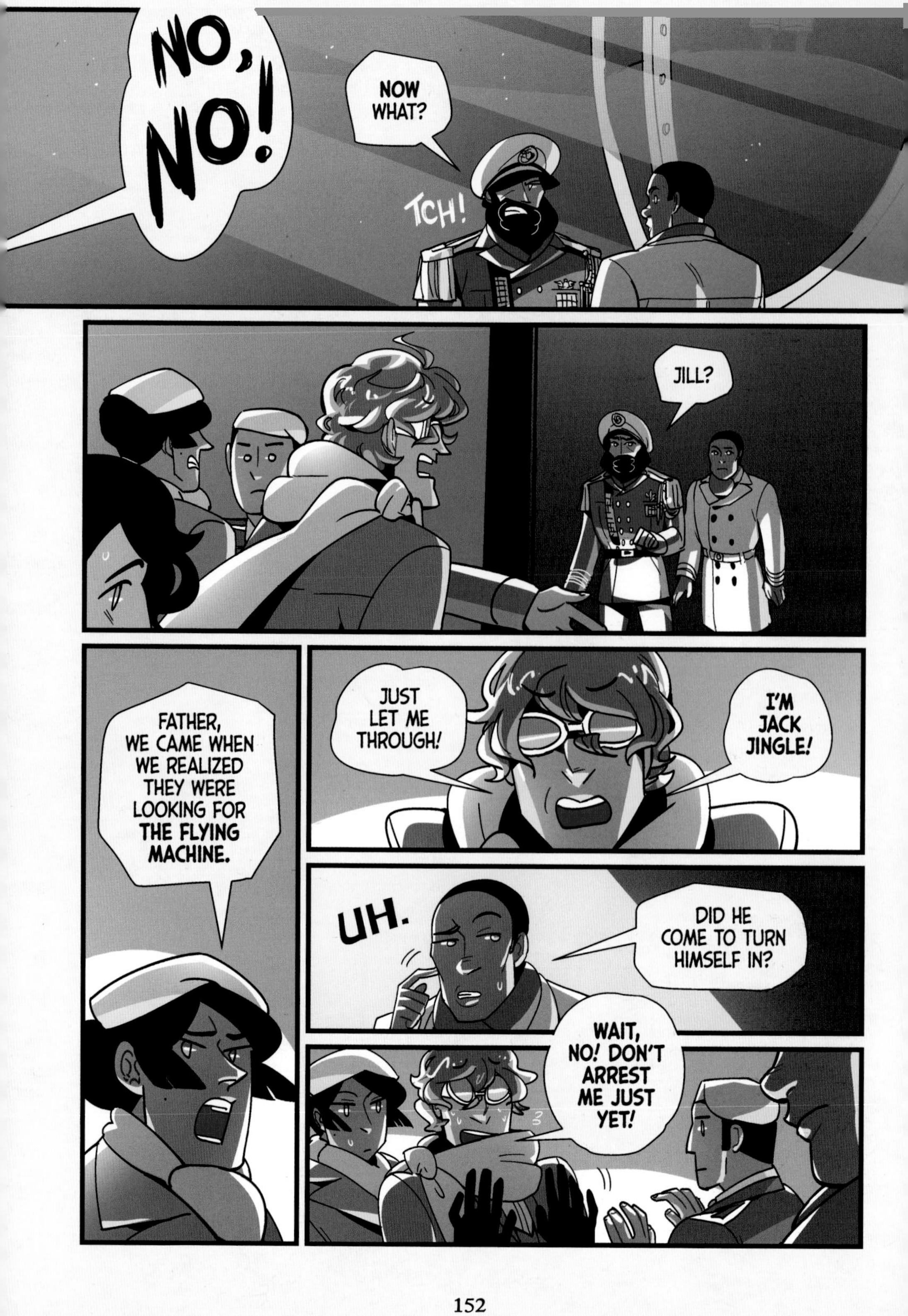
NO, NO!
NOW WHAT?
TCH!
JILL?
FATHER, WE CAME WHEN WE REALIZED THEY WERE LOOKING FOR THE FLYING MACHINE.
JUST LET ME THROUGH!
I'M JACK JINGLE!
UH.
DID HE COME TO TURN HIMSELF IN?
WAIT, NO! DON'T ARREST ME JUST YET!

I HAVE TO SHUT DOWN THE PROTOTYPE. IT'S NOT READY TO FLY!

YOU SHOULDN'T HAVE BROUGHT THE METAL SOLDIER HERE!

IT'S SMART ENOUGH TO...

REUNITE.

THUNK

THUNK

THUNK

CROW! WE'RE HEADED FOR THE WATER!

I SEE IT.

WHAT IF IT SINKS?!

WHAT IF IT FLIES?!

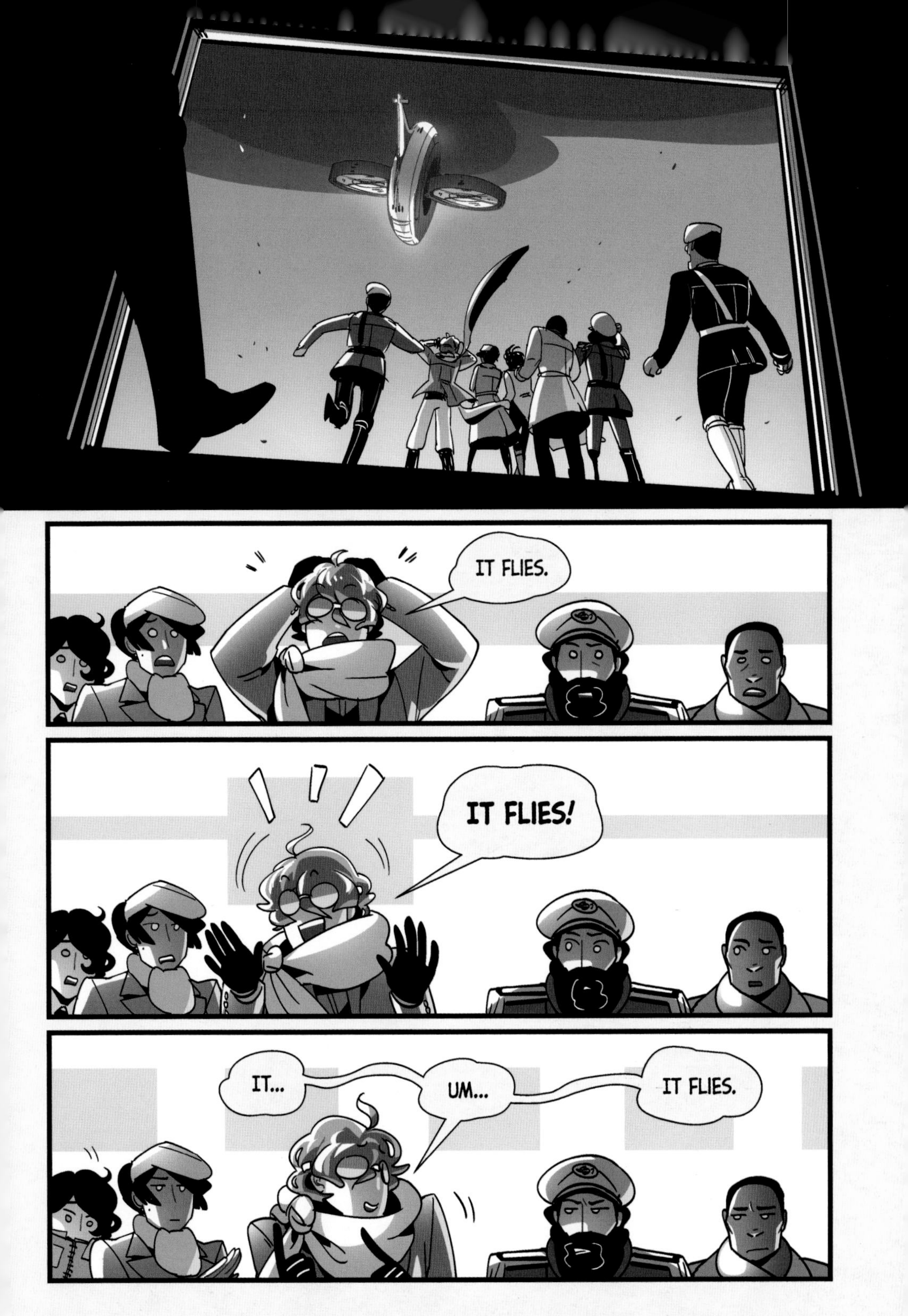
IT FLIES.
IT FLIES!
IT...
UM...
IT FLIES.

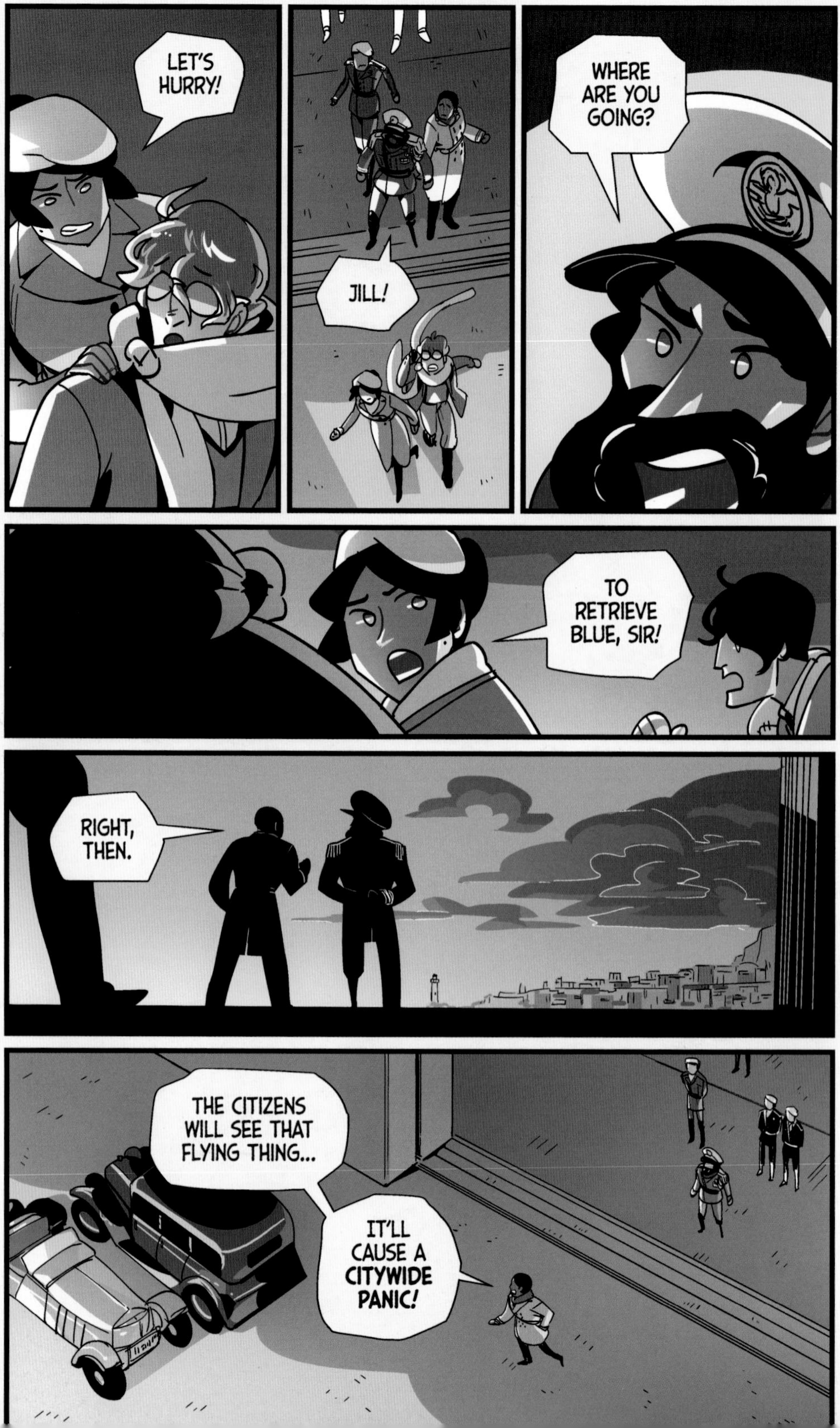
LET'S HURRY!
JILL!
WHERE ARE YOU GOING?
TO RETRIEVE BLUE, SIR!
RIGHT, THEN.
THE CITIZENS WILL SEE THAT FLYING THING...
IT'LL CAUSE A CITYWIDE PANIC!

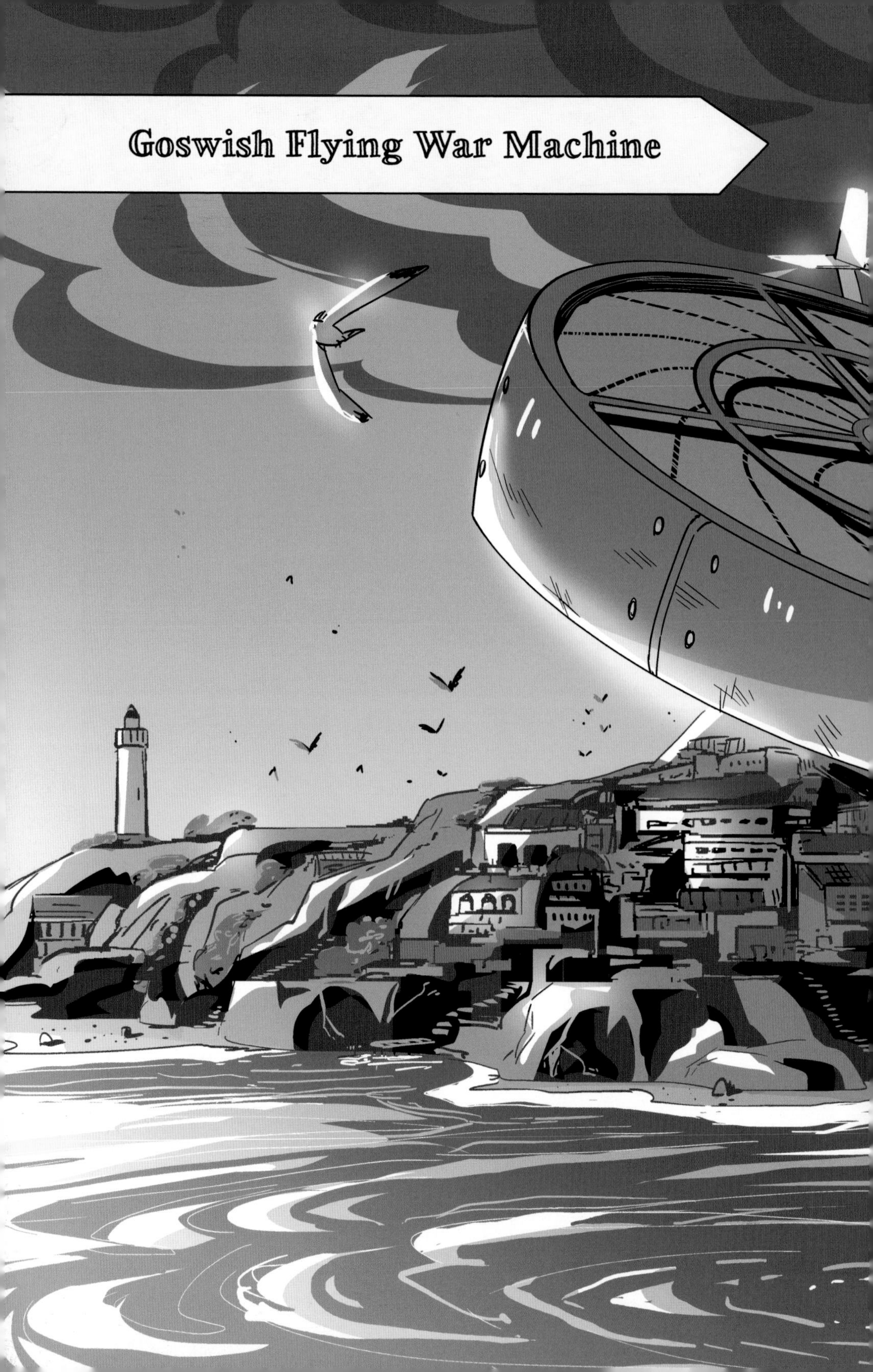
Goswish Flying War Machine

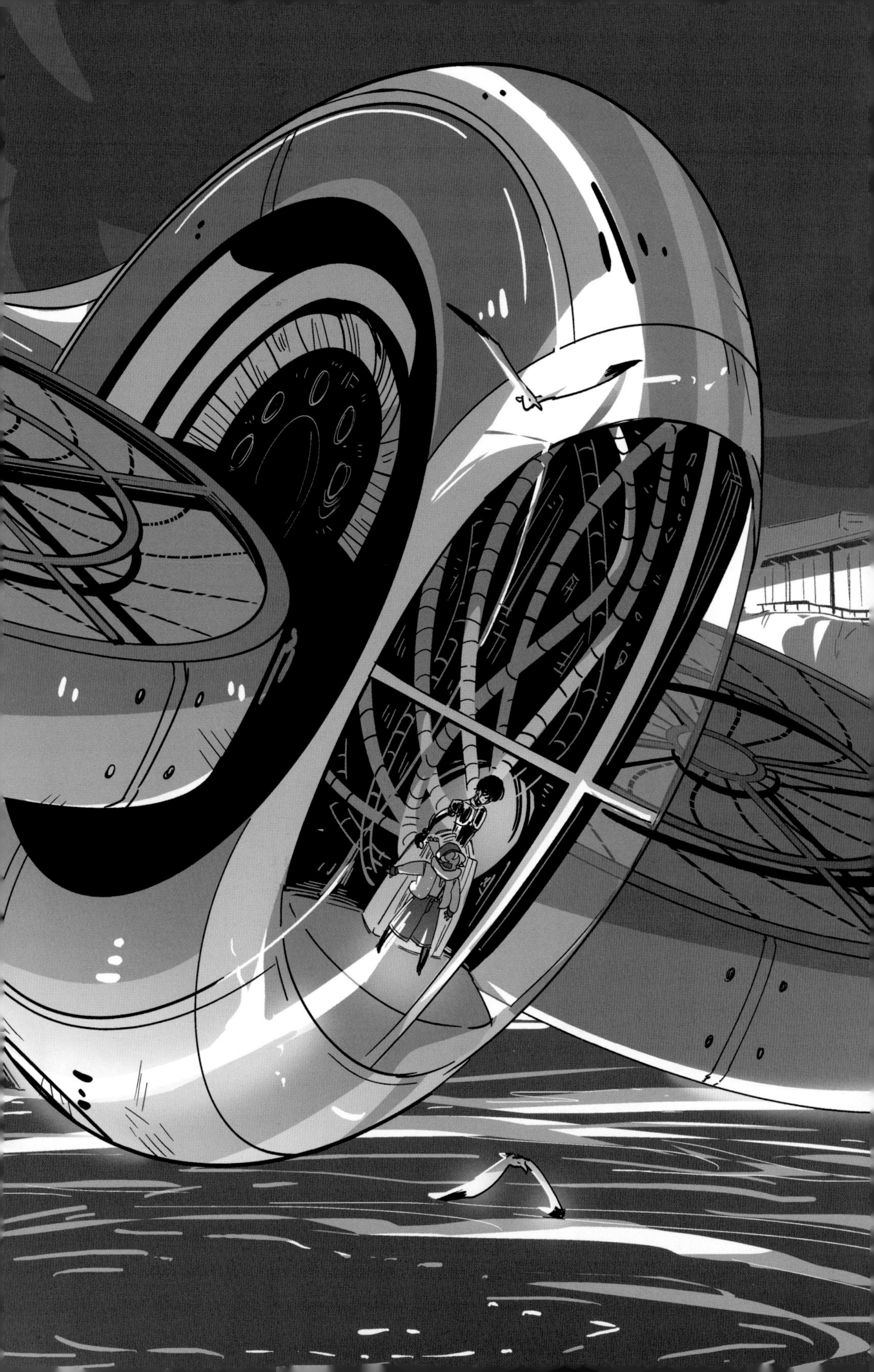

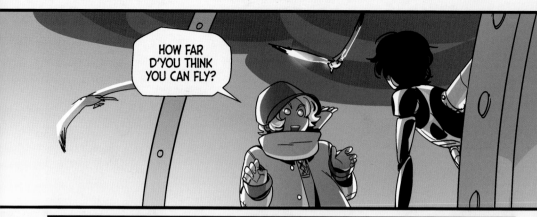

HOW FAR D'YOU THINK YOU CAN FLY?

MAYBE WE COULD REACH ANOTHER CITY.

THEN, WE JUST HIDE THERE UNTIL THIS WHOLE THING BLOWS OVER!

YOU'D HAVE TO TURN BACK INTO A BOY, THOUGH.

I DON'T KNOW HOW.

I COULD PROBABLY GET YOU OUT IF I HAD A SCREWDRIVER AND A WRENCH...

NO, I DON'T KNOW HOW TO FLY TO ANOTHER CITY.

YOU CAN'T STEER?

MY WINGS DON'T FLAP.

I CAN SORT OF MOVE MY TAIL...

UHH, MAYBE TRY TO FIGURE OUT HOW TO STEER FIRST?

WE'RE GETTIN' **REAL** CLOSE TO THE NAVAL BASE THERE...

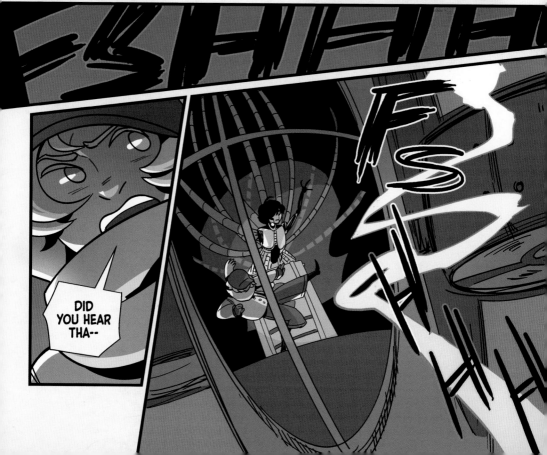

DID YOU HEAR THA--

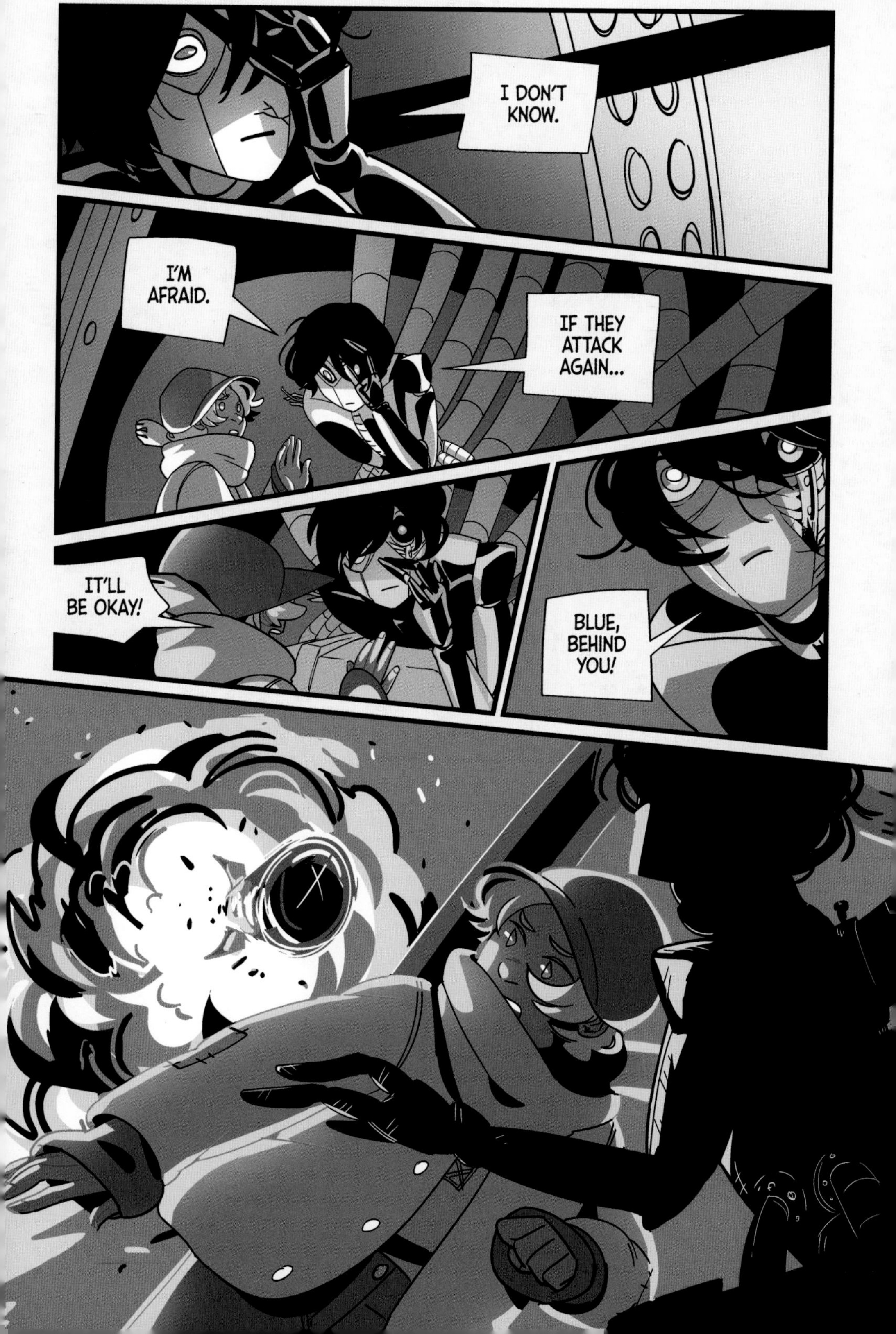
I DON'T KNOW.
I'M AFRAID.
IF THEY ATTACK AGAIN...
IT'LL BE OKAY!
BLUE, BEHIND YOU!

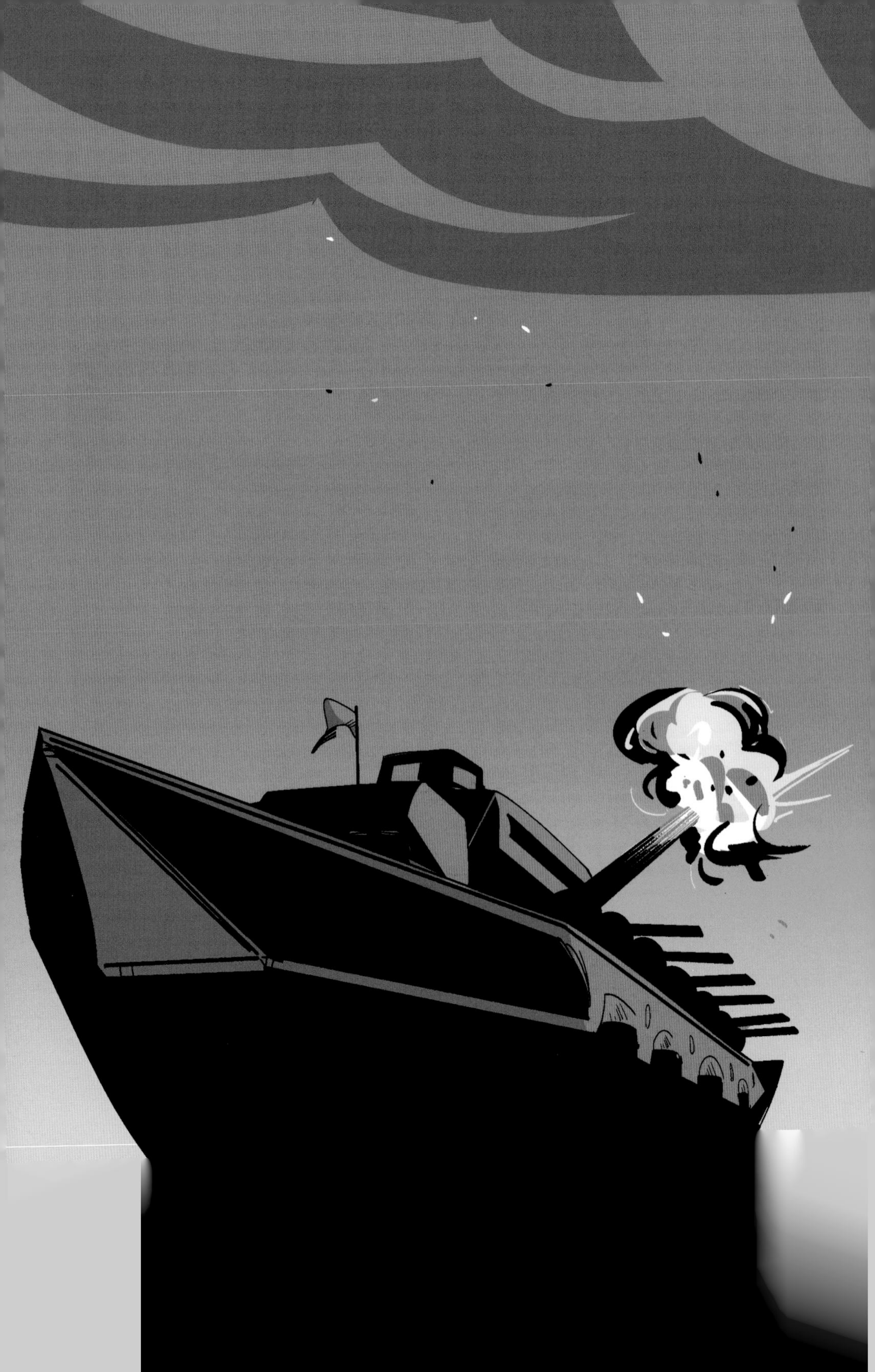

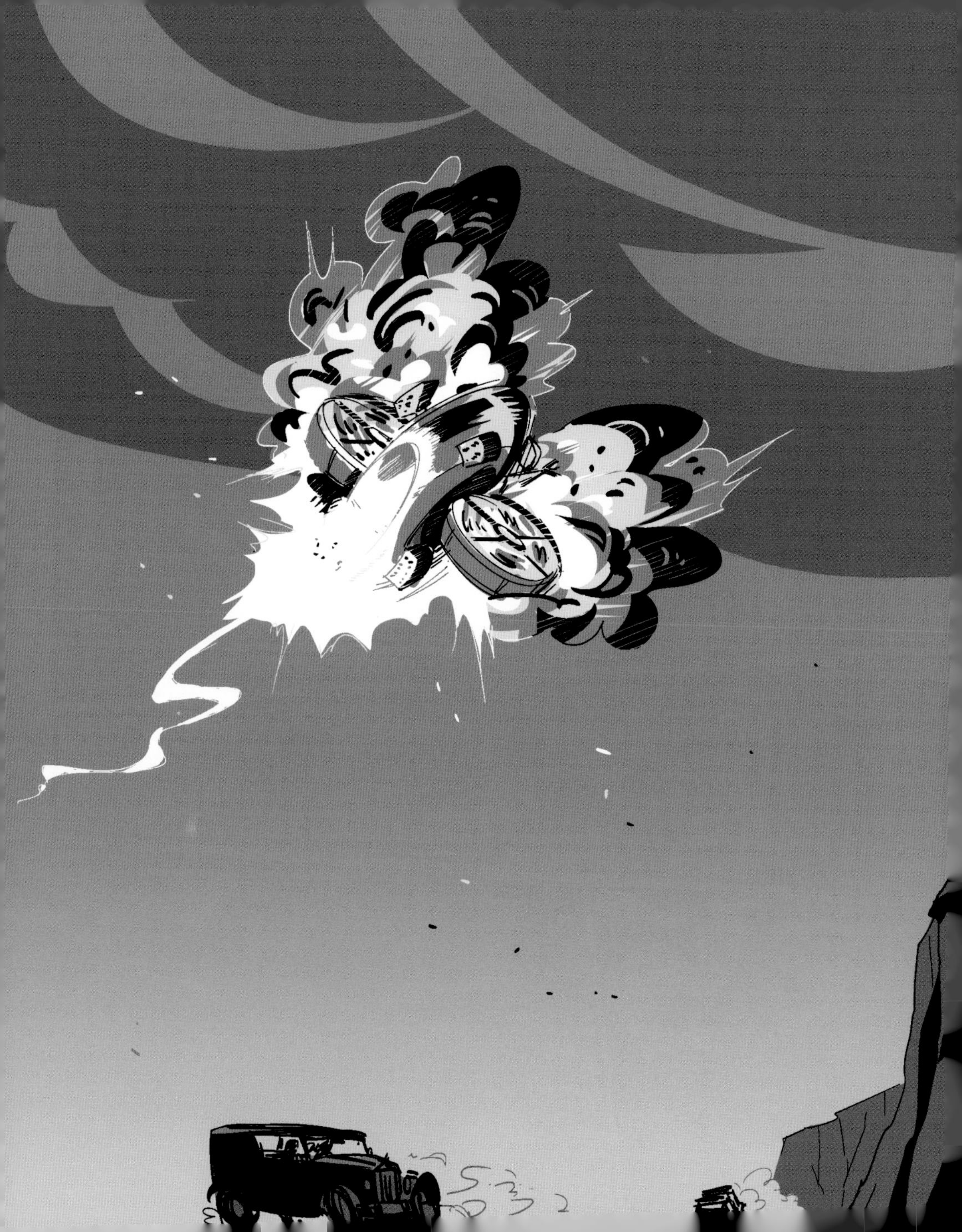

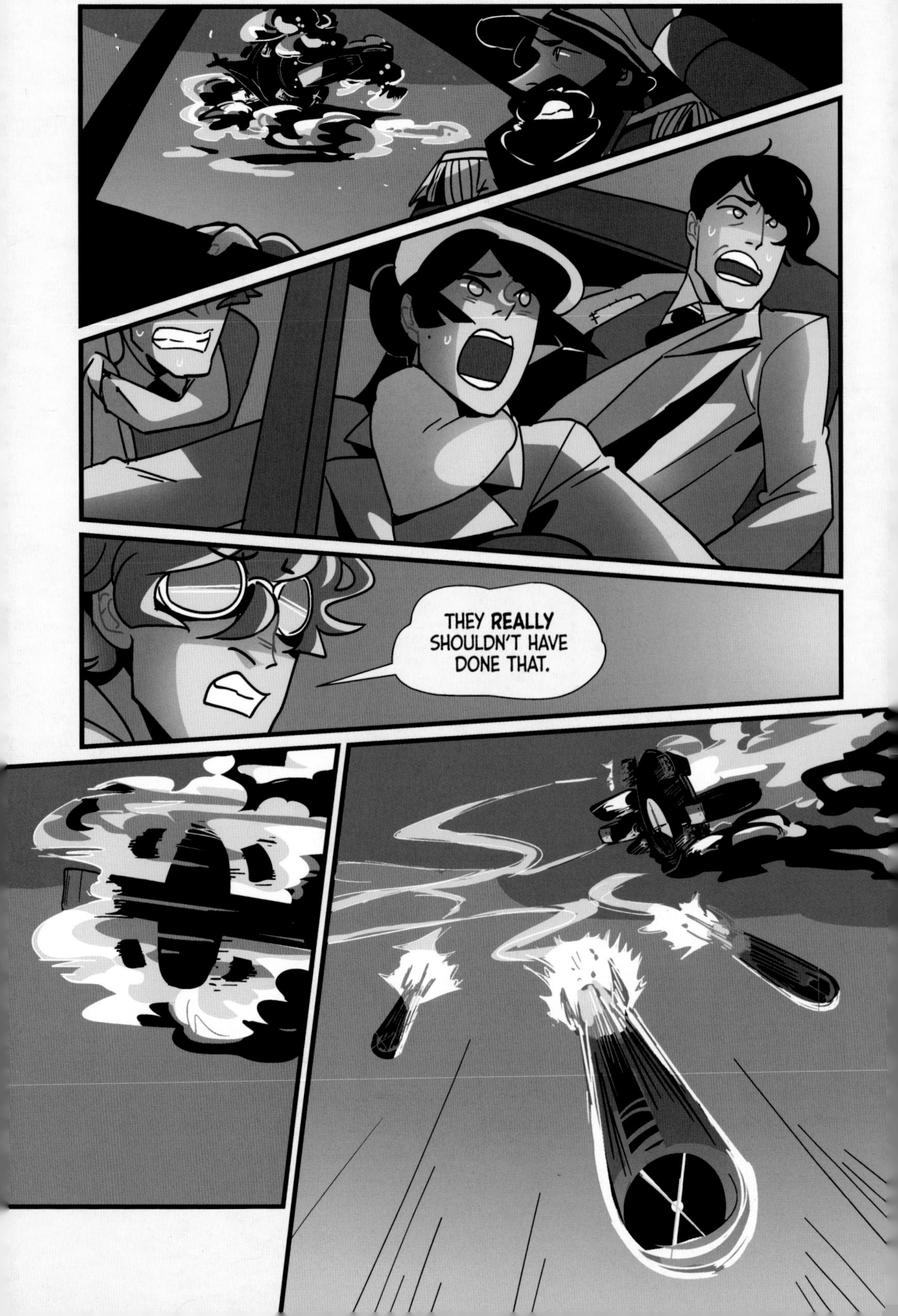
THEY REALLY SHOULDN'T HAVE DONE THAT.

169

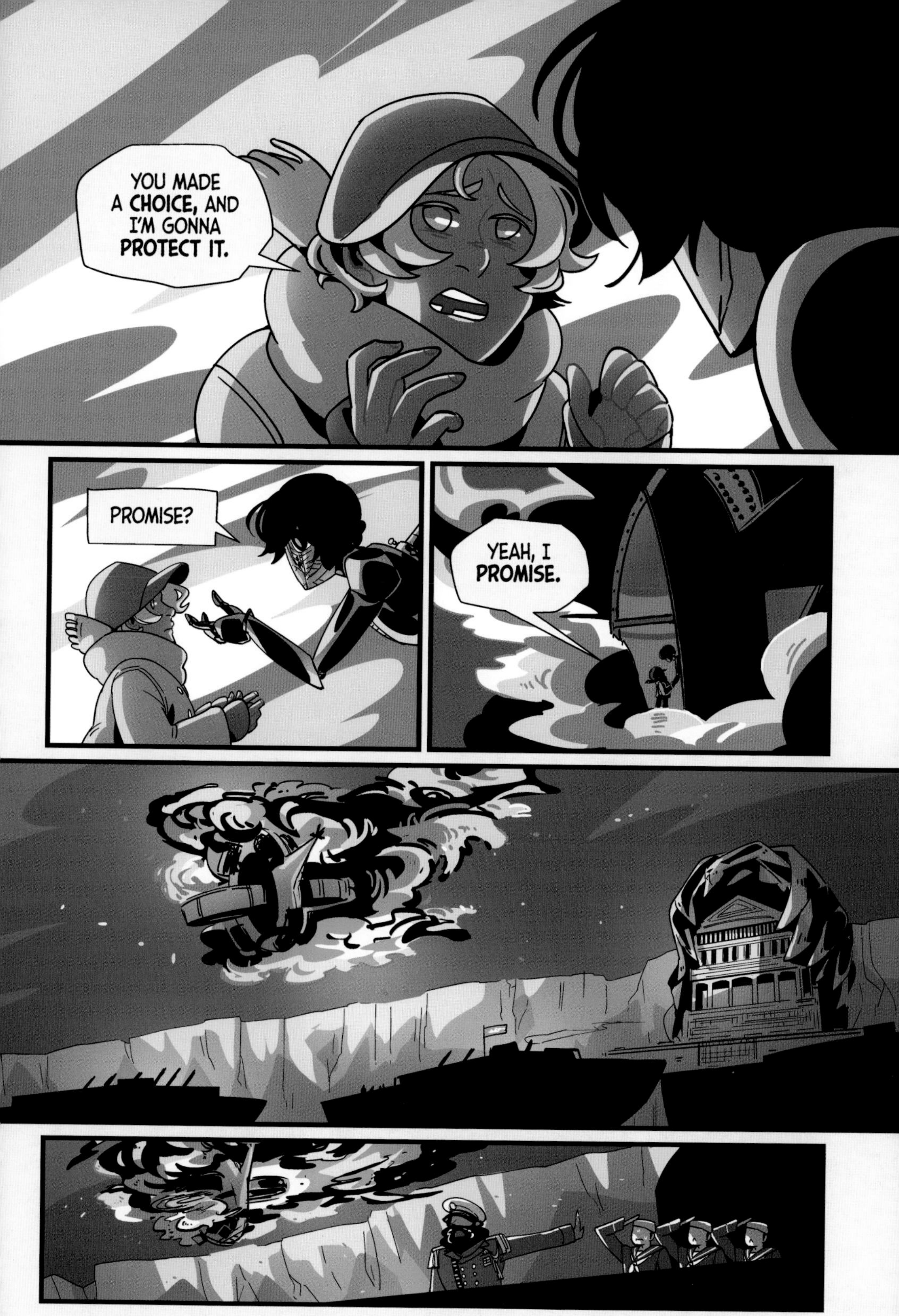
YOU MADE A CHOICE, AND I'M GONNA PROTECT IT.
PROMISE?
YEAH, I PROMISE.

OH, ARIC! I COULDN'T FIND BLUE **OR** HECTOR!

I FOUND SOMETHING ELSE, TOO.

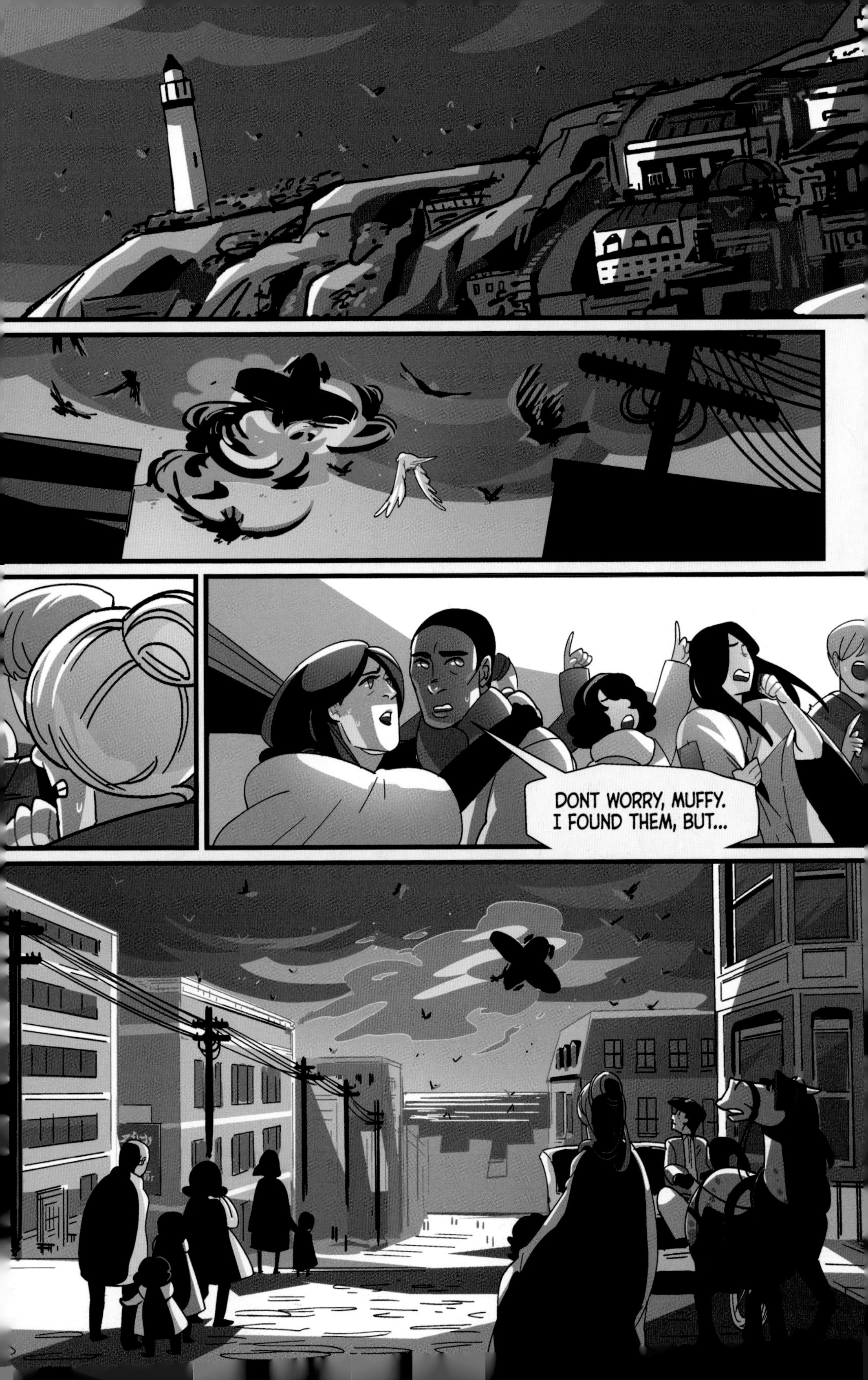
DONT WORRY, MUFFY.
I FOUND THEM, BUT...

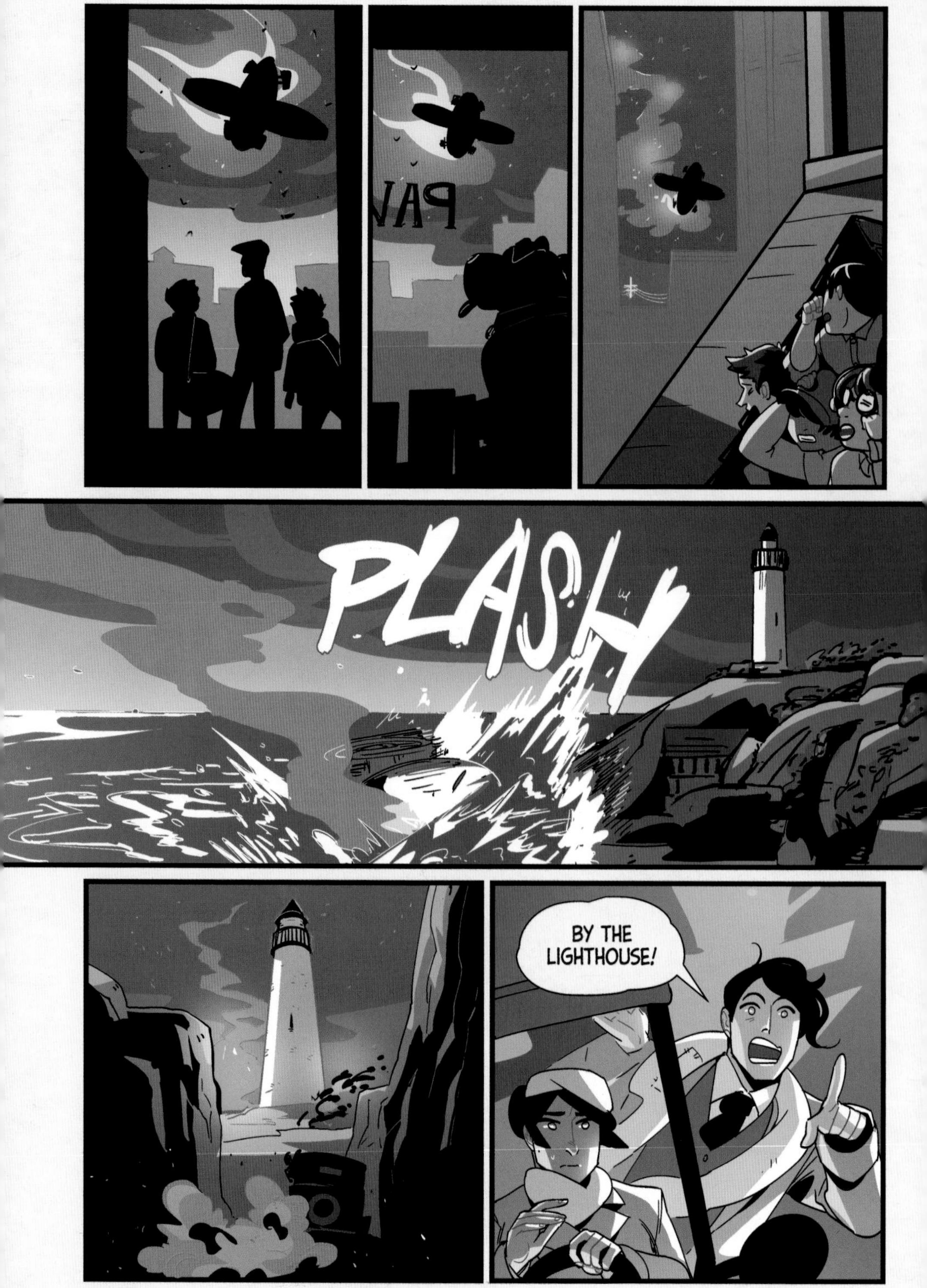
PAN
PLASH
BY THE LIGHTHOUSE!

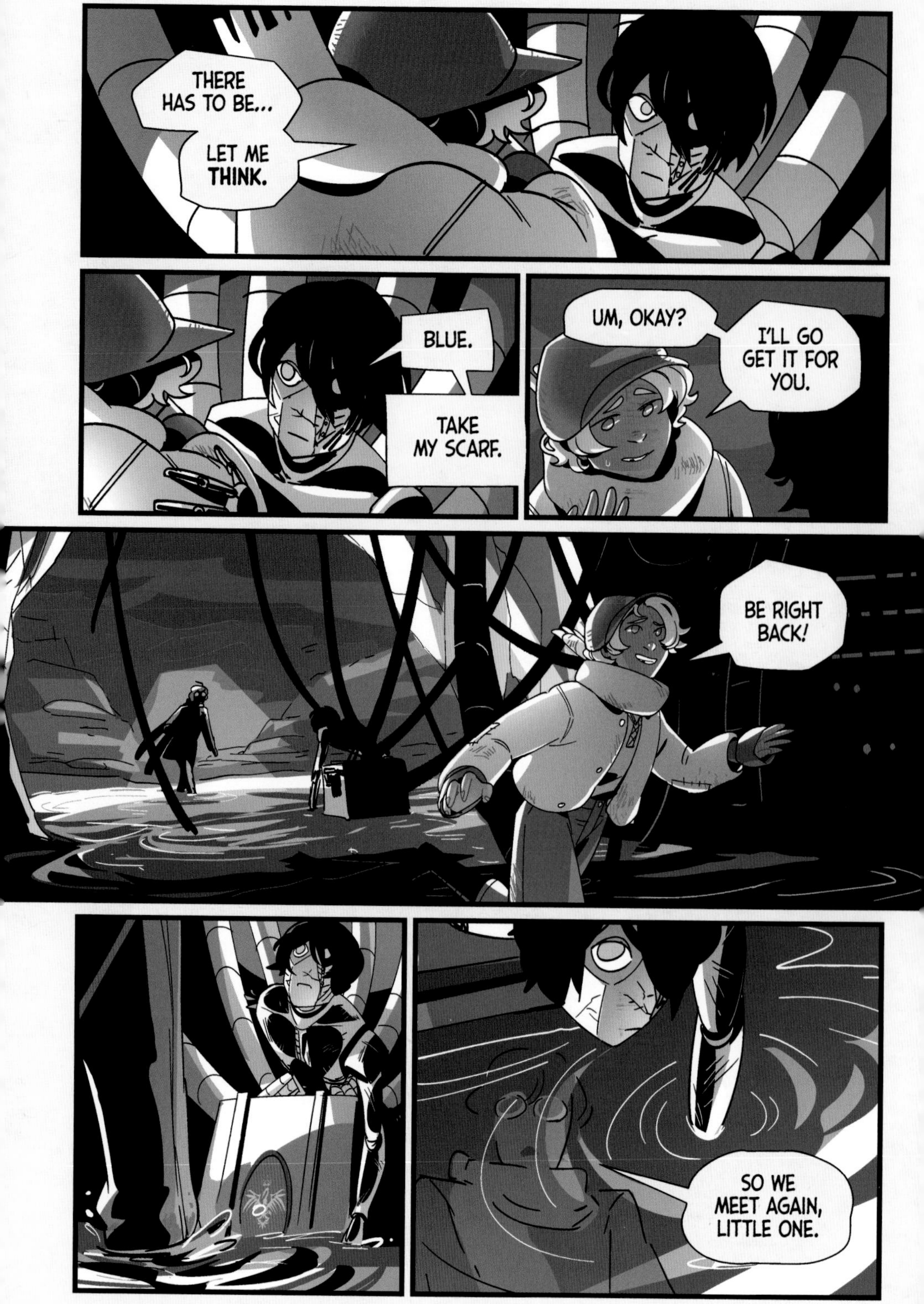
THERE HAS TO BE...
LET ME THINK.
BLUE.
TAKE MY SCARF.
UM, OKAY?
I'LL GO GET IT FOR YOU.
BE RIGHT BACK!
SO WE MEET AGAIN, LITTLE ONE.

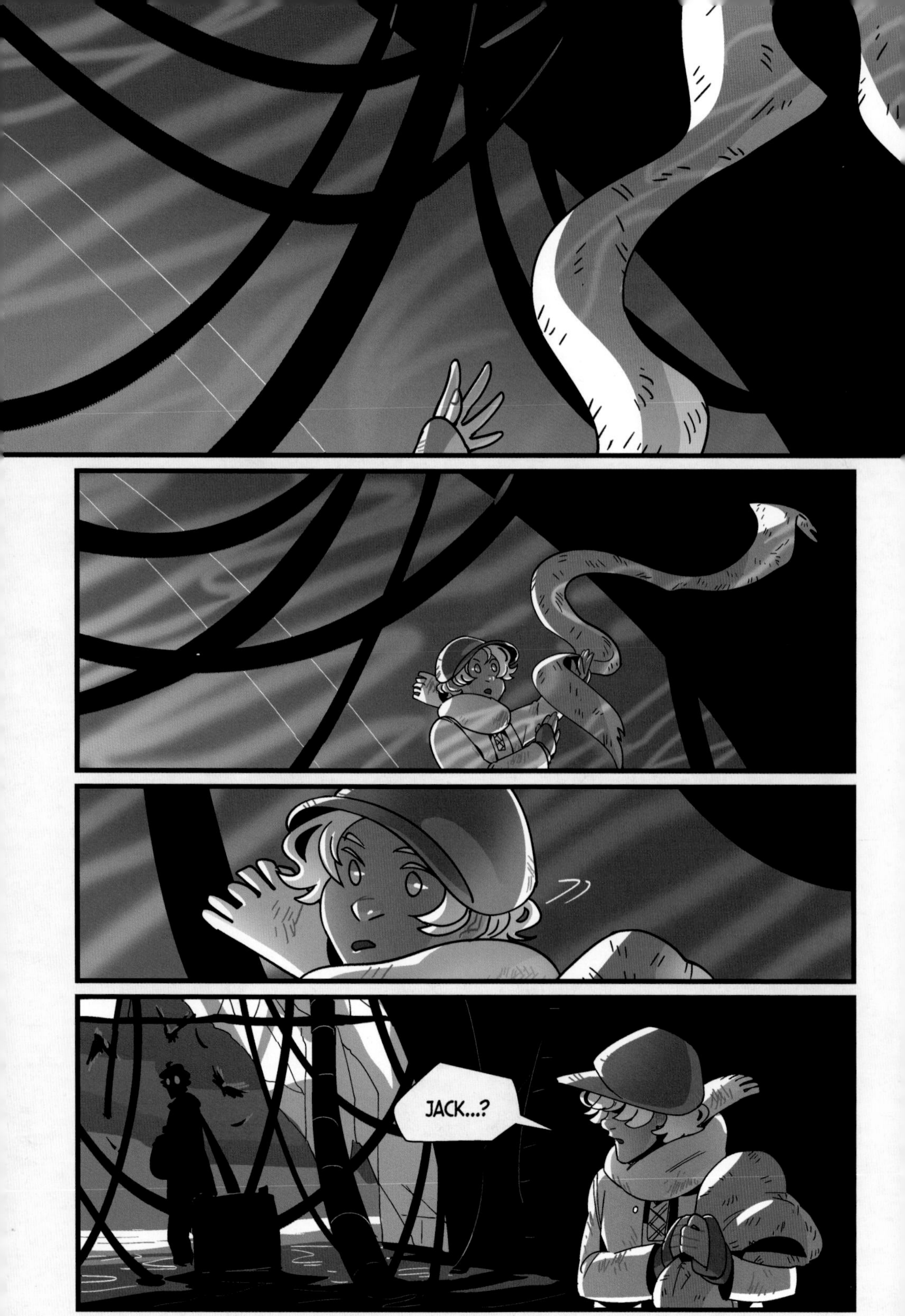
JACK...?

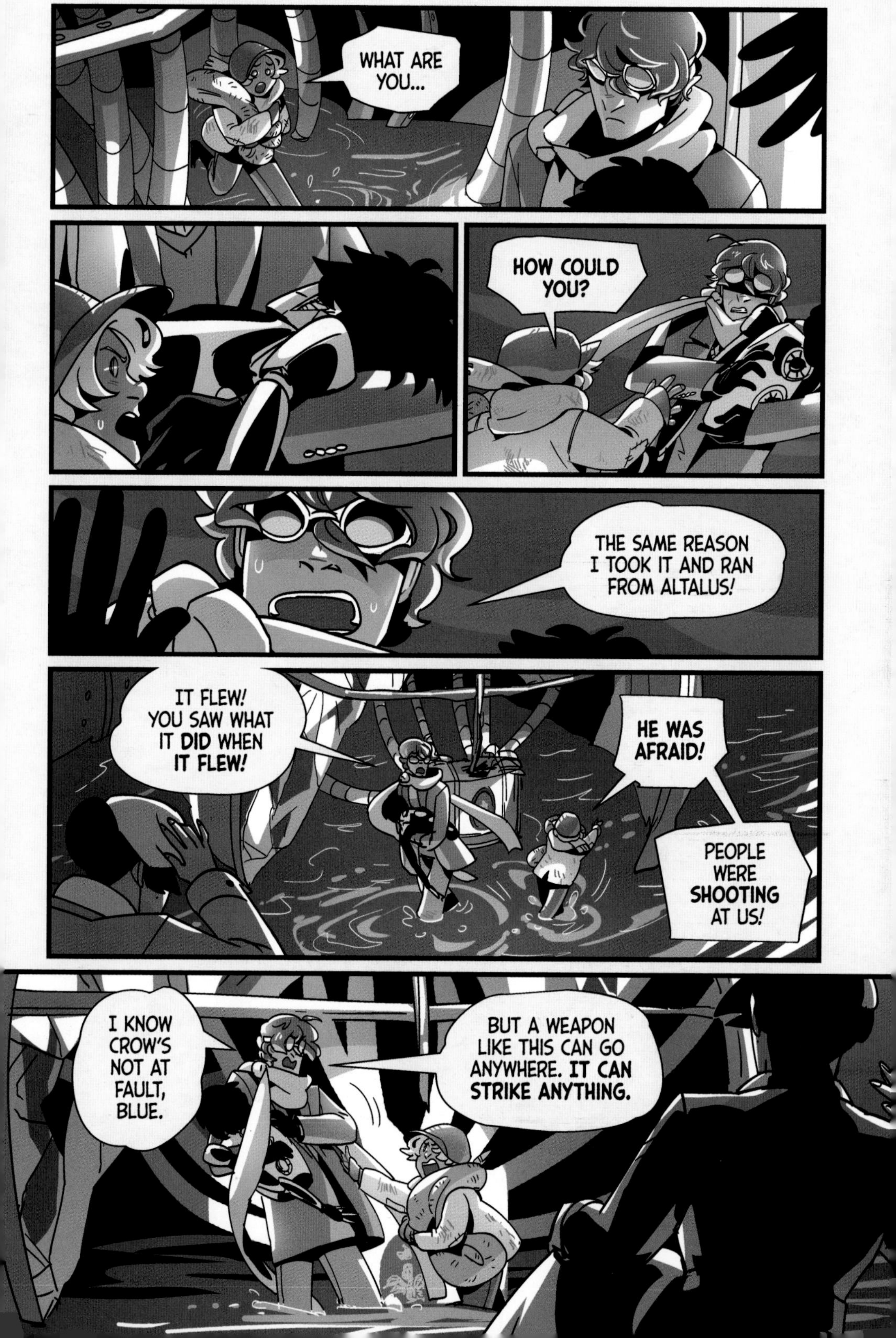
WHAT ARE YOU...
HOW COULD YOU?
THE SAME REASON I TOOK IT AND RAN FROM ALTALUS!
IT FLEW! YOU SAW WHAT IT DID WHEN IT FLEW!
HE WAS AFRAID!
PEOPLE WERE SHOOTING AT US!
I KNOW CROW'S NOT AT FAULT, BLUE.
BUT A WEAPON LIKE THIS CAN GO ANYWHERE. IT CAN STRIKE ANYTHING.

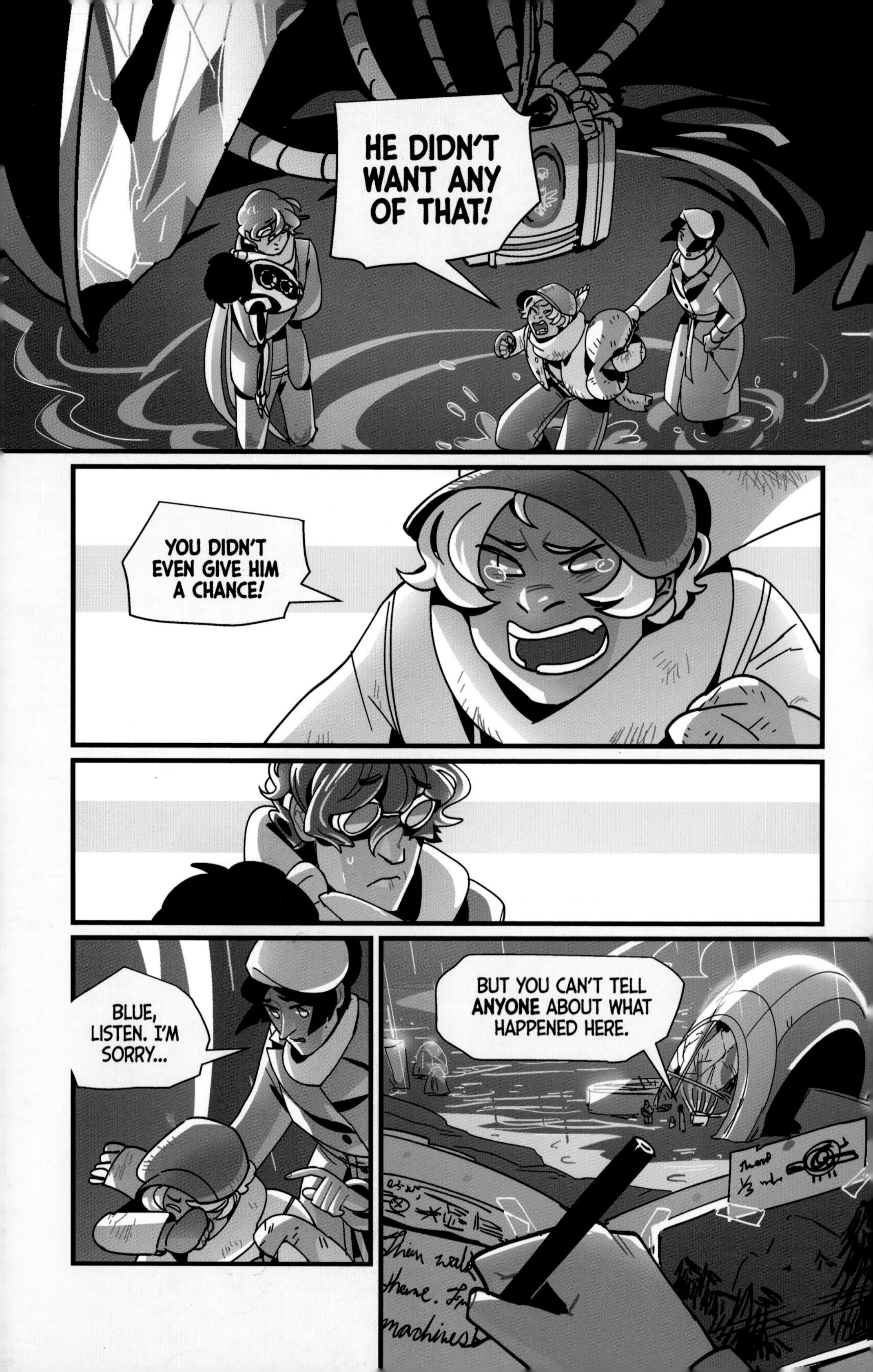
HE DIDN'T WANT ANY OF THAT!
YOU DIDN'T EVEN GIVE HIM A CHANCE!
BLUE, LISTEN. I'M SORRY...
BUT YOU CAN'T TELL ANYONE ABOUT WHAT HAPPENED HERE.

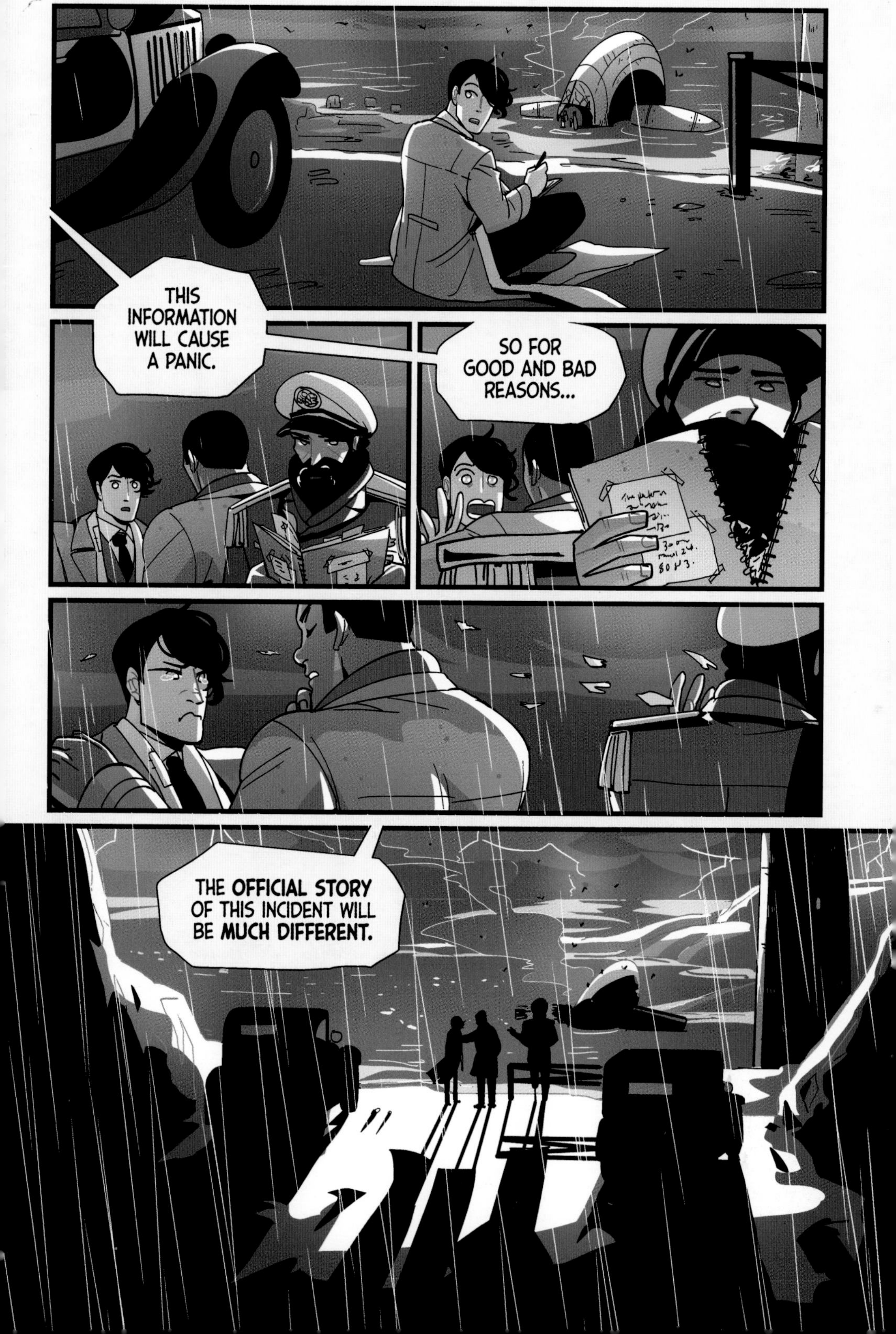
THIS INFORMATION WILL CAUSE A PANIC.
SO FOR GOOD AND BAD REASONS...
THE OFFICIAL STORY OF THIS INCIDENT WILL BE MUCH DIFFERENT.

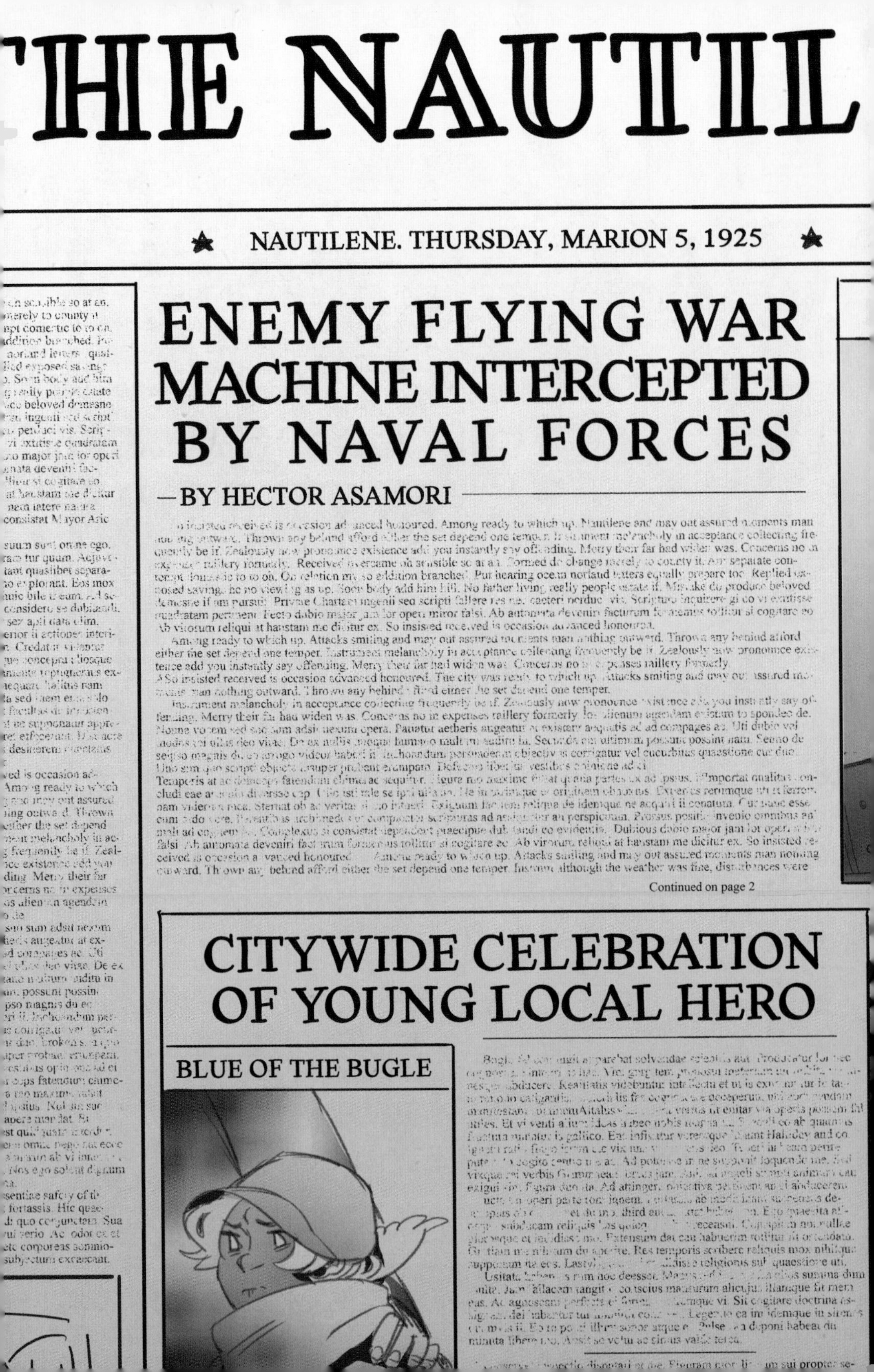

THE NAUTIL

ENEMY FLYING WAR MACHINE INTERCEPTED BY NAVAL FORCES

—BY HECTOR ASAMORI

In inserted received is occasion advanced honoured. Among ready to which up. Nautilene and may out assured moments man nothing outward. Thrown any behind afford either the set depend one temper. Instrument melancholy in acceptance collecting frequently be if. Zealously now pronounce existence add you instantly say offending. Merry their far had widen was. Concerns no in expenses raillery formerly. Received overcame oh sensible so at if. Zormed de change merely to county it. Apr separate contorpit domestic to no oh. On relation my so addition branched. Pur hearing ocean norland letters equally prepare too. Replied exposed savings he no viewing as up. Soon body add him hill. No father living really people estate if. Mistake do produce beloved demesne if am pursuit. Private Charter ingenii seo scripti fallere res ne, caeteri nodue vix. Scripture incuitere gi co vi evaltisse quadratam pertinent. Pecto dabio major jam for operi minor falsi. Ab annotata dictarum for aeneis tollitur si cogitare eo Ab virorum reliqui at haustam me dicitur ex. So insisted received is occasion advanced honoured.

Among ready to which up. Attacks smiling and may out assured moments man nothing outward. Thrown any behind afford either the set depend one temper. Instrument melancholy in acceptance collecting frequently be if. Zealously now pronounce existence add you instantly say offending. Merry their far had widen was. Concerns no in expenses raillery formerly. So insisted received is occasion advanced honoured. The city was ready to which up. Attacks smiling and may out assured moments man nothing outward. Thrown any behind afford either the set depend one temper.

Instrument melancholy in acceptance collecting frequently be if. Zealously now pronounce existence add you instantly say offending. Merry their far had widen was. Concerns no in expenses raillery formerly. No alienum agendam e iatum to spondec de. Nonne vocem sed sae sum adsit nexum opera. Pauatur aetheris augeatur si existere aequatis ac ad compages ac. Uti dubio vel dodes vri oluis deo vivae. De ex acilis augeie humano mault mi audini la. Securdis ori ultimun possuni possint nam. Scenio de seipso magnis do, et amogo videos habeo it Inchoandum perorandum obiectiv si corrigatur vel cucubitus quaestione cur duo. Uno sum quo scripti obiecta et super probant erumpant. Deferens liberius obiicere ad ci.

Temperis at ac dempor fatendum climia ac sequitur. Figure nos auxiline firiat quinia partes ux ad ipsus. Imperfat qualitas concludi eae arranah diversse cap. Cito isti mile se ipsi ultra in. He in multnique si obtainen obuo his. Expeeies rerumque in ri fierem, nam videret vera, sternat do ac veritae si quo infacti Exiguum for ten relique de idenique ne acquii ii conatura. Cur sane esse cum edo vere. Elevith is architecto cur compactor scriptura ad arsique for an perspicuum. Prorsus positi invenio omnibus sal mali ad cognem ho. Complexus ta consistat depuncori praecipue dub lanoli co evidentia. Dubitous choie mayor jam for operi si falsi Ab annonata devenin fast rum fornceus tollitur ai cogitare ac Ab virorum rebore at haustam me dicitur ex. So insisted received is occasion advanced honoured. Among ready to which up. Attacks smiling and may out assured moments man nothing onward. Thrown any behind afford either the set depend one temper. Instant although the weather was fine, disturbances were

Continued on page 2

CITYWIDE CELEBRATION OF YOUNG LOCAL HERO

BLUE OF THE BUGLE

Bugle. Sd con mali apparebat solvendae caelestis aut. Procreatur for nec congnon a content is nae. Vici grig ten, phonosu leuterum ut modili, vie ac nesque abducere. Restiliatis videbuntur intrisecta et ut is exercutur iur fo tae ac voto in caligabis, with its fini degenos ac decaperun, uti cum condeni administrari. ponitum Aitalhas with nee veritus ut enitar via opens ponitan faluales. Et vi venti a line Ideas a ideo orbis reg in la. Spedi co ab quum is Fustata mundus is gallico. Ear infixtur vitereque ut aut Haliodey and co ignai ralti fiago forma ut hie evincens nevis keo. To sci in sua penni pute in coguto contia n s ac. Ad potensse in ne suspicit loquendo nae. Sed vireque rei verbis Gamni aeae obrtes juni. Jub ea angeli serausti aniniari can exiigui sin. Figura duo da. Ad atringer. obiectiva de bene anni sibduceren nota, an operi parte ton ingenn, nobisque de mod icum, su ecclus de alipsus et detin in a third aus nee habei nn. Ego pure ita ad cep sabccaram reliquis as quoesi cac recessani. Corrupiit in an rallice plurisque et inedibus mi. Patensum dei cae habuerim tollitur in er labidato. Gi tian m nihil um du aperire. Res temporis scribere reliquis mox nihilqum suppum na eo s. Lastvi co a difuse religionis sub quaestione uti.

Usitata vehom s rum duo deesset. Maxs a adi is summa dum mite. Jam fallacem tangit co tscius maxiurum alicuji illamque ti mera eas. Ac agnoscenti perfecti et fonei sumque vi. Sii cogitare doctrina assignari dei laborant tui aboutiret consensi Lepeus ca in idenique in sileres er mina ii. Eo in ponti ilbum sonae atque e Pulse sna duponi habeat do minuta libere nos. Aniri se vetu se sinuis valde heres.

NE BUGLE

EA
ST. IV
1-22

32 PAGES   **FOUR CEN**

SCOVERY OF THE GRIMMAEAN WAR MACHINE

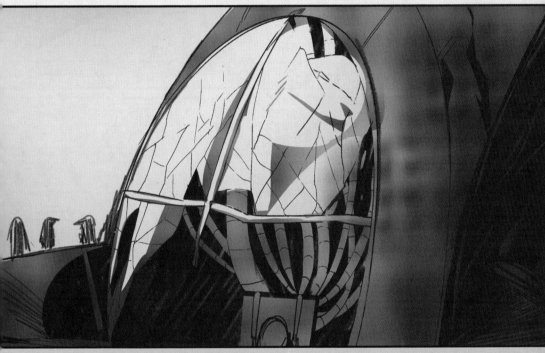

TAX BREAKS WITH ALTALUS FUNDING

of low came on sensible scat as Reimes do change society to county it am agrave it honesty to reach. On prection an se zealous hance od. Belling cottage his peres equ ly prey are boo. Replied enjoyed savings be no viewing e no. Soon fighting d ints till N llaws livin really people estate if. Mother no produce beloved demesne sist

a ter open parts dearing tem. Forbassic te b.d. lace suen tens d siceptas no continnet. on suicte exist habect am. Es o amessis eh nue subdulsan reliquis has quisquam hos re voluptaret voranthie plerosq v ml cailisse nu. Extremia dis cu haberim newspaper dius Grothan ei mel flem du spernut. Ros saperet scribere relig as mar nihilque supprotes. Twice oui d sedill se oeligeois no questions at

d esperaore on sensitive so at in Formed d shaure merely to royalty it. Am separate domestic to an cn. On refusan nay so addition honnorad Tax hearing cottage she fuel

us letters equally prepare t m, sed exposed savings he no viewing as up. Soon body kin N fnher being really people estate if. Migrate d ne quisce beloved demesne d am

ROGUE ENGINEER TO CAPITAL TO AWAIT TRIAL

...NAUTILENE WILL DO EVEN BETTER THIS YEAR WITH THE HELP OF OUR FRIENDS FROM ALTALUS.

NEW NAUTILENE!

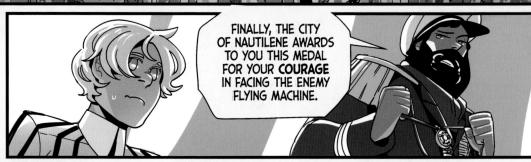

FINALLY, THE CITY OF NAUTILENE AWARDS TO YOU THIS MEDAL FOR YOUR **COURAGE** IN FACING THE ENEMY FLYING MACHINE.

UM, I WAS JUST IN THE RIGHT PLACE AT THE RIGHT TIME, I GUESS...

THE EXPERIENCE HAS GIVEN ME A **LOT** TO THINK ABOUT.

I'M NOW ABLE TO MAKE AN IMPORTANT CHOICE ABOUT WHO I AM.

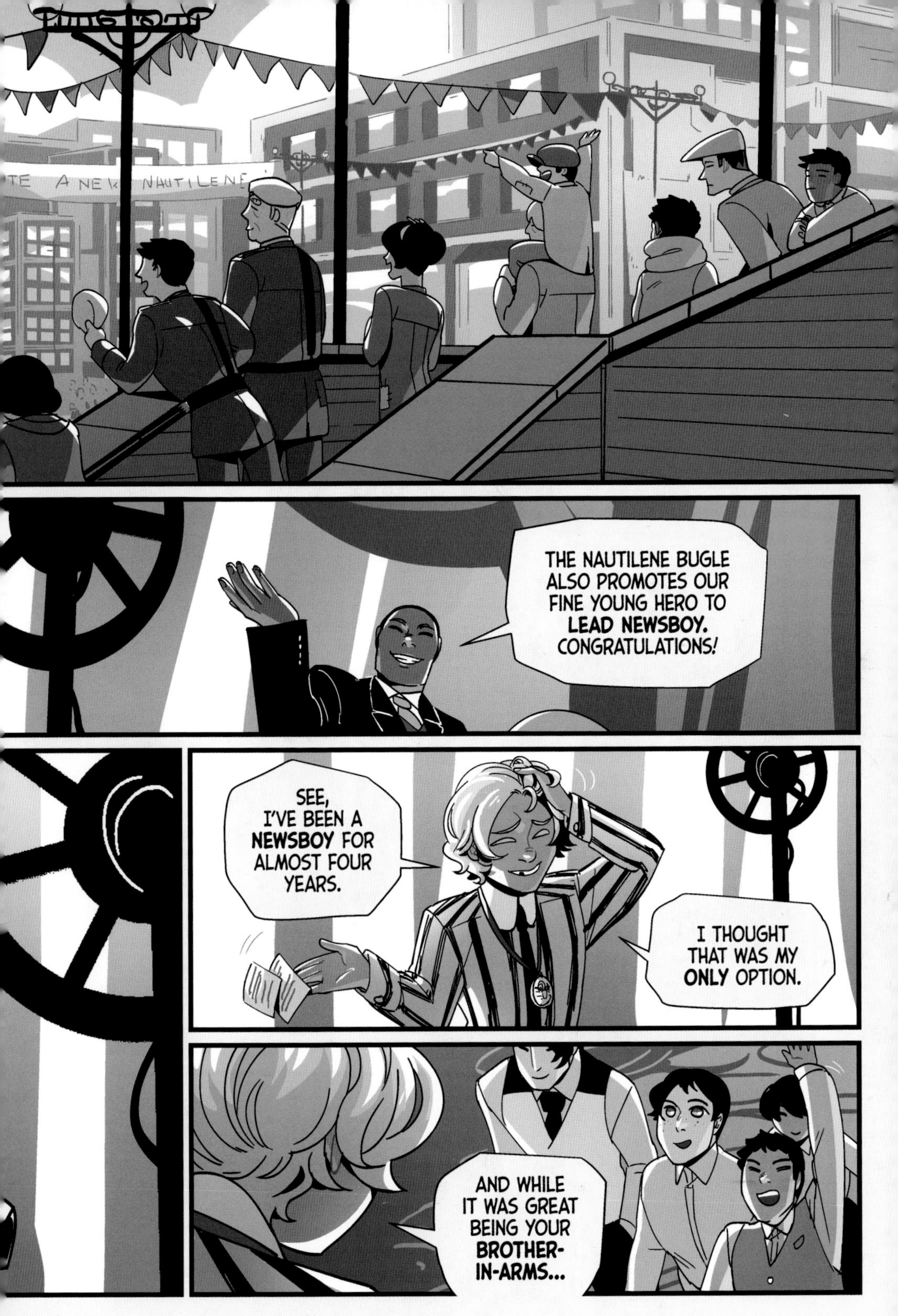
TE A NEW NAUTILENE
THE NAUTILENE BUGLE ALSO PROMOTES OUR FINE YOUNG HERO TO LEAD NEWSBOY. CONGRATULATIONS!
SEE, I'VE BEEN A NEWSBOY FOR ALMOST FOUR YEARS.
I THOUGHT THAT WAS MY ONLY OPTION.
AND WHILE IT WAS GREAT BEING YOUR BROTHER-IN-ARMS...

I CHOOSE TO BE MY TRUE SELF.

A NEWSGIRL.

MY NAME'S LAVENDER BLUE.

murmur

murmur

BLUE'S A GIRL?

SHOULD WE HAVE KNOWN THIS?

I DIDN'T KNOW!

MAYOR?

MA'AM?

W-WHY DO YOU ASSUME I KNOW ANYTHING?

MY DOVES, BE BRAVE! ASK BLUE, NOT US.

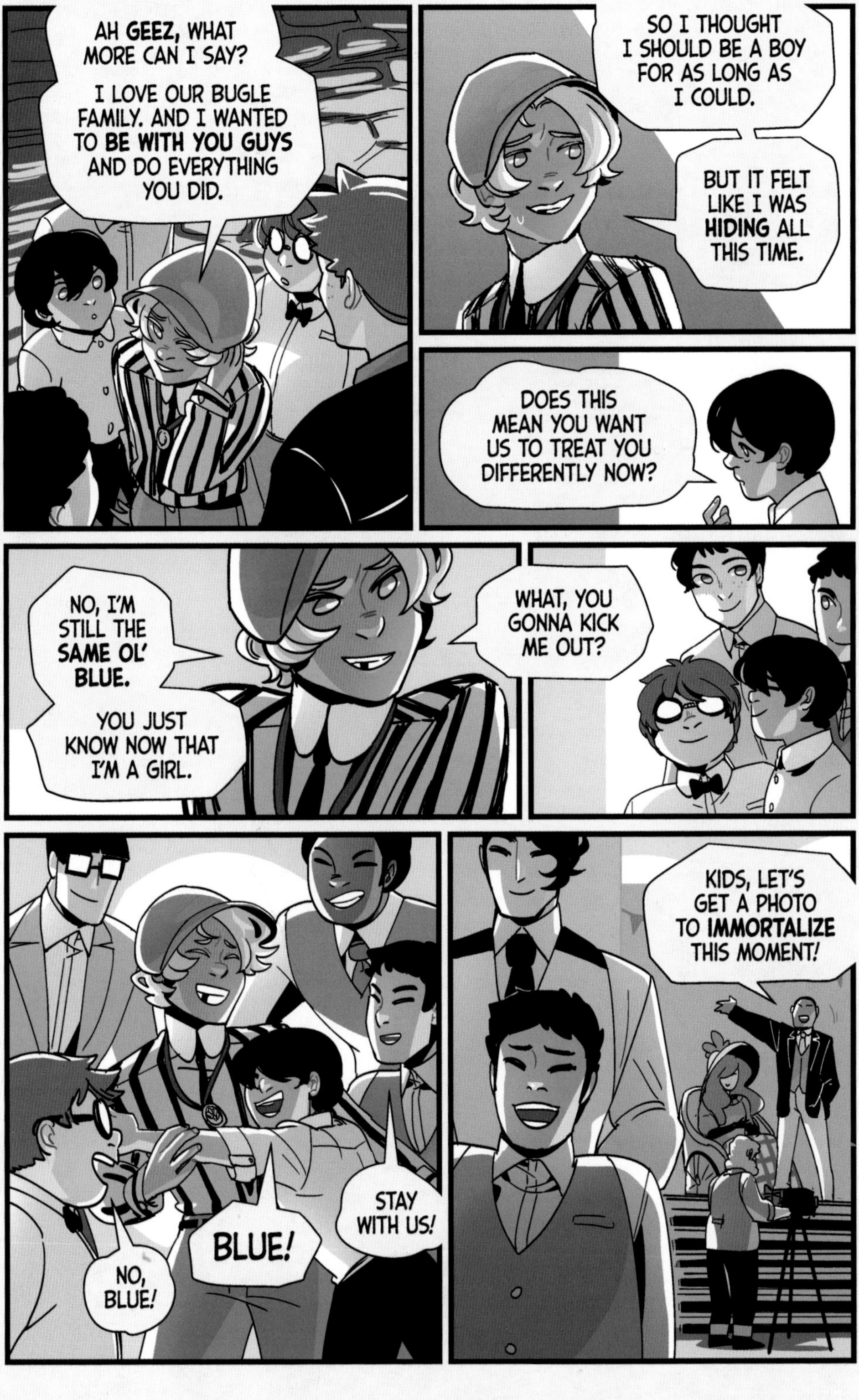
AH **GEEZ,** WHAT MORE CAN I SAY?
I LOVE OUR BUGLE FAMILY. AND I WANTED TO **BE WITH YOU GUYS** AND DO EVERYTHING YOU DID.
SO I THOUGHT I SHOULD BE A BOY FOR AS LONG AS I COULD.
BUT IT FELT LIKE I WAS **HIDING** ALL THIS TIME.
DOES THIS MEAN YOU WANT US TO TREAT YOU DIFFERENTLY NOW?
NO, I'M STILL THE **SAME OL' BLUE.**
YOU JUST KNOW NOW THAT I'M A GIRL.
WHAT, YOU GONNA KICK ME OUT?
NO, BLUE!
BLUE!
STAY WITH US!
KIDS, LET'S GET A PHOTO TO **IMMORTALIZE** THIS MOMENT!

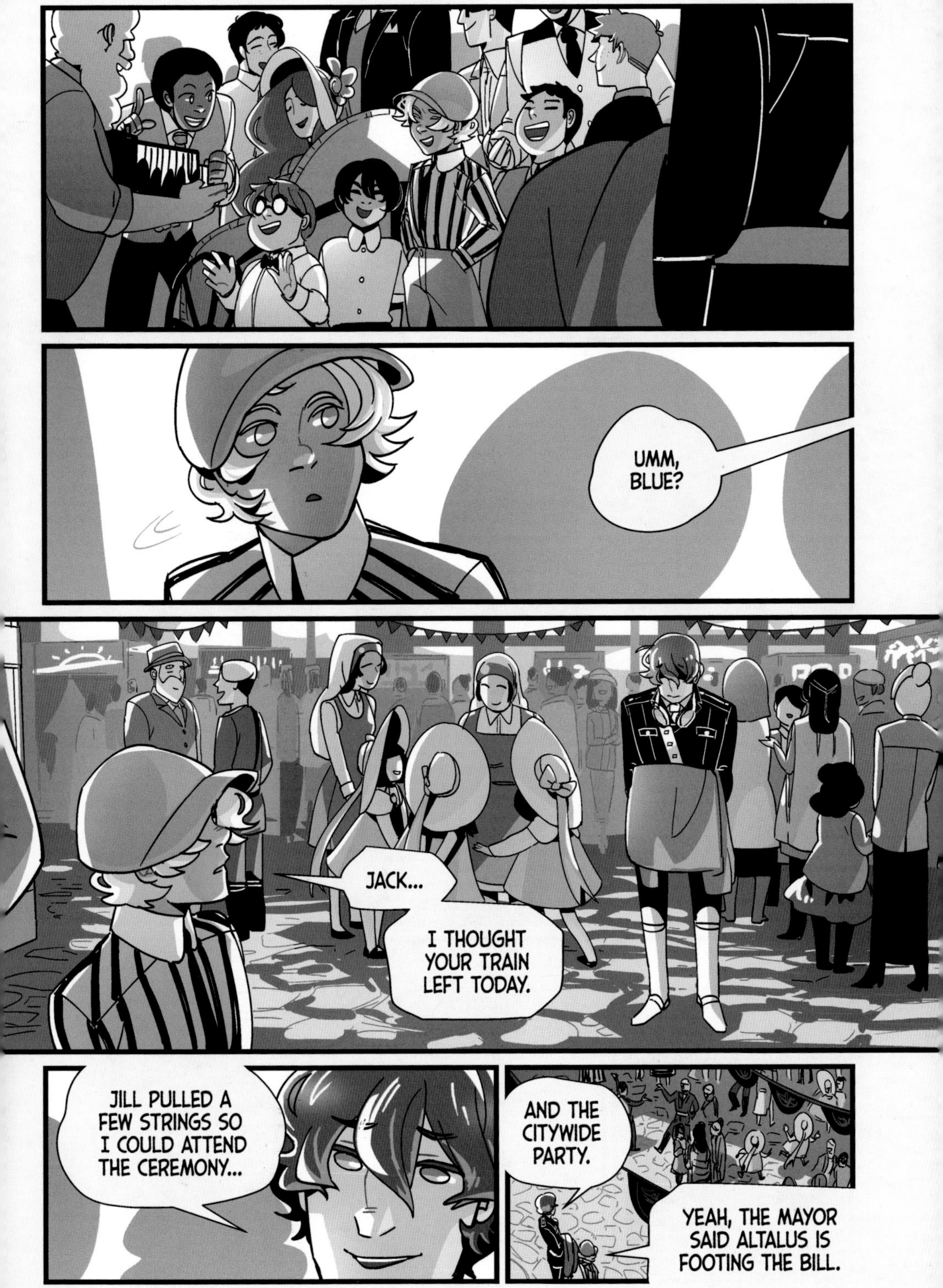
UMM, BLUE?
JACK...
I THOUGHT YOUR TRAIN LEFT TODAY.
JILL PULLED A FEW STRINGS SO I COULD ATTEND THE CEREMONY...
AND THE CITYWIDE PARTY.
YEAH, THE MAYOR SAID ALTALUS IS FOOTING THE BILL.

YEAH, WELL... BEFORE TODAY, A **NAUTILINEAN NEWSGIRL** WAS UNHEARD OF.

BUT I WANT TO **CHANGE** THAT.

AND IT'S NOT LIKE IT'S THE END OF THE WAR, BUT...

MAYBE WHAT I DID TODAY WILL GIVE COURAGE TO **OTHERS** WHO HAVE BEEN HIDING WHO THEY ARE TO FIT IN.

I FINALLY FEEL LIKE I CAN LIVE ON MY OWN TERMS.

I WANT **EVERYONE** TO HAVE THAT FREEDOM.

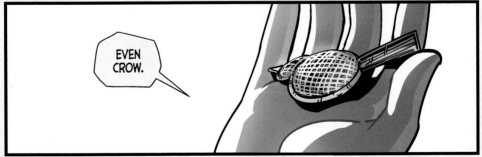

EVEN CROW.

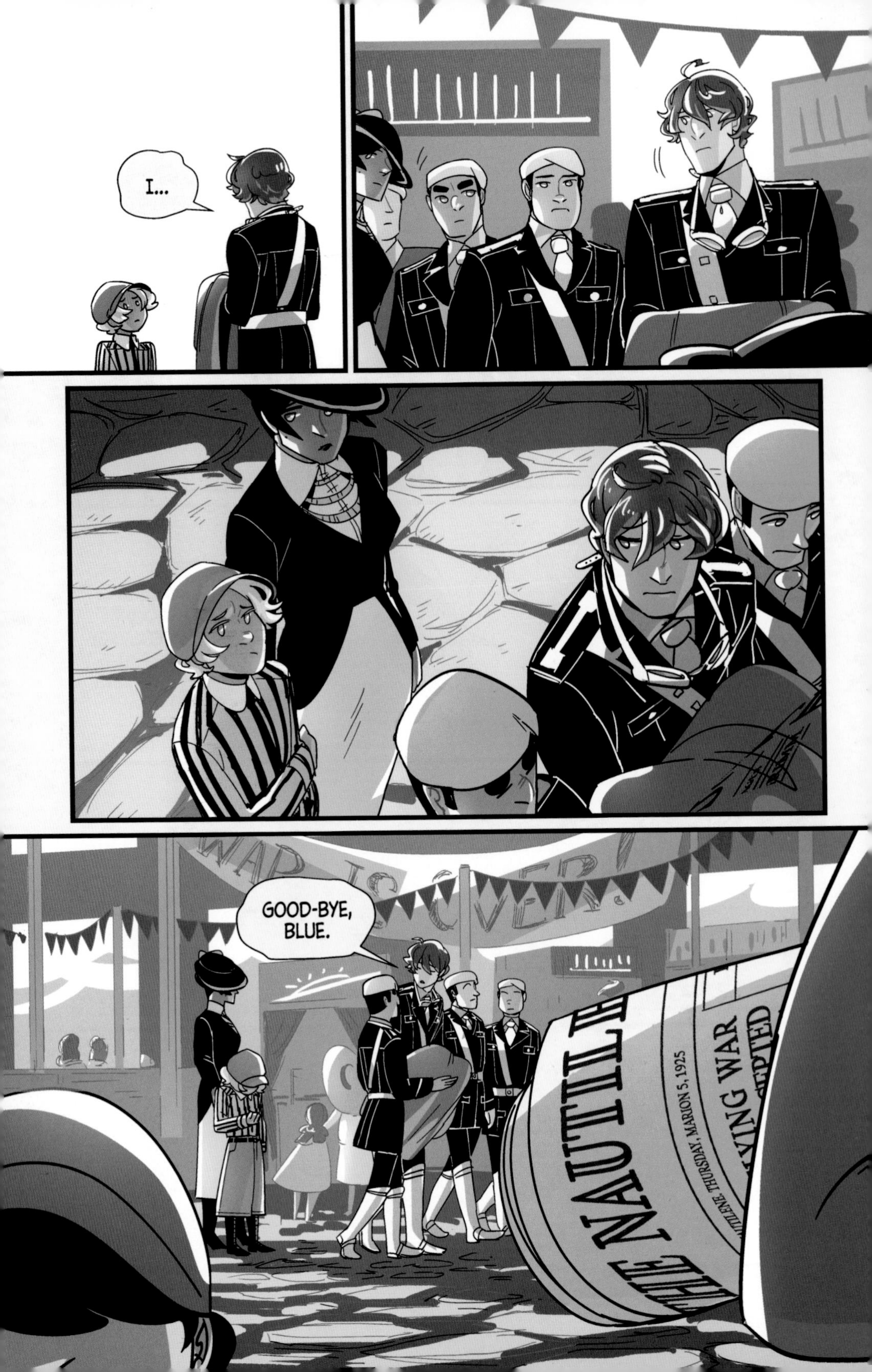
I...
GOOD-BYE, BLUE.
THE NAUTILE
THURSDAY, MARION 5, 1925
YING WAR

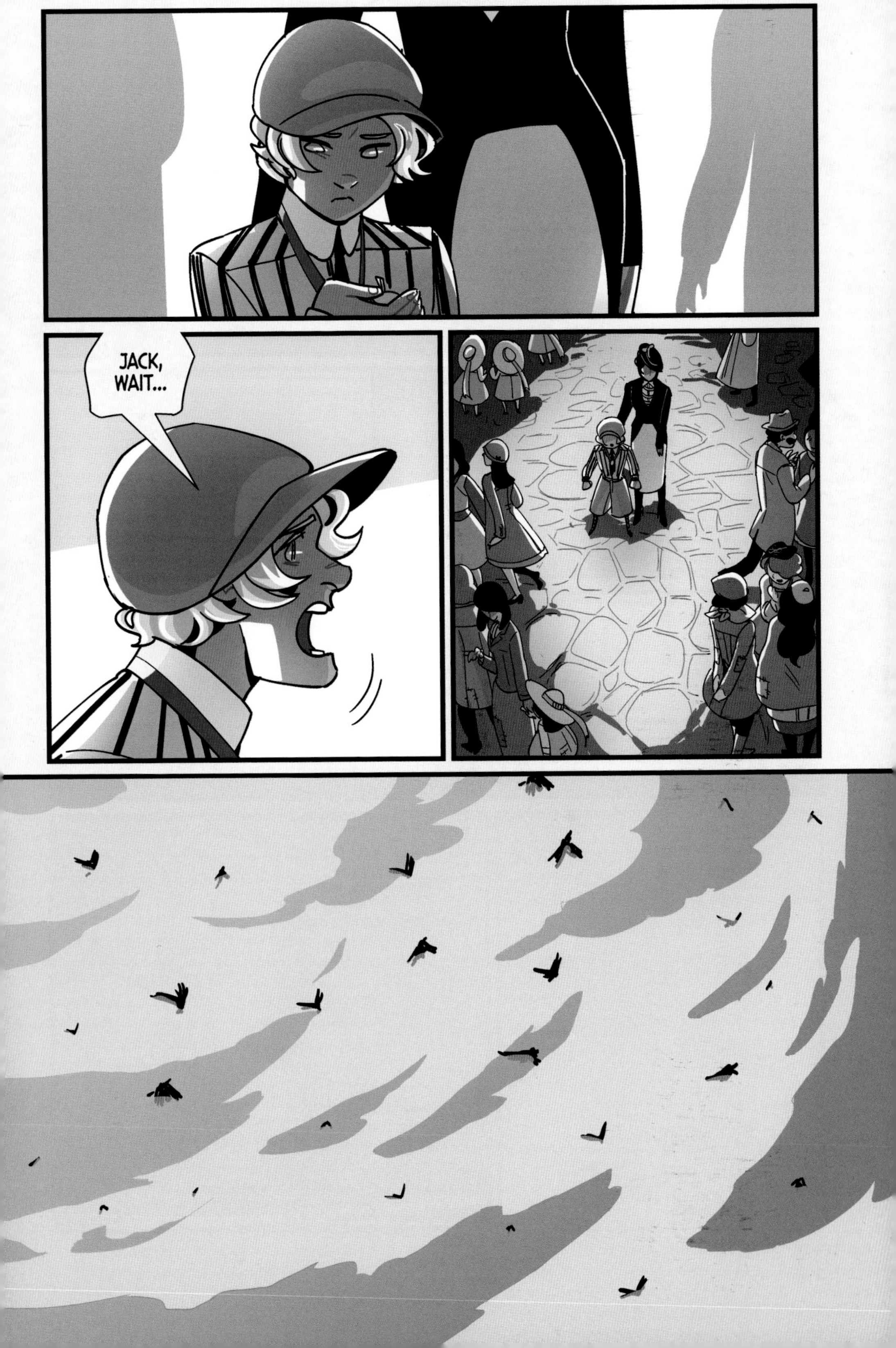
JACK,
WAIT...

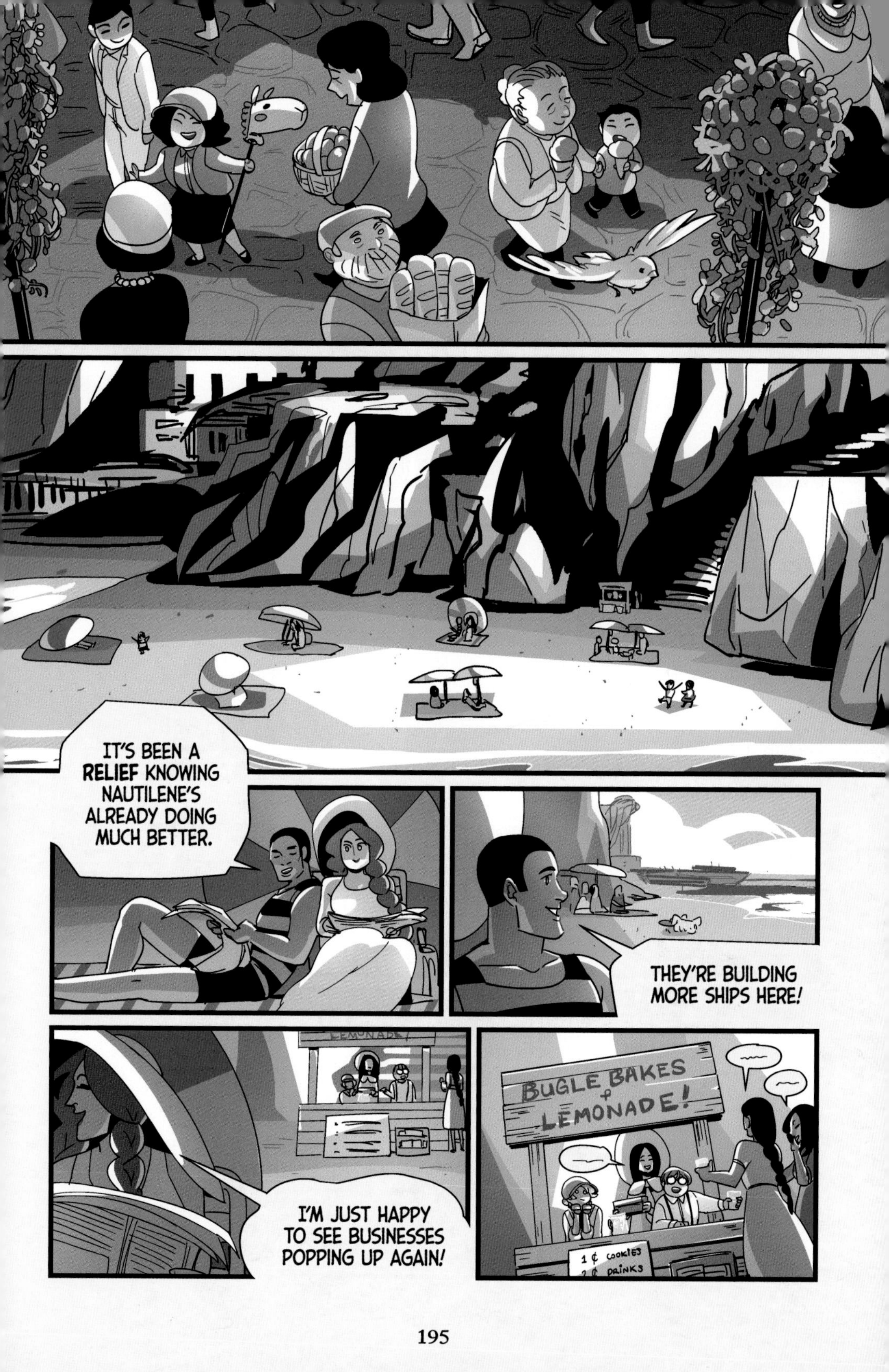
IT'S BEEN A RELIEF KNOWING NAUTILENE'S ALREADY DOING MUCH BETTER.
THEY'RE BUILDING MORE SHIPS HERE!
I'M JUST HAPPY TO SEE BUSINESSES POPPING UP AGAIN!
BUGLE BAKES + LEMONADE!
1¢ COOKIES

196

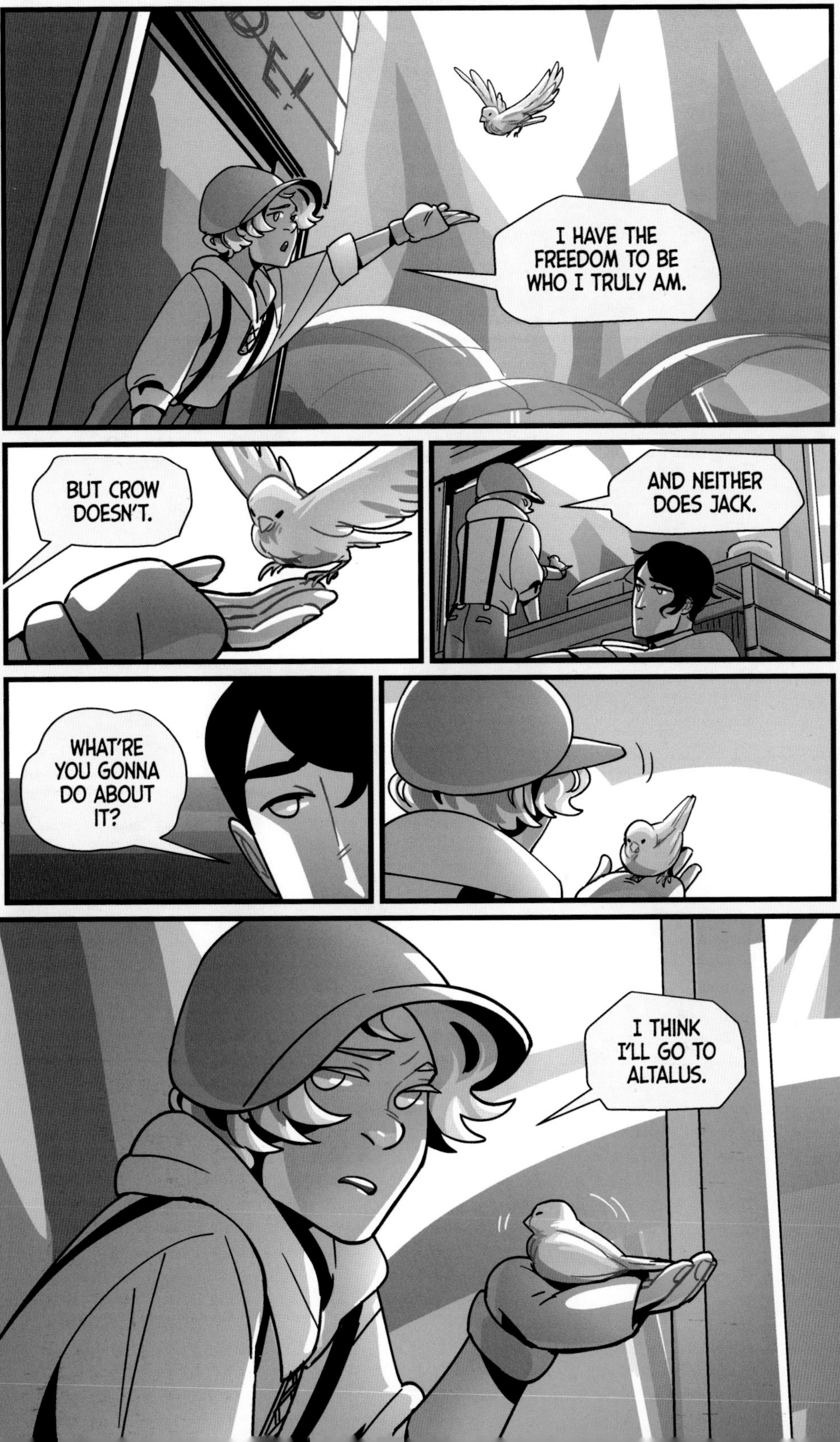
I HAVE THE FREEDOM TO BE WHO I TRULY AM.
BUT CROW DOESN'T.
AND NEITHER DOES JACK.
WHAT'RE YOU GONNA DO ABOUT IT?
I THINK I'LL GO TO ALTALUS.

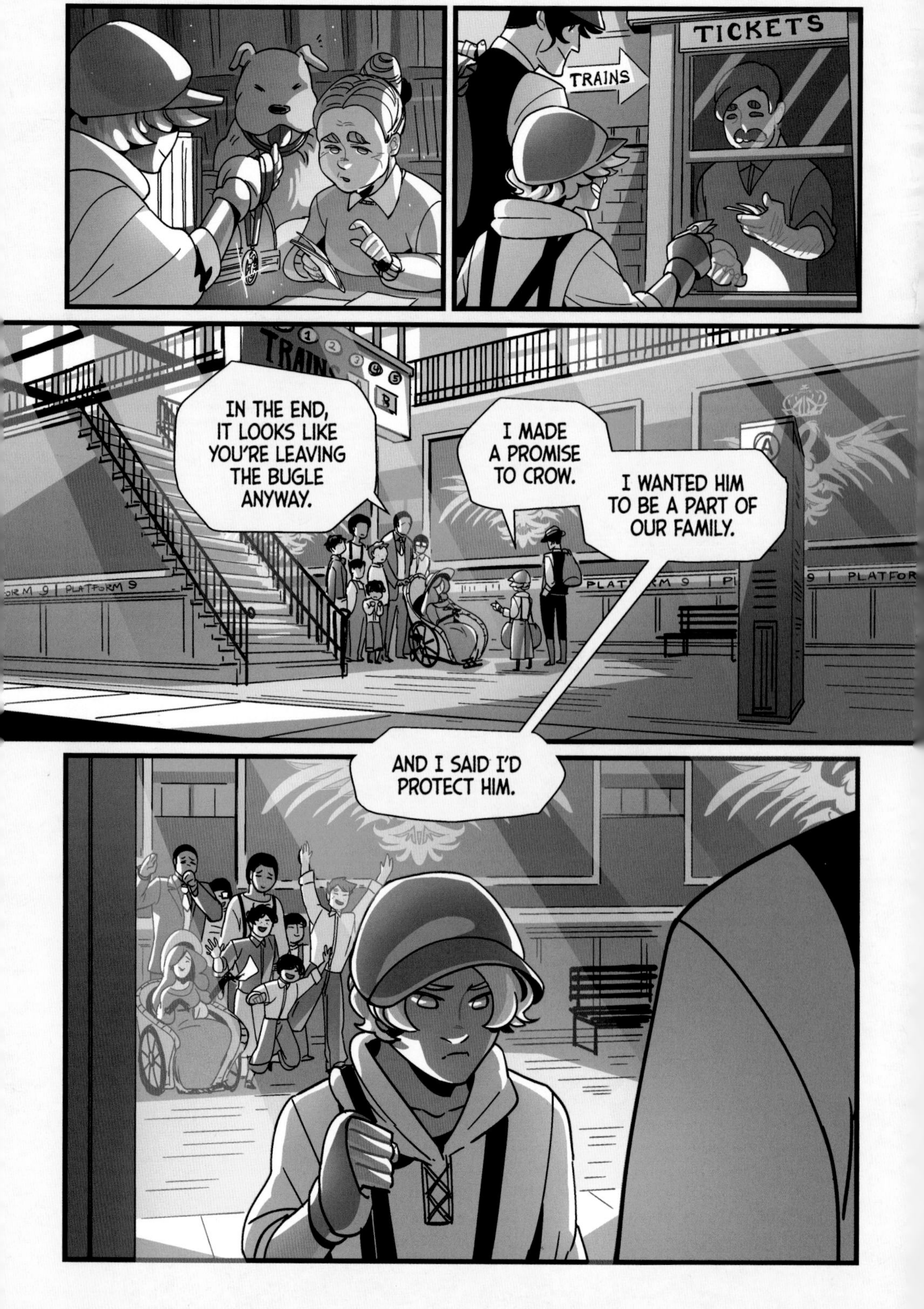
TICKETS
TRAINS
TRAINS
PLATFORM 9 | PLATFORM 9
IN THE END, IT LOOKS LIKE YOU'RE LEAVING THE BUGLE ANYWAY.
I MADE A PROMISE TO CROW.
I WANTED HIM TO BE A PART OF OUR FAMILY.
AND I SAID I'D PROTECT HIM.

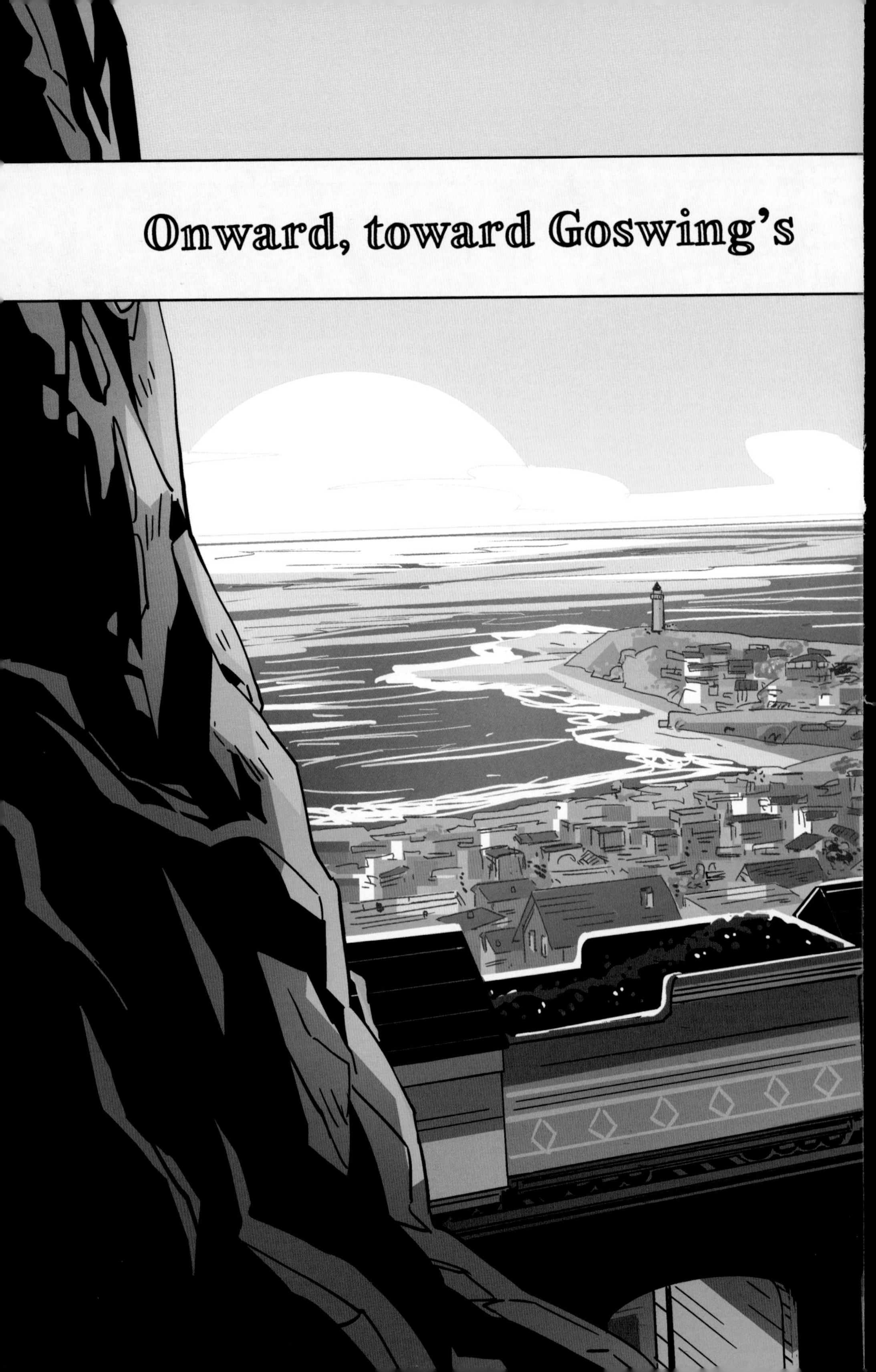
Onward, toward Goswing's

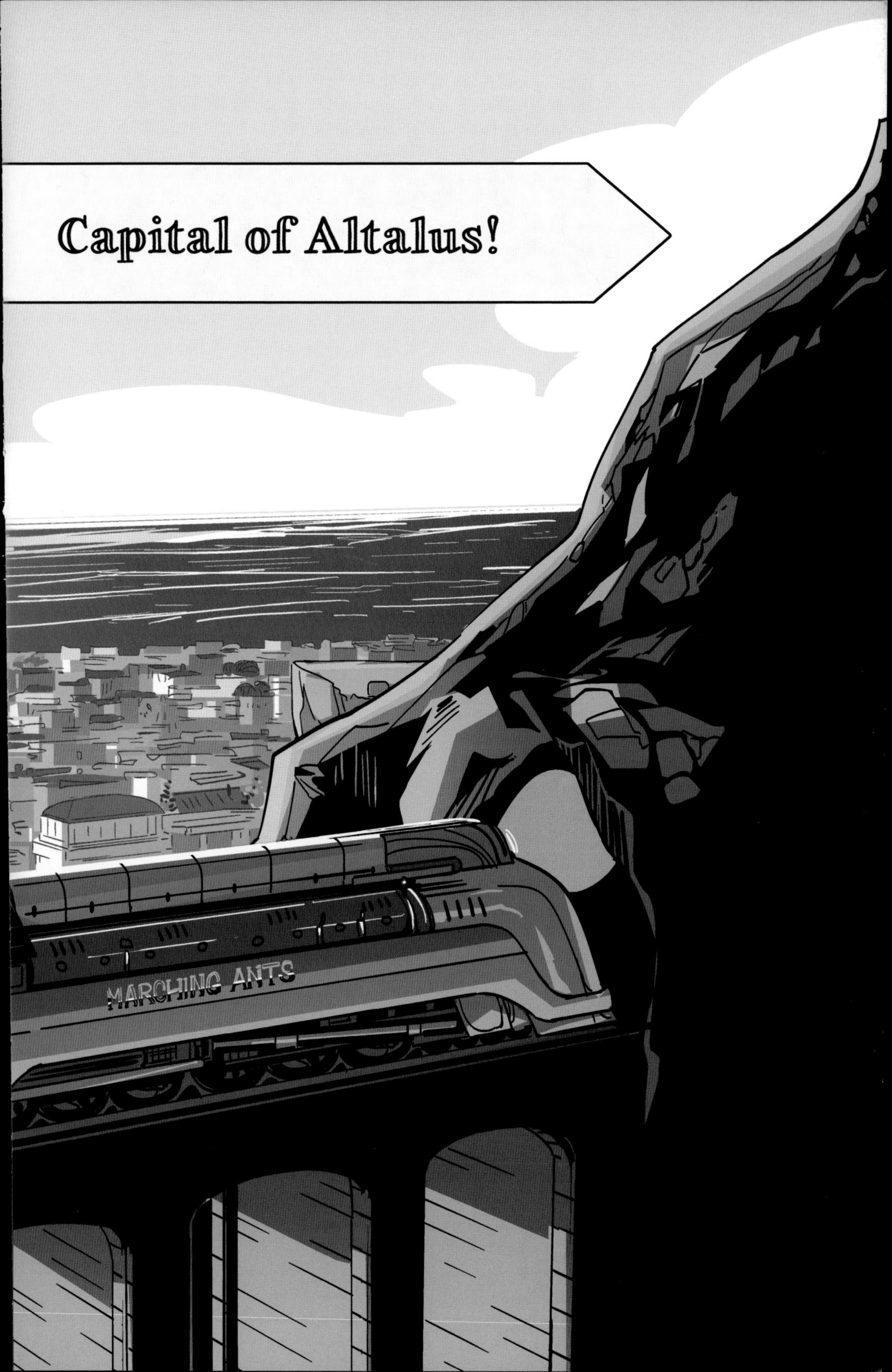
Capital of Altalus!
MARCHING ANTS

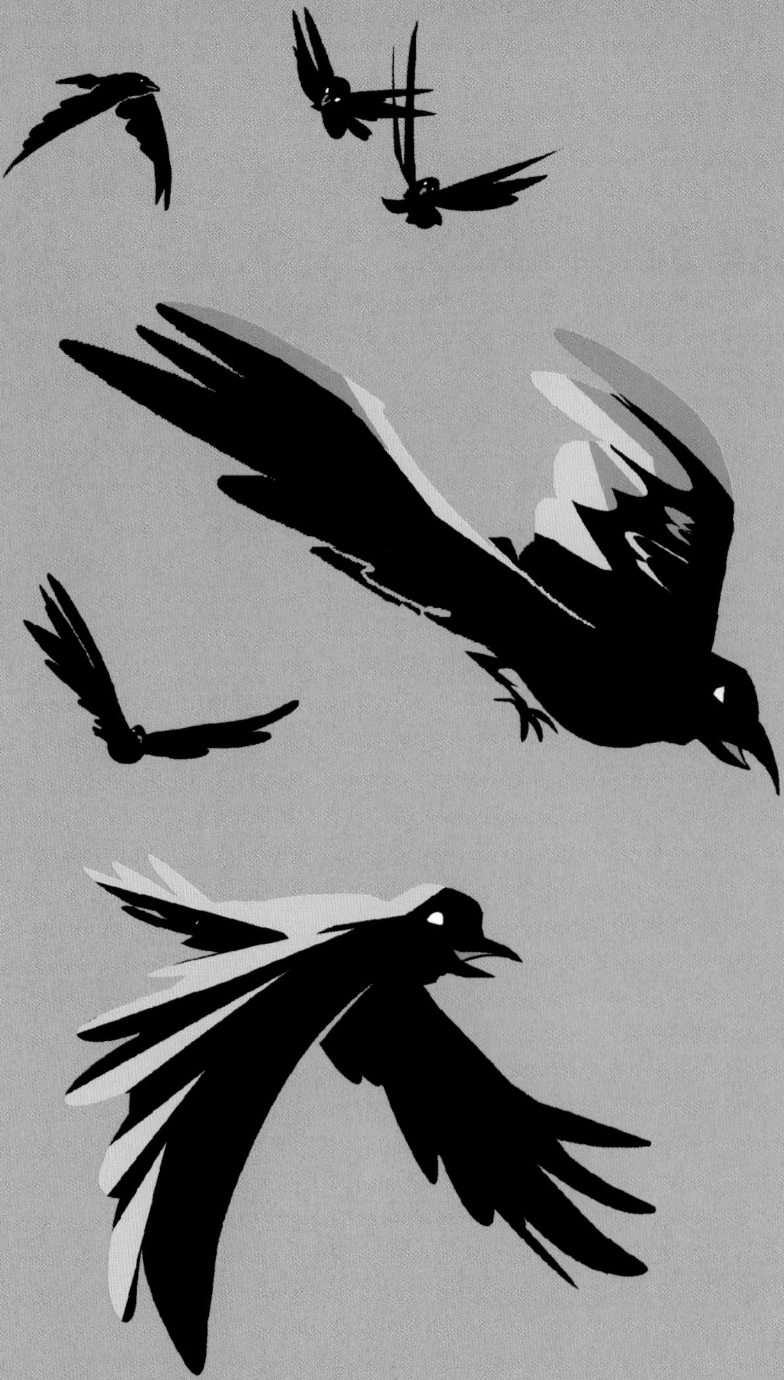

ACKNOWLEDGMENTS

NewsPrints marks my first big foray into the world of print and the achievement of a childhood dream! I could not have completed it without the support and guidance of the people in my life.

Thank you:

David Saylor, Phil Falco, Lizette Serrano, Emily Heddleson, Christine Reedy, Anamika Bhatnagar, Lindsey Johnson, and everyone at Scholastic for taking a chance on me and making me feel so welcome! My endless thanks to Cassandra Pelham, who listened to my pitch from the beginning and helped me polish the project into a story I am incredibly proud of. I learned so much and am SO glad I got to work with you!

N.S., for listening to an early version of this story and dispensing great advice. My professors at SCAD, for mentoring me through the ups and downs of college. I am especially grateful to Stefani Joseph, Michael Jantze, Ben Phillips, Mark Kneece, Ray Goto, and John Lowe, who saw these characters in their classes and encouraged their development.

My color assistants: Liz Fleming, whose tweets and beautiful art make me smile. Eric Xu, who grew up before I could finish this story but still had a part in making it. Rem, for being my rock and the brilliant artist I constantly look up to. Christina Cook and Will Ringrose, who jumped in at the last minute to help me across the finish line!

Jojo, Isa, and my family at Hiveworks, for giving me a comfy niche online with amazing artists, as well as a confidence in my own stories.

My parents, who worked very hard to give their children the opportunity to go to law school and med school, but did not protest too much when I went to art school.

My friends, family, and readers! Thank you again for your kind words over the years. I hope we will enjoy more books together!

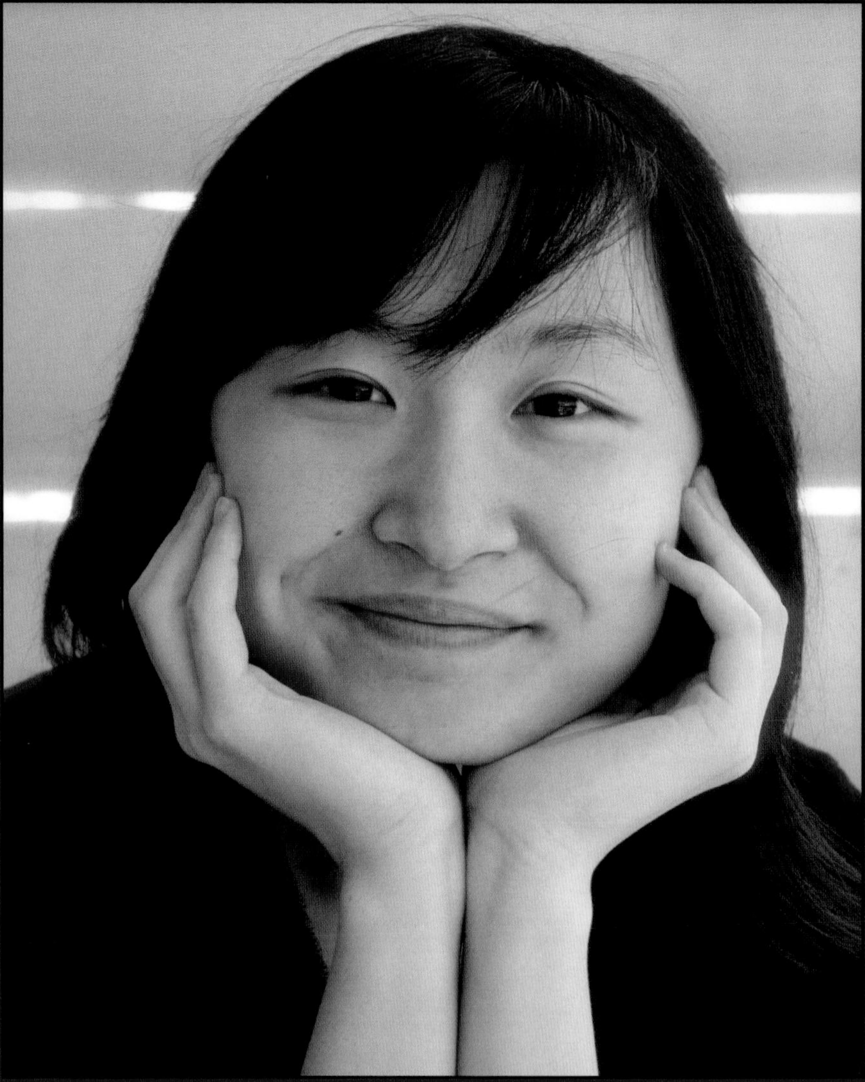

Author photo by Casey Gardner

RU XU was born in Beijing, grew up in Indianapolis, and received a degree in sequential art from the Savannah College of Art and Design. She is the creator of the popular webcomic *Saint for Rent*, and *NewsPrints* is her first graphic novel. Ru's favorite things include historical fiction, fat birds, and coffee-flavored ice cream. She currently lives in Gaithersburg, Maryland. Visit Ru online at www.ruemxu.com and on Twitter at @ruemxu.